Praise for *North by Northanger*

"Bebris captures Austen's style and the Regency period perfectly, drawing her characters with a sure hand. Her plot is poignant and gentle and will appeal to readers who prefer their mysteries without murder or violence."

—*Library Journal* (starred review)

"The writing is crisp, dryly humorous, and consistent with Austen's style. This book is the best of the three mysteries so far. It is tightly and credibly constructed down to the last detail, heavy on danger and intrigue, historically accurate, and engaging." —*VOYA*

Praise for *Suspense and Sensibility*

"The author smoothly combines characters from *Pride and Prejudice* and *Sense and Sensibility* while remaining true to Austen's originals." —*Publishers Weekly*

"No evil is a match for the witty and happily married Darcys."

—*Kirkus Reviews*

Praise for *Pride and Prescience*

"Thoroughly 'light and bright and sparkling,' in the best Austen tradition, with a dollop of murder and mayhem to leaven the whole. A delight." —Stephanie Barron, author of the Jane Austen Mystery series

"Well crafted . . . Bebris works her own brand of Austen magic, whetting the reader's appetite for a sequel. . . . Taking a lighter approach than Stephanie Barron's sleuthing Jane Austen series, this one should appeal as much to Regency readers as to Austenites." —*Publishers Weekly*

"Mannered prose, Regency backdrops, moody country houses, and delightful characterization place this new series high on the to-buy list." —*Library Journal*

OTHER MR. & MRS. DARCY MYSTERIES BY CARRIE BEBRIS

Pride and Prescience
(Or, A Truth Universally Acknowledged)

Suspense and Sensibility
(Or, First Impressions Revisited)

North by Northanger

(OR, THE SHADES OF PEMBERLEY)

A Mr. & Mrs. Darcy Mystery

Carrie Bebris

TOR®
A TOM DOHERTY ASSOCIATES BOOK
NEW YORK

NORTH BY NORTHANGER (OR, THE SHADES OF PEMBERLEY)

A Tor Book
Published by Tom Doherty Associates, LLC
175 Fifth Avenue
New York, NY 10010

www.tor.com

ISBN-13: 978-0-765-35274-3
ISBN-10: 0-765-35274-5

First Edition: April 2006
First Mass Market Edition: April 2007

Printed in the United States of America

0 9 8 7 6 5 4 3 2 1

For my mother

Acknowledgments

Anyone who imagines that a book is written in isolation has never written a book. While I may have been on my own side of a closed door while committing most of the words to paper, many people have contributed to the creation of this novel by sharing specialized knowledge, editorial feedback, encouragement, and other aid vital to the care and feeding of authors and the creative process.

I, first of all, thank my family for their patience and support; this includes not only my immediate family, who kept me grounded in the twenty-first century, but also my parents and siblings, who lent me quiet places to write when I had to escape to the nineteenth.

I also thank Anne Klemm: friend, brainstorming partner, critical reader, and intrepid travel companion. By the time I sent this manuscript off to my editor, I felt as if I had given birth along with Elizabeth Darcy, and if the book had a midwife, it was Anne.

Speaking of my editor, I appreciate Brian Thomsen for his guidance and suggestions; his assistants, Natasha Panza and Deborah Wood, for helping shepherd my "baby" through the publishing process; and David Moench and Fiona Lee for their enthusiastic promotion of the Mr. & Mrs. Darcy series. I thank Teresa Fasolino for her lovely cover art and for inspiring my use of Madonna lilies in the plot. And I am grateful to my agent, Irene Goodman, for her advice, sagacity, and belief in me and my writing.

Many fellow authors lent support in various ways. I thank Maddy Hunter for her friendship, cheer, and for sharing a story one afternoon about her grandmother's lost rings. Victoria Hinshaw, Dee Hendrickson, and other members of the Beau Monde Society offered Regency-era expertise. Susannah Fullerton sent her book *Jane Austen & Crime* express from Australia just when I needed it, then graciously answered a multitude of follow-up queries.

Experts in numerous fields kindly answered countless research questions. I am grateful to Canon Chancellor Edward Probert, Salisbury Cathedral; Dr. Tim W. Machan, professor and chair, Marquette University Department of English; Professor John Childs, School of History, University of Leeds; Professor William Cornish, Faculty of Law, Magdalene College, University of Cambridge; Susan Haack, M.D.; horticulturist (and dear aunt) Ann Wied, University of Wisconsin Extension; lily growers Ed McRae, Darrel Roeder, and Eugene Fox; quilters Rebecca Murphy and Reesa Evans; and horse enthusiast Linda Gies.

Appreciation goes across the Atlantic Ocean to Sue Hughes and the staff of the Jane Austen Centre in Bath, England, for their warm reception, and to members of the Jane Austen Society of North America, Wisconsin Romance Writers of America, and the Great Dames for their support closer to home.

Finally, I thank the librarians, booksellers, and readers who have embraced the Mr. & Mrs. Darcy mysteries and shared their enthusiasm with others. You make writing the series a true pleasure.

"Your alliance will be a disgrace. . . .
Are the shades of Pemberley to be thus polluted?"

—Lady Catherine de Bourgh to Elizabeth Bennet,
Pride and Prejudice

North by Northanger

One

At that moment she felt that to be mistress of Pemberley might be something!

—Pride and Prejudice

Less than a year into the marriage that made her mistress of one of England's finest houses, Elizabeth Darcy knew she still had much to learn about the place she now called home. Of one thing, however, she was certain.

A ghost haunted Pemberley.

She was not a ghost in the traditional sense. She did not moan, or shriek, or rattle chains. She did not cause rooms to grow cold, objects to fall, or fires to sputter. She did not manifest at midnight to pace on creaking floorboards, visiting in death the rooms she had occupied in life.

Yet the continued presence of Lady Anne Fitzwilliam Darcy was as real and pervasive as that of any spectre. And far more difficult to exorcise. Though her corporeal form had been laid to rest nearly twenty years earlier, she inhabited the estate as if it were still hers, casting a shadow so long that her daughter-in-law wondered whether she would ever escape it.

Elizabeth had known coming into her marriage that she

entered a family and a house with a long, respected history. She had embraced that history, and her new place in it, as she had embraced her husband and the life he had offered her when they wed. She had thought she was prepared for her new role as mistress of Pemberley. She had not realized that the previous occupant had not yet vacated it.

"You are—you are *certain,* ma'am?"

Elizabeth left the corner of the small parlor and crossed to a spot nearer the center of the room. "Yes," she assured the housekeeper. "Quite certain. I would like the desk moved over here, facing the window."

"Of course. I will summon the footmen directly." Despite her statement, Mrs. Reynolds made no move. The white-haired housekeeper lingered in the doorway of Elizabeth's morning room, worrying her lower lip, apparently wishing to say more but holding back out of deference to her employer.

Circumstances had prevented Elizabeth from spending much time at Pemberley since marrying Fitzwilliam Darcy nine months ago, but in that period she had come to respect Mrs. Reynolds's intelligence and opinions. One did not casually dismiss the concerns of a trusted servant with twenty-five years' tenure, and the housekeeper's advice had proven critical in easing Elizabeth's adjustment to overseeing a house far grander than the ones she had known growing up. Mrs. Reynolds was both extremely capable and unquestionably loyal to the Darcy family.

Sometimes *too* loyal. Guessing the source of the housekeeper's reservations, Elizabeth nevertheless asked, "Is there any reason not to move the desk, Mrs. Reynolds?" She resigned herself to the anticipated reply.

"Her ladyship preferred it in the corner. At certain times of year, this part of the room receives very strong sunlight. Lady Anne found the glare unpleasant."

Lady Anne, Elizabeth had been given to understand by various members of the household, had also found the Wedgwood breakfast set superior to any of Pemberley's many others, particularly the Royal Worcester china Elizabeth had thought to use last week. The fortnight previous, she had learned that the pattern of the music room's wallpaper was the only possible one that could adequately complement the view from that chamber's windows. The bird motif of the conservatory, another selection of her predecessor's, Elizabeth did not dare touch. Further, Lady Anne's taste in decorating had apparently been matched by equal excellence as an art collector, hostess, domestic manager, and philanthropist. As a result, Elizabeth had begun to find the glare of Lady Anne's perfection growing unpleasant.

"Thank you for the information, but I do not care to face a wall when I write," she said. "I would much rather look out. Pemberley has such beautiful grounds. I am exceptionally fond of the south garden."

Mrs. Reynolds smiled wistfully. "So was her ladyship. Lady Anne planted that garden herself—selected all the plants and put them in the ground with her own hands. But I am sure you already knew that."

"It might have been mentioned to me previously."

The housekeeper withdrew, and minutes later two footmen arrived to relocate the rosewood writing desk. As weary as she had become of most things related to Lady Anne, Elizabeth had to concede her own partiality for this particular furnishing. The graceful Chippendale piece practically beckoned one to take a seat and invent cause for correspondence.

The footmen lowered the desk to rest in its new position, then replaced the items they had removed from its top during the transfer. As soon as they left, Elizabeth rearranged the quill stand, wick trimmer, and wax jack, the latter of which she managed to drop in the process. She seemed to be dropping a lot of things lately. She bent to retrieve it—a motion more difficult now than it had been mere weeks ago—and positioned it to her satisfaction. The glass inkwell she then slid into place rather than trust herself to lift.

She sat at the desk, admiring the prospect from its chair. From her new vantage point, she could see not only the river and valley, as she could previously, but also the south garden. Though Michaelmas approached, the roses yet held their own, the marigolds vigorously announced their intention to stay until kissed by frost, and the morning glories climbed heavenward. The blooms' gentle perfume wafted through the open windows, dominated by a particularly sweet fragrance. As she attempted to identify it, her husband entered.

She held her breath as he silently noted the desk's new location. Though Darcy had given her leave to make any changes in the house she wished, and had especially encouraged her to remake Lady Anne's former rooms into her own, she could not escape consciousness of the fact that any alteration of hers severed another small tie to the mother he had lost at far too young an age. Fitzwilliam Darcy had been but eleven when Lady Anne died giving birth to his sister, Georgiana. Their father, George Darcy, had left most of his beloved wife's effects untouched, and his son had made minimal changes in the six years since he inherited the estate. Out of sensitivity to her husband's feelings, and those of Georgiana, she hesitated to adapt much at Pemberley to her own taste. A lifetime stretched before them—time enough for a gradual transformation. She need not sweep in and obliterate all traces of the first woman he had loved. If not yet secure in her role as Pemberley's mistress, she was secure enough in Darcy's affections to share them with his mother's memory.

If only that memory were not so idealized. Lady Anne had been loved not only by her family, but also by friends, neighbors, tenants, and servants. She had been a paragon of grace and lived an idyllic life. How Elizabeth would ever find her own place here, she could scarcely imagine.

Darcy at last nodded at the desk in approval. "You shall enjoy a finer view."

She exhaled. "I am glad you agree. Mrs. Reynolds so disapproves that I thought I might have to move the desk myself."

"I hope you jest. No mistress of Pemberley should be pushing furniture across a room, but especially not one in your condition."

"Of course I jest. If the servants mutinied, I would have prevailed upon you."

"And if I resisted?"

"I might have threatened to name this baby something ridiculous, such as Nancy."

"Nancy Darcy? You would never saddle a daughter of yours with such a singsong name. Besides, you carry a boy. The Darcys for countless generations have fathered boys as their first offspring, so it only stands to reason that we would continue the family tradition."

"Very well, then. Quincy Darcy."

"You do not frighten me."

"Chauncey? Percy?"

"Enough. We shall name him something that sounds well with Darcy. Richard, perhaps."

"Nay, not Richard. That, *I* could not countenance."

"It is a perfectly respectable name. In fact, it is the name of the physician I wish to engage for your lying-in. Dr. Richard Severn."

"The London doctor? I thought we agreed our child would be born here?"

"I will arrange for him to stay at Pemberley during your confinement. He already divides his time between London and Bath, where he is at present, so I am certain he can be persuaded to come to Derbyshire this winter."

"Should we not meet Dr. Severn first? What if we do not like him?"

"He has an excellent reputation."

"So does the village midwife."

His expression grew shuttered. "I do not want to entrust your safety to a country midwife."

"I do not want to entrust it to a doctor I have never met."

He regarded her quietly a moment, his air grown serious. "Very well," he said finally. "When we have concluded our visit with the Bingleys, we will return home via Bath—provided you feel well enough to prolong our travel."

"Our little Darcy has been behaving herself much more of late."

"I am glad to hear it. You have looked rather green these many weeks."

"I feel quite better." The morning queasiness that had plagued the early weeks of her condition had nearly abated—a fact for which she was grateful. Her sister Jane, who had just delivered her first child, had suffered nausea right up until the day she was brought to bed. Though Elizabeth remained hypersensitive to scent, only a few smells yet set her insides quaking. "In fact, just now I am famished. If I ring for nuncheon, will you join me?"

"It is only half past ten."

"Your child cannot yet tell time." She headed toward the bellpull, discovering on her way a folded sheet of paper on the floor. Certain it had not been there during her conversation with Mrs. Reynolds, she took it up.

"What have you found?" Darcy asked.

"A letter."

"On the floor? The servants are seldom so careless."

The note was sealed with the cinquefoil symbol from the Darcy crest. She turned it over and discovered her name on the front: Mrs. Fitzwilliam Darcy. She smiled softly. Had her husband, intending some surprise, dropped it for her to find? "It is addressed to me," she said, studying his expression closely.

"Indeed?" His countenance remained open, revealing mild interest but betraying no prior knowledge of the note. "From whom?"

Perhaps he had not authored the letter, or its sudden appearance, after all. Now that she looked at it again, the handwriting resembled Georgiana's more than his, but was not quite his sister's hand, either.

Her curiosity piqued, she broke the seal and unfolded the paper. The lines began neatly but became progressively uneven and blotted. She quickly scanned to the end, then lifted her gaze to Darcy in astonishment.

"It is from your mother."

Two

"Painful recollections will intrude which cannot, which ought not, to be repelled."

—Mr. Darcy, Pride and Prejudice

Pemberley
20 January 1796
Dear Mrs. Darcy,

Should this letter reach your eyes, it is because I no longer live to deliver its message in person. I know not who you are—what name you bore before taking that of Darcy. I know only that by addressing this letter to you, I write to the woman who has wed my son. For that reason alone I entrust to you the stewardship of something most precious, for as my Fitzwilliam's wife you already hold in your power that which I value above all else: my son's well-being and happiness.

Pardon my poor hand—my pains cause me to blot my words on the page. They follow hard upon each other—my time quickly approaches—already the midwife bids me come to the bed. I pray this babe survives. I cannot bear to bury another—

I had at Fitzwilliam's birth a . . . an heirloom from my own mother—I want it now, but it has become lost. If only I could find it, I would trust that I will be safely delivered. But I hid it too well, beyond my own reach. You—you must look if I cannot, for I want you to have it when . . . Valuable in itself . . . find it and you will hold the key to greater gifts—

Pain floods my mind—I cannot think for it. If you are my niece, my namesake, Anne, know that I guarded myself from my sister, not from you—

Mrs. Godwin demands that I set down my pen. On her alone I must depend . . . Search for me . . . My daughter, the only one I may ever have, start with the knowledge that love conquers all. I am—

Your mother,
Anne Darcy

Elizabeth watched Darcy read the letter in silence. His expression went from curious to clouded to somber as he reached its end. He stared at the note long after his eyes finished scanning its lines.

"Is it your mother's hand?" she asked.

He cleared his throat and handed the letter back to her. "It is."

"The date—"

"Is Georgiana's birthday. Yes, I noticed." His voice was thick, and he cleared his throat again. "The letter must have been lodged in some crevice of the desk and fallen when it was moved." He walked to the window and looked out upon the garden.

Elizabeth glanced once more at the note's address. *Mrs. Fitzwilliam Darcy.* How extraordinary, that at such a time Darcy's mother should have written to her, someone she would never meet.

But Lady Anne had not known that a stranger would read her words. Clearly, she thought she was writing to her niece, Anne de Bourgh. When Darcy and his cousin were infants, their mothers had planned a union between them. The arrangement had been an informal desire rather than an official betrothal, one to which Darcy had not been bound by honor, law, or inclination. But the wrath of his aunt, Lady Catherine de Bourgh, upon his engagement to Elizabeth had clearly demonstrated her assumption that those early wishes would be realized. Evidently, Lady Anne had expected his compliance as well. It was her sister's daughter, not the unheard-of Elizabeth Bennet, whom she anticipated would one day call Darcy husband and Pemberley home.

Elizabeth wondered whether Darcy's cousin Anne would have fared any better in escaping the influence of his mother's memory had they indeed wed. Sharing both Lady Anne's name and lineage, would she have slipped into her new role more easily than Elizabeth had? Somehow, Elizabeth doubted it. She had met Anne de Bourgh, a girl rendered so timid by growing up under the domination of her mother that she betrayed no hint of possessing a mind or will of her own. Were Anne now Mrs. Fitzwilliam Darcy, and this her morning room, the rosewood desk would have sat in the same location for at least another generation.

And Lady Anne's letter would never have been found.

Elizabeth again skimmed the lines—the last Lady Anne had ever written. She tried to read through the blots and scrawls to make out the missing words, but had no better success than upon her first reading.

She approached Darcy, who had fallen into reverie. He leaned against the window frame, his left hand yet holding the edge of the drapery panel he had pushed farther aside to widen his view of the garden below. To the world, the expression with which he quietly studied the landscape might appear impassive. But she could read in his stance and hear in his silence a depth of feeling he often found difficult to express, even to her at times.

She placed a hand on his back, and he turned his head to meet her eyes.

"I have always known my mother died in childbed, but I

never fully contemplated how painful a death it was." His tone, normally warm when he had occasion to speak of his mother, held the hush of one referring to someone recently departed. "My memories are of a woman who was always serene and in command—not someone enduring so much agony that she could not compose coherent sentences."

She felt acutely her own good fortune in yet having two living parents. "Those happier memories are the ones you should keep. She would not wish you to dwell on the circumstances of her death."

"It is not my mother's trial I have been contemplating most just now." He let the curtain panel fall back into place and took her hand. "It is yours."

Indeed, Lady Anne's letter had hardly made Elizabeth eager for the rite of passage that lay before her. But she did not care to fixate on the dangers of childbirth—at least, not this morning.

"My mother brought five babies into this world and has survived to see us all into adulthood. And my sister just safely delivered. I will be fine. Besides," she said with a smile she hoped would prove contagious, "there is no turning back now."

Her attempt at humor failed. Darcy regarded her with more seriousness than ever. "I am going to retain Dr. Severn." His tone brooked no opposition. Nor, looking at his face, did she wish to object.

"I still want to become acquainted with him before my confinement."

"You shall know him quite well. When we meet him in Bath, I will ask him to come to Pemberley immediately and stay until the child is born."

"For months? Darcy, that hardly seems necessary. What of his other patients?"

"I shall compensate him handsomely enough for you to be his only patient."

She opened her mouth to reply, but at the slight shake of his head she held her tongue. Darcy could be resolute with far less at stake—when confronted with the need to protect something precious to him, his drive was too fierce to redirect. Unable to remove a risk to someone he loved, he would do what he could to mitigate it. That trait was one of the things she admired most in him.

"Very well," she said. "Though I assure you, *this*"—she held up the letter—"will not become my fate. I am far too stubborn."

"My mother also possessed a strong will."

"So I surmise. She insisted on finishing this letter, after all, despite the circumstances." No doubt, her husband had inherited at least some of his determination from his mother. Like Darcy, Lady Anne had been trying to safeguard—or rather, recover—something precious to her right up until the end of her life. What could it have been, this object she wanted so desperately? Elizabeth could not imagine anything the faultless Lady Anne might have been denied, any object she could have lost that would not have been immediately replaced. "The item to which she refers—do you know what it is?"

"No. And I suppose we never shall."

She refolded the letter and offered it to Darcy. "Would you care to keep it?"

"She wrote it to you."

"She wrote it to the wife of her dear Fitzwilliam."

"Precisely. Which is why it rightfully belongs to you. Unless you do not want it?"

Elizabeth did not feel personally connected to the letter or its author, but would never admit as much to Darcy. "Of course I want it. It was written by your mother, someone important to you." She would keep it with the growing collection of Lady Anne's effects that she sought storage for—someplace safe but out of everyday sight. A house as large as Pemberley surely held room enough for two Mrs. Darcys.

If the former one would only leave her be.

Three

I give you joy of our new nephew, and hope if he ever comes to be hanged it will not be till we are too old to care about it.
—Jane Austen, letter to her sister, Cassandra

"This has been a pleasant visit," Elizabeth said, cuddling the tiny sleeping form against her shoulder one final time. The delight she experienced in holding her nephew was equaled only by that of seeing her sister Jane in good health and happy spirits following his entrance into the world. Nicholas Charles Bingley possessed the ideal attributes of a newborn: his mother's sweet countenance, his father's easy temper, and a love of attention that surpassed even that of his aunt Caroline. He seldom cried except when hungry—though on those occasions he exhibited a fretfulness almost certainly inherited from his maternal grandmother. Elizabeth and Darcy had been honored to stand as his godparents.

"If only you did not have to depart so soon," Jane replied. "I am sorry Lydia and Mr. Wickham arrived when they did. Had I known they were coming, I would have asked them to postpone."

"It is not your fault. At least we enjoyed some time together before they appeared." Their youngest sister and her husband, who had not been anticipated for the christening, had dropped in unexpectedly for a visit of undetermined duration, ostensibly so that Lydia could assist Jane. However, Lydia's aversion to useful occupation and insensibility to the needs of a new mother and child rendered any actual aid from her unlikely at best. This morning, she had quickly grown restless at the sisters' quiet conversation and had fled Jane's dressing room in search of superior distraction.

"But two days in the same house is as much of Mr. Wickham as Darcy can bear," Elizabeth continued. "He could scarcely endure him long enough for the ceremony to take place."

George Wickham, an army officer and a general reprobate, had a long and checkered history with the Darcy family. His father had been Pemberley's steward, and young Wickham and Fitzwilliam Darcy had grown up together. In fact, George had been named after Darcy's father, who had stood as his godfather. Regrettably, George Wickham did not share his godfather's noble character and had grown into a wild, selfish young man.

"Thank goodness Georgiana's previous engagement prevented her from accompanying you," Jane said, "or the situation would have been even more uncomfortable."

"Yes. Far better that she remains at Pemberley, safe from any encounter with Lydia's husband."

Jane was the only other member of Elizabeth's family who knew that upon the elder Mr. Darcy's death, Wickham had repaid his godfather's lifelong kindness and generosity by attempting to elope with Georgiana—then but fifteen years old—and thus acquire her inheritance. Luckily, her brother had learned of the plot before Wickham could execute it. Elizabeth's sister, however, had not been as fortunate. When Lydia fell prey to the scheming Wickham last year, he seduced her before anyone realized her danger. Though Darcy managed to restore the Bennet family's reputation by pressuring—and paying—Wickham to marry Lydia, his success came at the price of now tolerating a man he loathed as his brother-in-law.

"How long will you stay in Bath?" Jane asked.

"A fortnight. Long enough to meet Dr. Severn, though whether I like the man seems immaterial at this point."

"Does your reluctance stem from not desiring a man-midwife, or because you feel Mr. Darcy allows you no choice?"

"Both. Male accoucheurs might be fashionable among the *ton,* but I have never cared two pence for what is fashionable." Nicholas stirred against her, and she realized her voice had risen. She stroked his back, and he settled against her peacefully once again. "What I object to most," she continued more quietly, "is Darcy's treating me like an invalid. I do not need a physician to attend me around the clock from now until my lying-in."

"He loves you."

"I love him, too, but he may drive me mad before this child is born. If he worries this much now, I dare not imagine him when my waist has fully expanded. He will lock me in a bedchamber and shut out the sunlight. He will spoon-feed me barley water and blancmange. He will let all the servants go and replace them with medical men. Pemberley will be the only house in England where apothecaries sweep the fireplaces and surgeons polish the silver."

Jane laughed. "It will not be as bad as all that."

"You believe it may be worse? Indeed, I am in for a very long winter."

"Truly, Lizzy, you may find Dr. Severn's presence reassuring. Yes, women enter childbed every day, but we both know it can be dangerous, and I for one found the delivery itself rather frightening. Mama was here, but her nerves were in such a state that the midwife asked her to leave because she only added to my distress. So she went downstairs and shared her anxiety with Charles until *his* nerves nearly required a physician's care."

"My poor Jane! I wish I had been here with you, as we had planned."

"Apparently, Nicholas was so eager to meet his aunt that he wanted to greet you in person. But I shall come to Pemberley in time for your confinement. By then we will have settled in our new home, so I shall be but thirty miles distant—an easy journey, even with Nicholas."

After leasing Netherfield for two years, Jane's husband had finally found an estate that pleased them both. Just that morning, he had signed papers to purchase Ashdown House in Staffordshire. The sisters rejoiced that they would soon live in neighboring counties. Less frequent contact with Jane had been one of Elizabeth's few regrets upon quitting Hertfordshire.

"I know I can depend upon you. So long as Darcy does not smother me with solicitude before then."

"Has he been apprehensive since you first told him you were in the family way?"

"More so following our discovery of that letter from his mother. I must find something else for him to contemplate besides the possibility of my imminent demise."

"Perhaps the letter itself can help. Did you not say that Lady Anne mentioned a lost object? Mr. Darcy has a talent for solving problems—he located Lydia and Wickham in London after they eloped, and he apprehended that blackguard who tormented poor Caroline here at Netherfield. You could suggest he try to find whatever item his mother misplaced."

Elizabeth did not think she wanted Darcy dwelling on the contents of that letter any more than he already did. Further, while her husband indeed excelled at deducing answers, she herself had also played a crucial role in identifying Caroline Bingley's antagonist, as well as in solving another puzzle that had fallen their way this past spring. And Lady Anne's letter, after all, *had* been addressed to her.

"Lady Anne must have had a reason for writing to someone other than her son. Perhaps Darcy and I should seek it together."

"Seek what?" Lydia strolled in and dropped herself into a chair. "Lord, but I am bored! Wickham's off shooting and Mama has not come over from Longbourn yet. But you two seem to have finally finished talking about babies. What *are* you discussing? Who is Lady Anne?"

"Darcy's mother."

"I thought she was dead."

"She is."

"Then how could she write to anybody?"

Elizabeth summoned her reserves of patience, which always ran low in her youngest sister's company. Despite having acquired the status of a matron when she wed a year ago, Lydia had gained neither understanding nor discretion along with her wedding ring. At seventeen, she remained as immature and self-absorbed as she had ever been. "We found a note she wrote before she died."

"A note about what? You said something about seeking."

Elizabeth had hardly intended to discuss Lady Anne's letter with Lydia. "She briefly mentioned having lost some item or other. We do not even know to what she referred."

"But you're going to look for it? Oh—a treasure hunt! What fun! May I come help?"

Lydia's snooping around Pemberley was the last thing that would improve Darcy's mood. "It is not a treasure hunt. There is nothing to find."

"But you said—"

"There is no treasure," Elizabeth repeated emphatically. "Hence, no hunt. And no reason to discuss this further. It was just an old letter, that is all."

"Oh. Well, who cares about some old letter?"

"Precisely."

Nicholas opened his eyes, stretched, and let out a cry. Elizabeth tried to comfort him but he soon let it be known that he required more than a soft voice to satisfy him. "Jane, I think your son is hungry again."

"Good grief!" Lydia exclaimed. "Does he never stop crying? I cannot listen to it a moment longer. Lizzy, may I use your carriage to go visit Maria Lucas? I have not seen her since I reached Hertfordshire."

"I am afraid not. Darcy and I depart shortly. In fact, I have already been too long bidding Jane farewell." She brought the baby to Jane, kissed her sister's cheek, and stroked

Nicholas's downy hair one final time. "Take good care of your mama," she told her nephew.

Lydia pouted. "What about your carriage, Jane?"

Jane delayed a response, though Elizabeth suspected she would capitulate just to buy herself some peace. First, however, she addressed Elizabeth. "Write to me as soon as you meet Dr. Severn," she said. "I long to know what you think of him."

"So do I."

"Who is Dr. Severn?" Lydia asked.

"An accoucheur who might attend me in spring."

Lydia rolled her eyes. "Can *anybody* in this house speak of something besides babies?"

Four

"Oh! who can ever be tired of Bath?"
—*Catherine Morland,* Northanger Abbey

October marked the start of the official season in Bath, where members of the Polite World gathered in winter to improve their health and their social standing in a single convenient venue. Mornings were spent "taking the waters," either through immersion in one of the city's natural hot baths or by visiting the Pump Room to imbibe a draught of spa water. Evenings were devoted to concerts at Sydney Gardens, plays at the Theatre Royal, public assemblies at the Upper and Lower Rooms, and private parties in the stately town houses of the Crescent. In between, the streets themselves, designed for promenading and lined with any shop one could imagine, offered endless occupation and amusement. Yes, Bath held a cure for any ailment, whether one sought to fortify a weak constitution, a weak claim to society, or a weak wardrobe.

Though Darcy seldom visited Bath, he discovered many familiar names among the announcements of new arrivals in the *Chronicle* and the Pump Room's red book. Much of London's *haut ton* had migrated west for the winter, as had some prominent country families with whom he or Elizabeth were acquainted. They found, however, no close friends among those known to be in town. Save for their business with Dr. Severn, their two weeks' time in Bath was their own.

He had written to the physician immediately upon their arrival yesterday at lodgings in Pulteney Street. Dr. Severn had replied that the earliest he could meet with them was the following Monday. So today, Darcy and Elizabeth had elected to visit the Pump Room, where Elizabeth wished to sample the renowned water. Darcy, who had previously tasted the waters at Bath and other spas—and considered the experience sufficient indulgence for a lifetime—left his wife on one end of the busy room and went to procure a glass for her.

The burble of voices nearly drowned out the musicians playing a Hayden quartet. As he passed clusters of patrons, he caught snatches of conversation—if conversation it could be called. The exchanges among the *ton* while in Bath varied so little from day to day and year to year that its members could have been players delivering the lines of the city's longest-running dramatic production.

"Did you visit the Upper Rooms on Tuesday? It was a sad crush. . . ."

"There you are, darling! I declare, I have been waiting for you this age. . . ."

"For six weeks, I allow Bath is pleasant enough; but beyond that, it is the most tiresome place in the world. . . ."

Darcy reached the King's Spring, requested a single glass, and renegotiated the crowded room. He found Elizabeth near the great clock and handed her the water.

"Did you not bring one for yourself?" she asked.

"No, only you. And young William."

"Wilhelmina."

"Thomas?"

"Theresa."

"Francis."

"With an *i* or an *e*?"

"Drink your water."

She was prevented from doing so, however, by a bump from the side caused by someone pushing her way through the densely populated room. Water flew out of the glass, dousing her accidental assailant. The woman turned, and both Darcy and Elizabeth gasped.

"Lady Catherine!" Elizabeth stammered.

"Miss Bennet," spat out Darcy's incensed aunt. "Forgive me—*Mrs. Darcy*."

Despite the water dripping from her left side, Lady Catherine de Bourgh retained every bit of her usual imperiousness. From beneath her elaborate headdress she glowered at Elizabeth in furious silence for a full half-minute, then turned her glare on Darcy.

He offered a slight bow. "Lady Catherine." A movement to her right caught his gaze, and he realized his cousin accompanied her. Between her mother's overbearing presence and the noisy crowd, Miss Anne de Bourgh had practically faded from notice. Darcy and Elizabeth acknowledged Miss de Bourgh and Mrs. Jenkinson, Anne's companion, both of whom nodded meekly in response.

Lady Catherine removed a handkerchief from her reticule and attempted to blot the water soaking her sleeve. "I see you have not acquired any refinement along with your marriage, Mrs. Darcy."

Darcy bristled at the unfair attack on Elizabeth. "I believe it was you who jostled my wife."

"A lady does not jostle."

"No, she does not," Elizabeth said. She allowed the remark to hang in the air a moment. "Regardless of its cause, however, I am sorry for your unexpected shower. I understand one normally prefers to don a bathing costume before immersion in Bath's famous waters."

Lady Catherine issued a less than gracious reply and finished dabbing her gown. "I did not anticipate seeing you in Bath, Mr. Darcy. What brings you here?"

Though his aunt would learn eventually that they were increasing their family, he remained too vexed with Lady

Catherine for her rudeness toward Elizabeth to reveal the news. "Mrs. Darcy has never visited Bath before," he said.

"I suppose her father did not take the family to spas," she said to Darcy as if Elizabeth were not standing right next to her. "As you know, I bring Anne to Bath nearly every year for the waters. I believe them beneficial to her delicate health."

"We also have business with Dr. Richard Severn," said Elizabeth. Her openness with his aunt surprised him.

"A physician?" Lady Catherine continued to address only Darcy, but narrowed her gaze. "Are you ill?"

"Not at all."

"Is your wife?"

"I have never felt better," Elizabeth replied for herself.

Lady Catherine at last turned her sharp gaze on Elizabeth and subjected her to a thorough visual assessment. "You do appear in good health," she admitted grudgingly. "One might even say radi—" She suddenly looked as if Elizabeth had just splashed more water on her. "Mrs. Darcy," she said accusingly, "are you *breeding*?"

"I prefer the term 'carrying.'"

The news managed to render Lady Catherine speechless—never a small achievement, though the effect was momentary. Darcy and Elizabeth had, after all, been married nearly a year; their expectation of an heir could hardly have been unanticipated.

"I see." She stared at Elizabeth further, her expression revealing an inner struggle between equally strong drives to demonstrate haughty disdain and to demand every particular. Apparently, curiosity won out over pride. "We cannot discuss so delicate a subject in a public forum. But I grant you permission to wait upon me in Camden Place."

"You are too generous," Elizabeth said.

"How long are you staying in Bath?"

"A fortnight."

"So little time? You should remain at least six weeks. You cannot have any reason to rush home, and it is foolish to exhaust yourself with travel."

"I am sure a fortnight will prove quite long enough."

"Hardly. One requires twice that period simply to become oriented. Which baths have you tried? People speak highly of the King's and Queen's Baths, but the Cross Bath is superior. I have instructed Anne to use it exclusively. Have you gone into it yet?"

"No, I have not used any of the baths."

"None? But you have, at least, been imbibing the water."

"Actually, I was just about to sample it for the first time when you happened past."

"You will no doubt find its flavor unpleasant at first. It is an acquired taste. The water is quite fortifying, however. I insist that Anne drink a full pint each day."

"Indeed?" Elizabeth said. "And how much do you drink?"

"I consume a glass daily whilst in Bath, and I advise you to do likewise. It keeps one in good health."

Lady Catherine expounded another ten minutes on the benefits of regular pilgrimages to Bath before spotting an acquaintance amid the throng. Darcy took advantage of Lady Dalrymple's arrival to excuse himself and Elizabeth, citing a wish to take some air.

"I will expect you in Camden Place on the morrow, Mrs. Darcy," Lady Catherine said as they departed. "We have important matters to discuss."

The crisp air proved refreshing after the closeness of the Pump Room. They walked slowly, passing the abbey and crossing the churchyard to Cheap Street. The road teemed with carriages, horses, and carts, and they were some time waiting to cross it. Indeed, merely standing on the pavement, they found themselves quite in danger of being run over by a gentleman doing a rather poor job of driving four-in-hand, and swearing at his "deuced beasts" for their slow pace. Eventually, however, they traversed the thoroughfare and continued past the guildhall to amble over Pulteney Bridge.

Shops lined both sides of the stone bridge. Though they paused before several windows to admire the wares for sale, they found little to tempt them. The only shop that captured

Elizabeth's attention was one displaying gentlemen's walking sticks.

"Darcy," she said, pointing. "That cane on the right appears very similar to yours. Did you purchase it here?"

"Mine was a gift from my father when I left home for Cambridge. I do not know who made it." Darcy lifted his walking stick and held it across both palms. It was beautifully crafted and one of his favorite possessions; he carried it nearly everywhere. A cinquefoil, recalling the Darcy coat of arms, adorned the head of its silver grip, which ended at a wide band engraved with smaller cinquefoils. He kept its length so richly polished that he could almost see his reflection in the deep red-brown wood. A slight imperfection, where the grain widened around a shilling-sized whorl, marked the cane's sole flaw, but was scarcely noticeable unless one sought it.

"My father sometimes came to Bath. He might have bought it here during one of his stays."

"Shall we go inside and ask the shopkeeper whether it is his work?"

He shook his head and returned the cane to its usual position at his side. "I would much rather continue walking with you."

They journeyed only a few more yards, however, before another shop—a pastry-cook's—brought Elizabeth to a halt.

"Are you hungry?" Darcy asked.

"No, but your daughter is."

They went within and enjoyed strawberry ices as they watched passers-by through the shop window. When they had finished, they bought hot Bath cakes to take home. Darcy took her arm as they left the bridge and passed the fountain in Laura Place.

"I confess surprise that you chose to reveal your condition to my aunt, given her treatment of you since our engagement."

"She would learn of it soon enough. Meanwhile, admitting her into our confidence seemed the best means of making amends with her. She is one of your few remaining Fitzwilliam relations, after all."

The maternal branch of his family tree was indeed a small one. Lady Catherine was his mother's only sister. Catherine and Anne's brother—Lord Hugh Fitzwilliam, Earl of Southwell—had died not long after Lady Anne, leaving the earldom to his eldest son, Roger. Hugh's second son was a colonel in the army. A third son, a naval officer, had died at sea.

Darcy appreciated Elizabeth's willingness to forgive the many insults Lady Catherine had heaped upon her. The breach with his aunt had weighed more heavily upon him than he cared to acknowledge. He considered family connections of utmost importance, relationships to be preserved except in cases of dishonorable conduct that blackened the family name. In their commitment to protecting the family's reputation, he and his aunt agreed. They differed, however, in their definition of discreditable behavior. Darcy defined it as willful disregard for the legal and ethical rules of society; Lady Catherine, as disregard for the opinions of Lady Catherine.

"What caused you to believe that news of a child would repair a relationship my aunt herself chose to break? She appeared horrified by the very idea."

"Yes, you have chosen an unworthy vessel to bear your offspring. Our progeny will undoubtedly suffer from their inferior maternal ancestry." Elizabeth held his arm more tightly as they negotiated an uneven stretch of pavement. "However, Jane and my dear friend Charlotte Collins both tell me that the moment the world learns that a woman is in the family way, she becomes a lodestone for unsolicited counsel from all quarters on every possible matter related to her condition. Knowing Lady Catherine's propensity for instruction, I suspected she would prove unable to resist the opportunity to educate me in everything I have been doing wrong thus far, and to issue endless orders regarding my conduct and habits for the remainder of my wait."

"Perhaps you should take notes during your visit tomorrow. You would not wish to forget a valuable piece of advice."

"Should she offer one, I shall rely upon you to remind me of it. You *do* intend to accompany me?"

"Much as I long to enjoy Lady Catherine's hospitality, I believe she tendered her invitation solely to you. Besides, I would be completely in your way. My aunt seemed to have matters of a most particular nature to discuss with you, and the presence of a gentleman among the party might hinder even her outspokenness."

"That is precisely why I wish you to come."

"Did you not just say that you effectively solicited her ladyship's attention?"

"That does not mean I look forward to subjecting myself to it."

"So now I am to rescue you?" He assisted her up the steps as they reached their lodgings.

"I would do as much for you."

"Endure my aunt's condescension to spare my suffering? That is love, indeed. But I am afraid you are on your own for this conversation."

She looked at him coquettishly—a device so foreign to his straightforward Elizabeth that he nearly laughed to see it.

"Have you no compassion for the mother of your son?"

At that, he did laugh. "*Now* the child is a boy?"

He shook his head and led her into the house. "A noble attempt, Mrs. Darcy, but I am unmoved. Lady Catherine's summons was your own doing. As I intend to teach our young Henry or John, if you create a plight, you must see it through yourself."

"That is an important lesson for our child to learn." She stopped at the hall mirror to remove her bonnet, catching his gaze in the glass. "Little Henrietta or Johanna will thank you for it."

Shortly after they settled themselves in the sitting room, a note arrived. The servant informed them that its messenger waited for a response.

Darcy glanced at the direction. "I do not recognize the hand." He broke the seal, skimmed its content, then read aloud:

Edgar's Buildings
Bath, 6 October
Dear Mr. Darcy,

My discovery of your name in the Pump Room book prompts me to write. Though we are strangers to each other, I believe our families are acquainted. My late mother, Mrs. Victor Tilney, enjoyed the friendship of one Lady Anne Darcy, whom I believe to be your mother.

Though I understand Lady Anne has also passed away, I would take great pleasure in meeting her son. Unfortunately, my military duties obligate me to depart Bath this very day. However, I plan to return to my country home in Gloucestershire by 18 October, and shall remain there for some time. I would consider myself honored to receive you and Mrs. Darcy at Northanger Abbey as my guests for a se'nnight whenever you make your return journey to Derbyshire.

I hope your response names the date upon which I will enjoy the pleasure of your company. I am—

Yours most sincerely,
Captain Frederick Tilney

"An intriguing invitation," Elizabeth said when he finished reading. "Do you recall Mrs. Tilney?"

"I do not believe I ever met her," Darcy said.

"Are you inclined to accept?"

He thought a moment. "I am. If our mothers were friends, Captain Tilney must come from a worthy family. We can only gain from renewing the connection."

And she could only gain from Darcy's having the novelty of a new acquaintance to distract him from his well-meant but excessive concern for her health.

"I wonder how old a man he is. He might remember your mother." It was ironic that they should receive a letter mentioning Lady Anne so soon after discovering the one written by her, but she welcomed the coincidence. With luck, Captain Tilney would bring happier memories to the forefront of

Darcy's mind, and the desperate tone of Lady Anne's final note would recede from it.

"Whether he remembers her or not, I look forward to meeting him." Darcy cast her a look of enquiry. "Unless you would rather not delay our return to Pemberley? Perhaps it would be best for your health if we traveled straight home. We also have arrangements for the harvest feast to oversee."

Each autumn, Pemberley hosted a harvest feast for its tenants and villagers. The Darcy family had sponsored the event for generations. Elizabeth looked forward to this year's day-long celebration, her first as mistress of Pemberley. But they need not forgo the opportunity to meet Captain Tilney—the date of the feast was still many weeks distant, and their steward and housekeeper had preliminary preparations well in hand.

"No," she said quickly. "I think a stay in Gloucestershire sounds like a pleasant means by which to break up the long journey to Derbyshire. In addition to the diversion of meeting the captain, Northanger Abbey surely offers more comfort than an inn. And plenty of time remains before the harvest feast."

"All right, then," he agreed. "I shall advise Captain Tilney to expect us Tuesday week."

Five

Mrs Coulthard and Anne, late of Manydown, are both dead, and both died in childbed. We have not regaled Mary with this news.

—Jane Austen, letter to Cassandra

Enticed by a glorious autumn day—crisp air, warm sunlight, and not a cloud in the cerulean sky—Elizabeth elected to walk to Lady Catherine's lodgings the following afternoon. She had always preferred the use of her own ten toes to other forms of travel, but even more so since arriving in Bath. The enclosed sedan chairs by which residents moved around the city created in her such a sense of confinement that each time she hired one, by the time she reached her destination she could barely restrain herself long enough for the bearers to lower it before bursting from the tiny box. So she reserved the cramped, jostling conveyances for times when it rained hard enough to render walking unpleasant even to her—a frequent-enough occurrence in Bath.

Though not exactly anticipating unmitigated delight in her errand, she set out for Camden Place determined to enjoy the fine weather and opportunity for exercise. Accompanied by her maid, she crossed the bridge and entered Broad Street before turning up Landsdowne Road. Here, however, her pace slowed. Bath was a city of hills, some of them quite steep, but she had not realized that Camden Place sat atop one of the most extreme slopes. She found herself stopping to catch her breath as she toiled uphill.

The struggle surprised her. She considered herself in good form, and was not unused to exertion; she had expected the climb to challenge but not utterly wind her. She raised a hand to her chest and felt her heart racing beneath her fingertips. What was the matter with her today?

She responded to her maid's solicitous enquiries with a dismissive shake of her head, certain that she merely needed a few minutes to allow her pulse to resume a less frantic rate, and cited a desire to look in the window of the nearest shop. A display of dolls prompted her to consider the child she carried.

Would she bear a girl? For all her teasing of Darcy, she of course could not know with certainty. But if the ease with which she imagined the child as female and the difficulty with which she pictured it male meant something, if the midnight whisperings of her heart on restless nights could be trusted, if instinct counted for anything . . . she believed she carried a daughter.

The reverie lent her breathlessness context. Her body was no longer her own—she had a tiny passenger that would only grow larger in the coming months, and she would have to start remembering that. Meanwhile, her respiration steady once more, she completed the walk to Lady Catherine's.

Darcy's aunt greeted her with all the condescension Elizabeth had come to expect from her. She received Elizabeth in the drawing room, where Anne de Bourgh and Mrs. Jenkinson also sat. Elizabeth could not recall a single occasion upon which she had seen Miss de Bourgh without Mrs. Jenkinson at her side, and wondered whether the poor girl ever enjoyed a moment's solitude. Or whether Mrs. Jenkinson did, for that matter.

"You appear breathless, Mrs. Darcy," Lady Catherine observed.

"Camden Place is a steeper climb than I anticipated," she said. "But I was rewarded by the view as I reached the top."

"You *walked*?" Lady Catherine uttered the word as if Elizabeth had confessed to turning cartwheels. "For heaven's sake, why did you not hire a chair?"

"It is a fine day, and I wanted the exercise."

"And were repaid for your foolishness by fatiguing yourself. You are too headstrong for your own good—and that of the child you carry. Shame on you for thinking only of yourself. Does my nephew know how you conducted yourself here?"

He did not. Normally, Darcy encouraged her love of walking, but now that she was in the family way, she could not predict whether he would approve of her traveling by foot all the way up to Camden Place. So she simply had not told him of her intent before he departed their lodgings upon errands of his own.

Her silence proved answer enough for Lady Catherine. "I thought not." She turned to the other two ladies. "Mrs. Jenkinson, I have matters to discuss with Mrs. Darcy that are unsuitable for the ears of a young lady not yet married. This would be a convenient time for you to escort Miss de Bourgh to the Pump Room."

Mrs. Jenkinson, who had developed an intense interest in the carpet pattern when Lady Catherine began chastising Elizabeth, rose with alacrity. Anne appeared more reluctant to leave, the words "unsuitable for the ears of a young lady not yet married" having offered the tantalizing promise of conversation different from her mother's usual repertoire.

Her ladyship waited until they had departed before fixing Elizabeth with her gaze once more. "Now, then. When do you expect this child?"

Though she bristled at Lady Catherine's commanding tone, Elizabeth resigned herself to submission—within limits. Cooperating with the interrogation seemed the most efficient way to bring it to an end.

"March."

"When in March? March is thirty-one days long. Did not

your mother help you estimate any more precisely than that? When I carried Anne, I knew exactly which day the child should come."

"Early March."

"Hmph. I suppose that is the best you can do."

"The sixth of March at twenty-three minutes past four in the afternoon."

Her ladyship was not amused. "You will, of course, want to spend your confinement in London, where the best physicians may be found. Dr. Skinner in Harley Street is the man you want. He is an older gentleman, so he knows what he is about. He attended me at Anne's birth, and I advise all the young mothers of my acquaintance to use him if he will take them as patients. He attends mostly peers' wives, but I will speak to him."

"We are already engaged to meet Dr. Severn on Monday."

"And who is this Dr. Severn? I have never heard of him."

"He is highly recommended."

"Where does he practice? Here in Bath?"

"Mostly in London, though he comes to Bath each winter for the season."

"He is a poor choice, then. What if your child comes early and he is still in Bath while you are in London?"

"I do not intend to be in London at all. I shall remain at Pemberley for my confinement."

"Pemberley? Whatever for? Neither Dr. Severn nor Dr. Skinner can attend you at that distance."

"Mr. Darcy hopes to persuade Dr. Severn to come to Pemberley when my time approaches."

"And if this Dr. Severn will not?"

"Perhaps I shall simply ask the local midwife to assist me."

"A *midwife*?" From her ladyship's tone, one would think Elizabeth had said "milliner." "With the most learned physicians in the country available to you in London, you would settle for the aid of some provincial woman?"

"My mother delivered all five of her daughters with the assistance of our village midwife and had no trouble."

"Your mother was fortunate. Do you have any idea what can happen—to the child and to yourself?"

"I realize there are dangers, but—"

"You young women think you know what to expect, but you are entirely ignorant of the trial before you. I myself labored for a day and a half, and surely would have died of exhaustion without Dr. Skinner. Or take the case of my neighbor Mrs. Anderson, who lost a healthy son in a breech birth. Had she used a physician instead of a midwife, he might have survived. I could offer countless more illustrations."

Which she then proceeded to do.

As much as Elizabeth wanted to disregard these examples simply because it was Lady Catherine who offered them, she found she could not. She had heard similar stories, and had not been insensible to them, but today the cautionary tales seemed to settle on her heart in a way they had not previously. Her fatigue at climbing Landsdown Road had left her more aware of her increasing physical vulnerability, an unpleasant reality that she would have to take into consideration whether she cared to or not.

Nevertheless, she soon had heard as much from Darcy's aunt as anyone could be expected to tolerate for one visit. "Lady Catherine, I appreciate your concern and your counsel. I will accord the matter due thought." She rose to go.

"A London confinement, Mrs. Darcy," her ladyship repeated once more. "You cannot possibly contemplate anything else. Do not forget that my own sister lost three babes after Fitzwilliam, then bled to death bringing Georgiana into the world. Consider the effect the loss of you or your child would have on my nephew. Whatever my feelings toward you, I would not have him suffer the torment his father experienced."

Neither would Elizabeth. She also could not help but think that her own death would hardly be an altogether agreeable event for herself.

Her ladyship insisted on not only ordering her carriage for Elizabeth, but also accompanying her to Pulteney Street. Elizabeth supposed Lady Catherine wanted to tattle on her for having arrived in Camden Place under her own power, but as it turned out, she had an entirely different issue she wished to bring to Darcy's attention.

Darcy had returned from his errands and greeted Lady Catherine's arrival with evident surprise. "Mrs. Darcy and I had not anticipated the honor of a reciprocal visit so soon." He glanced to Elizabeth with amused curiosity as her ladyship settled herself in the sitting room. "You must have enjoyed a pleasant tête-à-tête."

"I have advised your wife on several subjects related to her lying-in. She would do well to heed my counsel." Lady Catherine waved her hand. "Mrs. Darcy, you may excuse yourself now. I have a matter of family business to discuss with my nephew."

Elizabeth stiffened. To dismiss her like a servant from her own sitting room! Though a moment ago she would have welcomed the opportunity to escape her ladyship's presence, she now wanted to remain in the room solely on principle.

Darcy's expression lost its amusement. "If it is family business, it can be discussed in the presence of my wife."

"It does not concern her."

"Then it does not concern me."

Lady Catherine bristled. She looked at Elizabeth resentfully, then back at Darcy with an air of calculation. Elizabeth sensed that Darcy's aunt wanted something from him and was weighing how much cooperation on her own part would be required to obtain it.

"Very well," she said finally. "I suppose you will only divulge our conversation to her the moment I leave." She spared Elizabeth one more glance, then declared, "Southwell is gone to France again."

The travel arrangements of Darcy's cousin hardly constituted the momentous news Elizabeth had anticipated after such a dramatic preface. Darcy, however, closed his eyes and sighed.

"Has he—"

"I have no particulars yet. But you know how poor his

judgment is, especially in regard to a certain individual. He narrowly avoided a scandal last time."

"I remember." He rubbed his brow wearily. "What does his brother think of this?"

"The news reached me only this morning, so I have had no opportunity to discuss it yet with Colonel Fitzwilliam. Even so, the colonel is needed with his regiment at present and therefore is not at liberty to sail off to France and serve as his brother's keeper."

"Neither am I."

"If you can idle away weeks in Bath, you can go to Paris long enough to make a few discreet enquiries. *Someone* must determine what his lordship is about and intervene if necessary to avert disaster. Else he could finally succeed in undoing himself, and all of us in the process. The political and social repercussions—"

"Would be grave indeed, I realize."

"Then we are agreed. You will go."

"No, but I shall send an agent in my stead. My solicitor, Mr. Harper, possesses sufficient connections in Paris to learn what we need to know. If my cousin indeed places himself in jeopardy once more, I will proceed as appropriate."

"I would prefer that a member of the family undertake this charge." Determination radiated from the former Lady Catherine Fitzwilliam with such intensity that Elizabeth thought the potted palm would bend under the force. But Darcy had inherited more than his Christian name from his mother's family.

"If you wish to journey there yourself, I have no objection."

Confronted with the resistance of her nephew's equally strong will, her ladyship was forced to concede—though with an expression that clearly indicated annoyance. "If you can testify to Mr. Harper's dependability and discretion, I suppose I am satisfied." She rose. "At present."

Before the wheels of Lady Catherine's departing carriage had rotated a full turn, Elizabeth sought an explanation from Darcy. "I do hope you intend to enlighten me as to the subject of that conversation?"

"You were likely able to surmise most of it. Have you ever wondered why, in entrusting Georgiana's guardianship jointly to me and one of my cousins, my late father chose Colonel Fitzwilliam instead of the earl?"

"I did find it curious." She watched Lady Catherine's vehicle enter Laura Place, then let the curtain fall and turned away from the window.

"Though Roger inherited a title, he did not inherit a great deal of sense." Darcy went to the decanter and offered her a glass of wine. Though she declined—the smell of liquor had troubled her since her pregnancy began—he poured one for himself. "To curtail a long saga, he has a habit of offending the wrong people and landing himself in political, social, and sometimes even physical danger. In the past few years, he has expanded his imprudence across the English Channel."

"Your unwillingness to follow him there displeased your aunt. Have you done so before?"

"Displeased my aunt?" He gave her a wry smile as he replaced the stopper on the decanter.

"Gone to France."

"The last time Roger tarried there, he nearly lost his life in a duel. I brought him home."

"Why did you not go on this occasion?"

"I am no longer a bachelor. While previously I might have placed myself at my aunt's disposal, I now have a wife and child who require my attention. I cannot allow Lady Catherine to consider me at her beck and call whenever the whim strikes her."

She crossed to him as he sipped his wine. "I am glad to hear it. I much prefer you at *my* beck and call."

"Indeed? And what whim presently strikes you?"

"You need not journey to France." She took the glass from him, deliberately brushing his fingers in the process, and set it down.

He regarded her warmly. "Why, Mrs. Darcy—"

"Only Pulteney Bridge."

At that, he chuckled. "We are returning to the pastry-cook's shop?"

"How ever did you guess?"

"We have not yet been there today. The proprietor might feel neglected." He took her hand, kissed it, and led her into the hall. "Is it to be lemon ice or strawberry this time?"

Six

I do not want people to be very agreeable, as it saves me the trouble of liking them a great deal.

—Jane Austen, letter to Cassandra

Dr. Richard Severn was a petite, wiry gentleman with a dark complexion and the eyes and nose of a hawk. He wore his black hair short, his sideburns long, and his vanity like a suit of armor. He entered the Darcys' sitting room with an air of command and proceeded to interview the couple instead of the other way round.

Rather, the physician proceeded to interview Darcy. He barely spared Elizabeth a glance, and she soon felt as if she could have left the room without the doctor's noticing.

"This is your first child?"

"It is."

"And your wife estimates it will arrive when?"

"Early March."

"I normally return to London on the first of March. She, however, should complete her travel much earlier. The roads, as you know, can be extremely hazardous in winter, and you would not want a rough carriage ride to cause premature birth. I advise you to install Mrs. Darcy in town well before Christmas." He withdrew a small notebook and pencil from his bag. "I will note in my calendar when you anticipate requiring my services. You have my direction in London—simply summon me when Mrs. Darcy's pains commence."

"My wife prefers our country home in Derbyshire for her confinement. I had hoped you might consider attending her there."

"Derbyshire? Impossible," he said, not looking up from his calendar. "It is too far from London. I could take on no other patients—I would have to arrive before I was needed and waste weeks waiting for Mrs. Darcy's delivery."

"I would make your sacrifice worthwhile."

The doctor paused, pencil still in hand, and studied Darcy appraisingly. "How worthwhile?"

"That depends upon how long you stay at Pemberley."

"Hold a moment!" Elizabeth drew their attention toward herself for the first time in the entire conversation. "Dr. Severn, before we make any arrangements, might you be so good as to describe what I can anticipate when you attend me?"

He regarded her with annoyance. "Have you not a mother or sister with whom you can discuss the particulars of lying in?"

"What I mean to say is, all the women of my family have been brought to bed with a midwife and other women attending them. As a physician, do you assist births differently?"

"My medical training is far superior to that of any midwife," he said tersely. "What midwife can boast a university education? Should the birth not proceed smoothly, has she the knowledge and instruments to save you or the child? The greatest families in England rely upon me to see their children into the world, but if you prefer the aid of an ignorant old woman—"

"I did not say that. I only wished to know the advantages of having a doctor present."

"I have assisted hundreds of births, Mrs. Darcy. I am an expert in my profession. Moreover, I am a man of science, equipped to handle not only the common emergencies, but also the unforeseen. I can tell you tales that would chill your soul about extreme measures I have taken to save a mother or her child after having given up the other for lost."

Which he then proceeded to do.

Apparently, a woman's expectant state ranked second only to All Hallows' Eve as inspiration for one and all to share horror stories. Elizabeth actually shuddered at one particularly disturbing example the doctor offered as evidence of his superiority. There would be no resisting Darcy's preference for a physician now, and, in truth, she herself had begun to think that perhaps engaging a male accoucheur was the wiser course of action. She could not say, however, that she cared for Dr. Severn himself.

The physician glanced from her to Darcy impatiently. "What is your intent? Do you wish to engage me or not?"

As much as she resented Dr. Severn's arrogance, she respected his knowledge. She met Darcy's gaze and read in it his desire to proceed. For Darcy's sake, she could tolerate him. Should the unthinkable occur, at least her husband would have the small consolation of knowing he had done everything in his power to prevent it.

She nodded her acquiescence.

Within ten minutes' time, all was arranged. Mercifully, Dr. Severn shared Elizabeth's belief that his coming to Pemberley immediately was entirely unnecessary—a view that somewhat mitigated her opinion of him. He consented to travel there if needed to respond to specific complaints, but otherwise he would arrive in February and stay until the birth. A monthly nurse—he could recommend several—would then oversee Elizabeth's recovery for the remainder of her lying-in. The gentlemen negotiated payment, and Dr. Severn departed.

"The interview proceeded more smoothly than I anticipated," Darcy remarked.

"You thought Dr. Severn would prove more difficult?"

"I was speaking of you."

Before she could reply, a servant entered and handed Darcy a letter that had arrived while they were engaged with the doctor.

"It is from Mr. Harper," Darcy said. "He writes that he will depart for France on the nineteenth, and assures me that he will conduct the business quietly." Darcy refolded the letter and set it aside. "So the matter of watching over my cousin is well in hand. If I know Mr. Harper, I will find an initial report waiting for me when we return to Pemberley."

"Do you anticipate Mr. Harper will learn anything unpleasant?"

"After nearly losing his life, Roger swore that he would not so hazard himself again. It is my hope that he meant it. Nothing would please me more than for Mr. Harper's journey to prove entirely unnecessary."

"I suspect your aunt, on the other hand, would be disappointed by the news that he is *not* courting trouble. She seemed so eager for a crisis about which she could declare her disapproval." She sighed. "Well, should Roger fail to provide, at least she has me to console her."

Darcy looked at her oddly. "Given your history with Lady Catherine, you expect your company would comfort her?"

"Not my company, dear, my condition. Instead of working herself into a bother over the purity of the Fitzwilliam name, she can fret over what my involvement has done to the bloodline. With our child not due until March, the vexation will happily occupy her for months."

Seven

Every bend in the road was expected with solemn awe to afford a glimpse of its massy walls of grey stone, rising amidst a grove of ancient oaks, with the last beams of the sun playing in beautiful splendour on its high Gothic windows. But so low did the building stand, that she found herself passing through the great gates of the lodge and into the very grounds of Northanger, without having discerned even an antique chimney.

—Northanger Abbey

"Thus far, I cannot say I find Gloucestershire entirely hospitable," Elizabeth said, drawing her cloak more closely about her.

Darcy silently agreed. The thirty-mile journey to Northanger Abbey had so far proven grey and wet. They had set out from Bath with overcast skies; by the time they reentered their carriage after a stop in Petty-France to take refreshment and exchange the horses, a light drizzle had begun. Thick clouds and rising fog shrouded the Gloucestershire landscape in gloom.

He drew Elizabeth against his side. It was unlike his wife to allow damp weather to dampen her spirits. "You are too harsh. Every county in England receives its share of rain."

"Oh, I have no objection to the rain—just its falling today." She settled against him. "Whenever one forms a new acquaintance, the parties cast about for innocuous subjects of conversation, and now when we meet Captain Tilney we shall be unable to rhapsodize over the beauty of his native region. We will be reduced to discussing the length of our journey and which plays we saw in Bath."

"But observations on the weather always offer a fallback for discourse. The rain is actually a boon."

"Nay, a bane. If the sun shone, we could praise the glorious day at length, as if our host were responsible. But what is there to say about foul weather, other than 'it rained,' that does not sound like complaint? No, I am afraid we are stuck, and I reserve for myself the theatrical reviews. You may narrate our travelogue."

Eventually, the somber atmosphere lulled Elizabeth to slumber. She had been sleeping more now that she was carrying their child, Darcy reflected. He drew her more tightly against him and rested his chin atop her head.

Now that their arrangements with Dr. Severn were in place, he had managed to leave some of his unease behind in Bath. He had secured for Elizabeth the best care his fortune could provide. They were headed back to Pemberley, where she could spend the rest of her pregnancy in the comfort of home. There was little more to be done than wait for March and pray that all went well. In the meantime, he would try not to ponder the irony that an event that promised such incredible joy also carried the threat of unimaginable sorrow. He would try instead to simply look forward to the arrival of their child.

The rain fell heavier, and Darcy heard the low rumble of thunder over the noise of the carriage. A louder *crack* a few minutes later woke Elizabeth.

"Is it possible that the sky is even darker than before I nodded off?"

"It is, but more than the rain is to blame. Dusk approaches."

"I wonder that the postilion can see anything in this mist. I hope he does not miss our turn."

Darcy hoped so, as well. "Northanger Abbey cannot be much farther," he assured her.

Just as he became convinced that they had indeed lost their way, the carriage passed through a set of great gates. An imposing Gothic structure, the pointed arches of its windows illuminated by candles, rose from the fog blanketing the valley.

"I believe we have arrived," Darcy said. He assisted Elizabeth from the carriage, and together they dashed to the shelter of an old porch, leaving their servants to attend to the luggage.

Northanger's housekeeper admitted them to a lofty hall. Darcy gave their names and enquired whether Captain Tilney was at home.

"Yes—he has been expecting you this age." Catching her reflection in a looking glass, the tall, thin woman adjusted her cap over blond hair starting to evidence grey. Darcy waited impatiently, reflecting that Mrs. Reynolds would never countenance a servant attending to her own appearance before guests at Pemberley, let alone do so herself.

When she was satisfied, the housekeeper returned her attention to them. She noted Darcy's walking stick and reached for it. "Do let me take that for you."

He relinquished the cane. When she made no move to also divest them of their cloaks, Elizabeth asked whether she would like to take those, as well.

"Oh, yes—I suppose so." She appeared less than eager to accept the wet garments, and held Darcy's greatcoat and Elizabeth's wrap as far away from herself as possible so as not to dampen her own clothing.

"Wait here a moment while I deposit your things. Then I will conduct you to your chamber. You no doubt wish to refresh yourselves—rain always makes everything so dirty."

She disappeared behind one of several doors in the hall, leaving Elizabeth and Darcy to exchange perplexed glances.

Elizabeth smiled. "Perhaps we should have paraded through the house in our wet things so as not to trouble her."

Darcy did not find their reception so amusing. "If her conduct is characteristic of servants here, I begin to share your opinion of Gloucestershire's hospitality."

"Now *you* are too harsh. A warm fire will set all to rights."

When the housekeeper returned, Darcy asked how soon they might have the pleasure of meeting their host.

"My master looks forward to welcoming you at dinner. We dine precisely at five o'clock every evening at Northanger Abbey. It is now half past four."

She led them up a broad oak staircase with a heavily ornamented rail. At the top, they entered a long gallery lined with windows on one side and doors on the other. Nothing could be seen through the windows but darkness and splattered raindrops reflecting the candlelight.

They passed to the end of the gallery, where she opened a pair of folding doors. These led into a narrower gallery, with a winding staircase and more doors. The first of these on the left, she opened to reveal a generously sized apartment, with mahogany wardrobes, painted chairs, a canopied bed, and two dressing-closets. A large tapestry hung on one wall. Their trunks, already open, waited for them.

The room was dark save for the light of the candle the housekeeper carried. Darcy and Elizabeth waited in expectation for the servant to light a lamp or candle in the chamber, but the thought apparently did not cross her mind. She stood gazing about the room as if appraising the furnishings.

"This seems a pleasant room," Elizabeth said. "Though perhaps a bit dim."

"Yes . . ." She suddenly seemed to remember herself. "Oh! Indeed." She crossed to the room's sole lamp to light it. For some reason, the task proved a challenge, and she struggled with it so long that Darcy found himself nearly overcome by the urge to seize the lamp from her and light it himself.

Eventually, she achieved success and set the lamp in the center of the table. It sputtered, not quite committed to remaining lit.

"This chamber belonged to the late Mrs. Tilney," she said. "The apartment has gone unused since she died, despite its being the nicest in the house. Can you imagine?"

Darcy had more difficulty imagining himself retaining her as a senior servant. Perhaps in her middle or late thirties, she was considerably younger than Mrs. Reynolds, but the true gulf between them lay in their professionalism. Captain

Tilney must maintain far more relaxed expectations than did Darcy.

"The master thought it was time the apartment saw some use," the housekeeper continued, "so we hope you find it comfortable."

The room was not remotely comfortable at the moment—the air within was cold. Though a Bath stove occupied the fireplace, it sat empty and unlit.

"If you do not require anything else—"

"A fire," Darcy said.

"Oh! Of course. I suppose someone will see to that while you are at dinner. I shall leave you now to dress and come back to escort you. As this is a large house, the master requests that you not wander it by yourselves."

She closed the heavy oak door. Thunder rumbled outside, drowning out the sound of her receding footsteps.

Elizabeth looked to Darcy with an expression of bafflement. "All right, I concede. Would you care to remark upon the oddity of our reception, or shall I?"

"I would, but we have not time."

Though their luggage was present, their servants were nowhere about—an unaccountable dereliction. They rang the bell, but with such a short span in which to make themselves presentable, they seized the first suitable clothing they could find in their trunks and began assisting each other while waiting for their summons to be answered.

Five minutes later, they were still waiting.

"I cannot fathom where our servants have gone," Elizabeth said as Darcy fastened the back of her gown. "And why has no one else answered the bell?"

Darcy could not spare a moment to formulate a guess. He had missed a button and had to fasten her gown all over again. "Captain Tilney will be enjoying dessert before I finish these buttons," he said.

"It seems rather inconsiderate of him to make us rush so."

"As a military man, he no doubt values punctuality."

"As a host, he ought to value the comfort of his guests."

She winced as she caught sight of her hair in the looking

glass. The damp weather had set each lock conspiring against the others. She left the mirror and pillaged her trunk.

"I cannot find my hairbrush."

"Is there not one on the dressing table?"

She glanced at its surface. "No. Perhaps in one of the drawers." She opened the dressing table drawers in rapid succession, but the search proved unsuccessful. Darcy, meanwhile, approached the looking glass and struggled to tie his neckcloth in record time.

A large, old-fashioned cabinet of ebony and gold stood in a nearby recess. "Should I try that cabinet?"

"Unless you have decided to accept the present state of your hair as satisfactory after all."

"I cannot meet our host like this. He will mistake me for one of the hedges."

She crossed to the cabinet. A key extended from the lock; she turned it and unfolded the doors to reveal a wall of small drawers. These she slid open one by one. "Empty . . . empty . . . handkerchiefs . . . gloves . . . empty . . . stockings . . . more handkerchiefs . . . oh, my!"

He glanced at her reflection in the looking glass. Her countenance held astonishment. "Have you discovered the crown jewels?"

"No. Only a hoard of diamonds."

"Is that all?" He made a final adjustment to his cravat.

"Darcy, I am quite serious."

He brought the lamp over and looked into the drawer himself. A diamond necklace, bracelet, and pair of eardrops glittered back at him. The set appeared very costly—hardly the sort of thing he would leave in such an unsecured location for years. "The family must have forgotten about these."

They closed the drawer. The next contained a superior treasure—a comb. Elizabeth seized it and hurried to the dressing table.

SOMEHOW, THEY MANAGED to achieve full dress by the time the housekeeper reappeared. Elizabeth enquired into the whereabouts of their maid and valet, and received a blank look in response.

"They are *your* servants—I am not responsible for supervising them."

"Nor did anyone answer the bell."

"It must have gone unheard in the bustle of dinner preparations."

Though she found these replies less than satisfactory, Elizabeth let the matter drop as they hastened to join Captain Tilney on time. She did, however, note the displeasure in Darcy's face as the housekeeper sprinted down the corridor expecting rather than inviting them to follow.

"Do you suppose all guests at Northanger are treated so attentively?" she said under her breath.

"If so, it is little wonder that our host seeks new acquaintances," he replied. "No one ever returns."

Despite the speed at which their guide led them, the housekeeper walked gracefully and carried herself with as much dignity as one would expect in a servant of her status. She conducted them back through the great gallery, past portraits of long-dead ancestors and paintings of the abbey's various incarnations.

"How long have the Tilney family lived at Northanger Abbey?" Elizabeth asked.

They reached the central staircase before she finally answered. "A long time."

Contrary to Elizabeth's expectation, they did not meet their host in the drawing room and proceed to the dinner table; rather, the housekeeper escorted them straight to the dining parlor. It was a spacious room, richly appointed, with an enormous chandelier overhead and a long table set for three. The chandelier was unlit, forcing the entire burden of illuminating the vast chamber on two candelabra standing at attention on the table and an indifferent blaze in the massive marble hearth. These lights made a noble effort at dispelling the shadows that cloaked the room's perimeter, but proved inadequate to the task.

One place setting rested at the head of the table, with the

other two across from each other about a third of the way down. The housekeeper directed them to the latter, informed them that her master would arrive momentarily, and departed.

They took their seats. Though Pemberley boasted a grand dining parlor and Elizabeth had enjoyed the hospitality of others similar in scale, she felt dwarfed by the proportions of the room.

"Perhaps it is the absence of our host," Darcy suggested in response to her observation.

"Or of proper lighting. I can scarcely see my silverware."

Lightning flashed. Elizabeth jumped at the sudden sight of the housekeeper behind Darcy. She had not noticed the servant reenter the room.

"Captain Tilney sends his most sincere apologies. He feels indisposed at present and must settle for a tray in his chamber. He urges you, however, to enjoy the meal after your long journey. He will meet you afterward in the drawing room."

"If the captain suffers indisposition, perhaps he would prefer to receive us in the morning," Darcy offered.

"No—he is quite decided upon meeting you tonight."

"I hope his complaint is of a minor nature," Elizabeth said. "Is the captain an older gentleman?"

"Not at all. He is of middle years, and still quite fine to look upon."

"Has he a wife?"

"No," she said sharply.

She brought in the first course—some sort of soup Elizabeth could not quite identify, though Darcy almost became far too personally acquainted with it when the housekeeper's inattentive serving threatened to pour it into his lap. They were soon left alone again, with only the sounds of the storm for company. Rain pelted the windows, and cracks of thunder punctuated their conversation.

Darcy met Elizabeth's gaze in the flickering candlelight. "And you thought a visit with Captain Tilney sounded intriguing *before* we left Bath."

"This is certainly one of the more interesting places to which you have brought me since our marriage."

"More interesting than Mr. Dashwood's town house?"

She smiled. "Mr. Dashwood's residence had only an antique looking glass to lend it character. Here we have already encountered a housekeeper who cannot keep house but who can materialize out of nowhere, been installed in an apartment last used decades ago by the home's dead mistress, and played hide-and-seek with a mysterious host who never appears. All this, and we have not yet been within these walls a full hour. Even Mr. Dashwood's town house cannot compete with the allure of Northanger Abbey. Indeed, I think only the castle of Udolpho holds more charm."

"Are you wishing we had declined the captain's invitation?"

"Indeed not! I find this all excessively diverting. But if we discover a black veil anywhere on the premises, *you* can raise it up."

She tested the soup and glanced back at Darcy. "Mock turtle?"

"Certainly a mockery of something."

The soup was followed by successive courses that invited speculation as to whether Captain Tilney's indisposition was merely an excuse to avoid the fare. Or perhaps a digestive ailment caused by it.

When they finished the meal, the housekeeper escorted them across the hall, through an antechamber, and into a grand drawing room. Pier glasses and other mirrors lining the walls endlessly reflected the light of dozens of candles, surrounding them with hundreds of tiny points of light that somehow did not seem to dispel the darkness.

In a chair near the hearth, partially shielded from their view by a firescreen, sat a figure swathed in bandages. Strips of white cloth wrapped his head and obscured most of his face, exposing only a single eye and his mouth. The coverings extended down his neck, where they met the edge of a blanket draped over his shoulders.

The housekeeper crossed to him. "Sir, Mr. and Mrs. Darcy are here."

"Excellent." He rose to his feet. "At last, I am able to bid you welcome." The blanket slipped off one shoulder of his stout frame, revealing that he had use of only one arm. The other was splinted and strapped to his side. He indicated two chairs on the other side of the fireplace and invited them to sit.

The housekeeper helped him back into his own seat and restored the blanket around his shoulders. She then placed a glass of port in his hand and brought another for Darcy.

"Thank you, Dorothy," the captain said. "You may go."

The servant appeared reluctant to leave. She repositioned the firescreen, nearly knocking it over in the process, to provide her master's damaged face more protection from the heat. When stable once more, the screen cast Captain Tilney's face in shadow. She then adjusted his blanket again, refilled his glass, and hovered about for another minute or two. Finding no further tasks by which to demonstrate her extraordinary domestic skills, she at last departed.

"Forgive my not greeting you upon your arrival," Captain Tilney said. "Find it difficult to move about the house these days—deuced injuries, but that is the risk one takes when serving His Majesty, hey?"

Despite the profusion of bandages, he spoke with ease. Elizabeth took this verbal facility as an encouraging sign that their host did not suffer too terribly from pain—unless drink dulled it. His one good eye, however, appeared bright and focused.

"I trust Dorothy saw to your comfort?" their host continued.

"Yes, although—"

"Capital. I intended to join you for dinner, but then discovered myself unequal to it. Feeling well enough now, though, to share a glass with you." He raised his wine in salute.

"Captain Tilney," Darcy replied, "if you would prefer to postpone—"

"No, no! Upon my soul, I have been looking forward to meeting you more than you can guess. Deuced poor luck, getting injured during the few short days I returned to my regiment last week." He muttered something about an accident. "Devil take me, I must look a sight, all bandaged up like this. I hope my appearance does not put either of you ill at ease?"

In such a potentially eerie setting as an ancient, shadow-filled room with a storm raging outside, a shrouded figure with a Cyclopean gaze could well have inspired discomfort in his unprepared guests. And Elizabeth indeed found herself disconcerted by Captain Tilney—but not because he seemed remotely ominous. The Eye, rather than fixing upon one of them with a penetrating stare that sent shudders down the spine, instead shifted rapidly between her and Darcy, never resting on either of them more than a moment. She had difficulty reading the captain's temperament with his gaze bouncing around so, and his manner—surprisingly animated given the extent of his injuries—contributed to the impression that he was exerting himself overmuch to win their amity. She felt herself and Darcy to be trespassing on the invalid's recovery by their very presence at Northanger. The poor man ought to be in bed, not forcing himself to fulfill his duties as a host.

"Your kind hospitality toward us cannot but render us perfectly easy," Elizabeth assured him. "However, we do not wish to begin our acquaintance by fatiguing you, and entertaining strangers can prove tiring for someone in the best of health. Perhaps Mr. Darcy and I should return, or you can visit us at Pemberley, on a future date, when your strength is restored."

"No, no—I care not a whit about fatigue. I could sprint from here to Gloucester if I chose. I do not wish to defer the pleasure of your society, and as I am injured, you must indulge me. Let us have no more talk of leaving. Do you find your quarters satisfactory? Northanger Abbey is an old house, but not too draughty. Been improved to offer modern comforts."

The old-fashioned comforts of a fire and adequate time to properly dress for dinner would have constituted sufficient improvements, but given their host's current state of affliction, Elizabeth no longer considered these matters deserving of mention. "Quite satisfactory," she said. "We understand our apartment was formerly occupied by your mother?"

"What's that? Oh, yes—I suppose it was." He swallowed more port. "It has been so long, you know. When I arrived yesterday, I thought it rather cork-brained to reserve those rooms from use any longer. The nicest rooms in the house, just sitting empty while everyone else is forced to make do with smaller. Why, dear Mother would not want that at all, I am sure. So I said to—to Dorothy, that the first guests to use them should be the son of her dear friend and his wife."

"We are honored," Darcy said. "But are you aware that some of the drawers and cupboards still hold her effects?"

"Oh, that is nothing. Feel free to use everything in the rooms as your own."

His nonchalance took Elizabeth aback. Surely the late Mrs. Tilney would not want strangers handling her possessions without her son having sorted through them first. "Perhaps you wish to remove her personal items, at least, to another location?"

"No, no. Not if any of them can be of use or interest to you."

Elizabeth blinked at his continued indifference. She glanced at Darcy, who appeared similarly dumbfounded by their host.

"You are most generous, Captain Tilney," she said. "But I cannot imagine a need of ours that would supersede the sentimental value your mother's belongings hold for you. And we found—"

"As I said, use everything as your own. By Jove, this is fine port, is it not, Mr. Darcy? I believe I shall have a second glass. Can I top off yours?" He began to rise, but Darcy stopped him.

"Allow me." Darcy refilled their host's glass but poured no more wine for himself. When he was seated once more, the captain took a long draught and settled more deeply into his own chair.

"Now, forgive me, Mrs. Darcy, if you feel excluded from the conversation for a few minutes. But there are many questions I wish to ask your husband here—"

"Of course." Elizabeth had expected as much. In fact, the conversational turn was about the only part of their visit that had met her expectations.

The Eye turned upon Darcy and remained fixed for the first time all evening. "So, Mr. Darcy—did you ever meet Mrs. Tilney?"

"Regrettably, I do not believe I had the honor. How long ago did she pass away?"

"Oh, twenty years at least." He took another sip of wine. "When did you lose your mother?" The casualness of his voice made it sound as if Darcy had merely misplaced her.

"Eighteen years ago this January," Darcy replied in a much more sober tone.

"And your letter said Mrs. Tilney never visited Pemberley?"

"I do not believe so. Unless I was too young to remember."

"Did your mother—what was her name—Lady Anne?—ever speak of her?"

"She would have had little occasion to speak to me about Mrs. Tilney. I was a young boy, more interested in my mother's nursery tales than in her social acquaintance."

The captain sat forward. "Come, now—did she *never* mention visiting Mrs. Tilney here at Northanger? Point out mementoes she might have received from her?"

"Not to me."

"Well, then, to anyone at Pemberley?"

"If she did, I have no direct knowledge of her having done so."

Even with only one eye showing, the captain's disappointment was obvious. The curl of his lower lip resembled nothing so much as a pout. "But they corresponded, yes?"

"One might presume they did. My mother engaged in frequent correspondence with many friends."

"Did she save her letters?—Upon my soul, of course she did! Women always keep that sort of thing. There must be a note or two from Mrs. Tilney somewhere at Pemberley. Nay, dozens! I should like very much to see them."

Though his glass remained half full, Darcy set it aside. "I am aware of none, but should we discover any, it would be my pleasure to return them to your care."

Elizabeth sensed an increase in her husband's natural reserve. He was, she knew, unaccustomed to answering so many questions about his family, particularly from someone of such slight acquaintance.

"Captain Tilney," she said, "did your mother preserve any correspondence herself? Might there be letters from Lady Anne here at Northanger?"

"Dash it, no. Nothing the old general kept for anybody to find, anyway. Did you ever meet him? Superior billiards player, though I could always best him. By Jove, once when I met him at—oh, but we were speaking of his wife, were we not? Well, one never knows when an old letter might be found. Or what interesting details it might contain about something everybody forgot about ages ago. Only think—a simple note that was nothing but tittle-tattle between friends could reveal some secret nobody else knew. Jolly intriguing things, old letters! I swear, I shall begin saving mine as of this moment just to entertain my heirs after I pop off."

Darcy's expression grew still more shuttered. Elizabeth wondered whether the captain's comment had inadvertently brought to his mind Lady Anne's final letter. Her husband had not found it entertaining in the least. It had revealed an extent of suffering on his mother's part that he would just as soon have never known about so vividly.

"A letter can communicate more than its author intended," Darcy said. "Particularly to those who were never meant to read it."

"My point precisely!" Captain Tilney drained his wineglass and set it down with so much force that Elizabeth briefly feared for its welfare. "Revelations just waiting to be uncovered!"

"To what purpose?" Darcy shook his head. "Some things are best left buried in the past."

"Some things should never have become buried in the first place, and ought to be brought to light."

A flash of lightning cast the room in sudden brilliance. The shadow eclipsing Captain Tilney's face momentarily receded, exposing the zeal that brightened his lone blue eye. An enormous boom followed. Rain pelted the windows with renewed fury.

The Eye now shifted back to Elizabeth. "What do you think, Mrs. Darcy? If you stumbled across some intriguing hint of forgotten treasure, would you search for it?"

Despite the casual character of his speech, Captain Tilney's statements held an undercurrent Elizabeth could not define, as if he and they were not quite participating in the same conversation.

"If I thought it could—and ought to—be found," she replied warily.

Darcy's jaw had acquired the rigid set she had come to recognize as a sure sign of his displeasure. "Forgive me, Captain," he said, "but my wife and I have endured a long day of travel, and I can see that she is weary. Would you take it amiss if we retired for the evening?"

The sudden request brought a look of surprise to their host's face—or, at least, to the Eye—but he recovered himself quickly.

"So soon? But you have not yet—that is, we were just becoming acquainted. Surely you will stay long enough to share another glass of port, at least? Mrs. Darcy may withdraw if she chooses."

Darcy stood. "Unfortunately, I must decline. Our journey fatigued me also."

"Well . . . if you must," he replied rather petulantly. There was something off-putting about their host. Although Elizabeth pitied the man for his injuries, she did not find him a pleasant individual. "I shall summon Dorothy to escort you."

He rose, but turned in the direction opposite the bell. He paused and glanced round the walls until he located it.

Elizabeth eyed his wineglass and wondered whether the port or his recent accident accounted for his absentmindedness. "Do let me ring it for you."

The housekeeper appeared almost before Elizabeth's hand released the pull. She seemed disconcerted to find the three of them standing, and looked at her employer as if demanding an explanation.

"The Darcys would like to retire to their apartment now," the captain said.

"Already? Have you finished your conversation?"

"We shall continue tomorrow."

Dorothy pursed her lips in the same sort of pout Captain Tilney had displayed earlier. "After I see the Darcys to their chamber, I shall return directly."

The housekeeper was silent as she conducted them through the corridors and galleries. They reached their chamber, which remained free of any hint that they had even brought their personal attendants to Northanger. At least someone had started a fire while they were at dinner, so the room had warmed.

"Our servants?" Darcy enquired again.

"They will turn up sooner or later. Ring the bell if you require anything."

Elizabeth harbored little hope of anyone in the house actually addressing a need of theirs, especially as the housekeeper immediately left them to themselves without another word. She stared at the door through which Dorothy had so speedily departed. "Just when one thinks this place cannot get any stranger—"

"We meet our host?" Darcy finished.

She turned. "Him, too." She shook her head in bewilderment at the whole evening. "One hesitates to criticize a man who has suffered such extensive injuries. But he is not at all what I expected a captain to be."

"Nor I." He removed his coat and tugged at his cravat.

"For a man of his years and occupation, I thought he would possess a graver manner—particularly after having suffered such serious injury. His speech and appearance formed an odd pairing. I suspect we were more afflicted by his accident than he was. Every time he turned his eye upon me, I felt a bit off balance. I was thankful when you begged leave to retire."

"I believed we had both answered enough of his questions for the present."

She went to her open trunk to retrieve her nightdress. "He certainly posed a great many of them, though I think most were to be expected. Your mother is the reason he invited us here, after all. Of course he would want to know more about her." She frowned. "I thought I had seen my nightdress toward the top of this trunk when we were dashing around here earlier."

"I saw it there, too." He draped his coat over the back of a chair and neatly folded the neckcloth.

She continued rummaging through half-folded stacks of clothing. She had not realized she'd made such a mess of her maid's packing in her haste to dress for dinner. "The captain is quite an enigma. I wonder what he looks like without the bandages. Oh—here is the nightdress, under my blue sarsenet. I thought that gown was in the other trunk." She held the nightdress by its shoulders and shook it open. "It was a little unsettling, was it not, that the captain should talk about never knowing when a letter might turn up, and about letters inspiring people to search for forgotten things, when we so recently found that letter of your mother's urging us to do just that?"

"That is a matter Captain Tilney need never learn anything about."

"Agreed."

He regarded her current gown with dismay. "I suppose you require assistance with those buttons again."

"Do not complain. They are easier to open than close."

He indulged in a wicked grin. "I know."

She laughed, pleased by the display of Darcy's less serious side. It had been little evident since their discovery of Lady Anne's letter, and she welcomed its return. Perhaps engaging Dr. Severn had helped improve her husband's humor by easing his anxiety. If so, she considered the change worth tolerating the physician's haughtiness.

"Shame on you, Mr. Darcy. We are in an abbey."

"A former abbey."

She came to him and offered him her back so that he could start on the buttons.

"All right, a former abbey," she said. "And one straight out of a horrid novel, I might add. The house is gloomy and dark, and we are not allowed to move about it freely. There seems to be a decided lack of servants—including our own. And for all we know, our host could be a phantom under those layers of bandages."

"I doubt a phantom would swear upon his soul quite so often."

Just as she finished changing into her nightdress, a thunderclap rent the air. It was another sound, however, that caused her to jump. "Did you hear that?"

"I expect everyone within twenty miles heard it."

"Not the thunder—over there." She pointed at the wall with the tapestry. She thought she had heard a thump from that quarter following the boom.

"Perhaps the force of the thunder shook some object."

"Are you not going to examine the tapestry?"

"I thought my investigative responsibility was limited to black veils."

"A tapestry is close enough."

He crossed the room. The large silk-and-wool tapestry depicted the Annunciation, and appeared old enough that it might have hung at Northanger in the days when the building had indeed been an abbey. Though the centuries had dulled most of the colors, the heavenly light radiating from the virgin and the archangel stood out brightly.

Darcy caught the edge of the tapestry and pulled it to one side. To their surprise, the fabric parted down the center, revealing a door in the wall behind it. The door's paneling matched that of the rest of the room, so that when closed—as it now was—it blended into the wall unnoticed. Such doors existed in homes throughout England; Pemberley had dozens.

"It is an ordinary servants' door, nothing more." He opened it to reveal a small, dark landing and narrow stair. "The thunder must have rattled it. You have nothing to fear but your own imagination." He closed the door and allowed the tapestry to fall back into place. When it hung properly, the center division was indiscernible.

She let out a long breath and realized she had been more alarmed than she thought. The atmosphere of Northanger Abbey was starting to play havoc with her nerves. She longed to be home, in the comfort of Pemberley, away from strange houses, strange servants, and strange captains.

"Darcy, despite our having discovered a servants' door rather than a skeleton, I must confess that I have not felt entirely comfortable at Northanger Abbey since the moment we entered it. There is something not quite right here."

"Nothing a competent domestic staff could not address. Though having now met Captain Tilney, I believe the master himself partially responsible for the lax standards. I suspect he fails to set the proper tone."

"Nevertheless, I cannot imagine enduring a full se'nnight of this."

"A premature departure would insult our host."

"Despite his assurances to the contrary, our presence is an imposition while he recovers."

"Even so, we cannot simply leave."

"Yes, we can. We can quit Northanger tomorrow morning—our trunks are even packed. Please, Darcy. We have been gone from Pemberley many weeks. I just want to go home." Away from Captain Tilney, away from Lady Catherine, away from Wickham and Lydia and all the other vexations that had comprised their trip.

Darcy studied her face a long time before replying. She knew that her request asked him to ignore his sense of propriety, to place her wishes above his natural inclination.

"Very well," he said finally. "In truth, now that we have

met Captain Tilney, I am not certain I want to cultivate his acquaintance to a high degree. Nonetheless, we must take care to avoid giving offense."

She thanked him with an embrace. "We shall invent a plausible excuse."

Outside, the wind moaned its protest and rain furiously assaulted the windows. Though morning offered the promise of returning home, it would be a long night.

"I suppose," he said, stepping out of her arms, "an early departure reduces the likelihood of our finding a black veil requiring my examination." He drew closed a set of curtains to shut out the storm.

"Not necessarily. This room holds numerous draperies, two tablecloths, and a canopy to occupy you before we leave."

"Those also fall under my province?"

"Your sphere includes all hanging fabric."

"All?" His eyes dropped to the hem of her nightdress. He released an exaggerated sigh and met her gaze. "With that much responsibility, I could be up half the night investigating."

Eight

Against staying longer, however, Elizabeth was positively resolved.

—Pride and Prejudice

Morning saw no end to the gloom that engulfed Northanger. Dawn could scarcely be said to have broken, so dark did the sky remain. The rain continued, less violent but steady, and one could not determine where the mist ended and the clouds began. An equally melancholy atmosphere pervaded the house.

Darcy and Elizabeth helped each other dress. Their personal servants were still nowhere to be found, and further enquiries to Dorothy regarding their whereabouts produced only more paltering. After dining alone in the breakfast parlor, they returned to the drawing room for another audience with the captain.

He sat in the same chair, his white bandages a stark contrast to the purple velvet. "Well, now, this is a dreary start to the day, is it not? Thought surely the storm would blow itself out after keeping me awake half the night, but the rain simply will not quit. I believe it continues solely to vex us. Oh, well—I suppose it saves you the obligation of asking for a tour of Northanger Park this morning, and me the trouble of showing it to you. We instead can remain indoors and talk more of your mother and Mrs. Tilney."

Darcy had little desire to reopen that conversation. He conveyed to their host that, to their deep regret, they would have to cut their visit short. "Business calls us home."

"No, no—I will not hear of it! Your business cannot be of great consequence. You must remain at least another day or two."

"I am afraid we cannot tarry."

"But this weather has made the roads unfit for travel. I would not take my carriage out upon them for anything! It will pour all day—see if it does not!"

Though Darcy himself harbored concerns about the condition of the roads, he held fast to his resolve. His own wish to leave had begun to match Elizabeth's, and increased with every hour. "Further, we would not intrude on your privacy whilst you recover from your accident—"

"Upon my soul, your presence is no imposition. On the contrary, it boosts my spirits! Would you abandon an injured man to recuperate in isolation, with none but servants for company?"

The thought of leaving the captain to the haphazard care of Dorothy indeed inspired sympathy on Darcy's part, but not a reversal. He again offered their apologies.

Captain Tilney became ill-tempered. "I can only interpret your insistence upon leaving as a rejection of my overtures of friendship. Is this how my hospitality is repaid? You discredit your mother's memory, Mr. Darcy, by inflicting such insult upon the family of her dear friend. Indeed you do! I would not behave so unkindly toward you for all the world."

"You are too hard on my husband," Elizabeth interjected. "Please do not blame him. Before coming here, I learned of a matter requiring my attention back at Pemberley. After our conversation last evening, I was kept awake by the storm and spent the night in contemplation. I awoke with the conviction that the matter ought not be deferred. In departing this morning, he indulges me."

"Indeed? Our conversation last night inspired this decision?" The captain studied her with his good eye. "Then go, Mrs. Darcy, and take care of your business. The devil take me, I would not cause a lady delay in attending to affairs urgent to her."

So released, Darcy wished to effect their exit without further delay. The horses were ordered. A final stop in their chamber discovered their missing servants, returned and repacking the disorganized trunks.

"Lucy!" Elizabeth exclaimed. "Wherever have you been?"

"It was the strangest thing, ma'am. When we first arrived, the housekeeper told me I was not needed in your apartment right away. I knew you were in haste to prepare for dinner, but—well, it would not be the first time Mr. Darcy helped you dress instead of me. So I stayed in the servants' hall, and the housekeeper gave me and Graham our dinner. Then she showed me where I was to sleep. I felt a little dizzy and shaky, so I sat down on the bed for just a moment. Next I knew, I woke up about half an hour ago. I am so sorry, ma'am! The damp ride yesterday must have given me a chill, I suppose. I still feel a bit shaky, but nothing of concern—I can travel."

Graham, Darcy's valet, reported a similar experience and offered his most humble apologies. It was the first time in twenty years of service that he had failed to perform his duties, and he felt the failure acutely.

Darcy accepted his apology and, assured of his fitness for travel, told him to not give it another minute's thought. Darcy did, however—many minutes' worth. He did not like the suspicion that formed in his mind upon hearing the servants' stories, and he found himself even more thankful that Elizabeth had pressed for an early departure from Northanger. When the housekeeper escorted them back to the hall, he enquired into the servants' accounts of their experience.

"I understand both Lucy and Graham were taken ill last night."

"Apparently so."

"Did no one think to check their quarters when Mrs. Darcy and I questioned their absences?"

"I thought someone had. There must have been a misunderstanding."

A misunderstanding, indeed. As Dorothy retrieved their cloaks, handed Darcy his cane, and disappeared once more, he reflected that she seemed to lack a great deal of understanding. He immensely looked forward to returning to a home maintained by a capable housekeeper. In fact, when they reached Pemberley, he would grant Mrs. Reynolds a raise in pay.

The wait seemed interminable. Though the postilion arrived with the horses, their carriage was not ready. No one came to offer them any reason for the delay, so they were left to their own speculation for over half an hour. Darcy grew more impatient with each passing minute, conscious that the later they set out, the fewer miles they would be able to travel before nightfall.

"You could have walked to Pemberley in the distance you have paced."

Elizabeth's observation stopped him short. He had not even realized he was pacing. "You know I abhor wasted time. I cannot imagine what causes this detainment."

"Perhaps our servants have not finished packing the trunks."

"As they were never unpacked, I do not know why that should take so long." He caught himself starting to pace again. "I shall go see whether that is indeed the case."

Cane still in hand, he mounted the stairs. He encountered no one on his way back to their apartment, which he found empty of both trunks and servants. He returned to the hall, where his wife informed him that the carriage was at last ready.

As they climbed inside, Elizabeth shared the explanation

she had been given. "Apparently, one of our trunks became misplaced."

"How does one misplace something as large as a trunk?" he asked.

"In this house," she responded, "I begin to think anything possible."

Nine

"How very little trouble it can give you to understand the motive of other people's actions."

—*Henry Tilney,* Northanger Abbey

Thunder rumbled in the distance as they left Northanger Abbey, passed through the gate, and started a slow ascent up the steep, woody hills. The mist seemed to swallow the house almost directly they left it, so they soon had nothing upon which to fix their gazes save those trees close enough to the road to stand out from the fog. The rest of the outside world was naught but a grey haze, creating the surreal sense that they had entered a realm where time and movement were suspended.

It was a protracted, arduous journey. Though the rain abated, it had fallen so hard and so long that it had littered the ground with fallen branches and piles of dead leaves, and turned the roads to muck. The horses struggled to keep a steady pace, and the carriage seemed in perpetual danger of becoming permanently stuck in the mire.

Darcy looked at the ever-darkening sky. They had set out from Northanger much later than he had intended, and what little light penetrated the murkiness would not last much longer.

"How far do you estimate we have traveled?" Elizabeth asked him.

"I thought we would have passed through Cheltenham before now. It cannot lie too far distant." He endeavored to withhold frustration from his voice. Not even to Cheltenham, and the day already nearly gone. "We will stop for the night at the next inn."

She put a hand to her back and stretched as much as she could in the close space. "I am just as content to avoid Cheltenham. I had enough of spas in Bath."

Despite his vexation, her response wrested a slight smile from him. "You do not wish to sample the waters for comparison?"

"I would sooner drink hemlock."

Just as the waning light failed, the inn presented itself. Though the ostler of the Golden Crown informed them that the next post stop would indeed bring them to Cheltenham, where all the luxuries of a spa town might be enjoyed, Darcy believed it unwise to proceed any farther. In fact, he secured lodging for two nights, to give the roads a chance to improve before they continued home.

Exhausted from the day's journey, they retired early and awoke to bright light streaming through the windows. Apparently, the gloom that had pervaded Gloucestershire from the moment they entered it had at last relinquished its hold, and now the sun's rays warmed and restored the landscape.

Having already committed to postponing their travel, they enjoyed an unhurried breakfast and were just discussing how to employ the day when they heard heavy footfalls on the stairs. Moments later, a loud knock sounded on their chamber door. Darcy opened it to discover a short, barrel-chested gentleman with a sword at his side. Sharp eyes peered from beneath the bushy grey eyebrows that dominated his ruddy face. Two other men, also carrying swords, accompanied him.

"Mr. Fitzwilliam Darcy?"

Darcy bowed.

"I am Mr. Chase, constable of this region. An unfortunate situation has come to my attention, about which I believe you possess information. Might I have a word with you?"

"Of course." Darcy admitted the constable and his companions. He moved one of the chairs away from the table, which still held the remains of their breakfast, and invited Mr. Chase to sit. Despite Darcy's gesture toward other chairs, the constable's associates remained standing. Darcy took a seat beside Elizabeth.

"I understand you reside in Derbyshire," Mr. Chase said. "What business brings you to Gloucestershire at present?"

"My wife and I are returning home from Bath."

"Upon which day did you depart Bath?"

"Tuesday."

"And when did you arrive at this inn?"

"Yester eve."

"Yesterday was Wednesday. Where did you pass Tuesday night?"

"At Northanger Abbey."

Although of substantial girth, Mr. Chase bore himself with the air of a little man with a lot of authority. It was a trait Darcy had encountered before.

"I am familiar with Northanger. It is remotely situated—certainly off the main roads for a traveler headed from Bath to Derbyshire. What business took you there?"

"We were the guests of Captain Frederick Tilney."

"Indeed? And what is your connection with Captain Tilney? How long have you been acquainted with him?"

Darcy disliked the tenor of Mr. Chase's enquiries. "Might I ask to what this interrogation pertains?"

"If you don't mind, Mr. Darcy, I shall ask the questions."

Darcy did mind, but saw little to be gained by antagonizing the local lawman. "We met Captain Tilney in person for the first time on Tuesday, but our families have a longer association."

"I see." The constable reclined against the back of his

chair and folded his arms across his ample belly. "So, passing through Gloucestershire, you decided to call upon him?"

"He invited us."

"Had you ever visited Northanger Abbey before?"

"Never."

"It is a large house, and your stay was rather brief. Where did you pass most of your time?"

"In our own chamber," Darcy said. "We had endured a long day's travel, due to the storm, and retired early."

The constable nodded, his second chin spilling over the folds of his simply tied neckcloth. "And where were your quarters?"

"Upstairs, in the back of the house."

"The late Mrs. Tilney's apartment?"

"So we were told." Darcy glanced at Elizabeth to see whether she seemed any better able to grasp Mr. Chase's purpose than he, but she appeared equally perplexed.

"While occupying the apartment, did you remove or relocate any objects?"

"No. We left all as it was."

"And you left in haste, did you not?"

The sharpness of Mr. Chase's tone raised Darcy's defenses. What intelligence did the constable truly seek, and why did he not simply ask for it? Darcy began to doubt whether full cooperation was in his and Elizabeth's best interest.

"What causes you to believe we departed in haste?"

"Perhaps I should have said 'urgency.' As you stated, the storm rendered travel hazardous. Only necessity could have induced you to risk the roads yesterday. What prompted your departure?"

Darcy hesitated to state that there had been no specific reason other than a sense that nothing at Northanger seemed quite as it should. "Business calls us home."

The constable gestured to the remains of their breakfast. "Yet I find you enjoying a leisurely morning. Are you no longer in a hurry to reach Derbyshire?"

"We thought it best to postpone further travel until the roads improve."

"They are greatly improved now—I just traveled them myself to come here. But I am afraid your journey home will be delayed regardless."

At a look from Mr. Chase, one of his companions moved to stand in front of the door. Too late, Darcy wondered whether Mr. Chase was indeed a constable. He instinctively shifted to place himself more squarely between Mr. Chase and Elizabeth.

Noting his movement, Mr. Chase chuckled humorlessly. "Fear not, Mr. Darcy. So long as you cooperate, this will not become a physical confrontation."

Darcy suddenly felt like cornered prey. His pulse quickened as his mind scrambled to assimilate the nature of the threat Mr. Chase posed.

"Cooperate in what?"

Mr. Chase rose, walked behind his chair, and rested his hands on its back. "I received an anonymous letter this morning advising me that a crime had been committed at Northanger Abbey. It seems that a collection of diamonds once belonging to the late Mrs. Tilney has vanished from the premises, and that their disappearance coincides with your visit at Northanger. Can you offer any enlightenment on this matter?"

Elizabeth gasped and looked at Darcy. "The diamonds . . ."

Mr. Chase seized upon the utterance as if it were a confession. He leaned forward and regarded Darcy with increased antagonism. "So you do possess information. Where are the diamonds?"

Initial relief that Mr. Chase indeed represented the law rapidly gave way to resentment at the suggestion that Darcy had broken it. "We know nothing about any missing diamonds," he said. "We discovered a set of jewelry in Mrs. Tilney's chamber, but we left it in the drawer in which we found it."

"When did you make this discovery?"

"Almost directly upon our arrival. My wife happened upon them while seeking a hairbrush as we dressed for dinner."

"Did you mention them to anyone?"

"I was going to mention them to Captain Tilney," Elizabeth said. "But he interrupted me and our discourse shifted to other subjects."

"You did not think the discovery of a valuable set of jewelry merited redirecting the conversation?"

"We were not in the captain's company much longer."

"By your own management. And you claim that the diamonds were still in their drawer when you left Northanger?"

"I presume so," Elizabeth said. "We never looked in the drawer a second time."

"You did not need to. The two of you discovered the diamonds and decided to take them for yourselves."

The accusation so appalled Darcy that he momentarily lost the power of speech. "Nay, sir," he practically sputtered when he recovered himself. "We most certainly did not."

"By your own admission, you spent the majority of your time in your chamber—even retiring early. Thus you not only had ample opportunity to hide the diamonds among your belongings, but your presence in the chamber restricted the access of any other party."

He could not believe his ears. How dare this self-important clod carelessly issue such a serious allegation? "We were absent from the room at dinner and breakfast, in addition to our time with Captain Tilney. Someone could have entered the apartment then. A servant, perhaps."

"Such as a housemaid? That is possible," the constable conceded. "Did you happen to encounter any of the servants who attended your chamber?"

Darcy paused. Revealing the lack of attention both they and their chamber had received from Northanger's staff did not seem likely to aid their cause.

Mr. Chase twisted Darcy's hesitation to suit his purpose. "You suspect one of your own servants, then?"

"No!" Elizabeth exclaimed. "One cannot imagine more trustworthy servants than Lucy and Graham. Beyond that, they both took ill upon our arrival and entered our apartment only to repack our trunks when we departed."

"When you departed as soon as possible to make good your escape—with the diamonds in your repacked trunk."

Darcy shot to his feet, unable to contain his outrage any longer. "Sir, you insult my honor as a gentleman. And you insult my wife."

"Then to prove your innocence, you will not object if we search your belongings."

He objected very much to Mr. Chase and his cronies ransacking their trunks. "I will not have my wife subjected to that indignity."

"Would you rather subject both her and yourself to the indignity of sitting in gaol while I complete my investigation?"

"Gaol?" Elizabeth exclaimed.

"On what grounds?" Darcy asked. "You have no evidence, only your own speculation."

"And the letter."

"A letter authored by someone too cowardly to sign his name."

"Darcy." Elizabeth had moved beside him and now touched his arm. "We can resolve this very easily. Let Mr. Chase search our things. We have nothing to hide."

Submitting to such an affront went against every natural impulse. But she was right—they had nothing to hide, and allowing Mr. Chase to determine that for himself was a more expedient way to acquit themselves of his ridiculous accusations than engaging in prolonged argument.

"Very well," he said stiffly.

A thorough examination of every trunk, case, and compartment—right down to Elizabeth's reticule and his coat pockets—commenced. Darcy observed in silent fury, thankful that Elizabeth had packed no diamonds of her own to confuse the search. Just as the offensive exploration seemed at an end, Mr. Chase's gaze came to rest on the umbrella stand, where Darcy's walking stick rested.

The constable withdrew it from the stand. Darcy resented the sight of him holding the cane.

"This is yours, I presume?"

"It is."

He inspected the grip, then twisted the cinquefoil band. To Darcy's astonishment, the cane separated into two pieces.

With a smug glance at Darcy, Mr. Chase set aside the grip, inserted two fingers into the shaft, and withdrew a long, narrow bundle wrapped in cloth. He set the shaft on the table beside the grip and, as Darcy watched in dread, unfolded the muslin.

"Well, now, Mr. Darcy."

The constable held up Mrs. Tilney's diamond necklace. Sunlight bounced off its many facets, splaying the walls with damning brilliance.

"What have we here?"

Ten

My hearing nothing of you makes me apprehensive that you, your fellow travellers and all your effects, might be seized by the bailiffs. . . .

—Jane Austen, letter to Cassandra

Darcy stared at the two pieces of the cane in disbelief. He had owned the walking stick for a decade. How could he never have noticed that it held a hidden compartment?

The still more obvious question—how the diamond necklace, bracelet, and eardrops had come to be inside it—he could not begin to contemplate.

Mr. Chase sent a servant to fetch the magistrate, who arrived quite put out that his hunting party had been disrupted. But a case of this magnitude, with defendants of the Darcys' social status, warranted immediate attention. Mr. Melbourne would determine whether sufficient evidence existed to commit Darcy and Elizabeth to gaol pending trial at the next assizes.

The magistrate held the proceedings in the common room of the Golden Crown before an audience of local tradesmen, merchants, and yeomen.

"Could we not discuss this matter in private?" Darcy said.

"Justice is a matter of public interest, Mr. Darcy," the magistrate responded. "I conduct all my hearings in full view of His Majesty's law-abiding subjects."

Though called in from the hunt to perform his duties this afternoon, Mr. Melbourne had taken meticulous care with his person before arriving at the Golden Crown. His clothes looked so freshly donned and his dark hair so neatly combed that one could scarcely believe he had traveled to the inn on horseback. Apparently, he ran his legal proceedings in the same exacting manner he applied to his appearance. Darcy actually found a degree of reassurance in this; he would rather deal with a justice of the peace who regarded his responsibilities seriously than one who approached them so sloppily as to not deserve the office.

"Mr. Chase, present the evidence against the Darcys," said Mr. Melbourne.

The constable strutted forward. "Mr. Fitzwilliam Darcy and his wife have committed theft against Captain Frederick Tilney of Northanger Abbey. After passing Tuesday night as guests in his home, they repaid his hospitality by stealing a set of diamonds from his late mother's chamber. I found the couple right here in this inn, with the diamonds in their possession."

Darcy rose. "Mr. Melbourne, we—"

"I shall inform you when it is your turn to speak, Mr. Darcy."

Mr. Melbourne asked to see the diamonds, and Mr. Chase readily produced them. The sight of the jewels raised a murmur in the crowd, which seemed to grow by the minute. Apparently, the arrest of a gentleman and his wife formed the most interesting event the village had seen in some time.

"They secreted them in a cane with a hidden compartment," the constable said as he handed the cane to Mr. Melbourne for inspection. "See here? The grip twists off like this. Someone less observant would have missed it altogether, but I figured it out." His chest swelled. "Mr. and Mrs. Darcy took the diamonds, hid them in the cane, and smuggled them out of the house."

The magistrate examined the pieces, then regarded Darcy coldly. "Is this true?"

"It is not, sir. My wife and I are victims of deceit. I assure you, we did not steal those diamonds." Darcy longed to inspect the cane himself. Mr. Chase had not allowed him to handle it since the diamonds were discovered.

"Do you admit to owning this walking stick?"

"I do, but I had no notion of its harboring a hidden compartment." He gestured toward the cane. "Might I?"

Mr. Melbourne considered a moment, then nodded his consent.

Darcy took up the two pieces. He tilted the opening of the shaft toward the light and determined that the hollow extended about twelve inches. Threads at the top and in the cinquefoil band enabled the shaft to screw into the grip. He fitted these together; when joined, they formed a smooth line that betrayed no evidence of the secret compartment within. He weighed the cane across his hands, then gripped it by the head. It felt familiar in his palm. How could he not have known?

He traced his finger along the length of the cane. And found his answer.

The slight imperfection in the wood was not there. The grain ran evenly down to the tip.

"This walking stick is not mine," he declared.

"Not two minutes ago you identified it as yours."

"It appears very much like mine—resembles it so closely, in fact, that I carried it out of Northanger Abbey and into this inn without realizing the difference. But my cane has a slight imperfection in the wood about halfway down its length, a widening of the grain barely noticeable unless one seeks it. This cane displays no such mark."

"How very convenient." Mr. Melbourne's countenance indicated that he did not believe a syllable Darcy had just uttered.

Darcy was not accustomed to having his word doubted. "My wife can attest to the marking on my cane."

"As your wife is also implicated in the theft, her confirmation means little. Further, you have now just admitted that you left Northanger with this cane, and the diamonds it contained, in your possession. If the cane does not belong to you, then you have stolen it, too."

"This is absurd! We did not steal the diamonds, and we did not put them in this cane."

"Then how do you account for Mr. Chase's having found them in your custody?"

"Someone else must have placed them in the walking stick."

"Someone else *gave* you these diamonds, and neglected to inform you of it? That is preposterous."

"Not nearly as preposterous as the notion that we stole them. I am a gentleman. I own an estate in Derbyshire larger than Northanger Abbey. If I wanted diamonds, I would purchase them myself."

"I have been practicing law and maintaining order in this county a long time, Mr. Darcy, and if there is one thing I have learned about human nature, it is that people often do not act according to sense. You are not the first gentleman I have encountered who stole something he could well afford to buy. Nor does England lack gentlemen who, through mismanagement or dissipation, have exhausted their own coffers and might find themselves unable to resist the temptation of an easy opportunity to refill them."

"I am neither of those sorts of gentlemen. I did not steal anything."

"I have a hollow cane and a handful of diamonds that suggest you did."

Darcy took a deep breath, attempting to cool his ire. He was beginning to wish that Mr. Melbourne were one of those more careless magistrates after all. Continuing the current line of argument would prove futile; he needed another tactic.

He wished he knew who had written the anonymous letter. Should he not have an opportunity to face his accuser? From the little Mr. Chase had revealed, the note must have come from someone at Northanger. A servant—the housekeeper, perhaps? Surely if Captain Tilney himself had thought they were departing his home with the family jewels, he would have stopped them. Or at least signed his name to the letter.

"Mr. Melbourne, does not a crime require a victim? If Mrs. Tilney once owned these diamonds, they now belong to her son. Let us go to Northanger Abbey and talk to the captain. Doubtless, he will assure you that this is all an enormous error."

The magistrate pondered the proposal. "All right," he said finally. "The jewels must be returned anyway. I might as well deliver them myself and allow you to accompany me."

"Thank you, sir—"

"Do not thank me yet. The day is now too far gone for us to journey all the way to Northanger and back before dark. We shall pursue this errand tomorrow morning. Until then, I must commit you both to gaol."

Darcy was filled with mortification and outrage. A member of the Darcy family passing a single night in gaol was inconceivable. His name would be tarnished, his reputation damaged. Physical discomfort he could bear with fortitude, but the injury to his honor would be a heavy blow to suffer. That Elizabeth, in her condition, could not possibly be subjected to the environment of gaol was beyond question.

"Might you consider permitting us to stay here at the inn? You have my word that we will not attempt escape, or even leave our room."

"You have just been caught with stolen diamonds in your possession. Why should I trust your word?"

"I am a gentleman."

"As I just explained, Mr. Darcy, your status as a gentleman means little. Perhaps the magistrates in Derbyshire treat persons of means more leniently, but in my jurisdiction the law applies equally to all individuals. In fact, as a gentleman myself, I hold those of our status to a higher standard, and condemn the actions of any gentleman who would taint our collective honor through conduct unbecoming. Ask those gathered here about the fate of Mr. Oliver Smyth, known in these parts as the 'gentleman bandit.' "

"Swung from a tree!" someone cried.

"I am no bandit," Darcy declared. "Do not treat me as one."

"You stand accused of theft—a hanging offense for an item as valuable as these diamonds. Until this matter is resolved, you and your wife shall be treated like any other criminals."

Another murmur swept through the crowd.

Darcy looked at Elizabeth. Her face was filled with anxiety. The thought of her sharing this shame was insupportable. He could not—would not—allow that to happen.

"I will go with you willingly, but for mercy's sake, please do not subject my wife to incarceration."

"If gentlemen do not enjoy exemption from the law, neither do ladies."

"Yes, but . . . a private word, please, Mr. Melbourne?"

"What is it?"

Darcy approached the table and leaned forward. "Mrs. Darcy is in a delicate state of health," he said in a voice audible only to the magistrate.

"You ought to have considered that before breaking the law."

"If anything happened to her or the child while in gaol, would you want that on your conscience?"

Mr. Melbourne folded his arms across his chest and studied Elizabeth for several long moments. Finally, he said, "Mrs. Darcy, was there ever a time when your husband was in Mrs. Tilney's chamber alone—without you?"

Darcy heard the question with relief and gratitude. The magistrate was offering Elizabeth a way out. But to accept it, she would have to cast even more suspicion on him.

She looked not at Mr. Melbourne, but at Darcy. He could read the reluctance in her eyes. She would not pronounce a word that might betray him.

"Speak the truth, Elizabeth."

She hesitated. He willed her compliance with his steady gaze. *I shall be all right. Speak the truth.*

She swallowed. "Just before we left Northanger Abbey, my husband went to the apartment alone to ascertain whether the servants had finished packing our trunks. He was gone but a few minutes—"

"Did he have this walking stick with him when he went?"

Her face filled with distress. "Yes."

"Then it is possible that Mr. Darcy committed this crime without your knowledge?"

"It is impossible that my husband committed any crime," she said fiercely. "He is the most honorable man I have ever known."

"An admirable display of loyalty, Mrs. Darcy."

Mr. Melbourne leaned back in his chair, his gaze shifting between Elizabeth and Darcy several times as he deliberated. Darcy, meanwhile, strove to mask his own apprehension. So long as Elizabeth was spared, he could tolerate anything.

At last, the magistrate reached a decision. "Mrs. Darcy, your statement has sufficiently convinced me that your husband is the principal perpetrator of this plot. You may stay here under guard tonight. Mr. Darcy, the constable will escort you to gaol."

At the word "gaol," Elizabeth released a soft cry.

The eager Mr. Chase stepped forward. Darcy would go willingly, as promised. But first he needed to remove the stricken look from Elizabeth's face. "Might I have a few words alone with my wife?" he asked Mr. Melbourne.

"I suppose so. A few *brief* words."

Darcy went to Elizabeth and took both her hands in his. Despite the stuffiness of the crowded room, her hands were cold and betrayed a slight tremble. He held them tightly as he looked into dark brown eyes that had never before reflected such turmoil.

"Darcy, I—"

"Hush. I would not have had you say anything else. I will be fine, and this is one instance in which I do not desire your company."

"But gaol!"

"My first concern is for you and our child. Knowing you are safe, I can endure a night of the gaoler's hospitality until this matter is sorted out." He longed to touch her face, to smooth away the anxiety that furrowed her brow. But consciousness of their audience forced him to settle for pressing her hands in reassurance.

"Shall I contact Mr. Harper?" she asked.

"Mr. Harper cannot be reached in France, let alone assist us, between now and tomorrow morning—when our return to Northanger will resolve this affair."

If it did not, he would summon Mr. Harper posthaste.

Darcy prayed events would not come to that. He wanted no one else to learn of this embarrassment. Though he trusted his solicitor implicitly, the *haut ton* was a gossiping beast that fed on the adversity of others. Somehow the news would leak, and Mr. and Mrs. Fitzwilliam Darcy would become the topic du jour in every club, parlor, and assembly room of the Polite World. He could not bear the thought of his name being bandied about London, of other people—persons with whom he might not even be acquainted, who had no interest in his welfare—using his misfortune to increase their own social capital by trumping their listeners with the most dramatic *on dit*.

How Darcy now regretted sending his solicitor abroad! If only, as his aunt had requested, he had personally undertaken the errand of ensuring his cousin Roger did not sully the family reputation.

Instead, he had stayed behind to ruin it himself.

THE FOLLOWING DAY DAWNED brighter than any day so begun had a right. Darcy watched the sun rise through the small window of his cramped room in Mr. Slattery's house. Once at the county gaol, Darcy's status as a gentleman had spared him from confinement with the common criminals, but he'd had to pay generously for the privilege of being accommodated with the gaoler himself. Given the vulgar, dirty conditions in which Mr. Slattery lived, Darcy had been only slightly better off.

He had slept little, his mind too active to permit rest. He had entered the gaol bewildered, the circumstances in which he found himself too far removed from his realm of experience to be immediately comprehended in their entirety. But now having had an opportunity to fully contemplate recent events, he emerged from his imprisonment even more outraged than he had entered it.

Outraged, and wary. This was no mere misunderstanding. Someone had gone to considerable trouble to make him appear guilty of theft, to damage his reputation in society. The charges themselves he did not fear; he had enough influential connections who would believe in his innocence that an acquittal was almost assured. But the cost would be dear. While the faith of his most intimate acquaintances might remain steadfast, all others who heard of the affair would forever suspect his integrity.

Yes, someone worked against him, for reasons mysterious and inconceivable. And Darcy had concluded that his attacker could be none other than Captain Frederick Tilney.

He kept this deduction to himself as the gaoler escorted him to Mr. Melbourne's waiting carriage. The magistrate had with him the condemning walking stick, and Darcy wondered how and when such a close replica had been crafted. How could Captain Tilney have known Darcy's own cane so particularly?

They reached the inn without incident or delay. Elizabeth opened the chamber door herself, and the sight of her did more to counter the indignity and discomfort of his ordeal than any concession his money had been able to procure from the gaoler.

Her gaze anxiously assessed him. "You appear unaltered," she said.

"Indeed, I am entirely unchanged." Right down to his clothing.

She took his hands and pulled him inside, where Mr. Melbourne had granted him permission to don fresh attire while the constable and Elizabeth's guards waited in the corridor. As soon as the door closed, she was in his arms.

"I wish you had allowed me to visit you."

"Gaol is no place for a lady, particularly one in your condition." He indulged in her embrace but a moment before setting her away from him. "You must permit me to wash away its taint." He stepped to the basin and stripped to the waist. In truth, even if the environment had not been so wretched, his pride could not bear the idea of his wife entering a gaol to see him.

"Was it very bad?"

"It could have been worse." He could have been housed in the common gaol, in conditions so squalid they bred gaol fever. At least he had not spent the night amid prostitutes, vagrants, and murderers.

She helped him into a fresh shirt. "You are confident that Captain Tilney's intercession will resolve the matter?"

"*If* he intercedes."

"You suspect him of dealing falsely with us."

It was a statement, not a question, leading him to infer that her thoughts paralleled his.

"I have done nothing since leaving here but ruminate on the whole affair, and I cannot otherwise explain our present circumstances," he said. "Even if a servant or other member of the household acted without the captain's knowledge in actually planting the diamonds, I fail to see a way he could not have been involved in some part of the business."

"I reached the same conclusion. What I cannot determine, however, is his motive. You have had no previous intercourse with this man, no occasion to give him offense. Why should he lure us to his home and enact such a scheme?"

They were interrupted by Mr. Melbourne's knocking on the door to hurry them along. It was just as well; Darcy had no answer to give. He found himself equally unable to divine Captain Tilney's intent.

The journey to Northanger required a fraction of the time their exodus had. They raced along through a landscape cheerfully disrespectful of their serious errand. When they passed through the gates, a noble structure, for once not obscured by fog and mist, greeted them.

Dorothy, however, did not. Instead, a butler appeared at the door the moment the carriage stopped. The white-haired servant bore himself with the air of a domestic who has served a home and family so long that he feels ownership of it.

"Is your master within?" Mr. Melbourne asked.

"He—" The butler stopped, appearing to reconsider what he had been about to say. "Yes, I suppose he is."

They entered the hall, where sunlight streaming through the high arched windows lent the lofty space a much happier air than the gloom that had pervaded it during their stay. The butler left them to themselves and passed through a door that had remained shut throughout the Darcys' previous visit. He returned shortly. "Mr. Tilney will receive you in the drawing room. May I relieve you of that, sir?" He gestured toward the damning cane, which Mr. Melbourne carried.

"No. This remains with me."

Expecting to follow the familiar route to the stately room where they had first met the captain, Darcy was surprised when the butler led them through the door he had just used. It indeed opened into a drawing room, but one of much more modest proportions and modern furnishings. Upon their entry, a tall, slender man came forward to greet them. He had dark hair touched with grey and a pleasing countenance, though the latter presently bore a somber aspect that matched Darcy's own mood.

The gentleman acknowledged Mr. Melbourne with a familiarity that suggested casual acquaintance, then bowed to Darcy and Elizabeth. "Welcome to Northanger Abbey. I am Mr. Henry Tilney. What may I do for you?"

"I beg your pardon, Mr. Tilney," said Mr. Melbourne. "We did not mean to disturb you—the servant must have misunderstood. We are here to speak with your brother."

"I am afraid that he is beyond speech."

"Oh, dear," Elizabeth said. "The captain appeared to be

recovering from his injuries. I hope his health has not failed?"

Mr. Tilney regarded her curiously. "One might say so, madam. My brother is dead."

Eleven

"You are describing what never happened."
—Catherine Morland, Northanger Abbey

"Dead?"

Elizabeth's exclamation held all the shock Darcy felt. Captain Tilney, the one person who could elucidate this whole affair—silent forever. Though Darcy regretted the lost life, in truth he regretted still more the lost enlightenment their late host might have provided regarding the diamonds. His death was most untimely, for more persons than the captain.

"We received word this morning that Frederick died from injuries sustained while serving with his regiment," Mr. Tilney said. "I am just arrived myself to begin settling his affairs."

Mr. Melbourne muttered some appropriate sentiment of sympathy, which Darcy and Elizabeth recovered themselves enough to echo.

"This is astonishing news, indeed," Darcy added. "Though his injuries were extensive, he bore them with such fortitude that we had no notion his survival was in question."

Mr. Tilney studied Darcy as if attempting to make out his meaning. "You speak as if you had seen my brother recently."

"We last saw him on Wednesday."

"Wednesday!" Mr. Tilney's keen eyes widened. His expression of surprise, however, lasted but a moment—it quickly gave way to one of doubt. "Where?"

"Here at Northanger. We took our leave of the captain after having spent the previous night as his guests."

Mr. Tilney stared at Darcy, seeming to have not quite heard his reply. His countenance, which upon their introduction had been open and genial—if subdued by sorrow—became guarded.

"Forgive me—you say you passed Tuesday night here, at Northanger Abbey, in my brother's company?"

"You must think us extremely inconsiderate to have intruded on your brother's privacy whilst he was so afflicted," Elizabeth said. "I assure you, we never intended to do so. We were not aware until well after our arrival that our host had recently suffered injury. By then, night had fallen and the storm raged at full strength. We could not depart until the following day—which we did."

"Yes," said Mr. Melbourne. "With Mrs. Tilney's diamonds." The magistrate withdrew a cloth bag from the pocket of his coat and handed it to Henry. "After the Darcys departed, these were found in their possession. I understand they belonged to your mother."

Mr. Tilney loosened the drawstring and lifted out the necklace. "It has been so many years since I laid eyes on this set that I had utterly forgotten about it." He turned an inquisitorial gaze on Darcy. "How did you come to have these?"

Darcy hesitated. He still suspected Captain Tilney had orchestrated the setup, but he could hardly malign a dead man to his brother without evidence to support his theory. Henry Tilney had no reason to believe him, and every reason to distrust him.

"I wish I knew. But I assure you, I did not steal those diamonds. Though my wife and I did happen upon them in your mother's chamber, we left them untouched."

Now Mr. Tilney's increasing displeasure encompassed Elizabeth, as well. "What cause had either of you to enter my mother's chamber?"

"We passed the night there," Elizabeth said.

His posture stiffened, and he regarded her incredulously. "You *slept* in my mother's apartment?" He blinked several times before adding, in a quiet yet angry tone, "On whose authority?"

"The captain's."

"Impossible!"

"Consult the housekeeper," Darcy said, attempting to deflect Mr. Tilney's ire away from Elizabeth and upon himself. "She installed us there."

"Northanger has no housekeeper at present. The previous one retired six weeks ago and has not yet been replaced."

Darcy exchanged glances with Elizabeth. While Dorothy had not possessed the competence of a senior servant, she had certainly seemed to possess the authority of one. They must have erred in their assumption of her status.

"We mean the servant Dorothy," Elizabeth clarified. "We took her for the housekeeper."

"I do not believe Northanger Abbey has ever employed a housekeeper named Dorothy," Henry said. "But there are many things about your story I find difficult to believe. Very well, let us summon this 'Dorothy.' "

Mr. Tilney rang for the butler, who denied the existence of any Dorothy among the household staff.

Elizabeth frowned, her countenance reflecting Darcy's own increasing frustration. "She is perhaps five- or six-and-thirty," she said.

The butler shook his head.

"A tall, blond woman with a handsome countenance?" Elizabeth pressed. "Not particularly attentive?"

"I am sorry, madam. I cannot think of a servant at Northanger who could be so described."

Mr. Tilney crossed his arms and cast Darcy a look of impatience. "Perhaps you would like me to summon all the female servants for your inspection?"

"Most of the maids are still away, Mr. Tilney," said the butler. "As I was explaining before your visitors arrived, the captain's military duties kept him from Northanger for such long spans of time that we have been operating with a reduced staff, and he recently granted the remaining household servants an unexpected holiday."

Darcy could not help but interrupt. "The entire staff—at once?"

"Indeed, one seldom hears of such liberality on the part of any employer. But Captain Tilney sent me at the same time to Lincolnshire to interview a new housekeeper, so I was able to make the journey without leaving a house full of servants unsupervised."

"When did you return from Lincolnshire?" Darcy asked.

"Wednesday night."

Darcy's thoughts tumbled one upon another as he watched the butler depart. If Dorothy—or whatever her name might be—was not Captain Tilney's servant, who *was* the woman who had led them around Northanger and settled them in Mrs. Tilney's apartment?

"Mr. Darcy, it seems that this Dorothy person does not exist," said Mr. Melbourne. "You have been caught in one lie. Do you care to recant any of the others before they are disproved as well?"

Indignation nearly robbed Darcy of speech. He could not bear to have his integrity so challenged. "I have told no falsehoods."

"I would venture to say that you have spoken little else since arriving here," declared Mr. Tilney. "To begin with, my brother could not possibly have received you here on Tuesday."

He turned abruptly and crossed to a far door. He flung it open and strode rapidly through an antechamber to a set of pocket doors. These he slid wide. "Is this where you claim to have met with him just two days ago?"

They followed him into the grand drawing room. It was indeed the chamber where they had first met Captain Tilney—but much altered. Sheets, not candles, covered the table surfaces. They had been draped over all the furniture to protect it from dust and sunlight. The fireplace was swept so clean that it appeared disused for months. A small firescreen stood beside the hearth; the large one that had shielded the captain was nowhere in sight.

"This room was fully fitted out for use," Darcy said. "As much so as the dining room and breakfast parlor."

"You must consider me a poor host compared to my brother. I should have invited you to take refreshment, but those rooms appear the same as this. We can visit them, too, if you like," Mr. Tilney said. "The state of this house contradicts your claims of what occurred here. My brother obviously has not entertained guests, or even resided here himself, for some time."

Elizabeth pointed to a covered piece of furniture that, from its shape, must certainly have been the purple velvet chair the captain had occupied. It now rested some distance from the fireplace. "He was sitting in that chair. We conversed with him. On Wednesday."

"Not unless you spoke with a spectre, Mrs. Darcy. Frederick died far from here, accidentally killed in a training exercise with his regiment. According to his commander, he died the very day he suffered injury. Though the dispatch reached us only this morning, it was dated well before Wednesday."

"If the gentleman we met was not Captain Tilney, then with whom were we here?" Darcy asked.

"A good question, Mr. Darcy—with whom *were* you here? In my brother's house? Taking advantage of his absence to steal my mother's diamonds?"

"We did not steal the diamonds. Indeed, we are as much victims of this fraud as you. Someone has conspired to make us appear guilty—lured us here under false pretenses, replaced my walking stick with a duplicate, deposited the diamonds within it. Do not you"—Darcy turned from Mr. Tilney—"or *you,* Mr. Melbourne, recognize that?"

"If there was a conspiracy, you were part of it," said Mr. Melbourne. "It is terribly convenient, all of this happening while the servants are gone, nobody who can confirm your story—nobody who witnessed what you did. Except for whoever wrote the letter Mr. Chase received."

"That the letter is anonymous supports my claim. Has it not occurred to you that the very person who planted the diamonds could have also written the letter? Is not Mr. Chase's having received it 'terribly convenient'? Please—all of you, consult your reason. I am a gentleman with an estate, a family, and a reputation to protect. Why would I risk them all for a set of jewels?"

"I do not know, Mr. Darcy," said Henry Tilney. "But then, I do not know you." Something on the floor caught Mr. Tilney's gaze. He reached down and picked up a dry oak leaf. "Did Frederick? Were you even acquainted with my brother?"

Damning as it would sound, he could not speak other than the truth. "I was not."

"Then on what pretext did you come here?"

"My late mother enjoyed the friendship of yours. Captain Tilney invited me here in their memory."

He cast Darcy a dubious look. "That does not sound like Frederick." Mr. Tilney suddenly looked very tired. "Mr. Melbourne, thank you for returning the diamonds. If you will excuse me, the day grows short, and I need to make arrangements for my brother's memorial service."

"Of course, Mr. Tilney. Forgive us for taking up so much of your time." He motioned toward the door with the walking stick. Darcy had grown to detest the sight of it. "Come along, Mr. Darcy. It's back to gaol for you."

"You cannot be serious!"

"I am quite serious."

"After everything we have just learned?"

"I have learned nothing to convince me of your innocence. Something peculiar occurred here—that is certain—but I am going to let the judge sort it out."

A judge. Please God, let it be someone who holds his position on merit. Someone intelligent enough to recognize that Darcy and Elizabeth were targets, not the perpetrators, of this bizarre affair.

"How soon may this matter be presented to the court? Can we resolve it soon?" Darcy began to calculate how quickly Mr. Harper could be contacted. The solicitor would need to engage a barrister on their behalf to argue their case at the bar.

Mr. Melbourne barked out a laugh. "The assize judge has just come and gone through Gloucestershire. It will be spring before he returns for you to stand trial."

Twelve

"Consider the dreadful nature of the suspicions you have entertained. . . . Could they be perpetuated without being known, in a country like this, where social and literary intercourse is on such a footing; where every man is surrounded by a neighborhood of voluntary spies, and where roads and newspapers lay everything open?"

—*Henry Tilney,* Northanger Abbey

Elizabeth and Darcy managed to snatch a minute's private speech as Mr. Melbourne took leave of Mr. Tilney.

"The moment you return to the inn, write to Mr. Harper," Darcy said. "Advise him of this calamity and call him here straightaway."

She nodded dutifully, grateful she would have a useful task to occupy her when the magistrate's carriage left her at the Golden Crown and departed with Darcy still inside. The thought of him spending even one more night in gaol was too awful to contemplate. "Have you his address in France?" she asked.

"No—as we were ourselves in transit from Bath, he was to direct all communication to Pemberley. But his clerk will know where he can be found." He gave her the solicitor's London address. "Send the letter express to his office with instructions to forward it by the swiftest possible means."

Tense silence dominated the journey back to the inn. The

presence of Mr. Melbourne stifled conversation between husband and wife, and Darcy fell into a state of deliberation so deep that Elizabeth doubted she could have elicited more than one-word responses from him had she tried. She passed the time in meditation of her own, attempting to comprehend how a crisis of this magnitude had sprung into being in so little time.

Who could ever have suspected that a simple invitation to renew an old acquaintance would lead to their potential ruin? But the entire visit had been an elaborate hoax, and all the evidence had vanished with the imposters. The only tangible reminders of that night at Northanger were the diamonds themselves.

Had the jewels been left in Mrs. Tilney's apartment in the first place to tempt them? And then, she and Darcy not taking them on their own, planted in the duplicate walking stick? In whatever manner the diamonds were originally intended to find their way out of Northanger, obviously Mr. Chase had been meant to find them.

Or had he? Darcy believed the author of the anonymous letter and the person who had hidden the diamonds were one and the same, but what if they were not? Had someone wanted to get the diamonds out of the house—either to be discovered by Darcy upon realizing the canes had been switched, or secretly collected later by their concealer—only to be thwarted by the letter writer?

To Elizabeth's admittedly inexperienced eye, the necklace, bracelet, and eardrops comprised a lovely set but nothing extraordinary. For a family as wealthy as the Tilneys appeared, the sentimental value of the diamonds likely equaled or exceeded their monetary worth. They had belonged to a departed mother, one who had been friends with Darcy's own.

And the false Captain Tilney had been very interested in the history of that friendship. Why? Of all subjects, why had the perpetrator of this scheme sought information about two women who had been deceased for decades?

To unravel this intrigue, to exonerate themselves, she and

Darcy needed to learn more about Lady Anne's connection to Mrs. Tilney. They had hardly formed a cordial new acquaintance with Henry Tilney today, and thus were unlikely to learn anything more about Mrs. Tilney from her surviving son. They had access only to information about Lady Anne's life, and those clues lay back at Pemberley.

Who knew how long it would take their letter to reach Mr. Harper, and how much more time would pass before he could effect Darcy's release? Somehow, Elizabeth needed to get herself and her husband home.

She studied Mr. Melbourne in the waning light. She had to persuade him to discharge Darcy from gaol, but how? Reason had failed. Compassion had won only limited liberty for her that was unlikely to be extended further. How was this man best worked upon?

An idea occurred to her. By the time the carriage pulled to a stop in front of the Golden Crown, she had formed a desperate resolution.

"Mr. Melbourne, might my husband accompany me to our chamber? If he is to be incarcerated until spring, I imagine he might like to retrieve a change of clothes."

"No. I will accompany you upstairs and inspect whatever you wish to send. He can wait here with your guard."

"Very well." She had not expected the luxury of another private conversation with her husband. Nevertheless, the magistrate's refusal disappointed her.

Mr. Melbourne permitted Darcy to hand her out of the carriage. As they parted, she met his gaze. They could not take proper leave of each other with the magistrate hovering impatiently. She wanted to hear Darcy's thoughts on what they had learned today. She wanted to ask what he intended to do once Mr. Harper returned to England, and whether he wished her to take any additional actions now. She wanted to say things of a more personal nature than Mr. Melbourne needed to overhear.

She read in his eyes the same number of unspoken thoughts.

"May I visit you tomorrow?" she asked.

"Absolutely not." His grip on her hand tightened. "I will not have you or our child anywhere near that place."

She would not have Darcy anywhere near that place for long, if she could help it—which she was determined to do.

Mr. Melbourne hurried her up to the chamber, where she gathered she knew not what garments into a valise for Darcy. She could have called Graham and asked him to select the attire, but she wanted to handle his clothing herself, as if some part of her would be packed along with the shirts for Darcy to keep with him.

Mr. Melbourne accepted the bag from her. "Can I trust you to stay in this room while your guard and I exchange places?"

She would rather not have the magistrate's agent monitoring her every move. "You can trust me to stay indefinitely. A guard is unnecessary."

"Just because I permit you to remain here at the inn instead of joining your husband in gaol, that does not mean you have been cleared of charges. I cannot risk your fleeing."

"Mr. Melbourne, you are holding my husband in prison. Where on earth do you think I might go?"

"You could go anywhere, Mrs. Darcy."

She raised her chin and summoned her most dignified air. She was mistress of Pemberley.

It was time she acted like it. Time she parlayed the weight of that station into something useful.

"No, I cannot, and neither can my husband," she said. "Mr. Darcy is responsible for a huge estate. Many people—hundreds of people—depend upon him for their livelihoods. He cannot sit in gaol until the spring assizes. Allow us to go home while we await our day in court."

Mr. Melbourne actually laughed at her. "Do you believe me so gullible as that? If I permit you to leave, Gloucestershire will never see the pair of you again. And when someone comes looking for you at Pemberley, you will not be there, either."

"Mr. Darcy and I will swear an oath to return."

"Oaths can be broken. As long as your husband resides in gaol, I am certain he will appear at his trial. What to do with *you* until spring, I have not yet decided. But do not hope, Mrs. Darcy, to see this Pemberley place of yours anytime soon."

"Can we not post a bond to assure our cooperation?"

"Your husband has already asked that. No."

"But why—"

"Good evening, Mrs. Darcy."

She maintained her composure until the door was shut and she heard his tread on the stair. Then she picked up a discarded shirt and crumpled it in frustration.

She had tried to act her part and failed. She was yet too new in her role as mistress of a great estate, as matriarch of a powerful family. She had not yet learned how to project a commanding presence, one that garnered the respect of listeners and inspired them to follow her lead. And perhaps she never would. Perhaps it simply was not in her nature. After all, she had gone two-and-twenty years without feeling its lack.

Until today.

Today she felt weak. Inadequate. Overwhelmed. Indeed, the strain of recent events was beginning to take a physical toll in the form of an intermittent quaking in her lower abdomen. She had not said a word to Darcy—even had there been opportunity, she did not want to add to his troubles. But the fluctuations were occurring too close to the baby for her own peace of mind. Even now, she felt a small quiver.

She carefully folded the shirt, placed it back in Darcy's trunk, and brought her portable writing desk to the table. She wrote the letter to Mr. Harper as Darcy had directed. But it would be some time before the solicitor could arrive. And she did not know how much more of this anxiety she could tolerate.

She withdrew another sheet of paper and began a second missive.

It was time for the strategy of last resort. She might not herself possess the air of indomitable authority required to free her husband.

But she knew someone who did.

Thirteen

"I came here with the determined resolution of carrying my purpose; nor will I be dissuaded from it."

—Lady Catherine de Bourgh, Pride and Prejudice

"*Where is my nephew?"*

The voice reverberated off the walls and every other hard surface of the room. It set Elizabeth's spine tingling—and she had been anticipating it. Best of all, its sheer authority sent Mr. Melbourne scrambling to attention. He stood up behind his desk as Lady Catherine and Elizabeth entered the library of the magistrate's home.

Elizabeth had not been entirely certain how Darcy's aunt would respond to the second express she'd sent the night before. Given the vigilance with which her ladyship protected the Fitzwilliam name from the slightest threat, Elizabeth hoped she would offer assistance in liberating Darcy as quickly as possible. Her optimism had not been in vain. Lady Catherine had sallied forth so swiftly to defend the family honor that she arrived at the Golden Crown before Elizabeth had finished her breakfast.

"Lady Catherine de Bourgh," Elizabeth said, "may I present Mr. Melbourne?"

He stretched to his full measure and squared his shoulders. "Good afternoon, your ladyship." Mr. Melbourne bowed.

Lady Catherine acknowledged the introduction with a nod so cool and slight that it could have been mistaken for simply adjusting the balance of her hat.

"My nephew. Mr. Fitzwilliam Darcy. What have you done with him?"

"He is currently in gaol awaiting trial for grand larceny."

"Inconceivable! And entirely unacceptable. A gentleman of his stature, sitting in a common gaol for a crime he did not commit—it is not to be borne!"

Her indignation washed over Mr. Melbourne as easily as had Darcy's. Though he maintained his deferential stance, the magistrate was clearly unimpressed.

"Bear it he must."

"Not any longer. Mrs. Darcy has communicated to me the particulars of these ridiculous charges against him. They have no foundation."

"Mr. Darcy had stolen diamonds in his possession."

"Do you know who he is?" Lady Catherine strode closer. Were it not for the great walnut desk between them, she and Mr. Melbourne would have stood nose to nose. "Mr. Darcy descends from a noble and ancient family. He is the grandson of an earl. His estate rivals that of any in England. A paltry set of diamonds is nothing to him. He could not possibly have taken them."

"The trial will determine that."

"His great-uncle was a judge. A good one. He knew a false case when he heard it, and this one is as false as they come." She rapped her walking cane on the floor. "I want these charges dropped."

Mr. Melbourne stepped back from the desk. "I will not do that. Mr. and Mrs. Darcy stand accused of a grave offense. I take justice very seriously, and so does the assize judge." His voice had lost some of its power.

"Then release him until the trial."

"I cannot."

"Name the price."

The three small words hung in the air as the startled Mr. Melbourne stepped back a second time. "With all due respect, your ladyship, I hope I have not given the impression that I accept bribes."

Lady Catherine huffed with impatience. "I am not offering one. I wish to post a bond."

"No." Mr. Melbourne repeated the denial with a shake of his head. "If Mr. Darcy forfeits, the judge will hang *me*."

"Mr. Darcy will not forfeit," she declared. "You will have his word and my money as assurance. My nephew would not jeopardize either."

"Nevertheless, I will not release him into his own custody. The risk—"

"Then release him into mine." Lady Catherine assessed him. Her gaze took in not just his person, but his surroundings—the document he had been writing when they entered, the law book lying open before him, the statue of blindfolded Justice on a shelf behind his desk.

"I see your position and the faithful execution of its responsibilities are very important to you," her ladyship said. "Have you trained at one of the Inns of Court?"

"Yes," he said, pride evident in his voice. "Middle Temple."

"Most local magistrates are not so well studied in the law. Have you ever aspired to administer justice in a more exalted role?"

The look of interest that flashed across Mr. Melbourne's countenance indicated that he had.

"You know," Lady Catherine said slowly, "many people owe their situations to me, either directly or through my influence. It is one of the duties of the privileged to help others find their place. I think your proper place is not here, serving merely as a justice of the peace. No—I believe a gentleman with your veneration for the law ought to be a judge."

"I consider the bench the most noble service to which one can be called."

"The lord chancellor would agree. Did I mention that I share acquaintance with Eldon?"

"Indeed?" His tone was nearly reverential.

"But we stray from the subject I am come to discuss. We were speaking not of Lord Eldon, but of Mr. Darcy." She gave him a meaningful look. "Your cooperation in the matter of my nephew would earn my personal appreciation."

He was silent a moment as he pondered the offer she had not—verbally, at least—made. "Perhaps," he said, "in light of your ladyship's willingness to stand surety for him, some accommodation can be made."

An expression of satisfaction spread across Lady Catherine's countenance. "I sensed that you were a reasonable gentleman."

"Even so, I hope I do not regret this." He cleared his throat. "There is also the matter of Mrs. Darcy."

Lady Catherine sighed heavily and cast a sideways glance at Elizabeth. "I suppose I will vouch for them both."

"Very good." He reached for quill and paper. "As soon as I have your signature, Mr. and Mrs. Darcy are in your keeping."

"ADMITTEDLY, ALL DID not transpire exactly as I had hoped."

"We are beholden to my aunt for our limited freedom. We are answerable to her for our every movement. And she is coming back to Pemberley with us until the trial. Who of sound mind would hope for that?"

Like Elizabeth, Darcy kept his voice low. Though they had returned to the privacy of their room at the Golden Crown, Lady Catherine had taken the chamber next door. His aunt had stated an intention to rest after her journey from Bath and liberation of Darcy, but they nonetheless did not wish to chance her ladyship's overhearing a conversation with herself as the subject.

"At least you are no longer incarcerated."

They sat by the fire, Darcy in a chair, Elizabeth on his lap. He tightened his arms around her as she leaned against him, grateful just for the ability to talk with her this way again.

"But at very dear cost. You *do* realize she will still be reminding us of this when our child enters Cambridge?"

"I did not know girls were allowed to enter Cambridge." She sighed. "Perhaps I made a poor decision. But Lady Catherine was the only person I could think of who had the force to sway Mr. Melbourne, the proximity to travel here quickly, and as much interest as we in preventing society at large from ever learning of the matter."

Darcy knew he could rely upon his aunt to keep silent—in that assumption, Elizabeth had been correct. Lady Catherine de Bourgh would never risk exposure, for the stigma of a family member tried for larceny would blacken her own reputation. But others—Mr. Melbourne and Mr. Chase, Henry Tilney, the audience of laborers at the Golden Crown—also knew of the affair, and they possessed no such motive for silence. He could only hope that Gloucestershire was far enough removed from London that word would not spread.

"Too," Elizabeth continued, "should diplomacy have failed, I thought perhaps Lady Catherine's dulcet tones alone could break you out of gaol. Either way, you would enjoy freedom more quickly than Mr. Harper could arrange it. How soon do you estimate we will see him at Pemberley?"

"It depends on whether he stops at his London office upon returning to England. If he receives the second letter I just sent, he will know to proceed directly to Derbyshire. If, having read only your missive, he travels here after landing, the detour will delay him." Darcy hoped to see his solicitor sooner rather than later, so they could immediately begin working on his case.

"He will be a welcome sight no matter when he arrives. I must confess, even your aunt was, today." Elizabeth smiled at some recollection. "Darcy, you should have heard the manner in which she manipulated Mr. Melbourne. It was really quite understated for Lady Catherine—a suggestion of future favor, but no actual commitment to ever do a thing for him. Do you expect she will indeed use her influence to win a place on the bench for him?"

"If there is one skill at which my aunt excels, it is putting people in their place."

A knock on the door forced Elizabeth to reluctantly relinquish her seat. Darcy rose and opened the door to one of the inn's maids.

"There's a gentleman downstairs, sir, wanting to see you. A Mr. Tilney."

Mr. Tilney? Darcy, having just started to relax the constant guard he had maintained since his arrest, braced himself once more. He doubted the visit would prove a cordial one. "Show him up."

Elizabeth's expression revealed similar concern. "I hope he has not come to express displeasure at your release."

"Quite the opposite," said Mr. Tilney as he entered the room and bowed to them both. He carried his greatcoat over one arm and his hat in hand. "I was glad to hear of it, as I went to see Mr. Melbourne with the intention of effecting it myself, if I could."

"I confess surprise," Darcy said. "When we parted, you did not appear so inclined."

Mr. Tilney seemed much more amiable now. His voice was warmer, his manner less reserved. "I am come to apologize for my incivility. I had, as you know, just learned of my brother's death, and I had not yet recovered from the shock of that news when the magistrate arrived with you—a stranger accused of stealing my mother's diamonds. The more you revealed, the harder it became to divide sentiment from reason and think clearly."

"Anyone receiving so much disconcerting intelligence in rapid succession would find himself similarly affected," Darcy said.

"You are more generous with me than I was with you. I am a clergyman; I make my trade in helping others cope with unpleasant news. I should be able to handle it better myself."

At Elizabeth's invitation, Mr. Tilney laid aside his coat and hat, and took a seat. He gratefully accepted her offer of tea, revealing that he had ridden directly from Northanger to

Mr. Melbourne's house to the Golden Crown without stopping for refreshment.

"We appreciate your trouble," said Darcy, "and your intention to intercede with Mr. Melbourne on my behalf."

"After I had time to consider your account more objectively, its full import struck me. I realized how unlikely it was that you invented so many of the particulars. Too, though I did not recognize your name upon first introduction, when you revealed our mothers had been friends I realized it had sounded familiar. Your mother was Lady Anne Darcy, was she not?"

"She was."

"I remember her. She visited Northanger once—I believe I was about twelve. I thought her very pretty." He smiled. "And her company made my mother cheerful—she valued their friendship. She was an estimable lady, your mother, and I cannot but expect that a son of hers resembles her in that regard. At a minimum, I presume you have better employment for your time than traveling all the way to Gloucestershire to steal a diamond necklace from our family."

Mr. Tilney paused. "There was also something else that countered my prejudice." He rose, went to his greatcoat, and withdrew from its folds a familiar object. "I believe this is yours."

"My walking stick?" Darcy had not expected ever to lay eyes on it again. "Where did you find it?"

"My butler came across it after you departed."

Darcy took the cane in his hands and examined it. The silver band was fixed—it hid no secret compartment—and the wood's signature flaw had never appeared so agreeable to his eye as it did now. "So you believe our account of events?"

"I do. Though it means something far more alarming than theft transpired at Northanger Abbey. In the fortnight since my brother died, someone sent his servants away, made free use of his home, enacted an elaborate masquerade for your benefit, and then erased all traces of their presence."

"Have you any idea who might have perpetrated this scheme?"

"None. I hoped perhaps the two of you could assist me. May I impose upon you to repeat your tale, from the beginning? You said Frederick—or someone claiming to be Frederick—first contacted you in Bath?"

"Yes," said Darcy. "We received a letter—"

Elizabeth rose. "We still have it." She retrieved the note and handed it to Mr. Tilney.

"It is dated before Frederick died." He studied the lines closely. "And this appears to be his hand. If not, it is a convincing forgery." He set the letter aside. "What occurred next?"

They described their reception at Northanger, their encounters with the false captain and housekeeper, and their premature departure. When they finished, Mr. Tilney asked whether they had been able to discern any of the captain's features beneath all the bandages.

"He had blue eyes," Elizabeth recalled. "At least, the one we could see was blue."

"Frederick's eyes were brown," Mr. Tilney said. "Not that there is otherwise any doubt that the man you met was an imposter. Can you remember anything he said that might provide some clue to his true identity?"

Both Darcy and Elizabeth shook their heads. "Nothing obvious comes to mind," Elizabeth said. "The whole interview was exceedingly odd, though the knowledge that our host was not in fact Captain Tilney now explains much."

"Obviously, I have an interest in finding this man," Mr. Tilney said. "And so do you, for Mr. Melbourne told me the larceny charges will not be dropped even though I have withdrawn my interest in the matter."

"We are to stand trial for a crime with no accuser?" Darcy asked.

"He claims the letter provides sufficient accusation."

"But the writer is nameless and suffered no damages." While Darcy himself placed high value on justice, he believed it must be tempered by reason. He could not comprehend the magistrate's zeal.

"I can only guess that this whole scenario has provided Mr. Melbourne an opportunity to demonstrate his passion for the law. I am sure, however, that if the man who posed as Frederick can be identified, what tatters of a case now exist will fall apart completely, and you shall be spared the inconvenience and insult of a trial. Can I persuade you to return to Northanger Abbey with me? Perhaps working in concert we can find our answers more quickly, and I would appreciate your aid."

Assist Mr. Tilney? Without question—for in doing so, he helped himself and Elizabeth. The false Frederick Tilney held the key to their freedom, and Mr. Chase and Mr. Melbourne certainly were not going to do anything toward identifying and arresting him.

But return to Northanger? To this he could not agree. He would not subject Elizabeth to additional time in that house, nor risk her being anywhere near it should the imposter return. He needed to get her to Pemberley, where he could keep her safe while awaiting the arrival of their child. And, much as he hesitated to leave the investigation entirely in Mr. Tilney's hands, he needed to escort her there himself. Not only did the conditions of their release demand that they remain proximate enough for Lady Catherine to supervise them both, but his own heart demanded that he entrust Elizabeth's care to no one but himself.

"I freely pledge our cooperation, but I fear we cannot delay our return home."

Mr. Tilney nodded sympathetically. "Were I you, I should not wish to linger in Gloucestershire, either."

Darcy actually wished he *could* linger. Though Pemberley offered a safe haven where he could retreat and regroup, he could not conduct his own investigation as effectively from Derbyshire as from here. He would have to rely heavily on Mr. Tilney and Mr. Harper to carry out actions he would otherwise perform himself—and to do so as successfully.

"Let us keep in close communication," said Darcy. "My wife and I will review our memory of events for anything else that might prove useful. We will also speak with our servants, and I advise you to do the same. Though Northanger's household staff has been on holiday, one of them might have perceived something unusual upon resuming his or her duties. Also talk with the groundskeepers and stablehands. I cannot believe that the imposters arrived at Northanger and set up housekeeping without somebody taking notice."

After a quarter hour's further discussion of strategy, Mr. Tilney, eager to begin his share of the investigation, departed for home.

"I trust Mr. Tilney," Elizabeth declared when he had gone. "He seems an intelligent man. But we leave great responsibility with someone we do not know well, and that is unlike you."

Yes, it was. And it bothered him more than he could reveal to her. "After I confer with Mr. Harper, I will send him here to work with Mr. Tilney. In the meantime, we must get you to Pemberley."

"I will not enter my confinement for several more months. We can stay here awhile until we find the imposter and clear our names."

He studied her face—the anxiety lines that creased her forehead; the troubled expression of her eyes and the dark smudges under them. She looked as if she had not slept since Mr. Chase arrested him. "No, we cannot. You need to be home, where you can take proper care of yourself and our child. Not at some inn, or at Northanger Abbey."

"But what of the investigation?"

"We are going home. Trust me, Elizabeth. Once we reach Pemberley, all will be well."

Fourteen

"And is such a girl to be my nephew's sister? Is her husband, is the son of his late father's steward, to be his brother? Heaven and earth!—of what are you thinking?"

—Lady Catherine de Bourgh, Pride and Prejudice

Derbyshire in any season was magnificent country, a landscape of wind-carved tors, rocky cloughs, deep wooded glens, and winding streams. Just shy of a year into the marriage that had made the Peak District her permanent residence, Elizabeth still surveyed it with the awe of a visitor each time she traveled its terrain. Nothing in her native Hertfordshire could compare to the imposing crags and lonely moors of the Dark Peak, nor the limestone plateaus and narrow dales of the White.

Today, however, as the Darcys completed the last leg of their journey, Derbyshire's distinctive grids of drystone walls partitioning rolling hills welcomed her with their familiarity. Though a great part of her felt they ought to have stayed behind in Gloucestershire until the Northanger matter was resolved, she had to concede solace in their homecoming. As their carriage wound its way through the wooded parkland of Pemberley, Elizabeth found herself watching for a glimpse of the noble house with as much anticipation as she had upon her first visit to the estate. Pemberley stood as a fortress, a bastion of stability. Surely the trouble that they had just endured could not reach them here.

Indeed, when a bend in the road at last revealed dignified walls framed by trees still stubbornly clinging to golden leaves, the nightmare just past took on the sense of having been only that: an unpleasant dream from which they had finally awakened. The anxiety of their recent ordeal receded, and Elizabeth felt herself able to breathe freely for the first time in over a se'nnight.

She noted a similar look of calm on Darcy's countenance. Pemberley was his foundation, a source not only of strength but also, to a considerable extent, of his very identity. Here he would figure out how to set their world back to rights.

"What will you do first, now that we are home?" she asked.

"What I always do upon arrival at Pemberley after a long absence—hear Mr. Clarke's report. And yourself?"

"What I do upon arrival anywhere these days. Visit the convenience."

The barest hint of a smile—the first she had seen on him since his arrest—touched the corners of his mouth.

"I suppose if you intend to closet yourself with the steward, that leaves me the entire pleasure of ensuring that Lady Catherine is comfortably settled," she said.

"My aunt is rarely comfortable anywhere but at Rosings. She will not hesitate, however, to inform you of how she might be made more so."

Elizabeth dreaded the weeks, perhaps months, of Lady Catherine's visit that lay ahead. She doubted even Pemberley would prove large enough to make her ladyship's indefinite stay tolerable. At least Darcy's aunt had come alone—her daughter would return to Kent with Mrs. Jenkinson—and in her own vehicle. Sharing a carriage all the way to Derbyshire might have driven one of them past the bounds of the tacit truce they had established in Bath.

"I eagerly await her counsel," Elizabeth replied. "Having witnessed her attention to the most minute details of Charlotte Collins's housekeeping at Hunsford parsonage, I anticipate she will have twice as much wisdom to impart regarding my management of Pemberley. Though how she will advise me to remove the pollution wrought upon the estate by my inferior relations, I cannot guess." Of the many objections Lady Catherine had voiced to a marriage between her nephew and Elizabeth, one of the most strenuous had been the connection it created between Darcy and George Wickham.

The carriages came to a halt, and soon Elizabeth and Darcy entered the house with her ladyship. Lady Catherine surveyed the hall with the air of one determined to find fault.

"I see you have painted in here since I last visited Pemberley," she declared. "By your initiative, Mrs. Darcy?"

"No, mine," Darcy said.

"I approve the color. Though were the blue a shade lighter, it would lend the room an even more regal air."

"Perhaps your ladyship would like to wait in the yellow drawing room while your belongings are brought to your chamber," Elizabeth suggested. "We might find Georgiana there—no doubt she will take delight in the discovery that you accompany us."

"Georgiana is a charming girl. I look forward to her performances on the pianoforte in the evenings. You would do well, Mrs. Darcy, to practice the instrument more assiduously yourself. You will never match my niece's talent, of course, but your execution would benefit from more serious application. I still cannot comprehend why your parents did not insist on better musical training for you and your sisters. It is one of the most basic accomplishments of a gently bred young lady. It instills discipline. Your youngest sister would not have turned out so wild had she engaged in serious musical study."

"Not everyone possesses the temperament for serious musical study." They started walking to the drawing room, where Elizabeth hoped to deposit Lady Catherine and win herself a temporary reprieve. "Lydia certainly does not."

"From all reports, Mrs. Wickham does not possess the

temperament for any serious undertaking, save a determination to engage in scandalous behavior with no regard for the consequences to herself or her family." She stopped a few feet before the drawing room door and addressed Darcy. "I do hope you have ordered your wife to cut off all communication with her?"

"I have done nothing of the sort."

A look of horror crossed Lady Catherine's countenance. "You do not *receive* the Wickhams here?"

"Of course not. But Mrs. Darcy is free to correspond with or visit any of her sisters as frequently as she chooses."

Upon entering the drawing room, they found not one but two young ladies passing the morning: Georgiana and a visitor. Elizabeth stopped just inside the doorway, astonished beyond measure.

"Lydia?"

"Lizzy! You are home at last!" Lydia sprang from her seat and hastened to Elizabeth. "Is not this an excellent surprise?"

"Lydia—" Still stunned, Elizabeth could only blink as Lydia grabbed her hands.

"Ha! Look at your face—I laugh just to see it!"

"Lydia, what are you *doing* here?"

"Lord almighty, Lizzy—after you left Jane's, things were dull as dishwater! Our sister's head is full of nothing but that baby. Did he eat enough? Does his napkin need changing? Is that a smile? Hush, he is sleeping. And Mama is just as bad! Whose eyes does he have? Whose nose? Whose ears? Bringing up relations dead so long I do not know who she talks about. Good grief! I could not stay one day more."

Lydia's boredom was easily believed, though it did not explain what had led her to arrive, unexpected and unwelcome, on *their* doorstep. "But, Lydia, why did you come to Pemberley?"

"To visit you, silly goose! You keep forgetting to invite me, so I decided to surprise you. Was that not a delightful scheme? Only you were not here. Did not you tell Jane you would stay in Bath but a fortnight? It must have been so jolly! Did you actually go bathing in public? Did you ride in a sedan chair? I always imagined it would be ripping fun to be carried around town in a sedan chair. Oh—you must tell me all the latest fashions you saw! La! I long to go to Bath! I keep asking Wickham to take me, but he says we have not got the money."

Here Lydia paused for air just long enough that all heard the snort of derision issued by Lady Catherine, who had observed the sisterly reunion in stony silence.

Georgiana crossed the room to greet her ladyship. "Good afternoon, aunt. Your arrival here is an unanticipated pleasure." Her expression suggested that she meant it. As Lady Catherine was nobody's favorite relation, Elizabeth presumed poor Georgiana welcomed not so much her aunt as the distraction from Lydia her presence offered.

"Aunt?" Lydia asked in a whisper so loud that it excluded no one. "Lizzy, is this the famous Lady Catherine?"

Though her ladyship had not requested an introduction, Elizabeth now felt obliged to attempt one. "Lady Catherine de Bourgh, may I present—"

"No, you may not." She abruptly turned to Darcy. "I would go to my chamber now."

"Allow me to accompany you," Georgiana offered.

Lady Catherine spared Lydia a final glance that left no doubt of her contempt, then turned her back and marched from the room.

"Well!" Lydia said. "What got under her bonnet?" She laughed at her own remark.

Darcy merely regarded his sister-in-law in weary silence as Elizabeth pondered how to remedy this unforeseen turn of events. The presence of Wickham's wife at Pemberley created awkwardness even without Lady Catherine among the party; the two could not possibly coexist in one house. Lydia would constantly expose herself to ridicule. Lady Catherine would surpass all known measures of insolence. And Elizabeth, caught in the middle, might well begin to consider gaol a not-so-dreadful alternative after all.

"Look at you!" Lydia exclaimed. "Your face is still all amazement. What an excellent joke we have played!"

Apprehension passed through Elizabeth. "We?"

"Wickham and I."

Darcy stared at her. "Mr. Wickham is not *here*?"

"Of course he is. The scheme was half his idea—he could not send me off to enjoy it alone!"

His expression hardened. "Where might I find him?"

"Oh, he's somewhere about. In the billiards room, I think. Or perhaps the saloon."

Darcy met Elizabeth's gaze. "Excuse me." He departed with such purpose that Elizabeth almost pitied Mr. Wickham. It would not be a pleasant meeting.

"I declare, Lizzy, I do not know how you managed to marry into such a disagreeable family. None of them ever talk, they simply glare. Mr. Darcy—"

"Mr. Darcy cannot and will not receive Mr. Wickham at Pemberley, for reasons your husband full well understands." To Elizabeth's knowledge, Lydia remained unacquainted with Wickham's attempted elopement with Georgiana, and she did not intend to share with her sister information so sensitive to Darcy. But Wickham himself knew better than to blacken their door. Elizabeth marveled at his temerity. Surely he realized how Darcy would respond to his unauthorized presence at Pemberley? "What were you thinking in coming here?"

Lydia pouted. "I wanted to help you, is all. You know—with the baby coming."

Given Lydia's lifelong preoccupation with herself, Elizabeth found it difficult to believe that altruism motivated her, especially since among the five sisters, they two were probably the least intimate. Elizabeth had possessed little patience for Lydia's silliness and selfishness before her elopement, and lost all tolerance afterward. She studied her sister's face to divine her true purpose. "My confinement will not begin for another few months."

"I thought I could help you prepare. I suppose the baby will need clothes and such."

If she relied upon Lydia to complete her infant's layette,

she might as well name the child Godiva. "You came to Pemberley to sew?"

"Yes! I have improved at it, you know. I had to tear apart half my gowns this season and make them over because the linendrapers will not let me buy any more material until Wickham pays for what I have already purchased. Wickham says he will, as soon as he has got the money, but in the meantime I could not go to the officers' balls in last year's gowns with all the other wives wearing new. Only imagine how everyone would talk! I think their husbands must receive better pay than Wickham, though I do not understand why. He is such a favorite in his regiment. He is always drinking with the other officers."

No doubt.

"I told him he should just inform his captain that he deserves better pay. It is unfair, you know, not to be able to buy the things my friends do, and never to go to places like Bath. But Wickham will not ask. He says someday we shall have pots of money. But in the meantime it is quite vexing to have Mr. Lynton calling all the time."

"Who is Mr. Lynton?"

"Oh, someone Wickham knows. I think he loaned Wickham a bit of money. What a horrible little man! I wish he would just leave us alone. Why, we no sooner returned from Jane's than he was pounding on our door again. I think the best part of visiting you is not having to see *him* every day."

At last, they had reached the real motive for Lydia's visit. Its revelation came as no surprise. The Wickhams had once again landed themselves in financial distress.

She wondered whether Mr. Lynton was a moneylender. Extravagant habits and an immature disregard for their consequences saw the couple constantly living beyond their income, and Lydia had often applied to Elizabeth and Jane for relief. Though Lydia had chosen this life through her own recklessness, Elizabeth did not want her sister to suffer. She would never ask Darcy for money to give to the couple—he had advanced thousands of pounds just to bring about Lydia's marriage after her scandalous elopement—but she herself made them presents out of her pin money.

The couple's current circumstances must be bad indeed to send them fleeing to Pemberley to avoid their creditors. Nevertheless, Wickham certainly could not stay, nor did she expect Lydia truly wanted to. In comparison to her usual society, the entertainments of Pemberley would not long satisfy her. Both sisters—not to mention everyone else in the household—would be happier if Lydia returned to the company of her friends.

Elizabeth sighed. "How many pounds do you need this time?"

DARCY DID NOT find Mr. Wickham in the billiards room, nor in the saloon. He found him in the library. *His* library. As if Wickham's mere presence at Pemberley were not sufficient insult. This was a trespass not to be borne.

Further, he did not discover Mr. Wickham alone. As Darcy entered the room, a housemaid quickly stepped away from Wickham's side. She moved too fast for him to determine whether he had interrupted a clinch, but the libertine had obviously been making himself too free with one of the servants. Again.

"Darcy! I had no idea you had returned." He leaned casually against one of the bookcases and offered an insincere grin. Darcy wanted to strike it from his impudent face.

"Obviously."

Before dealing with the reprehensible Mr. Wickham, Darcy turned his attention to the housemaid. She was a young slip of a girl, easy prey for a lothario as charming and practiced as Wickham. Darcy's mere gaze froze her in place.

"What is your name?" he asked.

She required a moment to find her voice. "Jenny, sir."

"How long have you been employed at Pemberley?"

"I just started this week, sir."

"Mrs. Reynolds no doubt advised you of the conduct expected from all servants here, but I shall ask her to remind you. If you want to keep your place at Pemberley, I suggest you listen carefully this time."

"Yes, sir."

"You may go."

Without another glance at Wickham, Jenny darted from the room. Wickham chuckled.

"Ever the stern master. I see nothing at Pemberley has changed."

"Including you."

Darcy had learned, after the fact, that during the period George Wickham had lived at Pemberley, he had seduced several of the female staff. Then, the handsome young rake had merely been the steward's son—a status that, if higher than that of his paramours, had not been so very elevated.

And he had been a bachelor.

Now, Wickham was—he still recoiled at the thought—a member of the family. Darcy would never countenance a dalliance between him and one of Pemberley's servants.

Wickham chuckled again. "You frightened the poor girl half to death. We were only talking. I am wed to your wife's sister now, after all."

"I hardly need reminding of that unfortunate fact."

"Come, now. You cannot grudge me the connection you yourself went to such trouble to bring off."

Darcy reviled George Wickham. The scoundrel tarnished everything he touched, and had any other method existed by which he could have saved Elizabeth's foolish sister from utter ruin, he would have seized upon it. When he had found Wickham and Lydia unwed and cohabitating in London, he knew that by enforcing the promises of marriage through which Wickham had persuaded Lydia to run away, he was not securing permanent happiness for the bride. He had acted to rescue Lydia from social disgrace and from the danger that would have followed when Wickham eventually tired of her and moved on to his next conquest. Once fallen, she would have spent the rest of her life as the chattel of one rapacious man after another.

He had intervened not for Lydia's sake, but for Elizabeth's. At the time, Darcy had possessed no connection to Lydia; he and Elizabeth had not been engaged, nor anywhere close to an understanding. But he had wanted to spare Elizabeth the pain of having a sister so debased, and to salvage her own respectability from the ignominy into which it must necessarily have descended as a result of Lydia's degradation. One fallen sister would have precluded all the rest from ever marrying well, if at all.

"Sometimes one must tolerate a parasite so as not to kill its host."

At this, Wickham laughed openly. "Is that what I am? My dear Fitz, I regard myself more as your errant brother."

"You are far too familiar."

"Am I? We did grow up together." He gestured toward the window. "How many hours did we spend angling in that river? Coursing for hares? Shooting? Hawking?" A flash of resentment crossed his countenance. "But I was just a convenient companion, was I not? Someone for Master Darcy to play with when no boys of superior birth offered better company."

"You have not come here to reminisce—with you, an ulterior motive always exists. What is it?"

"Indeed, brother, your cynicism wounds me. I merely brought my wife to visit her sister."

"Even were that true, it does not explain your own presence in a house where you know you have no entrée." Nor how the rogue had gained admission in the first place. "Do not military duties summon you back to your regiment? I know that I, for one, rest easier at night in the knowledge that Mr. George Wickham defends England from invasion."

"Duty indeed calls. I am afraid I must depart on Saturday."

"You will depart *now.* Both you and Mrs. Wickham."

"But the day grows short."

"Lambton is but five miles. Stay the night there or continue on; I do not care."

"We have not ordered a carriage."

"My driver will convey you to the inn." The good of the Wickhams' immediately quitting Pemberley would more than mitigate the evil of suffering them to use Darcy's private coach.

"You are the soul of generosity." Wickham bowed cockily. "Until we meet again, then—wherever that might be."

Darcy vowed it would not be at Pemberley.

Within a quarter hour, Darcy watched with satisfaction as his coach carried the Wickhams through the gates and from the grounds of the estate. As he stood at the window, Georgiana came to him.

"I want to apologize, brother, for your finding them here."

He turned and embraced her. "It is I who must apologize for failing to protect you from exposure to Mr. Wickham. What you must have suffered! How did he even come to gain entrance? Mr. Clarke and Mrs. Reynolds—"

"It is my own fault. Mrs. Wickham called first, anxious to see Elizabeth. It was most awkward, but I felt I could not turn away Elizabeth's sister. I told her I expected you in a se'nnight and said she might stay. Before I realized what had happened, she had somehow construed my invitation to include Mr. Wickham, who happened to still be waiting in their hired carriage. When I saw him, I could not muster enough courage to ask him to leave."

Darcy doubted Lydia's interpretation had been a mistake at all. "My dear sister, I am sorry I was not here."

"I tried to send word to you at Northanger Abbey, as you had written that you would stay there for a week after leaving Bath, but the letter came back."

"Our plans altered unexpectedly. I had no opportunity to advise you of the change."

"I should say so. I certainly did not anticipate you would return with our aunt."

Until last night, neither had he. "Is Lady Catherine happily settled in her chamber?"

"As happy as she ever is. I heard more than enough, however, of her opinions regarding Mrs. Wickham. How long does our aunt intend to stay?"

Not wanting to alarm his younger sister, he, Elizabeth, and Lady Catherine had decided to keep the details of events in Gloucestershire from her—and everybody else in the family.

"Her plans are undetermined at present. Perhaps as long as spring." He hoped the business of the diamonds would find resolution far sooner, but he thought it best to prepare Georgiana for the possibility of a protracted visit.

"That long? Has she come to help Elizabeth prepare for her confinement?"

No, to help them both avoid a different one—in prison. Georgiana's innocent assumption reminded him of how closely the return of the assize judge to Gloucestershire would coincide with Elizabeth's lying-in. She could not possibly leave Pemberley at that time to appear for trial. And how could he? They must settle this matter expediently. He grew even more anxious for Mr. Harper to appear without delay.

"Has our aunt finally accepted Elizabeth?" Georgiana asked hopefully.

"Not yet. But living in the same house, they no doubt will soon become bosom friends."

Fifteen

"Pictures of perfection, as you know, make me sick and wicked."

—Jane Austen, letter to Fanny Knight

"You served too many dishes with each course at dinner last night," Lady Catherine declared. "Do you dine so elaborately every day?"

Elizabeth looked up from her letter but silently counted to ten before replying. She was grown quite used to counting. Ten usually proved sufficient, but sometimes her ladyship's remarks required fifteen. Once she had reached one hundred ninety, but she had been counting by decades for variety.

"We do not; our family dinners are generally simpler. But as I have not yet learned all your ladyship's preferences, I thought you might appreciate more selection."

"Do not trouble yourself on my account. I am easily accommodated."

To this statement, Elizabeth thought it best not to reply at all.

In the three days since their return to Pemberley, Lady Catherine had thoroughly dissected Elizabeth's household management. Convinced that Elizabeth's inexperience as mistress of a great house equaled incompetence and inelegance, she had embarked on a mission to save the venerable Darcy estate and family from the ravages of resourcefulness and ingenuity. No matter was too small to pass beneath Lady Catherine's notice; Elizabeth wondered not whether her ladyship would demand to inspect the dairy and still-room, but when.

She dipped her pen and went back to writing Jane. After breakfast, she had retreated to her morning room in hopes of gaining a brief respite from her houseguest, but Lady Catherine had followed her and made herself quite comfortable on the sofa. Her ladyship now performed a thorough visual assessment of the chamber.

"You have repositioned my sister's desk."

"As Lady Anne has not used it in nearly twenty years, I doubted she would mind."

Bless it, she had forgotten to count.

"You ought to demonstrate more respect for your predecessor in this house than speaking of her in such an insolent manner. You have far to go before you can even hope to measure up to the example she set."

Fourteen, fifteen . . . She inhaled deeply, released her breath, and inhaled again. As she did so, she noted a floral smell—Lady Catherine's perfume, she presumed, a sweet fragrance not at all suited to her ladyship's bitter mien. She had never known Darcy's aunt to wear it before today. Though not offensive in itself, the scent vexed her further. Lady Catherine was invading even the air she breathed.

"I have great respect for Lady Anne's example. It is constantly before me." She returned the quill to its stand. The letter to Jane would have to wait. Obviously, Lady Catherine would not allow her to compose it uninterrupted, and she now had lost the mood for writing.

Disinclined to leave the half-completed letter where it could fall under Lady Catherine's gaze—not, of course, that it might contain any candid sentiments about certain relations by marriage—she slid open the top drawer to safekeep the note until she could complete it. Another, much older letter bearing her own name caught her eye. Lady Anne's letter. She thought she had placed it in another compartment of the desk the day she'd discovered it, but so much had transpired since then that her memory must err.

Spying the letter pushed her still more out of sorts. Had Lady Anne not been acquainted with Captain Tilney's mother, she and Darcy never would have gone to Northanger Abbey, never would have become embroiled in an incomprehensible legal predicament, and never would have been forced to endure Lady Catherine's pompous presence in their home.

"Headstrong girl! Can you honestly believe that you know all you must to oversee a house as great as Pemberley?"

"I do not pretend to know everything, but—"

"I have seen the house your mother keeps, the style in which you were raised. You are as unequal to the duties your marriage demands as you are to the status it confers."

"I am well aware of your opinions on that subject, as you have never hesitated to voice them. But despite your wishes to the contrary, I *am* mistress of this house and I will not hear the expression of such insults in my own home."

"It is only through my intervention that you *are* in your own home at present, and not in a Gloucestershire gaol."

All the numbers of infinity could not count Elizabeth down to calm. She shut the desk drawer with more violence than she intended. A soft thump sounded beneath it.

Lady Catherine heard it as well. "What have you done? Have you damaged that desk with your tantrum?"

Embarrassed, Elizabeth did not respond. She glanced at the floor and spotted a silver object under the desk. A small key, perhaps an inch long. She leaned down and retrieved it, discovering as she did so that her expanding middle made the action more difficult than it had been when she'd picked up Lady Anne's letter from this same floor nearly two months ago.

Lady Catherine strode toward her, peering. "What is that?"

Elizabeth palmed the key. "Nothing with which you need concern yourself."

"Insolent girl. Does my nephew know you behave this way when he is not present?"

"My husband would not expect me to countenance such abuse from you at any time."

Elizabeth rose. She had to remove herself from Lady Catherine's proximity. Though her pride rebelled at leaving her own morning room—lest her exit appear a retreat—the chamber could not contain her agitation. Nor could she tolerate any longer the scent of Lady Catherine's perfume, which now suddenly assailed her with its intensity. Apparently, her all-knowledgeable ladyship could use some instruction of her own—in experimenting with new scents more conservatively.

She needed fresh air. Open space. Activity. She had been too long confined with Lady Catherine and her oppressive disapprobation.

A walk. She needed a walk.

With scarcely another two words to Lady Catherine, she headed outside in such a hurry that she did not even stop for a wrap. The heat of her irritation would provide more than sufficient warmth.

Pemberley boasted so many walking paths that she hardly knew which to choose. Her mind still restless, she in the end made no choice. Instead, she allowed her feet to determine their own course while she meditated by turns on insults and insolence, ladies and letters, Tilneys and tribulation. Eventually her anger at Lady Catherine abated to mere ire.

After a half hour's wandering, she found herself at the entrance to the south garden. Lady Anne's garden. When she had first left the house, this was the last place she would have come, but the interim exercise and contemplation had settled her temper enough that the garden now drew her in.

It was a walled garden, constructed of pinkish-grey bricks set in a geometric pattern that ran the full perimeter. Terracotta rosettes ornamented the walls and the arched gateway that marked the entrance. Rosettes also embellished the ironwork of the gate itself. When viewed from above, as Elizabeth could do from her morning room, the crushed-stone paths that partitioned the flower beds revealed themselves to form a four-pointed rosette as well. The entrance stood at one point, while the other three "petals" ended in alcoves with stone benches set into the walls.

The gate swung open easily. Little remained of the riot of color that had filled the garden throughout the summer. Now, asters and chrysanthemums reigned over an otherwise lonely court of fading foliage as the garden settled in for its long winter's sleep.

Despite the garden's breathtaking beauty at its peak, Elizabeth had come here perhaps three times during the summer. So much of Pemberley yet held Lady Anne's imprint that she had feared being consumed by it entirely if she spent much time in Anne's favorite garden. But today it somehow bade her welcome, promised to soothe her troubled spirits if she lingered awhile.

She headed toward the alcove on her right. Ivy clung to the columns and climbed to the top of the arch, nearly obscuring the brick beneath. Within the sheltered niche, the stone bench beckoned Elizabeth to sit. The bench was cold through her muslin gown, and as a cool breeze gusted in, she regretted her lack of a wrap. She contemplated retrieving her cloak, but the garden held such an atmosphere of peace that she hesitated to leave.

She opened her hand, which still held the key that had fallen out of the desk. Though she had gripped it tightly as she walked—marched—along Pemberley's paths, she had all but forgotten it as other thoughts tumbled through her mind. Now she turned it round in her hand, wondering what it unlocked. She could not recall any locking drawers in the desk, and the key seemed too short to correspond to a full-sized door.

A low fluttering sensation drew her attention away from the key. Instinctively, her free hand dropped to her abdomen.

There it was again. Stronger this time. Almost like a light tap. Or a tiny—

Kick.

She caught her breath. Could it be? Is this how it felt? A third movement answered her.

A soft smile spread across her lips. "My goodness," she whispered. "Hello to you, too."

She sat in stunned surprise as the wondrous moment of quickening drove all other troubles from her heart. Lady Catherine could criticize her from dawn until dusk. Let all at Pemberley canonize Lady Anne as a saint. The Northanger Abbey problem would resolve itself somehow. Her child had moved, and she had felt it.

No further tiny stirrings occurred to delight her, but those she had experienced suffused her with quiet joy. Eventually, however, she could no longer ignore the increasing chill of the stone bench, and with reluctance left the little alcove that had witnessed her momentous discovery. But she did not head directly to the gate. Though cold, she wished to delay her return to the house—and all it represented—just a little while longer.

The paths led her to another point of the garden's rosette layout, where a solitary laborer worked on hands and knees to dig up expired plants. She recognized him as Mr. Flynn, the head gardener, and wondered that he had not either delegated the task to his numerous assistants or employed their aid to hasten the chore. Mr. Flynn must have seen at least seventy summers, and while he tended the grounds as efficiently as his arthritic hands would allow him, his greatest value to the estate lay in the knowledge and experience with which he directed his undergardeners.

She walked toward him. He saw her approaching and started to rise, but she stayed him with a gesture. "Would not an assistant speed your task?"

"I always tend our lady's garden myself, ma'am. Lady Anne and I planned it and planted it together; somehow, it doesn't seem right for anyone else to work in it."

Our lady's garden. Even after nearly two decades, the servant spoke of Lady Anne as if she were Pemberley's mistress still. But somehow, coming from Mr. Flynn, or perhaps in the wake of her own happiness, the words did not bother her.

"Her ladyship certainly left her garden in good keeping," she said.

He wiped his gnarled hands on a rag so streaked with dirt that Elizabeth debated whether he removed or added to that on his fingers. "I suppose, though, it's time I trained somebody to take over for me." He released a weary sigh. "I know I'm slowing down. It's time I admitted these old bones don't have too many seasons left."

"Perhaps tomorrow someone can help you with this task."

"Oh, not tomorrow, ma'am. Tomorrow is the first of November. All Hallows' Day. The chrysanthemums must be prepared for placing on the family graves, and I'll do that myself until I lie in one of my own."

She had heard of people in some predominantly Catholic countries acknowledging All Saints' Day by placing flowers on graves, but not in England. She had not realized her husband's family followed the tradition.

"Do you lay the flowers now?"

"Only when neither the master nor Miss Darcy is at home. Lady Anne began the tradition at Pemberley the year—well, the first year she lost a babe. She used to lay bouquets of hothouse flowers, until the year we introduced the chrysanthemums to her garden. She would lay the flowers herself, accompanied by young Master Darcy from the time he was old enough to walk. The graves of her own children, though—those she visited alone. She would rise before dawn, cut the blooms with her own hands, and fair cover the three little graves with flowers as the sun rose."

This image of Lady Anne struck Elizabeth with surprising force. Lady Anne had been held before her as such a paragon that Elizabeth had not devoted much thought to her deeper feelings. *I cannot bear to bury another,* she had written. Now, having just experienced for herself the wonder of sensing a life growing within her, Elizabeth felt a sympathy for Lady Anne that had not touched her before.

She shivered. Mr. Flynn struggled to his feet.

"If you will pardon my saying so, ma'am, you look cold through. May I walk you back to the house?"

She accepted his advice but not his offer of escort, as she did not want to cause the elderly servant undue exertion on her account. Once more indoors, she returned to her morning room and was pleased to find it empty. Lady Catherine had apparently settled elsewhere in the house for the remainder of the afternoon. Or she had embarked on an inspection of every room and closet of Pemberley to determine whether Elizabeth had dared move any other pieces of furniture.

Key still in hand, she withdrew Lady Anne's letter from the desk and reread it. The words struck her more personally this time, stirred a stronger response within her. She wanted to reach back through the years and succor the writer, locate whatever it was she so desperately wanted and bring it to her.

But what on earth had Lady Anne lost? A maternal heirloom, hidden "too well." That could mean anything.

She glanced at the key again. Was it related to the present puzzle, or merely another curious find on a day full of discoveries?

Search for me. That seemed the place to begin—not seeking on behalf of Lady Anne, but to uncover the woman herself, to identify the person her mother-in-law had truly been beyond the image everyone remembered. If Elizabeth were ever to know what sort of object the former mistress of Pemberley had valued so highly and exhorted her to find, she would have to know more about Lady Anne Fitzwilliam Darcy.

"There you are." Darcy's voice drew her attention to the doorway. "My aunt informed me of your abrupt removal, and I was grown concerned by its length."

"I went for a walk."

"To London?"

"No, to the south garden. Though when I departed the house, I think I was vexed enough to march at least as far as London."

He entered and came to her side. "If it provides any consolation, you left Lady Catherine so incensed that she declares she will not leave her chamber until you apologize."

"Truly?"

He laughed at her expression. "Do not look so delighted."

"Had I known relief could be obtained so easily—"

"Elizabeth!"

"You are right; it cannot last. She must emerge eventually."

"Has it been so very intolerable?"

"I have been accused of thrift where I should be liberal and extravagance where I should exercise economy. I manage my servants ill, my time even worse, and if I have not already embarrassed myself as a hostess before the neighbors, I should consider myself fortunate."

"I had been meaning to speak to you about that last point. You really must refrain from resting your feet on the table when the Devonshires come to dine."

She shrugged. "As her ladyship perpetually reminds me, I simply cannot escape my common upbringing. Satisfy yourself that I have ceased hanging laundry in the sculpture gallery."

His countenance and manner became more serious. "Does she speak of nothing but your deficiencies?"

"I possess them in sufficient quantity that they alone could occupy her indefinitely, but she also offers her opinions on any subject that comes to mind. A need or condition does not exist for which her ladyship lacks a better prescription than that in current use. She has rattled off receipts for everything from preserving cut flowers to repelling moths."

"So essentially, my aunt conducts herself as usual."

He pulled a chair to the side of the desk and sat down near her. "Forgive me. I did not mean for the full burden of entertaining her to fall upon you while I attended to other matters. Has not Georgiana helped divert her?"

"Georgiana has earned my eternal gratitude for her efforts, but your sister is no match for Lady Catherine. I doubt that successfully managing her ladyship lies within the power of any sole person. And as for the other matters commanding your attention, I would much rather you spend your time preparing to meet with Mr. Harper when he arrives than listen to Lady Catherine's discourse. I can handle your aunt."

His gaze fell upon the note in her hand. "You are rereading my mother's letter?"

"I spent a fair amount of time in her garden today, and came away wishing to learn more about her. Do you happen to know whether she left behind any other correspondence?"

"Given the amount in which she engaged, one could presume so. Whether my father saved it is another matter, but my guess is that he did. When she died, he was so distraught that I cannot imagine his discarding anything that had passed through her hands."

"Where might it be found now?"

"I was a boy. Mrs. Reynolds could best answer that."

"May I read through it—if it can be found?"

"Indeed, I believe at least one of us ought to read through it. Perhaps we might chance upon a letter from Mrs. Tilney that could illuminate our experience at Northanger."

"Have you heard from Henry Tilney?"

"I had a short report from him today. No new information, but he has not yet completed the enquiries we discussed. Once Mr. Harper and I have had a chance to confer, I intend to send him to Gloucestershire to work with Mr. Tilney."

"You mean, to *supervise* Mr. Tilney."

"To ensure all leads are followed."

Elizabeth knew how difficult it was for Darcy to delegate such a critical matter to others rather than performing every particular of it himself. He had been restless since their arrival at Pemberley, even though plenty of estate affairs had arisen during their absence to command what segments of his attention were not absorbed by the Northanger crisis.

"I am sure Mr. Harper and Mr. Tilney will conduct a thorough investigation in Gloucestershire," she said. "Meanwhile, I shall peruse your mother's missives with due diligence. The sooner all of us determine what truly transpired at Northanger Abbey, the sooner Lady Catherine can go home."

Sixteen

Elizabeth awoke the next morning to the same thoughts and meditations which had at length closed her eyes.

—Pride and Prejudice

Elizabeth's mind hovered in that state where dream and wakefulness merge and one cannot quite determine where one ends and the other begins. Images of infants and mothers, letters and locks, keys and chrysanthemums floated through her sleepy consciousness as the rest of her senses similarly teased her. She thought she heard a woman's voice, felt a gentle touch on the back of her hand, smelled the summertime flowers of Lady Anne's garden.

The scent of one flower in particular dominated the aromatic illusion. It was a pleasant scent, but unfavorable associations nagged as her foggy mind struggled to identify it. Several minutes passed before she recognized it as the same fragrance that had overwhelmed her as she'd argued with Lady Catherine. She groaned and tried to push Darcy's aunt out of her otherwise agreeable fancies. It was just like Lady Catherine to intrude where she was least welcome, even Elizabeth's dreams.

She opened her lids just enough to see that darkness yet cloaked the world. All Pemberley slumbered; even the servants had not yet risen. Only the infrequent pops of the diminishing fire broke the stillness. Despite the warmth provided by Darcy sleeping beside her, Elizabeth fought chill. She had never quite warmed up after yesterday's prolonged outing, and now that the waning flames of the hearth no longer generated much heat, the room felt especially cold.

Loath to leave even the inadequate heat of her bed, but still less willing to shiver through the unknown number of hours that remained until morning, she reluctantly parted company with the covers and crept across the chamber to bank the fire. She added the fuel, then lingered before the fireplace to let the warmth seep into her bones.

The nearest window faced southeast. Lucy had not completely closed one of the shutters, and as Elizabeth stood she noticed the barest hint of light starting to permeate the landscape. Clouds still stretched across the sky, promising an All Hallows' Day as grey and somber as had been All Hallows' Eve.

Her chill diminished, she went to the window and pushed the shutter fully open. The south garden lay in the same sleepy state as the rest of the grounds, but she knew that with dawn approaching Mr. Flynn would soon enter it to prepare the chrysanthemums. Indeed, were Lady Anne still alive, she would have already been within its gates.

Movement within the garden—a figure passing along its paths—caught her gaze. The garden walls and yew trees within its perimeter prevented her from obtaining more than a fleeting glimpse, and the faintness of the light further limited her view, but she presumed the head gardener had reported for duty. A desire to join him possessed her. If Lady Anne could not lay blooms on those three little graves herself, Elizabeth would do it for her. As the sun rose.

She dressed quickly and headed out. A surprised Lucy encountered her leaving her dressing room.

"You are awake early this morning, Mrs. Darcy."

She did not wish to reveal her errand to the servant, but neither did she want anyone to worry about her. "I could not sleep. Should Mr. Darcy enquire, tell him I thought I would enjoy the sunrise."

Upon reaching the garden, she found three bouquets of chrysanthemums, tied with ribbons, waiting at the base of a small statue. Mr. Flynn, however, was nowhere about. She glanced at the sky. The clouds had thinned at the eastern horizon, and those closest to the ground had a pinkish cast. Sunrise rapidly approached. If she were to reach the family graves before the sun broke across the horizon, she would have to go very soon. Though she hesitated to take the flowers without the gardener's knowledge—surely he would wonder what had happened to them upon his return—she picked up the bouquets.

She walked briskly to the churchyard where the Darcy family had buried its dead for generations. While the church that served the estate and nearby village stood near the house, she had been in the cemetery only once before, when Darcy had shown her his parents' final resting places during her early days at Pemberley. She easily identified the monument that marked Lady Anne's grave, and knew that his infant siblings lay close beside their mother.

She found the three little headstones: Gregory, Maria, and Faith. The inscriptions of each grey marble slab revealed ages heartbreakingly short—a day of life, an hour, a moment. Each bore a portion of verse from the Gospels. With a silent prayer for all three souls, Elizabeth laid the flowers on the small graves. Just as she placed the final bouquet, the first streak of daylight illuminated the markers.

The brilliant shaft brought out every subtle hue of the marble. Light and dark gradations became more pronounced, and the angle of the light defined the engraved epitaphs even more boldly. But beneath the inscriptions she had read before, a tiny word, previously unnoticed, appeared at the bottom of each headstone. Across the three markers they read, "Love conquers all."

So faint they were almost indiscernible, the three words appeared for but a minute against the pattern of each stone. When the angle of the climbing sun shifted, they faded altogether from view.

Elizabeth peered closely at the markers, trailed her fingers over the now-invisible words. The engravings were so small, so shallow, their strokes so thin that she could not feel any variance in the surface of the stone. Had she not been here precisely when sunrise broke, she never would have detected the words. Running as they did across all three headstones, they must have been inscribed sometime after the last of the three children, Faith, had been laid to rest.

She studied Lady Anne's memorial, read the epitaph that bespoke the heartache Darcy's father had suffered at her loss. This marker too bore the words "Love conquers all," but carved boldly into the marble. Elizabeth recalled that the words had also appeared in Lady Anne's letter to her. She had interpreted the line as a general expression of encouragement—perhaps written as much for the author's sake as the reader's as she faced her final trial. But now Elizabeth wondered at the connection between the words in the letter and the words on the headstones.

The subject occupied her thoughts throughout her walk back to the south garden, where she found Mr. Flynn just entering the gate. He carried a box of gardening tools and appeared freshly dressed; though she knew he had been working since before dawn, no dirt or other signs of labor yet streaked his clothing.

She hailed him, and he waited for her to pass through the gate.

"I hope I did not bewilder you when you discovered the chrysanthemum bouquets gone this morning," she said as they walked together toward the garden's interior. "I would have told you I was taking them to the cemetery, but I did not see you about."

Mr. Flynn appeared confused. He started to speak, stopped, and made a second attempt. "I was not about, ma'am. Mr. Darcy requested all the flowers be ready at noon, so I am only just now coming to prepare them."

"But—" Now Elizabeth regarded the gardener in puzzlement. "But from my window I saw someone in here before dawn, and when I reached the garden, three bouquets were waiting."

" 'Twas not my doing, ma'am."

"That is certainly curious. If you did not leave them, who did?"

A twinkle entered his clear blue eyes. "My da might have said a garden sprite, being as last night was All Hallows' Eve," he said. "But I suspect one of my assistants decided to spare my old bones a little work. They all think I'm too old to be up working before the sun, though not a one of them would be so bold as to tell me directly."

He surveyed the chrysanthemums, chose a grouping of plants, and settled down to his task.

"May I help?" she offered.

"You already have," he said. "It might not be my place to say so, ma'am, but I expect her ladyship appreciated your being there at sunrise."

Elizabeth returned to the house to find Darcy already dressed and breakfasting. Generally an early riser, he had become even more so since arriving home from Gloucestershire. She knew the unsettled state of affairs involving Northanger caused him restlessness that interfered with his sleep. Either that, or he wanted to be clear of the breakfast room before Lady Catherine entered it.

"I was wondering where you had hidden yourself this morning," he said when he saw her.

"Did not Lucy tell you?"

"I did not ask her."

As the room was empty of anyone save him, she kissed his cheek before heading to the sideboard. The morning's activities and unusually early start had left her famished. "I awoke with the sudden urge to beg your aunt's permission to name our child after her. I rousted her from bed to make my supplication, and was rewarded not only with her consent, but with pledges of her everlasting regard and affection for me. We have been closeted together these several hours planning her permanent residence at Pemberley so that we need never part."

She sat down beside him, and he covered her left hand with his. "As credible as I find your explanation, I believe you instead have been out walking again."

"How did you know?"

"Your eyes are brightened by the exercise. And your fingers are cold."

She snatched her hand away. "Here I thought you were being tender. You only wanted to gather evidence."

"There is also a flower petal in your hair." He removed the yellow floret and set it on the table. "Chrysanthemum?"

"I laid flowers on the graves of your siblings this morning." She watched his countenance as she spoke. "I hope I did not overstep?"

"No," he said quietly. "In fact, I am pleased that you wanted to do so. As matriarch of the Darcy family, you ought to take part in all our traditions. I should have told you of today's observance myself. How did you come to learn of it?"

"Mr. Flynn."

"Of course. You said you went to my mother's garden yesterday." He continued eating his breakfast. "Speaking of my mother, I have asked Mrs. Reynolds about her correspondence, and she believes it went to one of the attics in a trunk. Would you like it brought down?"

"Yes—to my dressing room." There she could read through it without fear of intrusion by Lady Catherine. "Would you care to read the letters with me?"

"I can join you this afternoon, but I must spend the morning in conference with Mr. Clarke regarding the harvest feast."

Mr. Clarke likely needed as little instruction in the feast

preparations as Mrs. Reynolds had—indeed, the servants were so well versed in their responsibilities that Elizabeth had felt more like a guest than the hostess when she had reviewed the details with the staff. She looked forward to the celebration as a welcome distraction from recent events in Gloucestershire. And from their current houseguest.

"Have you many particulars yet to settle?"

"Mr. Clarke has everything in order—I just want to review it all before Mr. Harper arrives. An express came while you were out, advising us to expect him on the morrow."

"Thank goodness. I suppose neither Mr. Clarke nor I shall see much of you while Mr. Harper is at Pemberley?"

"Yes, although once we confer, he is of most use to me in Gloucestershire and London, where he can build our case and engage a barrister to argue for us in court, if it comes to that."

"Perhaps he can also persuade Mr. Melbourne that this custody arrangement with Lady Catherine is entirely unnecessary."

"I thought you had become intimate friends?"

"An intimacy best enjoyed from a distance."

Though he had finished his own breakfast, Darcy remained in the room with her until she finished hers. She was happy for his companionship, as she felt as if she had not seen much of him since their return to Pemberley. When her appetite—both for food and for his conversation—was appeased, he rose.

"You will accompany me and Georgiana at noon, then?"

"I would not miss it."

After spending an hour in her morning room, she made her way back to their apartment. Mrs. Reynolds stopped her in the hall. "I have just spoken to Mr. Darcy. Lady Anne's papers are being brought to your dressing room now, ma'am."

"Already? Thank you."

"Ma'am?" She paused. "You did want *all* of her correspondence delivered there?"

"Yes, all of it." The unusually early start to her day had left her with several unoccupied hours until noon, and she looked forward to leisurely perusing the letters.

"Very good, ma'am. I just wanted to be certain."

"NINE?"

Elizabeth regarded her dressing room in astonishment. Or rather, what had once been her dressing room. It now resembled a coachyard full of luggage.

"There are two more trunks still in the attic, ma'am," said one of the footmen as he and a partner set their most recent burden on the floor.

"Leave them there for now, or I shall not be able to cross the room."

Indeed, when the men left, she barely had space to shut the door. Nine trunks, and more upstairs yet.

She lifted the lid of one and found it full of letters. How many letters could fit inside a trunk? One hundred? Three? This was not a task to be undertaken without reinforcements. Hearing sounds of movement in her bedroom, she maneuvered her way to that door. A housemaid tidied the chamber.

"Do you know whether Miss Darcy has risen?" Elizabeth asked.

The maid paused in sweeping the carpet. "I believe Miss Darcy is with her aunt, ma'am."

Elizabeth had no desire to interrupt that tête-à-tête. She would seek Georgiana later.

"Is there anything else, ma'am?"

"No. Yes—I do not believe I have seen you before."

"Just started recently, ma'am. Name's Jenny." She spoke in an accent that sounded even more northern than the Derbyshire inflections to which Elizabeth was becoming accustomed.

"Are you far from home?"

"A ways, ma'am. But happy to be here."

Elizabeth offered her a smile. "Welcome to Pemberley, Jenny."

With a deep breath, she turned back to the dressing room. Nine trunks, each likely containing hundreds of letters. Where did one begin?

"Jenny, when you have finished with the bedchamber, I believe I shall need some tea."

Seventeen

Where shall I begin? Which of all my important nothings shall I tell you first?

—Jane Austen, letter to Cassandra

We depart for London on Friday. How soon shall I have the pleasure of seeing you there? I understand G. D. is already in town. . . .

Yrs etc, A. Parker

Elizabeth stood, stretched, and rubbed her back. Save for a break at noon to lay the chrysanthemums with Darcy and Georgiana, she had done nothing all day but read through Lady Anne's letters. Her predecessor at Pemberley had, it seemed, single-handedly kept half the postal workers in England employed. She had maintained regular communication with dozens of correspondents—kin, friends, social acquaintances—had received intermittent notes from still more, and had apparently saved every letter that entered the house. With this many letters coming in, Elizabeth could only imagine how many must have gone out. How had Lady Anne ever set down her pen long enough to have something to write *about*?

Most of the letters Elizabeth had read so far largely contained the minutiae of daily life. Should she actually read through each letter in the trunks, she would probably come away with an intimate knowledge of every genteel family in Derbyshire and many prominent members of London's *ton*. Who had visited whom, who had become engaged, who had lately wed, who had been expecting, whose children had learned their alphabets, whose sons had left for Oxford, who had taken ill, who had just died.

As interesting a portrait as such news and gossip painted of the neighborhood—even if the details were over twenty years old—Elizabeth wished she could somehow read more of Lady Anne's own letters, the ones she had written and to which this mountain of correspondence responded. She could infer some of their content from the replies Anne had received ("I am sorry to hear Fitzwilliam suffers such pain cutting his third tooth. Have you attempted lancing the gum?"), but such surmises lacked Anne's voice.

She pushed a stray lock of hair away from her forehead with the back of her hand, careful not to touch her face or white cap with ink-stained fingers. Just then, Darcy entered.

He met the spectacle of Elizabeth amid the sea of open trunks with bemusement. "When you told me earlier that my mother had left behind such a collection of letters, I did not fully comprehend its size."

"It is a wonder your entire inheritance was not spent on postage."

"Have you found anything of interest?"

"Plenty of interest, though nothing related to Northanger Abbey yet. If Lady Anne did correspond with Mrs. Tilney, however, the letters must be here somewhere."

Darcy took off his coat. "Then let us devise a methodical plan for sorting through all of this."

"From what I have managed to determine, the trunks are loosely organized by date. That is, most of a given year's correspondence can be found in the same trunk, with some trunks holding multiple years. Your mother probably filled them gradually, storing the letters as they arrived and moving each trunk to the attic when it became full."

"That would explain why Mrs. Reynolds recalled that one trunk of correspondence went up there when her personal effects were packed away, yet nine came down today."

"Since we do not know when your mother and Mrs. Tilney formed their friendship, I began with the trunk that contained the oldest letters. They might be too old, however—most of them predate your parents' marriage."

"Perhaps, then, we ought to set aside that trunk at present and select another."

"Do you not wish to read the opinions of your mother's friends regarding their courtship?"

"I am not certain. Do I?"

"Most of them favored it. Lady Constance Richfield thought your father was terribly handsome, and so did Lady Amelia Parker. In fact, I just finished reading one of Lady Amelia's letters." She knelt down and retrieved a letter from one of several piles, then unfolded the note and skimmed to the middle. "Here it is—'I am all impatience to hear whether G. D. has declared himself yet. If he does, you *must* prevail upon your father to grant his consent. Your parents might favor an alliance with Lord E. for his title, but D.'s fortune rivals that of the marquess and E. cannot match him for looks. Were D. half so handsome, I would still consider his countenance the most pleasing of any gentleman I know.' "

The praise elicited a smile from Darcy. "I did not realize my father held such attraction for the ladies in his youth. Though Lady Amelia could not have found Lord E.'s profile too displeasing, for she is now a marchioness and bears the name Everett." He sat down beside her and picked up another letter. "What else have you found?"

"That one is from your aunt." Elizabeth hesitated, unsure whether Darcy ought to learn the opinions Lady Catherine had expressed about his father before the marriage. The knowledge might further tax their already tense relationship.

He noted her expression. "Allow me to guess—my aunt offered different advice?" He opened the letter. " 'If you can form an alliance with a man of both title and fortune, you should do so. It is your duty to your family, yourself, and your progeny to marry as well as you can. Reports have reached my ears that on the eve of securing one of the country's most eligible peers, you are encouraging the attention of a certain wealthy but untitled gentleman. Need I remind you that you are the daughter of an earl? Why settle for a mere gentleman when you could ally the Fitzwilliams with a man of both fortune *and* rank, as I have done? Do not argue that affection should be considered. Affection has no place in such an important decision as marriage.' "

"The view Lady Catherine expresses of your father in that letter varies radically from the manner in which she speaks of the Darcy family now. I wonder how much time passed before she resigned herself to the marriage?"

"Most likely, the day the engagement was announced. Though my father lacked a title, their marriage offered my mother and her family everything else they could desire in an alliance: fortune, land, and a connection with an old and worthy family. Once the decision had been made, Lady Catherine would have wasted little time cultivating the advantages of the connection." He reached for another letter.

"I have already read through those. Perhaps you could start reading some from another trunk."

"This one?" He slid forward a tooled leather chest about half the size of the others. "How old are these letters?"

She had not noticed the box before. "I cannot tell you. I must have overlooked that chest amid all the larger ones."

He opened the box. Two sets of letters, each tied with ribbon, rested within. He untied one of the ribbons and picked up the top letter. "This is my father's hand." He fanned out the bundle. "All of them are."

He untied the ribbon on the second packet. "And this is my mother's writing. These are addressed to him."

She opened several of Lady Anne's letters and quickly skimmed the pages. Darcy did the same with his father's.

"Love letters!" She whispered it like a secret. "Can you tell which is the oldest?"

"This one is dated the third of January, seventeen eighty-three. It is not exactly a love letter—it was written before their engagement, and is actually addressed to my uncle."

> *I return herewith your sister's volume of Chaucer, with gratitude for her having lent it to me. Please tell Lady Anne that at her behest, I reread the general prologue on my journey home, and find that her observations have enhanced my appreciation for the Tales. Whether that pleasure derives from the opinions themselves or the memory of the lively manner in which she delivered them, I cannot say. I shall, however, never again encounter Madame Eglentyne without recalling my visit to Riveton Hall. Nor shall I commit the error of expressing surprise that a friend's younger sister has read the great poet. If Lady Anne will indulge me, I look forward to continuing our discussion when I join your party at Riveton between Hilary and Easter terms.*

"Your father and uncle attended Cambridge together?" Elizabeth asked.

"Yes, that is how my parents met. My uncle brought a party of friends home with him one Christmas, my father among them. His first night there, he and my mother, who was a bit of a bluestocking, became engaged in a debate over something in *The Canterbury Tales,* to the amusement of all the gentlemen."

"They fell in love over poetry?"

"I believe it was more the badinage between them than the topic. My father appreciated her quick wit and animated spirit."

"Traits all men should prize," Elizabeth declared. Her own husband had once told her that he'd admired her for the liveliness of her mind. "Meanwhile, your mother's family worked to arrange a marriage between her and Lord Everett.

If your mother and father formed an attachment during his first visit, Easter must have seemed very far off, indeed—particularly since they could not with propriety correspond with each other directly. When and how did your father next write?"

The next letter on the stack was smaller than the others, and multiple crease lines indicated that it had once been well folded. He opened the note. "April."

> *Dear Lady Anne—Pray forgive the liberty I take in writing you this note. Though I depart for Pemberley today, I leave something behind at Riveton. As its nature renders a third party unable to transport it, your brother cannot bring it with him when we meet again at Cambridge. It therefore lies in your care. I hope it is not an unwelcome burden, and that one day you might return it. Believe me—*
>
> *Your most sincere and humble servant,*
> *G. Darcy*

Elizabeth smiled. George Darcy had not wanted to leave Riveton without ensuring that Lady Anne knew she had won his regard. In a house full of people on a busy morning of departure, how had George delivered the note? Had he pressed it into Anne's hand upon parting? Conveyed it through a servant?

"A clandestine letter. Are you shocked by your father's impropriety?"

"Yes." Darcy considered a moment. "And no. He was not a man to leave anything to chance. If something occurred shortly before his departure that caused her to doubt him, he would not have quit Riveton without finding some means by which to communicate his intentions. His persistence was one of the qualities I admired most in him." He refolded the letter, his expression contemplative.

She realized their discovery of his parents' private communication was no doubt triggering countless memories, and she hoped most of them were pleasant ones. She took her stack of letters and came to him so they could read them together. "I believe this note of your mother's responds to his. Apparently, your mother also was not one to leave anything to chance."

> *Dear Mr. Darcy—Hugh has agreed to bring these lines with him, but says he will deliver no others once at school. Know that I understand the worth of what you have entrusted to me, and that I shall safeguard it until such a time as it may be acknowledged.*
>
> *Yrs sincerely, A. F.*

There followed other letters from George and Anne's brief engagement and the first year of their marriage. The letters exchanged when business called George away or Anne visited a friend were few; once united, it seems the two had been nearly inseparable. More abundant were brief notes left, by the sound of them, on pillows and in pockets. One of these Darcy refolded without reading aloud.

She tilted her head to see his face. "Darcy—you are not blushing?" She took the note from him, read it herself, and giggled. "Oh, my!"

His countenance turned still more crimson. "One prefers to remain ignorant about some things regarding one's parents."

"Then we shall not leave such evidence behind for our own child to discover. She might figure out how she came to be."

The expressions of newlywed bliss gave way to anticipation of their first child. By the time Elizabeth and Darcy depleted the ribboned stacks, they had followed Anne and George through their eldest's first year. When Darcy's rich tenor voice ceased reading the final letter, she opened her eyes but remained curled against him, her head resting against his chest.

"They clearly had a happy marriage. And it sounds as if your arrival added still more to their joy," Elizabeth said. "Did you know they adored each other so?"

He held her tightly. "I could see fondness between them, but it was not the optimistic ardor of these letters. Something changed."

Elizabeth did not want to hear that anything had changed. As they had read the correspondence between Darcy's parents, Anne and George had become real people to her. Especially in the later letters, when Anne had been expecting their first child, her words had touched a response in Elizabeth, created affinity between them as Anne voiced feelings that echoed her own.

"Perhaps their love merely matured," Elizabeth said, turning to face him. "Or they were guarded about displaying it before their son."

"No, it—" Darcy searched for words. "It altered. I do not want to say it diminished, for my father mourned her as deeply as you can imagine. But it had a different character than what these letters contain."

He gathered the letters he had read and stacked them neatly. "Now, we must find our way through this sea of stationery to our dinner attire, for the day grows late."

She had become so engrossed in Anne and George's story that she had lost track of the hour. Now she realized she was famished. "I hope Lucy can maneuver through the door when she arrives to dress me."

"I hope so, too." He stood and stretched. "Meanwhile, I am fleeing to the perfect order of my own dressing room."

"You would abandon the mother of your child to this?"

"Accompany me if you like."

"I shall. First, however, I want to return these to their case." She retied the ribbons around each stack of letters and opened the lid of the leather chest. A solitary letter lay in the bottom.

"We missed one," she said.

"We have read enough for one day. It can wait."

She unfolded the letter. George's handwriting met her gaze. The date was much later than the rest of the letters they had read, the lines more closely written. And the words were, as Darcy would say, of a far different character.

"No, it cannot."

Eighteen

I shall be glad if you can revive past feelings, and from your unbiassed self resolve to go on as you have done.

—Jane Austen, letter to Fanny Knight

29 April 1795
My beloved Anne,

I resent the business that forces me from Pemberley this morn. There is too much we need to say to each other, words that perhaps ought to have been spoken last night. You sleep so peacefully that I cannot bring myself to wake you. Yet I cannot leave without unburdening my heart.

Forgive me, Anne. Forgive my weakness. Forgive me for breaking a promise to you that I intended to keep for the rest of my days if you required it. Most of all, forgive me for not regretting its breach.

When we wed twelve years ago, neither of us knew then the course our life together would follow. We anticipated—and have known—great joy. But we have also known profound sorrow, and it has nearly undone us. Gregory, Maria, Faith, all the miscarriages in between—though you outwardly bore the losses with fortitude, I saw part of you die with each of our children. And I had no notion of how to comfort you.

When you came to me and asked for no more children, how could I withhold from you a pledge that might bring you the peace I so desperately wished you would find? I have never regretted our decision, nor resented you for having requested it of me. Nor have I ever been tempted to stray.

But nothing has been right since. Falling asleep and waking up together had formed the rhythm of our lives. Whatever else our days comprehended, they had begun and ended with each other. Now days pass in which we might not look upon each other until afternoon, or dinner, or not at all. We have fallen out of step, and the distance between us has increased these several years.

I have missed you, my wife. Dear God, how I have missed you. But last night we again found the perfect accord we once knew. And it gives me hope.

Anne, should last night's union bear issue, should your deepest fears be realized and we find you are again with child, I bid you to remember that "love conquers all." From the day we met, those words have directed our course. You argued them so warmly in our first conversation that you captured me. We believed them in the early years of our marriage, when Fitzwilliam was an infant and we saw nothing but continued joy on the horizon. It was when we stopped believing, when we allowed fear to dominate, that we lost our way. Yet still love conquered, for it finally wearied of our misguided attempts to deny it. Let us trust it to see us through whatever lies ahead.

Ever your devoted—
G.

Darcy and Elizabeth read the letter together in silence. When they had finished, her face held sorrow. She waited for him to speak.

He felt as if he had just witnessed the demise of someone

close to him. In a sense, he had. The letter not only explained the affliction his parents' marriage had suffered, but foretold his mother's death. Her deepest fears *had* been realized: The letter was dated nine months before Georgiana's birth.

"As I said—" He cleared the thickness in his throat. "Something changed. Now we know why."

"Losses such as theirs must transform any feeling person." She gently took the letter from his hand and glanced once more at its content. "But, really, it is not altogether a sad letter. It expresses hope—they found their way back to each other. They had a second chance at happiness." She looked at him expectantly. "Did they not?"

"They did not. Within a year, she was dead."

"What of the time in between? While she carried Georgiana? I must believe that receiving a letter such as this restored your mother's faith at least a little. She kept it with their love letters, after all."

He thought back to the last few months of his mother's life. They were so long ago. He had been but a boy, and what child of ten or eleven fully comprehends the complex emotions and interactions of the adults around him? "I cannot remember. I do not recall her plunging into despair, so perhaps she did find a measure of peace."

"And your father?"

His father he remembered more clearly—they'd had another eleven years together. "I think he anticipated Georgiana's birth with guarded optimism. Thank heaven Georgiana survived. He never fully recovered from my mother's death, and had he also lost Georgiana, the double defeat might have overpowered him."

A fierce protective instinct arose within Darcy. The expectation of their own child filled him with happiness. He looked forward to holding that child, teaching that child, recognizing in that child the best parts of himself and Elizabeth. But he could not give himself over to complete joy in the event until he had escaped his father's fate.

She took his hands in hers and caught his gaze. Her eyes, the eyes that had first captured his interest and then his heart, held confidence. "I have no intention of leaving you to raise this child alone, or of losing this child. And surely any child carried by me must inherit my stubbornness along with my better qualities. I can assure you that our daughter has already inherited my strength."

"How can you be so certain?"

"I felt her move." A quiet light entered her eyes. "Yesterday, in your mother's garden. And again just now."

The news swept away his melancholy. Almost shyly, he put a hand to her abdomen. "I cannot detect anything. Does she yet stir?"

She stood very still for a minute. He held his own breath, willing even the slightest movement to pass under his fingertips. To his deep disappointment, he felt nothing.

"I cannot detect anything now, either," she assured him. "And what I have experienced is such a slight sensation that I doubt you could perceive it from the outside yet. But I am certain it is our child and not bad mutton."

At her words, he sensed a small fluctuation beneath his hand. He looked at her hopefully. "Was that him?"

"I am afraid not." She suppressed a smile. "That was my stomach reminding us that the dinner hour approaches."

Nineteen

"He is the best landlord, and the best master . . . that ever lived. . . . There is not one of his tenants or servants but what will give him a good name."

—*Mrs. Reynolds,* Pride and Prejudice

Pemberley's annual harvest feast was a grand event, one to which landlord and tenant alike looked forward. Farmers, laborers, schoolchildren, villagers—all who lived on or near the estate and depended upon it for their livelihoods joined together to celebrate the end of the growing season. Weather permitting, the supper, children's games, and other entertainments took place under the open sky, and tradition held that once the date had been fixed each year, it could be counted upon to prove fair.

Today had been no exception. The sun had smiled upon the afternoon's entertainments and continued as the entire company crowded around a dozen long trestle tables to break bread together. Afterward, the dancing commenced in the rustic tenants' hall, with Elizabeth and Darcy leading off the opening minuet.

Elizabeth was happy to see Darcy relaxed and enjoying his duties as host, the strain of recent weeks having left his countenance at least temporarily. Mr. Harper had come and gone, and now worked to bring their legal difficulties in Gloucestershire to an end. He had also reported that his initial enquiries into the Earl of Southwell's activities in France had yielded nothing of concern. By all accounts, Darcy's cousin was enjoying a quiet visit to the Continent. Elizabeth and Darcy tried not to ponder too hard the irony that in sending their solicitor away to attend to Lady Catherine's groundless fears of family scandal, a true potential scandal had brought Lady Catherine under their own roof.

Indeed, Elizabeth forced all unpleasant thoughts from her mind as she surveyed the revels going on around her. She considered her first harvest feast as mistress of Pemberley a success. Sounds of merriment had filled the air all day. Supper for six hundred had been served with nary a mishap. And every single guest seemed to be having a delightful time.

Except one.

"I do not know how you can suffer so many people to overrun Pemberley in this manner. They trample the lawns. Their children hang from the trees. Their vulgar voices form a cacophony. I shudder to see this noble house subjected to such indignity."

Lady Catherine observed the spectacle from an out-of-the-way chair to which she had fled the moment supper ended. Though she often boasted of her own far-reaching benevolence, she preferred to demonstrate it from the farthest reach possible. Sharing a table with common tradesmen and farmers had very nearly put her in need of the services of the apothecary who had been sitting across from her. Elizabeth had endeavored to place her amid the company her ladyship would find the least objectionable—the minister, the schoolmaster—but the size of the crowd overall had convinced Darcy's aunt that she dined in a mob of the coarsest peasants.

"Pemberley could not exist without these people," Elizabeth said.

"The quantity of food they consumed was staggering. Not one of them exercised restraint. Commoners always take advantage of a free meal."

"This is a celebration."

"They will be celebrating with your ale until every barrel runs dry. I support the principle of noblesse oblige, but you cannot permit the lower orders to exploit your generosity."

"I shall hold your ladyship's advice in mind the next time we plan a gathering to demonstrate our gratitude to the very people who provide what we have to give."

Elizabeth excused herself and began a slow weave across the crowded hall. Perhaps she ought to exhibit more patience with Lady Catherine, but the days leading up to today's festivities had seen a surfeit of her unsolicited counsel. Her self-imposed exile following their quarrel had lasted but a single day; unable to resist involving herself in an event of so large a scale as the harvest feast, she had soon emerged to perform her sacred duty to criticize and command. She had been full of opinions regarding the preparations and censorious of Elizabeth for not dictating every particular to her staff. Elizabeth, however, had defined her proper role differently; given her inexperience at hosting gatherings for hundreds, she thought it prudent to let the servants perform unhampered the tasks they had been doing for years, while she largely observed and learned. She had expressed her preferences on plenty of points, but postponed significant changes until next year when she would possess a better understanding of what had gone before.

At last, she reached the other side of the room. The noise and heat and closeness of the hall had conspired to render her light-headed, and she sought air and a little space. The doors leading outside stood open to welcome cool evening air into the crowded hall, and to these she headed.

She stopped suddenly. A trickling sensation brought her hand up to her nose. Drops of blood landed on her fingers.

An older woman standing nearby hurried over with a handkerchief, which Elizabeth gratefully accepted.

"Just pinch it for a few minutes, Mrs. Darcy. Here—let us sit down."

She led Elizabeth out of the hall to a set of steps where she might attend her nosebleed without the entire community in audience. The stone step chilled her through her dress but she was glad for its solidity beneath her shaky legs. Instinctively, her free hand dropped to her abdomen.

The woman noted the protective position of her hand but quickly raised her gaze back to Elizabeth's face. Elizabeth recognized her rescuer as Edith Godwin, the village midwife. She had met Mrs. Godwin at a similar fête Darcy had thrown last winter to celebrate their marriage and Elizabeth's arrival at Pemberley.

"There, now. I think we prevented any blood from landing on your dress. Has it stopped?"

Elizabeth pulled the handkerchief away. Crimson stained half the fabric.

Mrs. Godwin took Elizabeth's hand in her own and brought the kerchief back up to her nose. "Pinch here another minute or two." She placed her other hand on the back of Elizabeth's head for support. Her calm, comforting manner and sympathetic countenance put Elizabeth at ease despite the blood. While the nosebleed itself did not incite great alarm, the suddenness of it had startled her.

When the bleeding had stopped, she thanked Mrs. Godwin again. "I believe I owe you a handkerchief." She regarded the bloody cloth with slight embarrassment.

"Do not trouble yourself. I am glad I happened to be nearby."

"I do not know what caused it."

Mrs. Godwin gave her a swift appraisal that included a deliberate glance at her abdomen. "Pardon me for asking, Mrs. Darcy," she said kindly, "but there has been talk today that perhaps your family is increasing?"

"I am the subject of gossip?" Her surprise lasted but a moment. Of course such news would not remain secret. Pemberley's servants had been preparing the house in anticipation of the baby's arrival, and they interacted so frequently with local tradesmen that the whole village must know of her condition. Too, her middle had grown to the point where even the generous cut of her gown could not disguise her heavier figure. She was either expanding her family or simply expanding.

"Happy speculation. Folks are excited by the prospect of a new heir at Pemberley."

"We anticipate an arrival in early spring."

Mrs. Godwin smiled. "I am happy to hear it," she said. "And there is the cause of your nosebleed—many women in your condition experience them. It is perfectly normal. A woman in the family way produces additional blood for the baby, and her body does not always know what to do with it all. Simply get in the habit of carrying a spare handkerchief. Or two."

At the midwife's reassuring words, Elizabeth's whole body relaxed. She had not realized she'd been sitting so tensely.

Mrs. Godwin glanced up at the façade of the house. "It has been a long time since there was an infant at Pemberley."

"Indeed. Miss Darcy turns eighteen soon."

"I know. I delivered her." Though the corners of her mouth raised in a half-smile, her eyes were somber. "Your husband, too. Of course, his birth was entirely a happy occasion, while hers was bittersweet. A sad thing it is, when a day that ought to be joyful ends in such grief." Her face clouded. "In forty years of attending births, I have seen my share of sorrow in the birthing room. Sometimes the infants are dead while still in the womb, and sometimes problems arise during the birth that I cannot control. But Lady Anne is the only mother I have ever lost, and her death still weighs upon me."

Elizabeth recalled Lady Anne's letter and her mention of Mrs. Godwin. "She had faith in you. I am certain you did everything within your power to help her."

"Heaven knows I did. But it was not enough." She sighed. "Poor creature. After all her losses, she was so hopeful that this time her child would survive—and then she herself did not."

"Were you present at her other births—the ones between my husband and Georgiana?"

"I was. With the two girls, Maria and Faith, she brought in a physician and I merely assisted him. But the physician did not attend Lady Anne at Georgiana's birth."

"Why not?" Given Lady Anne's history in childbed, Elizabeth would have expected her to make use of every medical person in Derbyshire. Or to have gone to London for her confinement.

"He was away from home and could not be summoned in time," she said. "But she had not planned to use him. She was certain that the birth would go as smoothly as her firstborn's, and wanted, as closely as possible, to reproduce the conditions of his arrival. A good portion of her optimism came from an heirloom her mother had given her when she expected Fitzwilliam, which family tradition held to bring good fortune to mothers in travail. Unfortunately, when her pains started she could not find it, and its absence sent her into panic."

Surely Mrs. Godwin spoke of the same item Lady Anne had written of in her letter to Elizabeth. "Do you know the nature of the heirloom?"

"It was an ivory statuette of the Madonna and Child. Small—perhaps three or four inches tall. And quite old, from its appearance."

"Did she not have it at the other births?"

"No. I understand she gave it to her sister, who retained it for some time. After losing one child, Lady Anne was quite upset by its lack at subsequent births. But she regained possession of it while expecting Georgiana, and was convinced it would ensure the infant's survival."

Elizabeth hoped her face did not reveal the resentment toward Lady Catherine that this news provoked within her. Why had not Darcy's aunt returned the statuette sooner? Whether or not it indeed brought good fortune, the ivory had obviously been important to Anne. Why withhold such a simple thing that could have eased her mind?

Anne's letter to Elizabeth had mentioned something about guarding herself from her sister. She had also mentioned hiding the missing object. Little wonder—if it had taken her three pregnancies to get it back, Elizabeth would have hidden it, too. She resolved to reread the letter in light of Mrs.

Godwin's revelation, and to question Lady Catherine about the ivory. What a delightful conversation that would no doubt prove.

"Was the statuette ever found?"

"Not while Lady Anne lived. After that, I cannot tell you."

Elizabeth shivered. The sun had set, and although torches lit the grounds immediately surrounding the house, the night air was chilly now that she had left the heat of the hall. The stone step, once comfortingly solid, was now just plain cold.

"I have enjoyed talking with you, Mrs. Godwin," she said. She meant it—she instinctively liked the grey-haired woman. "But I should return to the rest of my guests."

"It has been my pleasure."

As they rose, the torchlight shone more fully upon Elizabeth's face.

"You have some streaks of blood around your nose." Mrs. Godwin reached for the handkerchief. "Here—permit me."

While the midwife dabbed Elizabeth's face, Darcy came round the corner. Relief flashed across his features upon sighting his wife.

"I have been searching for you. Georgiana observed you leaving the hall and said you appeared to be in some distress." He noted her bloody face and the soiled handkerchief with alarm. "What has happened? Are you all right?"

"A nosebleed, that is all. Mrs. Godwin has taken good care of me."

He acknowledged the midwife's aid with a nod. "I appreciate your attention to my wife."

"I am always pleased to be of service to your family, Mr. Darcy." Mrs. Godwin gave the kerchief back to Elizabeth. "Keep this in case you should need it before you have an opportunity to retrieve a fresh one. But I think the bleeding is ended." She regarded her warmly. "I am happy for your news. If I can assist you at all in the coming months, do summon me."

"I shall. Thank you."

As Mrs. Godwin departed, Darcy examined her face

closely. "Did you experience a mishap?" He withdrew a handkerchief of his own and wiped a spot the midwife had missed.

"No, my nose simply started bleeding. Apparently, your daughter caused it."

He paused mid-stroke. Apprehension spread across his paling visage. "Has something happened to the baby?"

"Not at all. Mrs. Godwin assured me that this is normal for women in my condition."

"Bleeding for no reason is never normal. I shall send for Dr. Severn."

"That is entirely unnecessary. And there *is* a reason. Mrs. Godwin says—"

"I am sending for Dr. Severn." His tone left little hope of compromise.

"But, Darcy, Mrs. Godwin says there is no cause for concern." She put a hand on his arm, not realizing that blood from the handkerchief had stained her fingertips. The sight of it unsettled him further.

"Dr. Severn can determine that when he arrives."

"The doctor will not appreciate coming all the way to Derbyshire to tell us nothing is amiss. Mrs. Godwin has known her share of expectant mothers. If she says all is fine, why trouble him? I trust her judgment."

"I do not. Edith Godwin failed my mother. I will not risk her failing you, too."

She recalled, then, that in the chronicle of birthing horror stories Lady Catherine had shared, she'd said that Anne had died in childbed by bleeding to death following Georgiana's delivery.

She released a weary breath. "All right," she conceded. "Summon Dr. Severn."

Dr. Severn, Lady Catherine—what a charming party they were assembling at Pemberley.

Perhaps she should invite Lydia back.

Twenty

When the ladies returned to the drawing room, there was little to be done but to hear Lady Catherine talk, which she did without any intermission till coffee came in.

—Pride and Prejudice

"You have, of course, already engaged a monthly nurse to assist with your lying-in?"

Elizabeth sipped her tea and tried to appear appreciative of Lady Catherine's latest probe into her arrangements for the baby. She had started to search for a recovery nurse who would assist her for the month following her child's birth, but had not proceeded further than sending out enquiries.

"I have not yet settled upon one."

"You should have secured a monthly nurse by now. The most competent ones are engaged months before their services are needed. Hmph. Well, I suppose your procrastination enables me to assist you in selecting her. Young mothers ought to seek the counsel of more experienced ones in such decisions."

Elizabeth had sought such counsel—from her aunt Gardiner, whose good sense she trusted. In fact, her aunt had helped Jane locate her monthly nurse, a woman who had impressed Elizabeth favorably enough that she hoped to engage her.

"The ideal nurse is between thirty and fifty years of age," her ladyship offered unasked. "Old enough to know what she is about, yet still vigorous enough to perform her duties. She must be quick to wake so that she can attend to your needs, or those of the babe, at any hour of the day or night. A mild temper is essential . . ."

Elizabeth half-listened, her mind less occupied with the present conversation than by the one she'd had with Mrs. Godwin yesterday. She wanted to ask Darcy's aunt about the statuette, but Lady Catherine had given her no opportunity to introduce the matter.

". . . moral character above question. A church-going woman. One cannot trust a person who does not regularly attend church. I was appalled by how few of the people who overran Pemberley yesterday appeared in church this morning. Did they overindulge to the extent that they could not rise from bed?"

"Many of them live in neighboring parishes. A few are Catholic, and attend a church in Lambton."

"Catholics?" Her disdain was evident. "Good English folk adhere to the teachings of the Church of England, not those of Rome."

Elizabeth, sensing the imminent eruption of a theological lecture, acted swiftly to contain it.

"Lady Catherine, I am most grateful for your advice on selecting a monthly nurse. As a new mother, I can indeed benefit from the wisdom of those more experienced. I imagine your own mother offered considerable guidance when you and Lady Anne were in my condition?"

Her ladyship's eyes narrowed. "Why should you enquire about my mother?"

"The countess was my husband's grandmother. I wish to learn more about his family."

"She was a lady of high principle and impeccable reputation," she declared defensively.

Elizabeth was uncertain how she had given offense. "I do not doubt her character. Did she take pleasure in her grandchildren?"

"She never knew them. She passed away shortly before your husband was born."

"Oh—forgive me. I did not realize." She poured more tea into Lady Catherine's cup and added the one lump of sugar her ladyship required. "The timing of her death must have been especially difficult for Lady Anne—to lose her mother during her own impending maternity. The heirloom she received from the countess—the Madonna and Child statuette—must have provided some comfort."

Lady Catherine looked at her sharply. "I have not thought of that statuette in years. But now that you have brought it to my notice, you may return it to me."

"It was my understanding that the ivory belonged to Lady Anne, and that she lent it to you when your daughter was born."

"She *gave* it to me. It ought to have been mine all along, as I was the eldest daughter. When my sister conceived first, our mother sent the ivory to her. But it was always my mother's intention that I should possess it."

Elizabeth suspected that was a matter of interpretation. It sounded like the same sort of "understanding" that Lady Catherine had claimed existed regarding a marriage between Darcy and her daughter, Miss de Bourgh. Had either existed beyond Lady Catherine's own mind? "Yet you gave it back to Lady Anne when she carried Georgiana."

"A loan—and only because she had plagued me for years about it. She regretted having relinquished it and asked for her gift back every time her husband got her with child again. She had some foolish sentimental notion of wanting it with her during her confinements. Finally I could bear her entreaties no more and surrendered it rather than receive another letter on the subject.

"But that ivory has been passed from mother to daughter for nearly three hundred years," Lady Catherine continued.

"Now that my sister is gone, its ownership is not in question. It is rightfully mine. Kindly retrieve it, for I want it back."

"I do not have it."

"Do you insult me with falsehoods? The statuette must be in your possession, or you would not know anything about it."

"Indeed, I have it not. I learned of it from others."

"Who?"

"Lady Anne herself. She mentions it in a letter I discovered."

"You have been nosing through my late sister's correspondence? Is *that* what you have been about in your dressing room in recent days? Oh, yes—I know about all the trunks delivered there. Do you think that servants do not talk? The presumption! To read my sister's private writings—you, who never knew her, who cannot begin to touch her excellence. Just because you have managed to snare her son and install yourself as mistress of Pemberley—assumed her role here—do not flatter yourself that you will ever fill Lady Anne's place. Does my nephew know of this?"

"He approves it. Indeed, I believe so does Lady Anne."

The remark nearly sent Darcy's aunt into apoplexy. "Your insolence surpasses anything I have heretofore witnessed. If Lady Anne somehow observes your conduct from above, I assure you, it does not please her to see you seize so much that by long understanding was to have belonged to another."

"Miss de Bourgh?"

"You have usurped my daughter's place here, the life that was intended to be hers. And you ruined my nephew's standing and reputation in the process. Why, he would not be in his current legal difficulties now—this business with the diamonds—were it not for you. He would have been nowhere near Northanger Abbey had he done his duty and gone to France as I asked."

"On an errand that has proven unnecessary."

"Just because no scandal presently brews, does not mean the errand was unnecessary. The honor of a great and noble family cannot be too vigilantly guarded. You would understand that, if you came from one yourself—if you had inherited a legacy, as my daughter has. But surely even you cannot justify the theft of her maternal birthright. The ivory statuette should ultimately fall to Anne, my sister's namesake."

"It was Lady Anne's to bequeath where she chose. But if it is a matter of maternal birthright, what about Georgiana's?"

"I am the elder of the sisters; my daughter is the elder of the cousins. Surrender the ivory."

"I told you, I do not have it."

"It must be here at Pemberley. Lady Anne would not have allowed it to leave her possession." Her eyes narrowed. "And you realize that, too. What else of hers have you rifled through besides her letters? Have you ransacked all her effects in search of the statuette?"

Elizabeth had reached her daily limit of Lady Catherine's abuse. "Not yet."

"Impertinent baggage! I demand your pledge that when the ivory is located, you will cede it to me."

"I make no such promise. Should the ivory be found, Mr. Darcy and I will do with it as we see fit."

Lady Catherine suddenly became very quiet. Scorn radiating from her, she gathered the full measure of her pompous bearing, rose, and made her way toward the door with deliberate steps. As she passed Elizabeth, she paused.

"Not if I discover it first."

Twenty-one

The Black Gentleman has certainly employed one of his menial imps to bring about this complete though trifling mischief.
—Jane Austen, letter to Cassandra

"You do not honestly believe my aunt came into this room and took the letter?" Darcy regarded Elizabeth skeptically.

She was in no mood to defend herself to him. Dr. Severn was due to arrive that day, and she anticipated enough disagreement ahead. Darcy had sent a note to the physician by express, and in turn received word that Severn would set out posthaste for Derbyshire. Severn meanwhile advised them to consult a local physician should her affliction continue or worsen until he could arrive. Darcy had been hovering over her ever since, staring at her nose so often one would think she had sprouted a wart.

"How else can the letter's disappearance be accounted for?" she asked.

He shook his head. "To enter your private dressing room and not only read a letter clearly addressed to you, but to purloin it . . . I simply cannot believe her capable of such conduct."

A few days ago, I would have said the same. But since Lady Catherine threatened to seek the ivory herself, I cannot shake the sense that someone is intruding in my personal rooms. Yesterday I had to empty the drawers of the desk in my morning room to find something I was certain I had left within easy reach. This afternoon I returned from my walk to discover a trunk lid open that I know I closed. And now the original letter from your mother is missing."

"Could you not simply have misplaced it? Thrice this fortnight we have had no tea after dinner because you mislaid the key to the tea caddy, only to find it again after we settled for coffee."

To Elizabeth's gratitude, Darcy was gracious enough not to add that on the second occasion she had discovered the key in the tea caddy itself, which had actually been unlocked. Or that her tea was almost too strong to drink some evenings because she could not seem to keep count of how many tea-ladles of leaves she added to the pot.

Though loath to admit it, she *had* become increasingly scatterbrained. The Wednesday before the harvest feast, she had entirely forgotten they were engaged to dine with the Vernons until the couple had arrived at Pemberley. And Thursday she turned her chamber inside out looking for her cap, only to spot it on her head when she passed the looking glass. Jane had complained of similar trouble when she was in the family way, and Elizabeth hoped her own distraction was indeed caused by her expectant state and nothing more serious. She also hoped it would not last beyond her confinement. The thought of losing more mental clarity with each successive pregnancy alarmed her—while casting the behavior of other women of her acquaintance in a new light. Perhaps her own mother had been a more sensible woman before giving birth to five children.

Then again, perhaps not.

Regardless, she felt certain that the missing status of Lady Anne's letter to her derived not from her own actions but those of someone else. And she could think of only one other person in the house with as much interest in it as she had. Lady Catherine had become uncharacteristically taciturn since their quarrel over the statuette, and Elizabeth believed Darcy's aunt genuinely schemed to find the ivory for herself.

"I have not completely lost my wits," Elizabeth said. "Lady Catherine was so adamant about her right to the statuette that I have little doubt she could justify, at least to herself, invading something so insignificant as my privacy. If she considered it beneath her to filch the letter directly, she would not scruple to delegate the task to her maid."

Darcy yet appeared doubtful. "Where did you last see the letter?"

"I moved it to the escritoire in here." She had wanted the letter more easily accessible while continuing to sort through Lady Anne's other correspondence.

He glanced at the desk. "Do you normally lock the fall front?"

"I thought the fact that this is my private dressing room was security enough. Apparently not."

The appearance of Mrs. Reynolds curtailed their conversation. "Sir, you had asked to be informed the moment Dr. Severn arrived. Do you wish him to attend Mrs. Darcy immediately?"

"No." "Yes." Elizabeth and Darcy replied simultaneously.

"There is no emergency," Elizabeth said to Darcy, "and he has traveled a great distance." With little cause, she refrained from adding.

"For the sole purpose of treating you." At her glare, Darcy relented. "I shall go receive the doctor and ask him to attend you in here as soon as he is comfortably settled."

After Darcy and the servant departed, Elizabeth's gaze swept the room once more. If Lady Catherine had not taken the letter, where had it gone? She had looked everywhere for it—half the horizontal surfaces in the room held stacks of papers she had sorted through, and several of Lady Anne's trunks stood open with more papers piled around them. Had she merely misplaced the letter, would she not have found it?

Further seeking would have to wait. In her determination to find the missing letter, she had not only left papers strewn about, but also had sent away the housemaid when she'd arrived to tidy the apartment for the day. If Dr. Severn were going to examine her in the dressing room, she needed to put it back in order. And she suspected Darcy would encourage the physician to consider himself "comfortably settled" in short time. She rang the servants' bell.

The new maid, Jenny, arrived quickly. In the time she had been at Pemberley, she had already impressed Elizabeth with her competence and conscientiousness. Whenever Elizabeth had need of a housemaid, she answered the summons with alacrity, and she performed her duties in a thorough but efficient manner.

Elizabeth organized the papers while Jenny straightened the chamber. She had managed to sort through two more trunks since the harvest feast, and had determined that they held no correspondence related to either the ivory or Lady Anne's friendship with Mrs. Tilney. In fact, these trunks could return to the attic, leaving the dressing room less crowded.

She heard Mrs. Reynolds pass and went into the hall to stop her. The housekeeper promised to send a pair of footmen immediately to relieve Elizabeth of the chests.

No sooner were the trunks removed and Jenny's tasks completed than Darcy reappeared with the physician. With few preliminaries, Dr. Severn set his medical bag on a table and unpacked several instruments from it. She had never seen some of the items before and could only speculate as to their various functions. Given their appearance, she had no wish to satisfy her curiosity through personal acquaintance with them.

"Mr. Darcy tells me you are experiencing incidents of bleeding."

"Merely a brief show from my nose."

He glanced at Darcy with annoyance. "From her nose? When you stated she was bleeding, I thought you meant something more urgent. I traveled here immediately upon seeing one patient through forty hours of travail, and left two more ready to be brought to bed any day."

"In the matter of my wife's health, I would sooner err on the side of caution."

"While caution may be warranted, I suggest that in the future you supply more particulars when summoning me." He motioned Elizabeth to the chair nearest him. "How frequent are these episodes?" he asked Darcy.

She would have preferred to remain where she was—far away from the devices still arrayed on the table—but moved to the seat he had indicated.

"It was a single incident."

"I see." He shot another impatient glance at Darcy, then made a show of padding his fingertips along the bone of her nose. "Did she suffer a bump?"

"No, her nose began to bleed spontaneously."

"Where was she at the time? Near a smoking fire or some other irritant?"

Though Lady Catherine had wrinkled her own nose throughout the evening of exposure to common humanity, Elizabeth doubted anything in the air that night had contributed to the nosebleed. "I was walking across a crowded hall. It was the night of Pemberley's harvest feast."

Her voice could have come from the chimney, for all that the doctor acknowledged her.

"Did she engage in dancing or other strenuous activity at the feast, or in preparation for it?" He lifted her wrist.

"She danced the opening set, yes."

"A staid minuet," Elizabeth interjected.

"Did my wife overexert herself at the celebration?"

"Shush." Dr. Severn continued monitoring her pulse.

Elizabeth had never before witnessed someone *shush* her husband. She had never known anyone who might have dared. Darcy himself appeared astounded but held himself in check.

The physician dropped her wrist. "I suspect that on the night in question she overstimulated her heart and veins through heedlessly vigorous motion."

She did not believe she had been recklessly active. Nor had Mrs. Godwin, who had directly observed her that night, implied that any part of her own conduct had been to blame. "I understand nosebleeds are common among women in my condition."

"Perhaps among *some* women, but not my patients," he declared. "Clearly, any woman who suffers such incidents cannot properly restrain her behavior."

To her mind, Mrs. Godwin's explanation had made much more sense. "Does not an expectant mother's heart produce extra blood?"

Her question met a look of derision. "Are you a physician now? Someone must have suggested that to you."

"The local midwife."

He turned to Darcy. "She consulted a midwife? I advised you to call a medical man if needed."

"Mrs. Darcy did not consult her," Darcy said. "She happened upon my wife during the episode."

"And you believe the conjecture of some old woman? Very well, Mrs. Darcy. If you think an excessive quantity of blood caused an overflow, I can apply leeches to draw off the surplus."

Elizabeth shuddered. "I do not consider that necessary."

"Nor do I. If you will lend me pen and paper, I shall write down a receipt for an unguent to apply to your nose. Your maid can easily prepare it."

Darcy went to the escritoire for the writing materials. When he opened the drop front, a faint chuckle escaped him. Elizabeth glanced at him curiously.

"The letter you have been seeking today lies right here."

"Impossible. I must have looked there half a dozen times, at least."

He held it up. "Evidence of your latest lapse." A look of anxiety crossed his countenance. "Dr. Severn, my wife has become increasingly absentminded of late. Do you consider that cause for concern?"

"It is nothing we need trouble the doctor about," Elizabeth said.

The physician studied her with something that passed for attention. "She loses items regularly?"

"I would not say 'regularly,'" she protested. "And I did not lose—"

"Between the spontaneous bleeding and the mental distraction, it sounds as if her humors are entirely out of balance," the doctor said to Darcy as he packed up his instruments of torture. "Curb her activity henceforth. No strenuous exertion—nothing more demanding than a leisurely walk."

"But I have engaged in my usual pursuits since the night of the harvest feast, with no repeat occurrences. The mental lapses are just trifles—"

"Mrs. Darcy, I have delivered hundreds of children. To how many have you given birth?"

She held her tongue but could not help glaring at the physician. Darcy, she could not even look at; she felt for all the world that he had betrayed her.

"You and your husband have brought me considerable distance to solicit my advice, away from other patients who are grateful for it. Accept it or not, as you choose, but if you are unwilling to follow my orders, do not summon me again. My time and expertise are too valuable to be wasted."

Dr. Severn left the room, stating his intention to pass just one night at Pemberley before returning to Bath. The short duration of his stay suited Elizabeth perfectly. Perhaps at dinnertime she would plead "unbalanced humors" and dine in her apartment rather than subject herself to further contact with the man. Sharing a meal with him and Lady Catherine at once would surely prove detrimental to her mental state, not to mention her digestion.

Still unable to turn her gaze upon Darcy, she went to the escritoire. The innocent-looking letter lay there, mocking her.

"It was at the top of those papers on the left," Darcy said.

She glanced at the papers, neatly stacked in one of the desk's many compartments—all of which she had thoroughly searched. How could she have missed it?

Darcy came up behind her and put his hands on her shoulders. She stiffened.

"Elizabeth—"

"Nothing is out of balance."

He was silent a moment. "*Everything* is out of balance," he said. "The business at Northanger yet weighs upon us. My aunt's continued presence makes our home a place of conflict instead of comfort. And now there is tension between us."

She picked up the letter. She knew he had not meant to discredit her with Dr. Severn, had not intended to injure her feelings. It was his doubt that most wounded her, for it echoed her own. She had been so certain the letter had gone missing, yet there it was, right where she had left it. Could she no longer trust her own perceptions?

"If my anxiety for you is also out of balance, I beg your forgiveness," he said. "But when I see my clever wife forgetting simple matters, I worry. When I find her hands smeared with her own blood, I worry. Every day seems to bring a new change in you, and it is difficult to stand by idly and watch."

She turned round to face him. "It is difficult to experience firsthand. Sometimes I feel as if I no longer know myself. That is why I need your confidence, the security that when I tell you something, I will be believed—" She held up the traitorous letter. "Even if I am later disproved."

"I shall try. I can promise that much."

"And I shall try to follow Dr. Severn's orders. That should put at least some of your apprehensions to rest." She studied his face. He seemed to have aged in the past two months, and she knew that nervousness over her condition constituted but part of the cause. Until their legal troubles were resolved, Darcy would not know a moment's peace. Neither would she. "I wish our concerns related to the Northanger crisis were equally easy to counter."

"I wish I could do more to address them from here."

"Have you received any recent news from Mr. Tilney or Mr. Harper?"

"Mr. Tilney has completed his interviews with the servants, but they yielded little. The butler reports that Captain Tilney—the real one—examined all of his mother's remaining effects on his last visit home, but why or what he sought, no one knows. A few of the grounds staff believe they saw the imposters, but from a distance. They could offer no description beyond ours, only that a man and woman arrived the night before we did and departed shortly after we left. The woman, they thought they had seen at Northanger before, but they could not be sure. Mr. Tilney is now making discreet enquiries to determine whether any of the neighbors might recognize her description."

"What of your own efforts?"

"I have been unable to think of anyone in our acquaintance who would be moved to such villainy against us. Mr. Harper reports that word of the matter does not seem to have reached London yet, so a deliberate campaign to discredit me appears an unlikely motive. He has, by the by, engaged a barrister to speak for us in court."

"Do you think we shall indeed stand trial?"

"Not before I have exhausted every possible lead and resource." He released an exasperated breath. "Though I could investigate this matter much more efficiently were I not trying to do so from here."

"Why do you not go? Surely Lady Catherine understands the importance of such a journey and would accompany you."

"I have broached the matter with her. She insists that as she stood surety for both of us, we both must remain under her direct supervision. You cannot travel; Dr. Severn has just ordered you to refrain from anything so arduous. And even if you could, I want you at Pemberley where you are safe. We will learn what we can from here." He gestured toward the remaining trunks of Lady Anne's correspondence. "Have you come upon anything related to Mrs. Tilney?"

"Not yet, but I remain hopeful. I have not yet sorted through all your mother's papers, though now that Dr. Severn has restricted my activity, I suppose I shall have little to do but examine the remainder."

He winced. "I *am* sorry for that."

"And I am almost ready to forgive you for it."

In fact, she already had. With Dr. Severn and Lady

Catherine determined to undermine her confidence, she needed Darcy on her side.

"What can I do to make amends?" he asked.

"I shall have to think of something," she said lightly. "Whatever I settle upon, however, will cost you far less than you deserve."

"Why is that?"

"Because, my dear Mr. Darcy, I suspect you are now married to the one woman in England who will never appreciate diamonds."

Twenty-two

"Everybody allows that the talent of writing agreeable letters is peculiarly female."

—Henry Tilney, Northanger Abbey

Now that Elizabeth and Darcy knew what they sought, a general hunt for Lady Anne's missing heirloom commenced. A statuette so small could hide in plain sight in a house as large as Pemberley, so they enlisted the aid of the servants. By the end of December, every room had been explored. The ivory, unfortunately, was not found. Lady Catherine took great interest in the proceedings and developed a penchant for happening into particular rooms as they were being inspected, but her hopes of a serendipitous discovery went as unfulfilled as those of her hosts.

Meanwhile, Elizabeth's diligent perusal of Lady Anne's correspondence was rewarded with a gradual increase of floor space in her apartment. One by one, the trunks returned to the attic as their contents were deemed irrelevant to her present needs. When all had gone back to storage, she asked Mrs. Reynolds about Lady Anne's other effects.

"Oh, there are plenty of them, ma'am. But do you want the remaining letters? There are two more trunks in the attic, you will recall. You had said to leave them there while the others were occupying your dressing room."

Elizabeth had completely forgotten about them—like so many other things of late. "Yes, please have them brought down."

After reading so many letters written to Lady Anne, she felt as if she knew Darcy's mother better than she knew her own. In the details of Anne's daily existence, in the notes of congratulation, commiseration, and condolence, the story of her life took shape. Elizabeth discovered a woman who, for all her life of privilege, was in essence not so very unlike herself. She had gone into her marriage with the same sense of certitude, the same expectation of serving as a helpmate to a partner she esteemed, the same commitment to taking seriously the duties associated with privilege. Yes, there were also great differences between them—from childhood, Lady Anne had moved in circles Elizabeth had only just entered, and had negotiated that world with the assurance of a native. But in her private life she had been, quite simply, a woman, with the same hopes and fears and dreams and desires and hurts and joys that cross class and time.

Though the trunks had contained no clues about Anne's friendship with Mrs. Tilney or the ivory statuette, for Elizabeth—and for Darcy and Georgiana, who had helped her intermittently—they held treasure of their own: a connection to a mother who had been taken from her family too soon.

The two remaining chests arrived. Elizabeth approached the first with the expectation of another afternoon spent with voices from the past sharing twenty-year-old gossip from London and news of the neighborhood. She opened the lid, withdrew a handful of letters, and settled before the fire to read.

No sooner had she unfolded the first letter, however, than she gasped. And then immediately summoned a servant to find Darcy. This chest did not hold the same "treasure" as the others.

This chest held gold.

Northanger Abbey
3 May 1784
Dear Mrs. Darcy,

We received with interest your letter regarding the statuette that has come into your possession and its possible association with Northanger Abbey. While we can offer no particulars about the specific item you described, General Tilney and I are happy to share our knowledge of the abbey's history in hopes that it might prove useful to your research.

Northanger Abbey has been the home of my husband's family for over two hundred years. It was built in the thirteenth century as a convent dedicated to the Blessed Virgin, and paintings of the original building depict it as a magnificent structure. Though a relatively small religious house when compared to such abbeys as those of Glastonbury and Bath, it enjoyed the patronage of some of England's wealthiest families and counted among its sisters many of noble lineage. For two centuries the nuns lived and worshipped in peace. Upon the Dissolution of monasteries, King Henry the Eighth sold Northanger Abbey and its lands to Sir Edmund Tilney, who converted it to a private home. It has since passed through many generations of the Tilney family, falling to my husband a decade ago. While a portion of the original building yet stands, much of the ancient structure had deteriorated by the time General Tilney's father took possession. He began extensive repairs and modifications that my husband continues.

We know little about specific treasures held by the convent before the Reformation. As the abbey was richly endowed, I imagine that it was as glorious within as without, filled with ritual objects, art, tapestries, and other gifts of great beauty and worth. Most of them, of course, were either surrendered to the bishop or seized by the Crown when the priory was disbanded; we do, however, possess several items uncov-

ered during renovations to various portions of the house. As the nuns apparently hid these items rather than allow them to be destroyed as idolatrous, it is entirely possible that they might also have secretly consigned other objects to trusted individuals. Perhaps the ivory statuette came into the care of your mother's family at that time.

Should you wish to come to Northanger Abbey and see where your mother's heirloom originated, I would take great pleasure in showing you the house and the few objects we have found. General Tilney suggests you bring the ivory, as your description of it has aroused his curiosity. Do consider our invitation. Your visit would be most welcome to—

Your servant,
Helen Tilney

Northanger Abbey
12 June 1784
Dear George,

I have safely arrived at Northanger Abbey. Mrs. Tilney is as gentle and amiable as her letter suggested, and we get on as if acquainted for years. Already we call each other by our Christian names, and I believe a lifelong friendship has been formed. General Tilney is a harder man to like—rigid and, I daresay, even oppressive at times—but strives to be an attentive host.

The abbey grounds are lovely. The many gardens abound with flowers, including some varieties with which I was previously unfamiliar, nurtured in the estate's succession houses. Helen has adopted one of the abbey's oldest gardens as her own. It is a meditation garden, designed in a rosette pattern and filled with the most beautiful, fragrant blooms. I am quite infatuated with her Madonna lilies, and am determined to have some of my own at Pemberley. She has instructed her gardener to send Mr. Flynn a quantity of bulbs when they are ready for transplant.

Despite the modernizations undertaken by the General and his father, much of the house retains its ancient character, and I can imagine these walls once having held my mother's ivory. Indeed, in one of the former chantry chapels, now an ordinary room, the walls are lined with ten small niches for which the ivory appears perfectly sized. The General, who had already taken great interest in the ivory, became even more curious about it upon this discovery. He has examined the statuette most closely and asked me a great many questions. Do I know exactly how my mother's family came into possession of it? Do we know the whereabouts of any others? Have we ever sought an appraisal? Though he is all politeness, I sense he resents my ownership of an item that, as it once belonged to the abbey, he believes should rightfully belong to him.

Helen has suggested that I might learn more about the ivory by visiting the nearby cathedral. Perhaps its treasurer might know of similar statuettes, or its library might contain a record of items held by Northanger before the Crown seized them. She has offered to accompany me, and we journey there on Wednesday.

I enjoy good health; the babe gives me no trouble. I look forward to returning home before my condition becomes apparent to the world. Though Helen, with three children of her own, soon guessed my secret.

I will write when I have more news. Until then, I remain—

Your Anne

Northanger Abbey
17 June 1784
Dear George,

What an extraordinary day this has been! We have returned from the cathedral, where we spent two dusty days in its library. Though its modern books are as well organized as those in Pemberley's library, records predating the Reformation lie jumbled in an old vault.

Thank goodness Helen accompanied me, or I should have been twice as long searching—especially with the reverend canon casting his suspicious gaze upon me all the while, as if I intended to smuggle one of the neglected volumes out of their tomb. I had to invoke my brother's title, which you know I am loath to do, to gain access at all.

After many hours' fruitless labor, we had despaired of finding anything pertaining to our enquiry, when I happened upon a mottled volume titled Inventorie of the Jewells and Riches Belonging to Northanger Abbey. *Dated 1536, it catalogued every item of gold and silver plate, every work of art, every saint's relic the abbey held. George, I read through the entire register, and I believe I possess a treasure more valuable than I ever imagined! The statuette was listed—one of ten ivory figures as old as the abbey itself. The fate of the others, one can only speculate.*

Helen is quite as thrilled by the discovery as I. She has given me a beautiful new strongbox in which to safeguard my treasure. It is a small rosewood casket with a Madonna lily carved on its lid and velvet cushioning inside. The statuette and its cloth mantle fit perfectly.

General Tilney's reaction to our findings was not nearly so gracious. I believe he envies me the ivory more than ever. Helen, however, managed to placate him by sharing the particulars we also learned about the items in his possession.

I depart here Monday. Though excited by my success and delighted in my new friendship with Helen, I look forward to returning home. I have missed you, and remain ever—

Your Anne

Twenty-three

"The vicious propensities—the want of principle, which he was careful to guard . . . could not escape the observation of a young man of nearly the same age with himself, and who had opportunities of seeing him in unguarded moments."

—*Mr. Darcy,* Pride and Prejudice

Darcy approached Elizabeth's dressing room with apprehension. His wife had sent word through the servant that he should come quickly, but had not indicated why. Though the maid had assured him of Mrs. Darcy's appearing perfectly well, the distance between his library and their apartment had never seemed so great as it did now, with one dreadful imagining after another flying through his mind.

He found her seated beside a trunk, one letter in hand and surrounded by others. Upon his entrance, she with obvious reluctance dragged her gaze away from the open letter.

"I hastened here directly you summoned me," he said. "Are you quite all right?"

She regarded him eagerly. "These are letters from Northanger Abbey." She made a sweeping gesture toward the piles of paper. "I tried to wait for you, but I could not help myself."

"Is that all?" Relief overtook him at the knowledge that her health had not created the urgency. He sat down beside her.

"Is that *all*? These are filled with information about your mother's ivory. It seems that the statuette once belonged to the abbey—before the Dissolution, when it was yet a religious house. Upon receiving the statuette, your mother contacted the Tilneys in hopes of learning more of its history, and a friendship formed between Lady Anne and Helen. Here—these two messages are the earliest."

She thrust the notes into his hands. They were dated the year of his birth. She watched him impatiently while he read. He had barely finished, and was yet absorbing the particulars, when she picked up a third letter.

"Now in this one, Lady Anne learns that her ivory is one of ten such statuettes. And here—listen to this. Helen Tilney gave her 'a beautiful new strongbox in which to safeguard my treasure. It is a small rosewood casket with a Madonna lily carved on its lid.'" She looked up at him excitedly. "*That* is what we ought to be seeking. We have been searching all this while for the statuette itself, not a rosewood box with a lily on top."

A sickening sensation began in the pit of his stomach as a long-buried memory forced its way into his mind. *A rosewood box with a lily on top.* Dread rapidly enveloped him. Oh, Lord. Oh, dear Lord.

"Darcy? All the color has drained from your face. What is the matter?"

He had held such a box in his hands that day.

The day Georgiana was born.

The day his mother died.

He swallowed, but the bile in his throat would not recede. "I have seen that box."

"Indeed? Where?"

"In the summerhouse of the south garden."

"Lady Anne's garden?" She reflected a moment. "I suppose it makes sense that your mother might keep it there. When her sister finally returned the statuette, she put it in a place significant to her but outside the main house, where Lady Catherine would be unlikely to casually notice it and revoke its 'loan,' or to seek it if the determination ever possessed her—which it has, nearly twenty years later. But Darcy, you appear quite distressed. This is a happy discovery, is it not? We need only go down to the garden now and— Oh! But when did you see the box? As a boy, or recently? It might not be there, as we know that when your mother went looking for the ivory, it was not where she had left it."

Because he had moved it.

Guilt suffused him, the overwhelming remorse of a child who has committed a deed so naughty he fears his parents can never forgive it. While his mother had been suffering, his actions had denied her the one item that might have brought her comfort.

"I came upon it that morning—the day of my sister's birth. My mother was short-tempered at breakfast that day. For a fortnight she had been expecting her pains to commence at any moment, but they had not, and I think she grew weary of the waiting. As soon as I finished my toast, I fled the house in search of more pleasant society. I found it in . . ." He shifted his gaze, unable to meet her eyes. "George Wickham."

The very thought nauseated him. Of all people whose companionship to prefer above his mother's on the last day of her life! With whom to have committed his folly!

"He has not always been the scoundrel we recognize him as now. He once was your friend."

"But even then, I sensed a wayward bent to his character."

"You could not have known what he would become. Your own father did not, and he possessed the acumen of an adult."

She was too forgiving. But then, she had not yet heard the remainder of what he had to tell. Like a penitent to his confessor, he continued.

"We wandered into the garden. Wickham had entered it only once before and been run out by Mr. Flynn, who never liked him—in retrospect, the gardener had better judgment than any of us. But in my company, Wickham need not fear eviction. He had never been inside the summerhouse and wanted to explore it. Have you been within?"

She shook her head.

"There is a fountain in the center—a statue of a lily. When in operation, water spouts from its blooms. It was dry; my mother had decided it made the air in the summerhouse too damp, so it had not run all season. Wickham wanted to see how it worked. I was curious myself—I had entered a stage in my education where I took great interest in the physical sciences and I wished to examine its components. At the base of the fountain we discerned a section of loose bricks. Speculating that they concealed the fountain's mechanism, we removed them and discovered instead a small casket—the very one my mother's note just described. It was secured with a letter lock."

"I do not believe I have ever seen such a lock."

"Instead of requiring a key, it has moveable rings inscribed with letters that must be turned to the proper combination to open it. Wickham, of course, wanted to see what the strongbox held. He attempted to guess the code but was unsuccessful." Darcy recalled the scene with disgust; Wickham's failure had resulted largely from the fact that the lock had four rings, and he had amused himself by spelling all manner of vulgar words. "I indulged the experiment for a few minutes, despite uneasiness. The box did not belong to us, I told him, and should remain undisturbed. He responded that as heir to Pemberley, I had a right to everything on the estate. Then he challenged me, asking whether I was clever enough to puzzle out the combination."

"And you could not retreat from such a challenge, especially issued by Wickham."

"My pride would not allow it." Remorse washed over him. He had ignored his conscience and listened instead to the voice of conceit, allowed an unprincipled ne'er-do-well to goad him into conduct he had known to be wrong. "Wickham worried that Mr. Flynn would interrupt us, so we quit the garden and brought the casket into the woods. I tried all day to determine the code—I could not bear for Wickham to witness my failure.

"When the dinner hour approached, I was at last forced to admit defeat. We returned the strongbox to its repository and I left Wickham to go dress for dinner. Immediately upon entering the house, I learned that my mother's travail had begun some hours earlier." He shook his head, as if denying them now could change the events of the past. "She must have gone to the summerhouse while I was vainly using the thing most precious to her to prove to the worthless George Wickham that I was more clever than he."

"*You* were the thing most precious to her."

Elizabeth's statement only made him feel worse. "And I repaid that affection by stealing from her the one object that might have succored her." That might have saved her. Though Darcy did not believe the statuette or any other good-luck charm held any innate power of its own to affect one's fortune, he did believe it possible that the faith of its owner might influence a course of events. If his mother had held the ivory, might she have drawn on inner reserves she did not realize she possessed?

"You were a child."

"I was eleven years old. Old enough to know better than to take, even temporarily, something that was not mine. Especially at the very time it was most needed."

"You did not know what it was, and could not have known your mother sought it." Her eyes held the forgiveness he would never be able to beg from the person he had injured. "If you would blame anyone, let it be Wickham. He bears at least as much responsibility as you, and deserves so much censure for other offenses that he will hardly notice the addition." She took his hand. "Come, let us set aside these remaining letters for now and go to the garden to retrieve the strongbox."

The air inside the summerhouse had been cold on the January day Georgiana was born, and, the anniversary of that event approaching, the temperature was just as low when Darcy entered with Elizabeth. Not inclined to linger in a place that held a memory so repugnant to him, he immediately approached the fountain and located the section of loose bricks. Elizabeth stood behind him as he knelt to remove them.

The slight gap that had admitted his fingers as a boy now proved too small for him to obtain a grip on the initial brick. "I am afraid this requires a woman's hand," he said.

He helped Elizabeth lower herself to the ground. She grasped the brick and worked it out of its niche. Once it had been removed, the rest followed more easily. Soon the small cavity was exposed to view.

It was empty.

"Did you ever return for the strongbox?" Elizabeth enquired.

"No. My mother died that night, and I was so distraught, and the household in such chaos, that I forgot about it entirely. Indeed, it never entered my thoughts again until this day."

"Apparently, someone remembered."

Darcy suspected they need look no further than one individual. One who had been extremely disappointed at Darcy's failure to figure out the proper alphabet combination. Who had become surly when Darcy forbade him to smash the lock to discover what the box held. "I believe an interview with Mr. Wickham is in order."

"Agreed. But where? Will you summon him to Pemberley?"

"Certainly not." So long as the reprobate remained in England, he was already too close to Pemberley for Darcy's liking. Why could his regiment not be sent to India?

"Then a trip to Newcastle is required. I suppose Lady Catherine will insist on accompanying you to continue performing her duty to the courts."

"I will travel there alone. If Lady Catherine seeks the ivory for herself, we need not aid her by making her aware of this development. We must offer a plausible explanation for my journey and a compelling reason that she must stay behind with you."

"That will prove difficult. She will enquire into every particular of the business you undertake, and even then is unlikely to let you out of her sight with the courts providing such convenient justification for inserting herself into our affairs." She thought a moment. "I believe it is best she know nothing of your absence at all."

"But I shall be gone for several days at least—longer, should Mr. Wickham prove uncooperative. Surely she will notice my empty seat in the dining room."

Elizabeth contemplated, then looked at him archly. "Cough a bit at dinner tonight. Leave Graham behind at Pemberley. And trust the rest to me."

Twenty-four

This morning has been spent in doubt and deliberation; in forming plans, and removing difficulties.

—Jane Austen, letter to Cassandra

Northanger Abbey
19 January 1788
Dear Anne,

Your account of Fitzwilliam's latest caper amused me exceedingly. There is nothing quite like the mind of a child. He must be a source of happy diversion for you as you await the arrival of his sibling.

I confess, in the four years we have now known each other, I have formed an impression of your sister that is not quite favorable. I can scarcely believe your entreaties to Lady C. fall upon deaf ears. Even if convinced the ivory statuette rightfully belongs to her, can she not at least lend it to you, to set your mind at ease during your approaching confinement?

However, much as you want your mother's gift with you, do not persuade yourself that you can be safely delivered only through its power. Though it may, as your mother's female line has long believed, bring luck to women in travail, consider that I and all the other mothers of your acquaintance have brought healthy children into the world without benefit of such tokens. That you lost your last babe in the birthing room after surrendering the statuette to Lady C. does not mean you will lose this child. I understand how your previous grief creates in you foreboding over the trial to come, but do not invest all your faith in an object—even a blessed one. Have some in yourself and your own strength.

Trust me. For I am—

Your most devoted friend,
Helen Tilney

Northanger Abbey
30 January 1788
Dear Anne,

Today the west cloister wall was dismantled for repair, and can you imagine what was discovered? The other nine ivories, bundled in a tapestry! Once your statuette left the abbey, the prioress must have hidden these away—better for the Crown to remain ignorant of them all than for a partial set to draw attention to its missing member. The statuettes are exquisite, as detailed and well preserved as yours.

I have asked General Tilney if we might give one of these ivories to you, to replace the figurine your sister withholds. He will not hear of it, and forbids me to broach the matter again. I am sorry, my friend. I wish I could do more, but we have known each other long enough that you understand my real power in this house is nothing. . . .

I remain—

Yours most faithfully,
Helen Tilney

Northanger Abbey
16 February 1788
Dear Anne,

Last night General Tilney and I quarreled again over the statuettes. He intends to sell them! He says they are worth a great deal of money, and that he shall find a collector willing to pay him handsomely. How can he look upon these beautiful, sacred objects and see only their monetary value? I hope they fetch him thirty pieces of silver.

He departs tomorrow to join his regiment for a period of time, after which he intends to pursue the sale. I cannot countenance it. You have often invited me to visit you at Pemberley, and I have always deferred to General Tilney's preference that I not absent myself from Northanger. No more. If you will have me, I shall come within this fortnight. We will be merry as I help you plant your new flower garden and prepare for another Darcy. . . .

28 April 1788 . . . I have safely reached home, but a furious husband awaited me. It seems that during his absence, the statuettes disappeared from Northanger. He accuses me of authoring the business, but I said I could tell him nothing, having been away from the abbey myself these several weeks. He now levels accusation upon me with every glance. For my part, I am glad the ivories—wherever they might be—have escaped his mercenary grasp. . . .

13 May 1788 . . . Words cannot convey an apology adequate enough to address my husband's actions toward you. Please believe that I was ignorant of his journey to Pemberley until after he returned. When he revealed the nature of his errand to me, I was overcome with mortification. He had suspected me of delivering the missing ivories into your care—allegations which, being of course untrue, I repeatedly denied. But to descend upon you in your own home, and accuse you of harboring the statuettes! It is inexcusable. I am glad your husband ejected him from the house. I hope he did so before General Tilney's unpardonable conduct distressed you too greatly. What manner of friend am I, to have even inadvertently subjected you to such abuse in your condition?

The entire matter has so upset me that I have taken ill. The bilious fever that periodically plagues me has returned. It shall pass—it always does—but I shall rest easier if I knew a chance existed that my husband's unforgivable behavior has not cost me your friendship. . . .

21 May 1788 . . . I have recovered my health once more, aided in no small part by the assurance of your continued friendship. Your last letter provided more comfort than any apothecary's physic, and for it, and the generous sentiments it expressed, I thank you. Though you enjoined me to spare the matter of my husband's gross misconduct not another moment's regret, do indulge me in one final expression of most sincere apology. There—that is an end of it, and all is easy between us once more.

My harmony with General Tilney is not so simply restored. Though I say nothing about it to my husband, I have not yet forgiven him. He, meanwhile, continues glowering, but I am grown used to his moods. My recent illness has tempered his displeasure to a degree, and eventually he will find some matter besides the ivories to occupy his thoughts.

My pen moves on to happier subjects. The day you have anticipated these nine months cannot be long off now. I offer up prayers each morning and evening for your safe deliverance, but trust that all will proceed well this time. So certain am I, that I enclose this gift for the new child. Its creation has brought me many hours of pleasure, for I am continually reminded of our friendship and your new garden at Pemberley. How fare your marigolds? Though not yet blooming, I expect they thrive.

When your little one arrives, nestle this quilt around him or her and know that you are ever in my thoughts. . . .

2 June 1788 . . . I grieve with you and Mr. Darcy in the loss of your newborn daughter. I thought surely this time fortune would smile favorably upon you. Why God called Maria to Him, we cannot know, but doubtless Our Lady carried her to Him in Her own arms, and will watch over her with a Mother's heart until you see her again.

Perhaps in this dark time, your garden might bring you some small measure of comfort. The lilies of the valley—Our Lady's Tears—should be in bloom. Let She who knows a mother's sorrow bear some of yours. . . .

6 July 1789 . . . I find myself again unwell—my usual complaint has returned. My daughter is away from home, but Henry and Frederick are a comfort to me. I have not been able to enjoy my favorite walk, or even to sit in my garden. I can see from my window that the marigolds have bloomed. How do yours?

The effort of writing has taxed me beyond expectation, so I will close.

Ever your friend,
H. T.

Northanger Abbey
9 July 1789
Dear Mrs. Darcy,

I regret to inform you that my wife departed this life on the 7th of July, taken by a seizure brought on by fever.
Gen. Victor Tilney

Elizabeth set aside the final letter with a sense of loss, as if Mrs. Tilney's death had just occurred. Though she had known neither Helen nor Lady Anne, she imagined what Anne's feelings must have been upon receiving the general's curt note, and mourned the end of a friendship that had sustained the two women through periods of domestic unhappiness caused by lost children and a tyrannical husband.

With luck, the ivory statuette that had originally brought about their acquaintance would soon be found. Darcy had left Pemberley before sunrise to begin his journey to Newcastle. He had chafed at the necessity of sneaking away from his own home under cover of darkness, but avoiding Lady Catherine's observance required it. Elizabeth hoped his errand would prove successful and of short duration. Already, his absence had created restlessness within her; no sooner had his carriage slipped from view in the waning moonlight than, relinquishing all hope of returning to sleep, she had retrieved the remaining Northanger Abbey letters from her dressing room to peruse before the fire in their bedchamber. She had been eager to return to them since their fruitless expedition yesterday to the summerhouse, but preparations for Darcy's departure had consumed their attention. These had included giving over a large part of the evening to Lady Catherine's familiar orations, which had seemed to imprison them in the drawing room longer than usual after dinner. But the prolonged conversation had enabled Darcy to establish the pretense of developing a cold—a malady that, aided by the adroit management of appearances by Elizabeth and Graham, would grow so much worse this morning that it would require him to avoid company and take to bed for several days. Though not by nature inclined to or adept at artifice, Darcy had performed creditably enough to elicit an onslaught of suggested remedies from his aunt.

Indeed, it seemed that their scheme to keep Lady Catherine ignorant of Darcy's mission was off to a promising start. However, upon finishing her reading, Elizabeth wished they had studied the remaining Tilney correspondence before Darcy took leave. He would want to know about the additional statuettes found at Northanger Abbey; perhaps the ivories somehow pertained to their own recent misadventure there. The false Frederick Tilney had enquired about the existence of letters between Helen and Anne, and had spoken of searching for things long forgotten. Had he been alluding to the discovery and subsequent disappearance of the other nine ivories?

She would now have to wait until Darcy returned to share the news and puzzle over it with him. She had no means by which to contact him; he himself had been unsure how soon he would reach Newcastle and where he would lodge. Yet even if she had his direction, she would not commit such important intelligence to paper and risk its miscarriage.

Morning had broken. Lucy would arrive soon to open the shutters and bring her morning chocolate. Elizabeth wanted to intercept her before she entered the bedchamber and noted Darcy's absence. Although she fully trusted her personal maid, it was best that as few people as possible knew of the ruse, and Darcy's valet had already by necessity been taken into their confidence. While she thought of it, she rang for Mrs. Reynolds. The housemaids should also be kept from the bedchamber.

She gathered Helen Tilney's letters and returned them to the trunk in her dressing room. The housekeeper entered momentarily, bearing a large lily that filled the room with fragrance. Though lilies were long out of season, a memory of having encountered the scent somewhat more recently hovered at the edge of Elizabeth's consciousness.

"Mr. Darcy suffers a cold and wishes to rest in our bedchamber undisturbed," she said. "Relieve the housemaids of their usual duties in that room until further notice."

"Yes, madam. Shall I call for the apothecary?" Mrs. Reynolds crossed the room and set the plant on a table beside a large window.

"That is not necessary. Additional sleep and some of the cook's best broth should restore him within a few days. Graham may bring his meals on a tray."

"Very good, madam. Lady Catherine has instructed me in the preparation of some remedies and ordered them brought to Mr. Darcy as soon as he wakes. Shall I send them with his breakfast?"

Elizabeth assented. Graham would find a place to dump them out if she could not. She gestured toward the flower. "What is this?"

"Mr. Flynn sent it from the greenhouse, madam. He said he thought you would appreciate it."

She approached the table and touched one of the perfect white flowers with her fingertips. "I do." She inhaled deeply, trying to place the sweet smell. "It has an exquisite fragrance."

"That it does, madam. I have missed the scent. Madonna lilies were Lady Anne's favorite, and when they bloomed in summer she had them placed in nearly every room. This chamber and her morning room were practically filled with them. But I do not believe we have had one in the house since her death."

Anne's morning room—that was where she had smelled lilies. She had attributed the perfume to Lady Catherine, but come to think on it, she had not detected any fragrance on Darcy's aunt since. She smiled to herself. That day *had* been All Hallows' Eve. Perhaps the scent had been a ghostly afterglow.

Apparently, Lady Anne had received not one, but two gifts as a result of her friendship with Helen Tilney: a crib quilt, and a love of Madonna lilies that had lasted till the end of her days. "Mrs. Reynolds," Elizabeth said suddenly, "you once told me you came to Pemberley when my husband was four years old. Were you here when Lady Anne was expecting her daughter Maria?"

"Aye, madam. I arrived just before her birth."

"I understand she received a quilt at that time from her friend Mrs. Tilney. Do you know what became of it?"

"Oh, indeed, madam. After Maria's death, Lady Anne packed it away. That was such a sad time, losing Maria, and then another baby *and* her friend Mrs. Tilney the following year. When she was expecting Miss Darcy, however, she brought the quilt out again. She did not want to use it for the new child—she felt it had been created for Maria—but she treasured it for the memories it held of her friend. She displayed it in the nursery, where it hung until Miss Darcy grew too old for that room. When the nursery fell into disuse, I stored it away again."

"I should like to see it," Elizabeth said.

"Of course. It is a lovely quilt, covered in flowers. Shall I bring it to you here, or would you like it rehung in the nursery?"

She thought a moment. "The nursery."

"I shall do so directly, madam."

Lucy arrived and helped her dress. Afterward, Graham appeared with Darcy's breakfast and an assortment of unpleasant-looking concoctions. She invited him to dispose of the remedies in whatever manner he saw fit and to enjoy the food while allegedly attending his master—in other words, while standing watch over the empty bedchamber.

After breaking her own fast, Elizabeth went to the nursery, where she found the quilt hanging between two windows overlooking the south garden. She was struck by how many of Pemberley's rooms central to Lady Anne's life shared a view of the garden that had also meant so much to her, and felt certain the placement had been deliberate when the garden was created. But whereas Lady Anne's apartment and morning room viewed the garden from an angle, the nursery aligned with it almost directly.

The quilt, as Mrs. Reynolds had declared, was indeed lovely. Its beautifully detailed blocks depicted a large central four-pointed rosette filled with flowers of numerous types against a white background stitched in a crosshatch pattern. Lilies, roses, morning glories, marigolds, and more were rendered in cheerful colors undiminished by the score of years that had passed since the quilt's obviously loving creation. A larger version of each flower, with ivy interlacing them, formed the border.

An octagon of less vibrant hue occupied the very center of the rosette, with the outline of a lily stitched upon it. The grey object amid the riot of color gave Elizabeth a moment's pause—until she glanced from the quilt to the window and back. The octagon was the summerhouse; the lily, the fountain. The entire quilt was a representation of Lady Anne's garden.

Helen Tilney, who had helped Anne plant her garden and prepare for Maria's birth during her visit to Pemberley, must have looked out this very nursery window. She had then carried the view home with her to create a baby quilt in its image. It was little wonder that despite her grief over the child for whom it had been intended, Lady Anne could not keep the quilt packed away from sight forever. Such a heartfelt gift was meant to be seen and used.

The Madonna lilies gracing one petal of the rosette reminded Elizabeth of the gift she had received from Mr. Flynn that morning. With a last admiring look at Helen Tilney's handiwork, she went in search of the gardener. She found him in one of the hothouses instructing a boy of about twelve or thirteen as he transplanted a seedling to a larger pot.

So engrossed was Mr. Flynn in the lesson, that his apprentice noticed Elizabeth first. At the sight of Pemberley's mistress, the boy became self-conscious and scattered soil across the table. Mr. Flynn glanced up, ascertained the cause of his distraction, and sent his pupil off to water yesterday's transplants.

Wiping his hands on a rag, the master gardener acknowledged her and asked how he might be of service.

"I require nothing at present," she said. "I merely came to thank you for the lily."

" 'Twas my pleasure, Mrs. Darcy. Now that Pemberley has a mistress once more, it seemed the house should also have Madonna lilies again."

"It is an unexpected delight to enjoy the fragrance of summer in winter."

"Lady Anne would have surrounded herself with lilies all the year through, if I could have provided them. While she lived, I tried to force the bulbs to produce blooms out of season, but never with success. She's a temperamental flower, the Madonna. More particular than other lilies. But if you're patient and care for her with love, she'll respond in the end." A twinkle entered his eye. "Like any lady, I suppose."

Elizabeth smiled. "Obviously, you eventually mastered her, if you have lilies flowering now."

"One cannot master her. When I stopped trying, and learned to accept her blooms as the heavenly gift they are, that is when she rewarded me. Each year since Lady Anne died, I have been able to leave a Madonna lily in full bloom upon her grave on the anniversary of her death." An expression of uncertainty crossed his countenance. "Perhaps it is presumptuous of me to do so—I was but a servant to her."

On the contrary, Elizabeth admired the gardener's loyalty. "I think it a fitting tribute," she assured him.

"I always try to force several bulbs in anticipation of the anniversary, but somehow only one thrives. This year, however, two plants flowered. Lady Anne will receive hers on Friday, but I thought perhaps Miss Darcy might enjoy it until then?"

"I am sure she would. Is it here? I can take it back to the house with me now."

"No, it is in one of the other greenhouses. I shall go retrieve it."

Elizabeth did not want to trouble the elderly man to bring it all the way back to her. "I will accompany you," she offered. She also had a secondary motive for seeking out the gardener this morning.

"I understand," she said as they walked, "that Lady Anne came to appreciate Madonna lilies through her friend Mrs. Tilney."

"Aye. She returned from Northanger Abbey with her heart set on seeing their blooms at Pemberley. At first we grew them in the east garden."

"Why?"

"The south did not yet exist—it was only an expanse of lawn. 'Twas Lady Anne's idea to create a garden there, similar to Mrs. Tilney's. She and her friend invested considerable thought in its plan—we were two years designing and building it—and it remains today almost exactly as she envisioned it. Most of the same flowers, though I have had to switch some of their beds over the years. The marigolds thrive much better in the south bed, and the violets prefer the north. We added the chrysanthemums her final year."

"Lady Anne helped plant the garden herself?"

"She did. I never saw a lady more willing to dirty her hands—or at least, soil her gloves—than she was for that garden. Until her friend Mrs. Tilney came. Now *that* lady, she was all eagerness to feel the soil beneath her fingers. She came to the garden each day directly from breakfast, and one morning I actually found her at work when I arrived just after dawn. The two of them—" He shook his head in fond recollection. "Well, it was a pleasure to see Lady Anne so happy with her friend. I believe she enjoyed our lady's garden all the more for the memories it held of Mrs. Tilney's visit."

Elizabeth suppressed a smile. "You still refer to it as 'our lady's garden,' though Lady Anne has been gone these many years."

He glanced at her in puzzlement. "Why would I not? Our Lady—Oh!" He stopped as comprehension caught up with him. "I refer not to Lady Anne, but to the Queen of Heaven."

She was not confident she understood his meaning. "The garden is consecrated to the Blessed Virgin?"

"No, not consecrated. But inspired by her. All of the flowers within Our Lady's garden are associated with Mary—Madonna lilies, roses, lilies of the valley, cornflowers . . ."

She recalled Mrs. Tilney's reference to lilies of the valley as Our Lady's Tears, and enquired about the cornflowers.

"They are also known as Mary's Crown," he said.

"And the morning glories?"

"Our Lady's Mantle."

"Marigolds? Oh—allow me to guess. Mary's Gold?"

He smiled. "That is a simple one."

She could have quizzed him further—she felt as if she had stumbled upon a hidden code, and looked forward to discovering more as spring and summer brought the garden into full bloom. "Are there many others?"

"I wager I could name near a hundred. We did not use that

many in the south garden, of course—Lady Anne selected her favorites from among the flowers she had seen in the Mary garden at Northanger Abbey. That garden has existed since the nuns were there, and its beauty saved it from significant changes by later owners."

"I wonder that during the Dissolution, a garden devoted to Mary was not uprooted on principle."

"Mrs. Tilney said that statues and other obvious objects in the garden had been confiscated. But most people do not know the symbolic names of all the flowers it contained, so their association went unnoticed. To the unfamiliar, it was merely a pretty garden. Mrs. Tilney herself did not realize upon first coming to Northanger that the abbey's former Mary garden yet held connections to the Virgin. But she knew something of flowers, and after spending much time in the garden, became curious enough to learn more. When Lady Anne found the garden at Northanger very peaceful, Mrs. Tilney revealed its connections."

"Did Lady Anne name her garden?"

"Her ladyship desired that her own garden's connection also be subtle. Though between ourselves we at times called it 'Our Lady's garden,' to everyone else it was simply the south garden, or Lady Anne's garden."

"Yet you called it 'Our Lady's garden' with me."

"I had not even realized I had done so until you drew my attention to the fact. I suppose there is a quality in you that reminds me of her."

They reached the greenhouse. "I shall just go inside and fetch the Madonna lily for Miss Darcy," Mr. Flynn said, and smiled. He remained within quite some time, prompting Elizabeth to wonder what took him so long.

When he at last emerged, he was no longer smiling.

Twenty-five

"I have a warm, unguarded temper, and I may perhaps have sometimes spoken my opinion of him, and to him, too freely."
—*Mr. Wickham,* Pride and Prejudice

Darcy waited impatiently in the corner of the Boar's Head common room. He had been informed that the inn was a popular gathering place for officers stationed in Newcastle, and that it enjoyed the patronage of one soldier of particular interest to him. Mr. Wickham had not yet entered the public house, but Darcy had been assured that his eventual arrival could be relied upon with a measure of certainty normally reserved for death and the likelihood of fog in London.

He might have saved himself wasted time by contacting Wickham to arrange a meeting, but Darcy wanted the advantage of surprise. Anticipation would allow the scoundrel to prepare his natural defenses—a scheming mind and forked tongue—before the interview. Better to catch him unawares if Darcy hoped to extract anything resembling truth.

And so he sat, slowly consuming a half-pint and watching the door. The room had been three-quarters empty upon his arrival, but had gradually crowded with redcoats who kept the young barmaid steadily occupied with ensuring their tankards never ran dry. She had a familiarness about her that Darcy attributed to her occupation—it often seemed that the same server waited upon the same patrons at every inn and tavern in England. If he had not seen her before, he had seen another girl like her, just as he had seen the officer whose mug she now filled.

At last, Mr. Wickham sauntered in, to a chorus of salutations. He approached a group of officers standing near the bar and immediately joined their jocular conversation. The barmaid also greeted him, offering a pint. Before she could deliver his beverage, Darcy approached from behind.

"Mr. Wickham."

Wickham turned around. His face registered astonishment upon finding Darcy behind him.

"Mr. Darcy!" He recovered himself and continued smoothly, "What business brings you to Newcastle?"

The barmaid gave Wickham his tankard, placing a hand on his arm as she did so. Darcy's gaze followed her as she walked away. He was reminded of the incident with the housemaid when Wickham had last intruded at Pemberley. He looked at Wickham pointedly. "I came to see how Lydia's husband conducts himself."

Wickham chuckled. "Most faithfully, I assure you. Can I help it if the ladies wish otherwise?"

Yes, he could help it. The worthless scapegrace could help a great many things. "I would have a word with you."

Wickham took Darcy's measure, his gaze sweeping Darcy from the brim of his hat to the tip of his walking stick, upon which it seemed to linger an overlong time until he finally met Darcy's eyes once more.

"And which word would that be?"

"One I prefer to speak in private, if your comrades would excuse us." He acknowledged Wickham's companions with a slight bow.

"Why, Fitz, you intrigue me." He studied Darcy's face, but Darcy maintained his impassive expression despite the scrutiny and the baiting address. "Very well," he said finally.

"Meg? Might I use the back room to confer with my brother?"

Darcy inwardly flinched at the word "brother," but betrayed no outward sign of the very response he knew Wickham had intended to provoke. The barmaid called back her consent and they stepped into a small area between the common room and the kitchen. It was empty of people, although through the doorway Darcy could see another girl, younger than Meg, stirring a pot. The din of the common room was slightly muted here, but still burbled steadily.

Wickham tossed back a swallow of ale and grinned. "Well?"

Darcy, abhorring the necessity of holding this interview with Wickham at all, did not prolong it with preliminaries. "Do you recall the day my sister was born?"

He smirked. "Which one?"

Darcy could not believe even Wickham had the effrontery to allude to his siblings who had not survived their own birth. He did not dignify the question with a response. "That day, you and I discovered a strongbox in the summerhouse of my mother's garden."

"Ah, yes—I recall that despite my reluctance to disturb the box, you were quite interested in proving your cleverness with locks."

"We have no audience, Wickham. And therefore no need to recast events in light more favorable to you. We both know what transpired."

He shrugged. "Apparently, our memories differ."

"After we restored the box to the summerhouse, did you ever return for it?"

"Now, why would I do such a thing? It was not mine, after all."

Darcy stopped speaking. Silence had the power to create discomfort, and could often provoke a response more effectively than words. Instead, he stared unwaveringly into Wickham's eyes.

Wickham tried to match his gaze. But the obvious effort required revealed to Darcy the answer he sought.

"You *did* return," Darcy said.

Wickham shifted his eyes, looking off toward the common room.

"What did you do with the box? Where is it now?"

"Damned if I know!" He finally returned his gaze to Darcy. "Yes, I went back. I planned to try my luck with the lock once more, and break it if I could not determine the combination. But as I was leaving the summerhouse, that old crosspatch Flynn came upon me. He gave me a wigging and took the box." He shrugged. "I do not know what happened to it after that. I sneaked back into the summerhouse a few times, but never found it in its place again. The old man probably stole it for himself."

He took another swig from his tankard and studied Darcy's countenance. "Why these questions now, Darcy? That box, whatever happened to it, is long gone."

"Yes, it is." If Mr. Flynn confiscated the strongbox, Darcy trusted that the gardener had disposed of it responsibly. When he returned to Pemberley, he had only to ask the longtime servant its whereabouts. Wickham, however, did not need to know anything further about the matter.

Wickham drained his mug. "My tankard is dry. Have we finished reminiscing?"

"Indeed. We have quite done."

Darcy's gaze followed Wickham as he strolled through the doorway to the common room, threaded his way though the crowd to rejoin his comrades, and accepted another pint from the accommodating Meg. He did not wish to witness more. What he did not know about Lydia's husband, he would not have to withhold from Elizabeth.

The kitchen girl passed through, balancing three steaming bowls of a mixture his nose guessed to be mutton stew. Darcy started to make his exit behind her. As she reached the doorway to the common room, he looked past her to see the inn's outside door admit yet another person into the close quarters. A woman whose appearance so startled him that he gasped.

Dorothy.

No sooner did he identify Northanger Abbey's false housekeeper than she, happening to glance his way, caught sight of him. Her eyes widened in recognition.

He hastened to get around the kitchen girl, but she, oblivious to his urgency, blocked his path. Dorothy turned and fled out the door.

Just as the serving girl cleared the doorway, one of the patrons roguishly slapped her backside. The unanticipated prank caused her to drop the pewter bowls. Hot gravy and chunks of overcooked vegetables splattered across the floor.

By the time he got around the mess and stepped outside, he found exactly what he expected.

Dorothy was gone.

Twenty-six

We live entirely in the dressing room now, which I like very much; I always feel so much more elegant in it than in the parlour.

—Jane Austen, letter to Cassandra

Though sunlight streamed through the open shutters, it was the sounds of movement in her dressing room that woke Elizabeth. Still half asleep, she lay in bed listening, attempting to determine whether the noises were genuine or a continuation of the illusion she had experienced during the night.

She had dreamed of Lady Anne. In her imagination, Darcy's mother had come to her chamber carrying an infant wrapped in Mrs. Tilney's quilt. The image had seemed so real that Elizabeth had actually risen from bed to follow her into the dressing room, but only the fragrance of the Madonna lily and its ghostly white flowers gleaming in the moonlight had greeted her.

Afterward, she had been unable to return to sleep. Her now quite rounded belly prevented her from settling into a comfortable position. Within her, the baby had woken and decided that midnight was the perfect hour at which to perform a country dance. No longer producing only occasional light flutterings, the child moved constantly now, often keeping her awake with nocturnal gymnastics even Darcy could feel—when he was home. Apparently, their daughter was blissfully unaware of Dr. Severn's prohibition against prolonged exertion.

And so she had lain awake, alone in her bedchamber but with an entire host of visitors inhabiting her thoughts: Lady Anne and George Darcy, General and Mrs. Tilney, Henry and the mysterious Frederick Tilney, Wickham, Lady Catherine, Mr. Flynn . . . Though some of the figures lived in the present, her mind was most occupied with people and events of the past. If only she and Darcy could find Lady Anne's ivory, perhaps they could put some of the shades to rest and look toward the future.

It seemed she had just fallen back asleep when the noises in the next room intruded upon her consciousness. She assumed Lucy was in there preparing her morning toilette, but normally her maid performed her duties so quietly that her presence went unnoticed unless Elizabeth was already awake.

And normally her duties did not include opening a creaking chest lid.

At the telltale sound, Elizabeth hastened from bed and opened the door to the dressing room. The lid of the trunk fell shut with a *thud* as Lady Catherine jerked upright.

"It is about time you rose," her ladyship declared. "Did you intend to lie about all morning?"

Lady Catherine's audacity temporarily stunned Elizabeth into speechlessness. She had just caught Darcy's aunt intruding where she had no business, and somehow *she* was in the wrong? She stood in the doorway blinking until she became conscious that the door yet stood open—providing her unwelcome visitor with a partial view of the Darcy-free chamber beyond. She stepped into the dressing room, firmly shut the door behind herself, and donned the dressing gown Lucy had laid out the night before.

"Lady Catherine, I do not recall inviting you to my private apartment. Further, I do not recall inviting you to make yourself free in it."

"I am here for an explanation, Mrs. Darcy."

"And you hoped to find it in that trunk?"

Her ladyship drew herself up indignantly. "I hoped to find you prepared to account for the mischief visited upon me this morning."

"What mischief might that be?"

Lady Catherine thrust a handful of withered flower petals toward her. Ugly brown stains mottled the once-white edges. "I found these scattered on the floor of my bedchamber when I awoke. And the room absolutely reeked of lilies."

At the sight of the petals, Elizabeth's gaze immediately shifted to the Madonna lily beside the window. Though it had been perfectly intact last night, now one of its flowers was missing. Its petals, however, had been perfectly white and were unlikely to have completely deteriorated so quickly. Had Lady Catherine's petals come from another source?

When Mr. Flynn had gone to retrieve Lady Anne's lily for Georgiana, he had discovered it missing. The succeeding four days had evinced no sign of it—until this morning. The thief must have left the dead petals for Lady Catherine, but Elizabeth could not guess the prankster's identity. Before now, her ruminations had led her to consider Lady Catherine a likely candidate for having stolen the bloom, as her ladyship seemed to take proprietary interest in anything related to her sister. If Lady Anne was to be remembered with a lily, Lady Catherine would covet one, too. But unless Darcy's aunt presently enacted an elaborate ruse, this development left Elizabeth without another suspect.

"I cannot explain them."

"Do not pretend ignorance. Madonna lilies are well out of season, yet the housekeeper delivered that one to you early this week. From where else could these petals have come?"

The question sparked nervousness within her. If Darcy's aunt knew she had received the lily several days ago, how closely did Lady Catherine monitor her apartment and her movements? Darcy was still away from Pemberley—did she suspect his absence? Or was her surveillance motivated only by their race to locate Lady Anne's ivory?

"As you can see, the petals on my lily suffer no deterioration such as those exhibit." Thankfully, as later today she would give the flower to Mr. Flynn as a substitute for the one intended for Lady Anne's grave. "Those petals must have come from another lily." Elizabeth watched Lady Catherine as she made the last statement, but her ladyship's face did not hint at any knowledge of the missing plant. Nor did it suggest that Elizabeth's response had mollified her in the least.

"As if this day is not upsetting enough. You *do* comprehend its significance?"

"It is Georgiana's birthday."

"Also the anniversary of my sister's death."

"I have not forgotten." Indeed, she'd hoped Darcy would have somehow completed his errand and returned by today with enough information from Mr. Wickham to locate the statuette. Fulfilling Lady Anne's last request—that Elizabeth find the missing heirloom for her—seemed a fitting way to acknowledge the date. But Darcy had sent a brief message indicating he had been delayed. He had included no explanation, probably wise considering the tendency toward disappearance that letters and other items at Pemberley had begun to exhibit.

"I trust my nephew will exert some effort to remember his mother today? Emerging from his sickroom might form a start. This cold of his has gone on quite long enough. He *has* been taking the physics I provided?"

"They have all been put to use," she said quite honestly. Graham had discovered them particularly effective for polishing boots.

"Then he should not be ailing so. Perhaps he requires a doctor."

"I am sure one or two days more will restore him to perfect health."

She prayed Darcy would be home by then. Lady Catherine enquired more closely into his "illness" each day, and Elizabeth grew weary of keeping up the subterfuge. Upon receiving the news of his delay, she had taken Georgiana into her confidence to solicit her aid in distracting their aunt. Georgiana had surprised her by confessing that Darcy had already advised her of his journey—though not its purpose—and requested that she keep a vigilant eye on Elizabeth's health in his absence. Elizabeth appreciated the solicitude of her husband and sister-in-law, but believed herself equal to monitoring the changes within her. She grew larger each day, and her shifting center of gravity sometimes left her feeling less than steady on her feet, but otherwise she felt fine.

"Tell my nephew I would see him later today. Perhaps he can provide a satisfactory explanation for these petals, as you have not."

"And perhaps you can offer an acceptable justification for trespassing in here. What were you seeking in that trunk—Lady Anne's ivory?"

"I have told you, that ivory was not hers, but mine."

"I will spare you further trouble. It is not in that trunk, nor anywhere in this apartment. And when I do find it, I shall not leave it in a place vulnerable to your avaricious reach."

"Insolent girl! Valuable as the statuette is, I do not prize it for its pecuniary worth alone."

"You believe, as Lady Anne did, that it brings good fortune to mothers?"

"Of course not! That is absolute rubbish—Popish idolatry! Anne must have misunderstood whatever it was that our mother told her about the statuette. No, I referred to its sentimental value."

"Naturally. Whatever was I thinking?"

"Do not adopt sarcasm with me."

"Do not enter my apartment under the misapprehension that you have license to take or examine anything within it. In fact, do not enter it again at all."

"Mr. Darcy?" Lady Catherine called toward the closed bedchamber door. "Do you hear the way your wife is speaking to me?"

"My husband does not display good humor when ill. Disturb his rest and he will speak to you even more strongly than I."

"Not so long as he requires my cooperation in a certain legal matter. You would do well to remember that yourself."

"Your standing surety for us does not grant you the privilege of inserting yourself into any of our other affairs."

"Does it not?"

Elizabeth was so angry that she could hear the blood rushing in her ears. She went to the hall door and flung it open. "Kindly spare us both the unpleasantness of my having to ask you to leave."

Her ladyship gathered her indignation about her like a mantle and departed. Elizabeth left the door open, not trusting herself to close it without slamming it shut. Lady Catherine's arrogance needled her under the best of circumstances, but Darcy's aunt had become positively insufferable at a time when Elizabeth's ability to tolerate her shrank in direct proportion to the size of her increasing belly.

This latest outrage, however, was beyond anything she could have anticipated. Though she had harbored suspicions about Lady Catherine when Anne's letter had disappeared, Darcy's disbelief in his aunt's capacity for such invasive conduct—combined with the letter's rediscovery and the subsequent doubts it had raised regarding Elizabeth's own perceptions—had persuaded her that in her pursuit of the ivory Lady Catherine would at least adhere to basic standards of decorum. Such as observing the implicit rule of hospitality that guests respect the privacy and possessions of their hosts.

But apparently, Lady Catherine's practice of minding everyone else's business in addition to her own had been tolerated by so many for so long that the transition to physical intrusion had been an easy step. How long had she been in the room before Elizabeth caught her disturbing the trunk, and with what else had she meddled?

Elizabeth went to the escritoire and unlocked the drop front. Lady Anne's letter to her lay where she had left it, as did the mysterious key that had fallen from the desk in the morning room—and whose purpose she still had not determined. However, the most critical letters of the Tilney correspondence, which she thought she remembered transferring to the escritoire for greater security, were no longer at hand. Had she forgotten to move them? She checked the trunk, but they were not there, either. Had Lady Catherine taken them, or had Elizabeth simply misplaced something yet again?

After several more minutes of additional frustrated searching, she turned her back on the matter and headed toward the window. She wanted to more closely examine the lily's missing flower. But the moment she took a step, her right leg buckled under her.

She managed to grab the back of the escritoire chair and prevent herself from falling. Her leg had gone numb. She fought panic as she gripped the chair tightly to support herself.

"Elizabeth?"

Georgiana paused but a second in the open doorway before hurrying toward her. "Elizabeth, are you unwell?"

"I cannot feel my leg."

"Here, lean upon me." Georgiana offered her shoulder and assisted Elizabeth into the chair.

Elizabeth sank into the seat and stretched out her leg. Through her dressing gown, she rubbed the limb. Although the nerves of her fingers acknowledged her touch, those in her leg were utterly insensate.

Georgiana regarded her with alarm. "Did you injure yourself?"

She shook her head. "I was simply standing here. When I moved and put my weight upon the leg, 'twas as if I had no limb at all."

"We must send for Mr. Monroe."

Elizabeth offered no protest, only wondered how quickly the Lambton apothecary could arrive. Georgiana pulled the bell to call Lucy, then issued the summons through her.

Lucy returned a few minutes later. "Mrs. Reynolds says

we cannot send for Mr. Monroe," she said. "We called for him yesterday when one of the scullery maids suffered a burn, and learned he is gone to Sussex this fortnight."

Georgiana's expression became fretful. "It will require hours to fetch the closest doctor. What shall we do?"

Elizabeth massaged her leg, willing sensation to return to it. The baby kicked—a message from her daughter that she was well, or a sign of distress? The anxiety she had struggled to suppress now threatened to overcome her. She wanted someone to explain what was happening, to reassure her that whatever infirmity claimed her leg did not also trouble the child. And she wanted that someone now.

"Send for Mrs. Godwin," Elizabeth said.

Lucy departed again. Georgiana suggested that she ought to move to her bed while they waited for the midwife to arrive. Elizabeth almost agreed until she recalled that she still had to maintain the fiction of Darcy's presence at Pemberley. Lucy knew of the deception—Darcy had been gone less than a day when Elizabeth realized that keeping her personal maid in ignorance was impossible—but she could hardly be attended by Mrs. Godwin, or waited upon by other servants, in the chamber where Darcy allegedly lay on his own sickbed. It would no doubt appear odd enough that he had not emerged from it to aid her.

Georgiana gently insisted. "My brother would not countenance your neglecting your own health or comfort for the sake of perpetuating this illusion."

She supposed Darcy could just as easily not exist in one room as another. "Very well. Let us say that Darcy has elected to remove to a different chamber for my comfort. Graham can contrive the means to make it appear so."

"My brother should be advised of this so he can return posthaste. He will regret not having been here when this occurred." Georgiana appeared pensive. She worried her lower lip and studied Elizabeth's face as if scrutinizing every pore.

Lucy returned with warm compresses and confirmation that a servant had been dispatched to Mrs. Godwin's house. She and Georgiana assisted Elizabeth into bed, propping pillows behind her so that she could sit up. While Lucy busied herself with the compresses, Georgiana sought out Graham.

Elizabeth closed her eyes and tilted her head back against the pillows. Application of the compresses induced a slight tingling in her upper leg that slowly spread down the limb. The response relieved her in more ways than one.

Mrs. Godwin arrived. "Good morning, Mrs. Darcy. I understand you are having a bit of discomfort today?" The midwife brought with her an air of calm competence that was a remedy in itself.

"My right leg fell numb. I feared it might have something to do with the baby."

"Well, let us have a look at you." Mrs. Godwin removed the compresses and palpated the limb. "Have you experienced pain in your legs?"

"No, simply numbness."

"How does the limb feel now?"

"It improves. Some sensation returns."

The midwife nodded. "You have grown considerably since the harvest feast. Does the child move a great deal?"

"Oh, yes."

She felt Elizabeth's belly. A sharp kick met her palm, evoking a smile from Mrs. Godwin. "Apparently so."

After a few minutes' further examination and gentle queries, Mrs. Godwin asked Elizabeth to test her leg. The numbness had ceased, and she found she could stand on it steadily once more. Georgiana returned and looked as relieved by the sight of Elizabeth standing as Elizabeth herself felt.

"Numbness such as this, even sharp pain in the legs, I have seen with other mothers," Mrs. Godwin said. "It came and went, and disappeared entirely after their babies were born. And the infants themselves were fine."

"Should she refrain from standing?" Georgiana asked.

"Most mothers of my acquaintance do not have that luxury," Mrs. Godwin said. "Though indulging in extra rest before the birth is never unwise. Use your own good judgment, Mrs. Darcy."

After Mrs. Godwin departed, Georgiana insisted that Elizabeth return to bed for the remainder of the day. Elizabeth resisted, certain that a day so spent would bore her into mental numbness.

"I shall remain here to keep you company," Georgiana said.

"Today is your birthday. You can hardly wish to spend it in my bedchamber."

"Better the bedchamber with you than the drawing room with my aunt."

They struck a compromise: Elizabeth would submit to breakfast in bed and Georgiana's fussing over her until it was time to dress for dinner, whereupon if her leg had given her no additional trouble she would pass the evening as usual.

She settled back against the pillows and arranged the blankets while Georgiana momentarily withdrew to the dressing room. Darcy's sister reappeared carrying the Madonna lily, which she placed on the bedside table to cheer the room. Elizabeth welcomed the sight and scent of it. In a couple of hours she would return it to Mr. Flynn so that he could honor Lady Anne through his customary gesture.

"I also brought your book," Georgiana said. "Would you like me to read to you? I can begin wherever you left off."

Elizabeth regarded the book with confusion. She had read nothing but old letters for weeks, and the volume in Georgiana's hands did not look at all familiar. "I am not currently reading any book."

"Oh? When I saw this in your dressing room, I presumed you presently enjoyed it."

"Which book is it?"

"Geoffrey Chaucer."

She had never read Chaucer, let alone this particular copy. Though she had become mildly curious about *The Canterbury Tales* after learning it had inspired George and Anne's courtship, she had not yet got round to seeking it on the shelves of Pemberley's library. "Where, exactly, did you find the book?"

"On your dressing table."

When she had readied for bed last night, no book had been on her dressing table. How this one had found its way into her apartment, she could not fathom.

Georgiana regarded her uncertainly. "Shall I return it to the library?"

"No," she said, thinking of the idle afternoon ahead. Lady Anne and George had found enough of interest in the *Tales* that they had engaged in a debate over them. Surely the poem could provide a few hours' diversion today. "I believe I should like to become more familiar with Mr. Chaucer."

Georgiana began reading. One by one, Elizabeth was introduced to the pilgrims making their way to Canterbury. The knight was introduced, the squire, the yeoman, the prioress. When Georgiana said the name Madame Eglentyne, her listener bade her slow down. George Darcy's first letter concerning Anne had referred to Madame Eglentyne, the prioress.

Chaucer painted a vivid, if not entirely flattering, picture of Madame Eglentyne, who seemed to have suffered from a broad forehead and was not, as he put it, undergrown—a trait for which Elizabeth felt increased sympathy with each passing day. But he did compliment the prioress's manners and morals, her ability to eat without dropping food all over herself, and a trinket on her arm: a gold brooch engraved with " 'a crowned A. And after,' " Georgiana continued reading, " *'Amor vincit omnia.'* "

"Unfortunately, I do not know Latin," Elizabeth said. "Will you translate for me?"

" 'Love conquers all.' "

Twenty-seven

But I will not torment myself with conjectures and suppositions; facts shall satisfy me.

—Jane Austen, letter to Cassandra

Dorothy's name was not Dorothy.

Her name was Mrs. Stanford, and she was the widow of Colonel Reginald Stanford. When the colonel made the ultimate sacrifice for king and country, Mrs. Stanford had continued his service to the military . . . in a manner of speaking.

By all reports, the merry widow had been prostrate, though not necessarily with grief, in the days following her husband's demise. Apparently the companionship of the colonel's fellow officers had assuaged the pain of her loss. Her name had been linked first with that of a lieutenant, then with a major, before she embarked on a long-term campaign with one officer in particular. A man of fortune, he had set her up in the style to which she'd always yearned to become accustomed, and they had carried on a relationship that lasted two years. Content to enjoy his company when he made himself available to her and his money when he did not, Mrs. Stanford lived as independent a life as any kept woman could. She was in Newcastle only when her paramour was; the rest of her time was divided between London and various spa towns.

Four days of investigation had turned up that much intelligence on the lady who had fled the Boar's Head inn, but Darcy had been unable to locate the woman herself. Recently, her lover had also been killed in the line of duty, and upon his death she had quit Newcastle. Darcy's sighting had marked the first time since October that anyone in town had caught a glimpse of her. Once outside the inn again, she had disappeared without a trace.

Darcy had never expected to encounter the mysterious Dorothy while in Newcastle. But he had been less astonished upon learning the name of her longtime paramour.

Captain Frederick Tilney.

Darcy now traveled to Northanger Abbey. He needed to apprise Henry Tilney of Dorothy's identity and determine whether Henry possessed additional information about her. Much as he wished to avoid the trip to Gloucestershire for any number of reasons—the length of the journey, the increased separation from Elizabeth, not to mention the legal trouble that stalked him—this new intelligence required him to speak with Henry in person, and as expediently as possible. They needed to converse candidly about his brother's mistress, and they needed to do so soon, before Mrs. Stanford's trail grew colder.

He had dashed off a second brief note to Elizabeth before leaving Newcastle. He would not stop at Pemberley en route, refusing to delay by even a day the accomplishment of his mission. Better to travel straight to Northanger, complete his business, and return home to stay. He hoped that, meanwhile, Elizabeth could maintain her skillful management of Lady Catherine. He trusted his wife's ability to capably handle his aunt, but with her lying-in looming ever closer, he regretted causing her the additional vexation his absence produced.

Apprehension crept over Darcy as he entered Gloucestershire. Instead of returning with the information he needed to clear his name, he instead arrived with more queries than answers, and without his legal chaperone. He resented the feeling of skulking into the county, of trying to avoid encountering Mr. Chase or the magistrate as if he were—well, as if he were some sort of criminal. Darcy was used to moving freely in the world, as any gentleman ought.

He reached Northanger and was immediately received by Henry Tilney, who greeted him with eager surprise and conducted him to the library.

"You must have learned something?" Tilney said.

"Dorothy's identity. I saw her in Newcastle less than a se'nnight ago."

"Newcastle? Frederick's regiment is stationed there. Did you go to enquire after him?"

"I went on family business, in the course of which I happened to spy the woman who posed as your brother's housekeeper. She fled, but my enquiries yielded intelligence of interest. Do you recognize the name Mrs. Stanford?"

"I am afraid I do not. Was she acquainted with Frederick?"

"*Very* well acquainted."

Henry caught his meaning. "Well, now. That *does* add an interesting element to this business, does it not?"

"Were you aware that your brother maintained a mistress?"

"I suspect he kept a succession of them. Our father harped on him to marry and produce an heir, but Frederick never found a lady who could hold his interest long enough. So he dallied with a woman until one or the other of them grew bored, and then moved on to another. To his credit, at least he did not marry for convenience only to commit adultery for passion, as many gentlemen have done."

"Some men conduct love affairs openly—indeed, it required little time in Newcastle to link Captain Tilney's name with Mrs. Stanford's. Did he ever mention his paramours to you or bring them to Northanger?"

Henry raised a brow. "Discuss his liaisons with his brother the minister? No. And if he ever brought any of the women to Northanger, I would not know, for he certainly did not introduce them to me. Perhaps, however, the servants might be of assistance." Henry rang for the butler.

"If Mrs. Stanford had previously accompanied Captain Tilney here, that would explain her familiarity with the house the night Mrs. Darcy and I met her. She could pass herself off as the housekeeper—if not altogether creditably."

"And that would explain the reports of the servants who took her for a woman they had seen here before."

The butler arrived, and Mr. Tilney enquired whether a Mrs. Stanford had ever visited Northanger Abbey.

"Once, sir. She accompanied the captain about six months ago. She did not stay long—they had a falling-out one day and she departed in a fit. He never brought her back here."

"How do you know they quarreled?"

"The argument occurred during dinner, so I was in and out of the room." The butler cleared his throat. "It was not my intention to eavesdrop, but sometimes people ignore the presence of servants. Mrs. Stanford spoke freely and, by the end, rather loudly. Though she pretended to elegance, she was not the most genteel lady who ever dined at Northanger. I could not help but overhear." He bowed. "I assure you of my discretion, sir. I have never repeated my employers' business as gossip."

"Of course not," Henry said. "This, however, is a matter of importance involving a wrong done to my brother, so answering my questions does not place your loyalty in doubt. About what did they quarrel?"

"She suggested some improvements she planned to undertake as mistress of Northanger. Captain Tilney informed her that she would never be mistress of Northanger and appeared surprised that she had ever expected more than their present arrangement. She replied that he owed her a great deal more, that she had twice passed up comfortable situations with other gentlemen for him, and that if he would not make an honest woman of her he would have to make her a rich one. Then she threatened to depart that very day if he would not treat her as well as she deserved."

"How did Frederick respond?"

"He wished her a fair journey."

Henry asked the butler a few more questions, then dismissed him from the room.

"So," Henry said, "Mrs. Stanford aspired to become Mrs. Frederick Tilney, and when my brother disillusioned her, they parted ways."

"Not necessarily. The information I obtained in Newcastle suggests that they reconciled. By all accounts, they were still together when Captain Tilney died. Either Mrs. Stanford accepted the limitations of their relationship, or thought that given more time she could change his mind."

"But she ran out of time. My brother was killed, and she was left with nothing."

"So she enlisted an accomplice to pose as Captain Tilney and—" And do what? Here, logic failed for Darcy. How did any of this pertain to him and Elizabeth? "If she believed herself entitled to part of your brother's fortune, why did she not simply steal the diamonds for herself? Why concoct an elaborate scheme involving me, and what did she accomplish by it?"

"Perhaps you were not meant to be caught with the diamonds. You did not know your walking stick had been replaced, or that the substitute contained them. Perhaps she planned to retrieve the jewels later, with you none the wiser for having transported them."

"Again, for what reason did she select me—Fitzwilliam Darcy—as their unwitting conductor? I, who had no connection to her, and only the slightest one to your family. How could she even have known our mothers shared a friendship three decades ago?"

"Yet that was the subject of your conversation with Frederick's imposter, was it not? Did he not enquire about letters between them?"

"Yes—which, by the way, we have discovered."

"Indeed? Might they bring anything to bear on this puzzle?"

"I have not read them all, though I expect Mrs. Darcy has by now. Apparently, the acquaintance between our mothers began when my mother contacted your parents for information regarding an ivory statuette that had belonged to Northanger Abbey before the Dissolution. The figurine entered her family's possession at that time, though I understand there were nine others."

Henry rolled his eyes. "Indeed, there were—I cannot tell you how often we heard about them. They were quite valuable, and my father hoped to sell them for a handsome sum. But before he found a buyer, they disappeared from the house."

"Had your father any notion of their fate?"

"He most certainly did. My mother had opposed the sale, and he accused her of having hidden the statuettes or given them away. If she did, it was the one time she ever defied him. But he never found them, and he resented the loss of those ivories to his dying day. I think he complained about them to my poor brother even more than to my sister or me. He often said that my mother had robbed Frederick of part of his inheritance."

"Did Frederick share that opinion?"

"I think he doubted her capacity to resist my father's will. She bore a great deal from him. His presence in this house was so strong that it eclipsed hers. While she lived, the house reflected my father's taste, not hers, and after she died hardly anything retained her influence. Her apartment went untouched, but her favorite garden gave way to a pinery, and even her portrait was removed from the drawing room. Very few of her effects remain—we have, for instance, no letters written to or from her such as you were so fortunate to discover at Pemberley. I should like to see them, if I might."

"Of course," Darcy said. He paused as a thought struck him. "In fact, given the interest Frederick's imposter had in them, perhaps you would like to read them sooner rather than later. Your better knowledge of their author might enable you to discover something in them that my wife and I cannot. Would you care to come to Pemberley?"

Henry readily accepted, and they fixed upon a date in the near future. Darcy would have invited Mr. Tilney to accompany him back to Pemberley immediately, but when he departed Northanger on the morrow he would head south, not north.

He had one more stop to make.

Twenty-eight

There was a scarcity of men in general, and a still greater scarcity of any that were good for much.

—Jane Austen, letter to Cassandra

"Dr. Severn has arrived, ma'am."

Elizabeth almost poked herself with her needle. Her lying-in was not anticipated for another several weeks, and she doubted the physician had suddenly developed such interest in her as to journey to Derbyshire early just to lend his support. She would sooner credit him with intending to disrupt the impromptu concert to which Georgiana presently treated her and Lady Catherine in the music room.

"Dr. Severn? I did not send for him."

Georgiana's hands stilled on the pianoforte. "I did."

Elizabeth directed a questioning gaze toward her.

"I wrote to him the day your leg failed." Georgiana rose and crossed the room to Elizabeth's side. "Please do not be angry. Had I not, and something unfortunate happened, my brother would never forgive me."

She could not resent Georgiana for her concern, nor for the love and loyalty to her brother—and to herself—that had motivated the summons. "I am not angry. You acted as Darcy directed."

Part of Elizabeth was glad for the opportunity to confirm Mrs. Godwin's assessment with the doctor. The rest of her dreaded the conversation. She always left their exchanges with the sense that Dr. Severn considered her ignorant, incompetent, and insignificant. "Settle him in the guest wing," she told Mrs. Reynolds. "I will receive him in my dressing room afterward."

"It is about time someone in this house summoned a doctor," Lady Catherine declared. "My nephew must be at death's door. I have not seen him since—I cannot recall. It has been well over a se'nnight. As soon as this Dr. Severn finishes with you, I insist he cure Mr. Darcy's cold."

Darcy's "illness" *had* lingered so long that the excuse was becoming increasingly difficult to maintain. Lady Catherine grew more suspicious by the hour. Perhaps Elizabeth needed to adjust her strategy.

"Mr. Darcy is much improved today. In fact, he rose early and went shooting."

Lady Catherine eyed her skeptically. "So I may look forward to seeing him at dinner?"

So much for cleverness. As Darcy still had not found his way back to Pemberley, Elizabeth could not possibly produce him by dinner for his aunt's benefit. "He declared himself so in want of fresh air and activity that he might not return in time for dinner."

"Hmph."

Elizabeth went to her dressing room, where she found the housemaid just finishing her duties. Jenny greeted her cheerfully. At least someone in the house offered a pleasant word.

"How are you finding life at Pemberley, Jenny?"

"I like it very well, ma'am."

"I am glad for it." She crossed to the window that overlooked Lady Anne's garden. The snowdrops were beginning to bloom, just in time for Candlemas.

" 'Tis a pretty garden," Jenny said.

Elizabeth agreed. "Prettier when in full flower, of course. Was there much in bloom when you first arrived?"

"Chrysanthemums. And a few others still holding their petals. There were some bright orange flowers over in that part of the garden off to the right—near the yew. I could not tell from this distance what they were."

"I believe you refer to the marigolds."

"Well, they were lovely, whatever they were. Not," she hastened to add, "that I spend my time gazing out the windows when I am supposed to be working, ma'am."

As Jenny left, Elizabeth rang for Lucy. She wanted her maid present primarily for propriety's sake during the doctor's examination, but the moral support would not be unwelcome. She arrived just before the physician. Though only three of them occupied the room—Lucy as unobtrusively as possible—Dr. Severn's presence made it feel crowded.

"Miss Darcy wrote that your leg troubled you," he said. Without Darcy in the room, he for once had no choice but to actually address her.

"Yes. Earlier this week, it went numb."

"Then why do you stand upon it presently?"

"Because presently it is not numb."

"And what were you doing when the numbness occurred?"

She hesitated. "Standing."

He jerked his chin toward the chaise longue. "Sit down."

She followed his order, extending her legs along the seat. He approached and began to examine her left leg.

"It was the right leg that lost sensation."

He made no reply, only a cursory assessment of both limbs.

"A hot compress helped," Elizabeth offered.

He rose from her side and straightened his coat. Apparently, his examination was concluded. "When do you expect the child?"

Was it not his duty to remember such a vital detail? "Early March. You are coming to Pemberley two weeks hence in anticipation, correct?"

He withdrew a small notebook and pencil from his medical bag and made a note. "I believe I just accepted another patient due about that time, who has chosen a London confinement. I shall have to reconcile my schedule."

"Have you not reserved several weeks for us? Mr. Darcy and I both understood you would arrive at Pemberley a fortnight prior to the expected date to ensure you are present when my travail begins."

"Right. Yes." He released a disgusted sigh. "This would all be much simpler if you had arranged a London confinement."

So he could disregard her even more efficiently? "This would all be much pleasanter if you would consider me a patient instead of an inconvenience."

He looked at her coldly. "Fortunately, Mrs. Darcy, I am grown used to the temperamental outbursts of women in your condition." He shut his bag and prepared to leave. "Restrict yourself to the house. No walks. Except for moving from one room to another, remain seated so as not to tax the leg."

"For how long?"

"Until after your lying-in."

She put a hand to the base of her spine and stretched her back. Already, she had grown uncomfortable maintaining one position. How could she sit still for weeks?

"Sitting for prolonged periods causes its own discomforts. Might I at least stroll in the gallery with care? Mrs. Godwin advised—"

"Mrs. who?"

"The midwife."

"You have been consulting some uneducated gossip again?"

"Our apothecary is away, and I desired counsel while waiting for you to arrive."

"Now that I have come, you can dismiss whatever ignorant advice she provided."

"She merely said that—"

"In fact, Mrs. Darcy, to avoid your having to call upon her, or me, again between now and the day you are brought to bed, I order you to take to your bed now. That should prevent you from experiencing the numbness or any other problems."

"I am to remain in bed for weeks before my child is even born?"

"Yes. You—" He addressed Lucy. "Assist your mistress into bed."

"But I do not want to go to bed. I—"

"Do you want something to happen to that child?" The indifference in his voice indicated that he personally did not care whether a mishap occurred or not.

Her hand dropped to her belly—whether to instinctively protect her daughter from the suggestion or the physician himself, she was unsure. "Of course not."

"Then do not endanger it with foolish resistance to the best medical advice available to you." He abruptly turned his back and left.

In the heavy silence that followed, Lucy approached. "Shall I help you into—"

"No!"

Elizabeth immediately regretted the outburst. It was Dr. Severn who had deserved it. She apologized to the maid.

"It is not my place to say so, Mrs. Darcy, but if I were headed for childbed, that man is the last person I would want helping me."

Elizabeth was inclined to agree. Dr. Severn was an arrogant misogynist. He made her feel small. His latest advice seemed motivated more by his own convenience than her well-being. Yet he was an authority whose expertise she needed. Her hand stroked the baby. Did she dare violate his instructions?

She no longer trusted her own instincts. Frustration, anxiety, fatigue—not just from the interview, but the accumulation of months—overwhelmed her.

"Forgive my saying so, ma'am, but you do look tired. Perhaps a nap might restore you."

"Perhaps."

She allowed Lucy to lead her to the bedchamber. Though she had surrendered the Madonna lily to Mr. Flynn days ago and its scent had receded soon after, the intoxicating perfume seemed to hang strong in the air once more.

Lucy sneezed. "My—I think Jenny overdid it."

"Overdid what?"

"I saw her remove a bottle of toilet water from the still-room. She must have sprinkled it on the sheets."

Elizabeth found the scent soothing. She would have to thank the housemaid for her thoughtfulness.

Lucy settled her into bed, but she sat up almost as soon as the maid left the room. She was too agitated to rest. Dr. Severn expected her to spend all her waking hours this way for the remainder of her pregnancy? Boredom would drive her mad. How many hours could one sit and stare at the same paneled wall?

At least it was an interesting wall, with carvings of leaves and birds standing out in relief. The pattern drew the eye from one figure to the next. Having nothing better to do, she allowed her gaze to rest on each image and was struck by the level of detail. Some long-ago artisan had expended considerable time and skill to surround her with beauty she had never before appreciated.

Each repetition of the pattern formed an exact duplicate, save one. On the panel directly across from the bed, a turtle-dove's wing cocked at an odd angle. She rose from bed for a closer look. Apparently, the wing had separated from the rest of the carving at some time in the past, and had been reaffixed with a small nail. The nail, however, was not perfectly centered, nor quite as wide as the hole surrounding it, so the wing had slipped askew—revealing a small keyhole.

And she knew just the key to try.

With steps as brisk as she could manage, she went to her escritoire for the key that had fallen from Lady Anne's desk. She found it beneath the small stack of Helen Tilney's letters.

She paused a moment. She'd misplaced those letters, had she not? Now here they were, precisely where she had last seen them.

She would not contemplate her forgetfulness just now. Key in hand, she eagerly returned to the bedchamber. The key slid perfectly into the small hole, and as she turned it she heard a soft click.

The panel sprang open to reveal a shallow niche in the wall. Within rested a small, leatherbound book. She removed the volume and opened it to the first page.

Familiar handwriting met her gaze.

Twenty-nine

"My father . . . had also the highest opinion of him . . . As for myself, it is many, many years since I first began to think of him in a very different manner."

—*Mr. Darcy,* Pride and Prejudice

The old shopkeeper took the cane from Darcy. He held it in the light and examined it from grip to tip with the familiar touch of a craftsman. His fingers ran down its length until they reached the imperfection in the grain.

"Yes, this is my work. Made it—oh, must be ten, twelve years ago? I remember this little flaw. The gentleman who bought the walking stick hesitated over the purchase—said it was a gift for someone very dear to him and he wanted perfection. I explained that the beauty of wood lies in its variances." He chuckled. "Like people."

Darcy accepted the walking stick back. The detour to Bath had proven worthwhile if only to hear the paraphrase of his father's words about him. But he hoped to obtain more valuable information. "Have you made a similar cane recently? One with a hidden compartment?"

The shopkeeper regarded Darcy warily.

"My interest is in the purchaser, not the creator," Darcy said.

"Some years back, another gentleman came in here. Said he admired a walking stick bought here and was determined to have one just like it. Described this one perfectly. Then he asked if I could fashion his with a hollow center. He claimed it was for brandy."

"If he commissioned the walking stick, he must have left his name."

"He did. Let me see. It was Derby—no, Darcy. George Darcy."

"You must be mistaken. That was my father's name." Darcy held forward his own cane once more. "The man who purchased this walking stick."

The shopkeeper drew his brows together. "I am fairly certain. I do not receive many orders for canes with such compartments. I can check my ledger if you wish."

Darcy wished very much, indeed. The shopkeeper disappeared into his back room and returned a few minutes later with his record book. He paged through it, traveling back through the years—1810, 1809, 1808. . . . Darcy shifted his walking stick from hand to hand as he waited impatiently for the old man to locate the entry.

"Ah, here it is." The craftsman at last pointed to a line. "George Darcy, just as I recalled. Ordered the cane on the fourteenth of June, eighteen hundred four."

His father had still been alive then. "Was it the same gentleman who bought this walking stick?"

"No, a young man. University lad, I assumed, what with the brandy compartment and all."

"Can you describe him?"

The shopkeeper shook his head. "I cannot recall his features clearly. Mind you, ten years have passed."

Even without a description, an unpleasant suspicion of the gentleman's identity formed in Darcy's mind. Darcy had been at university himself at the time. Any one of his Cambridge acquaintances could have seen and admired his walking stick. A few of them might have thought it clever to own a cane with a hidden brandy compartment.

But only one would be so bold as to use the name George Darcy.

Thirty

Till she had made herself mistress of its contents, however, she could have neither repose nor comfort; and with the sun's first rays she was determined to peruse it.

—Northanger Abbey

I am once more with child.

My sentiments upon realizing my state have been jumbled. I never thought to carry a child again, did not believe I would ever feel another life quicken in my womb. The fear of losing this baby, as I have so many others, nearly paralyzes me. Yet it is only through risk that we can reap reward, and it would be a precious gift indeed to love another son or daughter as I adore my darling Fitzwilliam. . . .

I told George last night. He was quiet as he heard the news. I could see in his dear face that the expectation of another child brought him happiness, but that he hesitated to express it without first ascertaining my feelings. I confessed that I have reread his letter so often I have committed it to memory, and that I desperately want to trust once again the words that brought us together. He held me tightly and we talked long into the night, voiced many things too long left unsaid.

He believes this child is meant to be, and in his embrace, I believe it, too.

Even so, I cannot escape the apprehension that my heart will again be shattered. My thoughts stray to my own mother and the treasure she bequeathed to me. I remember her placing the ivory in my hands, and telling me, as I unwrapped the statuette, that the Madonna enfolded mother and child in a mantle of protection. I regret ever having relinquished it to Catherine. My sister does not know what she possesses. She cannot comprehend the true worth of what lies within the small casket. . . .

I have written to Catherine again. I have given up battling her for ownership of our mother's treasure and ask only for its loan. . . .

Catherine has agreed to lend me the ivory! She still claims it as her own, and insists upon its surrender after the birth. Very well. Once this child is born, she may keep the statuette for herself. Our mother's legacy, I will retain. . . .

George journeyed to Kent to bear the treasure safely home—I would entrust its transport to no one else. A peace I have not known for a decade suffused me as I opened the lid and saw the aged statuette enfolded in its old, tattered wrap. To repay my sister's kindness, I shall return the ivory in a new velvet cover, one better suited to her sensibilities. . . .

Catherine comes to visit. God forgive me for thinking so ill of my sister, but I worry that she has changed her mind about our mother's treasure and will try to take it back before I have done with it. I have moved the casket out of the house entirely, to a place she would never think to look should the whim seize her. I doubt anyone else would stumble upon it either, but in the event, I have taken the precaution of putting a lock on the casket. I felt somewhat impious, locking away the Madonna and Child, but I think Madame Eglentyne would approve. . . .

Catherine has left; the treasure remains safe. And so do the child and I.

Elizabeth closed the journal but did not set it aside. She absently held it against her chest, her thoughts occupied by its author.

Lady Anne had awaited Georgiana's birth with optimism. George had restored her faith in their bond, and the ivory had done the rest.

The blessed figurine had removed Anne's self-doubt. And when it disappeared, Anne had somehow known that she would never have an opportunity to reclaim it herself. So she had reached out to someone she would never meet, but whom she hoped would understand the value of her treasure.

Elizabeth understood.

She too yearned for assurance that all was and would remain well as she embarked on this journey of motherhood. The changes in her body, the growing child's toll on her own physical strength, uncertainty about the impending birth and how she would adjust to motherhood afterward . . . all conspired to assail her confidence. She had never felt so vulnerable in her life.

Lady Anne had faced this trial many times before her, had known the doubts a woman carries in her heart as she carries a child under it. In her own last hours, she had hoped to spare her daughter-in-law some of that anxiety. She had urged Elizabeth to find her missing treasure.

Find it she would. For them both.

Thirty-one

To be sorry I find many occasions. The first is, that your return is to be delayed, and whether I ever get beyond the first is doubtful.

—Jane Austen, letter to Cassandra

"Mrs. Darcy, where—precisely—did you say my nephew is at present?"

Elizabeth experienced a moment's panic. Where *had* she said Darcy was this morning? In the village, meeting with tenants? No, that was yesterday. Riding? Perhaps—she had used that excuse multiple times. Penning a letter to Mr. Harper? That seemed like a safe pretense. He had no lack of business requiring communication with his solicitor, as his aunt well knew.

She struggled to a standing position to acknowledge her ladyship's appearance in the doorway of her morning room. The baby was now so large that there was no truly graceful way to rise from her seat anymore. Were Lady Catherine a more sympathetic woman, she might have bade Elizabeth dispense with the formality—but then she would not be Lady Catherine.

"I believe he is in the library dispatching some correspondence," Elizabeth said.

"I have just come from the library; it is unoccupied."

Confound it. Ever since Dr. Severn had circumscribed Elizabeth's mobility, Lady Catherine was literally one step ahead of her. Though upon the physician's departure Elizabeth had reverted to his original dictate of restricting herself to sitting within the house—the subsequent order of confinement to bed having, in her mind, resulted solely from his fit of pique—the command had rendered it nearly impossible to monitor Darcy's aunt. Her ladyship moved about Pemberley too freely, and consequently had caught her in more than one falsehood regarding Darcy's whereabouts. If Darcy did not return home on the morrow, Elizabeth doubted her ability to maintain the façade any longer.

"He was there earlier. He must have completed his letter."

Lady Catherine stalked across the drawing room to plant herself in front of Elizabeth. "Does my nephew avoid me? Has he no respect for his aunt? No sensibility of the duties of a host to his guest? I have not seen him in weeks! Every time I seek him out, he has just left the room, or has requested not to be disturbed, or has retired for the evening. Is he truly so engaged every day that he cannot come to dinner?" She narrowed her eyes. "I begin to wonder if you play some game with me, Mrs. Darcy. I will not be taken for a fool."

"I assure you, Lady Catherine, I play no game." She found the burden of keeping up appearances not the least bit amusing.

"Hmph." Lady Catherine settled herself into a chair.

Elizabeth returned to her own seat and picked up her book. She had originally come to the morning room for a change of environs as she wrote some letters of her own, but the glare of the sun at this particular hour drove her from the desk. The other side of the room had proven more hospitable, so she had sent a servant to retrieve the Chaucer volume from her apartment. After hearing Georgiana read Lady Eglentyne's description from the opening of *The Canterbury Tales,* Elizabeth had thought perhaps the Prioress's Tale would provide amusement. It turned out, however, to be the grisly story of a murdered child, a theme not at all suited to her present spirits or general taste. At the moment she also lacked the patience and concentration that Chaucer's language required of her, and had been about to abandon the volume altogether when Lady Catherine entered.

"That is an enormous tome," her ladyship declared. "What on earth do you read?"

"Geoffrey Chaucer."

"Not those bawdy tales, I hope? Though I suppose *you* might find such matter diverting."

The appearance of Mrs. Reynolds provided a welcome distraction. "You have visitors, ma'am. Your—"

"Lizzy!"

Elizabeth's eyes widened. "Mama! What a"—she swallowed—"delightful surprise." Her father, an even more unexpected guest, also entered. "And Papa." She mustered a smile. "I did not anticipate you for another month, Mama."

"Now, Lizzy, you know babies come early sometimes. Look at Jane! If we waited another month I might miss all the excitement."

That had been the general idea.

Elizabeth extricated herself from her seat once more and waddled forward to greet them. An embrace with her father proved awkward—her protruding middle preceded her into it by some distance—so she settled for grasping hands with her mother.

"Look at you!" Her mother beamed. "So fat!" She reached out and patted Elizabeth's roundness. "Gracious, Lizzy, you are big as a house!"

Elizabeth's smile became still more forced. "Thank you, Mama."

Mrs. Bennet touched her belly again. "And you are carrying low—that means it is a boy! Mr. Bennet, we shall have another grandson!"

"Before you issue the announcements, my dear, I would remind you that you cited the same evidence five times to assure me *you* carried a son. And it all came to naught."

"Oh, but I was never as plump as Lizzy!"

Perceiving that her mother's hand threatened a third dart toward her abdomen, Elizabeth sidestepped the assault by turning toward Lady Catherine.

"Your ladyship, I believe you have met my mother."

Lady Catherine acknowledged Mrs. Bennet with a nod and displayed enough civility to submit to an introduction to her father. When the formality had been performed, Elizabeth invited her parents to sit.

Her father, in passing, caught her arm and winked. "Your mother was plumper," he whispered.

When all were comfortably settled, Elizabeth enquired after their journey.

"Oh, it was fair enough," Mrs. Bennet said. "Though long. Did it not seem long to you, Mr. Bennet?"

"Indeed, it seemed much longer than when I traveled alone in August."

"The roads were probably better in summer," Mrs. Bennet said. "Did your ladyship find them agreeable?"

"Perfectly agreeable. My carriage is well sprung and comfortably outfitted."

"Oh, yes! I recall admiring your chaise when you honored us with your visit to Longbourn."

Lady Catherine offered no reply. Mrs. Bennet, who could never bear silence, cast about for another topic.

"We did not expect the pleasure of finding you at Pemberley, your ladyship. Are you come in anticipation of Elizabeth's lying-in?"

Lady Catherine cast Elizabeth a pointed glance. "I have business with my nephew."

"Oh, yes. Of course." Mrs. Bennet smiled at Lady Catherine, but the disdainful stare she received in return discouraged her from gazing too long in her ladyship's direction. She instead focused her admiration on Elizabeth's belly. "Lizzy, how is Mr. Darcy? I hope he spoils you. A gentleman cannot indulge his wife too much when she is in a delicate condition."

"He is quite well."

"Surely he hopes for a son. Men always do, at least until

they have an heir." She sighed. "Lord knows we would have preferred to keep Longbourn in the family. Not that we begrudge Mr. Collins the entail," she said emphatically, looking at Lady Catherine. The Bennet heir served as her ladyship's rector back in Kent. "But for years I worried about what would become of us should misfortune take Mr. Bennet."

"It comforts me exceedingly to know you spent so much time contemplating my demise," he said.

"I never gave a thought to myself, mind you. But I agonized, as only a mother can—surely your ladyship sympathizes—over the futures of my five daughters, with no inheritance of their own and no brother to provide for them. What would have become of them? But now three are happily married, and Kitty too as soon as her young man is of an age to take orders. Poor Mr. Dashwood—he had a great fortune, but lost it in some confusing business in London last spring, so now he is gone into the church. However, with Jane and Elizabeth so well established, I hope Mary will find a rich young man who can hold on to his money."

"I imagine you do," Lady Catherine said coldly.

"Well, Lizzy, you shall have a boy, and Pemberley will be safe. Such a grand estate your Mr. Darcy has! I suppose he is off somewhere now attending to some important matter. Keeping track of all his money must occupy much of his time."

"Mr. Darcy does manage to fit other pursuits into his schedule on occasion." Such as clandestine excursions to Newcastle and Gloucestershire. Elizabeth hoped more fervently than ever that he would return soon. She did not feel herself equal to single-handedly entertaining both her mother and Lady Catherine at once.

"Papa, did you happen to visit Jane en route?" The Bingleys had recently quit Netherfield for their new estate in Staffordshire. Elizabeth anticipated with great pleasure a visit to her sister as soon as she was at liberty to travel once more.

"There, Mr. Bennet—see? Lizzy also thinks it would have been a good scheme. I long to see Jane's new home, Lizzy, but your father insisted we allow her more time to establish her household. And then Jane herself said she was departing within a fortnight to come here for your lying-in. But that cannot be correct—it is a full two weeks earlier than you advised me to arrive."

In sharing the estimated dates of her confinement, Elizabeth might have created a slight—and, of course, entirely unintentional—discrepancy between the information her sister and mother received. As if to reprove her, the baby awoke and practiced its pugilistic skills on the inside of her ribs, causing sharp pains that she was hard-pressed to conceal from her guests. Perhaps she carried a boy after all.

"Jane brings Nicholas, and wished to allow additional time to get settled at Pemberley before the arrival of a new cousin put the nursery at sixes and sevens."

"If only Lydia would come, also. Newcastle is not so very far." Mrs. Bennet addressed Lady Catherine. "My youngest daughter's husband is in the regulars, and his regiment has been stationed there over a twelvemonth. I miss her excessively, though she keeps so busy with her husband and new friends that I am certain she scarcely has time to give her mother a thought. She is so popular among the other officers' wives. Everybody adores her. What a wonderful thing it is to be young and carefree! I quite envy her sometimes."

Lady Catherine made not the slightest effort to disguise her contempt. She turned to Elizabeth. "Mrs. Darcy, I trust Mrs. Wickham will make no reappearance at Pemberley in the near future?"

Dear heaven, she hoped not. Adding Lydia to this delightful family assembly might send Elizabeth seeking asylum in her bedchamber for the remainder of her pregnancy. Already, Dr. Severn's order of bed rest held increased appeal.

"She has conveyed no such intention to me," she replied.

"Lizzy, why do you not write and invite her? Only think how merry we would be! Lydia is such a cheerful creature. Her companionship would divert us all. Mr. Wickham could bring her—did he not grow up at Pemberley? I am sure he would love to visit."

"Heaven and earth!" Lady Catherine exclaimed. "Have you no sense at all?"

Mrs. Bennet appeared confused and injured. "I—forgive me, your ladyship, if I somehow gave offense. I only meant that—"

"Mr. Wickham, invited to Pemberley? Could its woods be polluted any further?"

Though Mrs. Bennet's gabble often provoked impatience in Elizabeth, she could not countenance Lady Catherine so abusing her mother. "I daresay a home as venerable as Pemberley can survive the unbecoming conduct of any relations of mine—or of my husband's."

Lady Catherine huffed in disgust. "You are as common as the rest of them."

The baby, naturally, chose this moment to perform a somersault. Elizabeth gripped the arm of her chair in an unlikely attempt to maintain her composure. Could her situation become any more uncomfortable? Mercifully, Mrs. Reynolds interrupted.

"Another visitor, madam. Your sister has arrived."

Jane had come already? Relief flooded her. If Darcy could not be here to ease her suffering, Jane offered the most ideal substitute. "Do show her in." She eagerly fixed her gaze upon the door.

At the sight of her sister, something less than felicity seized her. Mrs. Bennet, however, sprang to her feet with glee.

"Lydia!"

SHE WAS IN hell.

Truly. Elizabeth thought she had glimpsed hell once before in her life, but nothing she had encountered during the last London social season could match the tribulation of her present circumstances. The conjunction of her mother, Lydia, and Lady Catherine was an event that ought to be described in the dire inflections normally reserved for doomsday prophecies. Even Pemberley was not large enough to contain three such forces of nature simultaneously.

Dinner had been an ordeal; the drawing room afterward, a crucible. Her father—lucky man—had withdrawn to the library for a time, leaving the ladies to divert themselves in the formal reception room until he joined them later. Both Lady Catherine and Mrs. Bennet had remarked on Darcy's absence from dinner, inspiring Georgiana to seat herself at the small pianoforte to offer a distraction. Her efforts, however, only resulted in allowing the married ladies to engage in discourse on topics that would have gone unmentioned in Georgiana's hearing and Elizabeth's preference. Mrs. Bennet had nearly nine months' worth of sage maternal advice to impart, and Lady Catherine, torn between impulses to demonstrate her superiority through haughty silence and to issue a contrary opinion on every matter raised, at last yielded to the latter. The pair of them commenced an inharmonious duet, each verse of which underscored Elizabeth's incorrect resolution on some issue related to her impending motherhood. Lydia chimed in with a descant voicing her disinclination for the entire theme. Elizabeth, though the chief subject of the opus, was all but drowned out by the more impassioned vocalists and contented herself with marking time. The performance reached a crescendo in a spirited arioso by Lady Catherine on the subject of wet nurses which almost drove Lydia to cover her ears before the entrance of Mr. Bennet ended the discordant concerto.

Now, just when Elizabeth thought she had escaped to the sanctuary of her bedchamber for the night, an incessant pounding rattled her door. Was it Lydia, come to hint that a spare twenty or fifty pounds would finance her extravagant habits for another few months? Beyond citing an implausible desire to be useful to Elizabeth during her confinement, her youngest sister still had not offered an explanation for her appearance at Pemberley, and Elizabeth had been too much occupied in maintaining civility between her and Lady Catherine to extract the truth. Perhaps it was her mother, come to rhapsodize further over how fat Elizabeth had grown. The subject had served as a refrain for every conversational lull at dinner. Pregnant pauses, indeed.

She donned her dressing gown and opened the door to reveal candidate number three: Lady Catherine. Of course. Who else would consider herself justified in disturbing her hostess after she had retired for the evening? Elizabeth had just been about to climb into bed and begin a futile attempt to find a comfortable sleeping position.

"Lady Catherine, what do you require at this time of night that a servant cannot procure for you?"

"My nephew. Hide-and-seek is a children's game, Mrs. Darcy, and I have done with it. If your husband is in fact here at Pemberley, he ought to be in his bedchamber at this hour. I demand that you produce him now."

"I would do so, your ladyship, but I am afraid he is—" She desperately sought an excuse she had not yet employed. "Exhausted."

"Exhausted?" Lady Catherine repeated scornfully. "In what has he engaged that left him exhausted?"

Elizabeth did not reply, only pulled her dressing gown more tightly closed and raised her brows innocently.

Lady Catherine's eyes widened. "In your condition!" For the first time in Elizabeth's recollection, the slightest tinge of embarrassment stained her ladyship's cheek. "You should be ashamed."

"Ashamed of what?" Lydia strolled down the hall. "Lizzy never does anything of which she should be ashamed." She giggled. "Though perhaps you ought to, Lizzy. It might be good for you."

"Brazen hussies, both of you!" her ladyship choked out.

Lydia giggled again, then disregarded her ladyship altogether. "Lizzy, the fire in my chamber has died."

"Lydia, it is late. I tire easily these days. Why do you bring this to me instead of simply ringing for a housemaid?"

"I *did* ring—she has not responded yet. Besides, I thought you ought to know. One cannot be too strict with the help, after all. Does your ladyship not agree?"

To be first ignored by someone she considered inferior and then solicited for corroboration on the subject of servants as if she and Lydia were on equal footing nearly sent

Lady Catherine into spasms. She cut Lydia from her view entirely. "Mrs. Darcy, I demand to see my nephew. Now."

"Oh, Lizzy! Thank heaven you are still awake!" Mrs. Bennet bustled down the hall toward them. "I have been thinking about your finding a husband for Mary."

"Lizzy, it is cold in my chamber—"

"—Are there any eligible gentlemen in the neighborhood?"

"Mrs. Darcy—my nephew!"

If she sank to the floor and began rocking with her head between her hands, would any of them notice? Their voices swirled around her like a maelstrom. And then, miraculously, the voice she most longed to hear broke through the cacophony.

"Perhaps this conversation can continue on the morrow."

She turned round to be certain she had not imagined it, so fervently had she wished for the sound. A set of dark eyes met hers, and order was restored to her world.

Darcy was home.

Thirty-two

Lady Catherine seemed quite astonished at not receiving a direct answer.

—Pride and Prejudice

Darcy wanted to spend a minute simply beholding his wife, but could not indulge the desire until their audience dispersed. So disperse it he would.

He took Elizabeth's hand and drew her back into their chamber. "My wife needs her rest. Whatever business you have with her can wait."

That statement alone proved enough to send Mrs. Bennet, who found him the most intimidating of her sons-in-law, scurrying back to her own bedroom. Lydia required only the addition of a disapproving look before muttering her intention to ring for a housemaid again.

Lady Catherine, however, remained, despite uncharacteristic discomposure. His attire seemed the source of her agitation. Unsure whether he yet suffered from a debilitating cold, he had taken the precaution of exchanging his clothes for a nightshirt upon reaching their apartment, so that he appeared to have just risen from bed and hastily donned a pair of trousers before coming to the bedchamber door. For some reason, his state of undress—hardly unexpected, given the hour—evoked Lady Catherine's disapproval.

"My business is with you, Mr. Darcy," his aunt declared.

"Then it, too, can wait. You may consider me entirely at your disposal after breakfast. Until then, I bid you good night." Without further ceremony, he shut the door. And closed his arms about his wife.

Impatient to return to her, Darcy had found the weeks of their separation long. Now it seemed as though twice as much time had passed. His embrace could no longer fully encircle her. He placed a hand on their son and was rewarded with a kick.

"Your child missed you," she said.

"Did his mother?"

"Oh—were you gone? I had not noticed."

If the scene to which he had returned were any indication, she'd had plenty of companionship to divert her. "Mr. Wickham did not accompany his wife, I hope?"

"He is not about Pemberley." She stepped out of his arms and looked up at him. Though the slight distance between them granted him a better view of the face he had longed to see, he did not want to let her go. "How did you come to be in our bedchamber without anyone's observing your entrance?"

"I entered my dressing room through the servants' door." He took both her hands in his, unable to completely break contact. He simply wanted to be near her. "I did not wish to risk encountering anyone before conferring with you, as I did not know whether you had been able to maintain our original pretext."

"Your illness lasted about a week. You recovered when your aunt began insisting that we summon a doctor."

"How have I busied myself since?"

"You have been conducting business in the village, visiting every part of the house Lady Catherine was not presently in, and engaging in all manner of outdoor sport. Then this evening you took to bed once more."

"What kept me there this time?"

Her eyes glinted with mischief. "Indoor sport."

He laughed. "I am sorry I missed it. I hope I acquitted myself well?"

"Tolerably."

"Only tolerably?"

"Your mind seemed to be elsewhere. So did the rest of you, for that matter. Where *have* you been?"

"Most recently, in Bath. After meeting with Henry Tilney at Northanger, I wanted to interview the owner of the shop where you noted the walking stick similar to mine displayed in the window. I decided that I was already so far south that I might as well continue on to Bath and conduct my business as efficiently as possible."

"And how did you come to visit Northanger Abbey? When you left here, you were headed to Newcastle to question Mr. Wickham about your mother's strongbox. From Pemberley, one does not travel north by Northanger."

"I did speak to Wickham. And no sooner did we finish our conversation, than I spied the mysterious Dorothy."

Her eyes widened in astonishment. "In Newcastle?"

"She was the cause of my first delay. She fled when she saw me, and I spent several days trying to locate her again. My search proved unsuccessful, but my enquiries revealed that she was in fact Frederick Tilney's mistress."

"Dorothy and Captain Tilney? My! That elucidates a few matters, does it not? She must have been a better lover than housekeeper."

"She was never a housekeeper at all, just the widow of one of Frederick's fellow officers. Until the night I sighted her, she had not been seen in Newcastle since Captain Tilney's death. I lost her trail there, so I went to report my findings to Henry Tilney and learn whether he knew anything of Mrs. Stanford."

"And did he?"

"No, but his butler recalled her having visited Northanger once. She and the captain quarreled when he abruptly dashed her hopes of marriage. Apparently, however, she decided to satisfy herself with his fortune if not his hand."

"Did he provide for her upon his death?"

"Not in any formal manner, according to Henry Tilney. Reports in Newcastle indicate that she quit her rooms there because she could no longer afford them."

"And headed straight for Northanger, where we encountered her before Henry received word of his brother's death. Hmm." She sat on one end of the chaise longue, making room for him to sit beside her. "You said she was the widow of another officer?"

"Yes, a Colonel Reginald Stanford."

"The dispatch to Henry Tilney did not reach him for two weeks. Might Mrs. Stanford have used her connections to delay the delivery?"

"That is quite possible. Apparently, she was well acquainted with a number of officers. She could have called upon one of them for a favor, or used her wiles on the messenger himself."

"Either way, the delay provided enough time for her and the false Captain Tilney to meet us at Northanger Abbey." She frowned. "But what interest had she in us?"

"I have been contemplating that point," he said. "Mrs. Stanford could have known of our expected visit and, for reasons of her own, wanted it to proceed."

"So she found someone to pose as the captain, and the two of them met us in Frederick Tilney's place."

"Precisely. After we departed and their objective—whatever it was—had been satisfied, the dispatch was delivered to Henry Tilney."

"Do you suppose their objective was at all related to the true Captain Tilney's original motive for his invitation? He cited a desire to renew the acquaintance between families, and the false captain seemed to know something of that history. Enough, at least, to enquire into the friendship between your mother and Helen Tilney, and whether Mrs. Tilney ever visited Pemberley."

"Which she did not."

"As a matter of fact, she did—and so did the general." Elizabeth rose and went into her dressing room. She returned a minute later with a handful of letters. "You were a boy of only four, so that is probably why you do not remember. She came to visit shortly after the other nine ivories that match your mother's were discovered at Northanger. While Mrs. Tilney was here, the statuettes disappeared from Northanger, and General Tilney, convinced she had given them to Lady Anne, descended upon Pemberley looking for them. Here—read for yourself."

He did, and wished he had possessed this information when he last spoke with Henry Tilney. "The statuettes were never found, and Henry Tilney told me that his father went to his grave resenting their loss. The general often spoke of them, especially to Frederick."

"Then at some point, he likely shared his suspicion that Mrs. Tilney brought them to Pemberley. Perhaps Frederick, upon noticing your name in the Pump Room book, was reminded of the lost ivories. He invited us to Northanger to learn what he could about them and, if they were indeed at Pemberley, request their return."

"And when he died before our meeting—"

"His mistress, having nothing but warm memories to show for her years of devotion to him, decided nine medieval statuettes would constitute fair payment if she could get her hands on them. She found someone to pose as Frederick long enough to meet us in his place. When the interview yielded nothing, she used your walking stick to smuggle the diamonds out of Northanger. If she could not have the ivories, she would console herself with jewels. What I cannot puzzle out, however, is how she obtained such a perfect copy of your cane in the short time we were at Northanger."

"I believe the substitute walking stick was made some time earlier. The Bath merchant recalled crafting it eight years ago."

"For whom?"

He set aside Mrs. Tilney's letters. "The gentleman who commissioned it gave the name George Darcy."

"Your father?"

"No. The purchaser was too young to be my father. The shopkeeper said he was a university student."

"A gentleman at university in aught-four . . . That would make him about your age. But who would take such liberty with the name George Darcy? I cannot conceive of anyone's attempting to conduct legitimate business in another man's name, except perhaps his son."

"Or godson."

Her eyes lit with sudden realization. "Mr. George Wickham."

"My father financed his education. Wickham may well have ordered the cane and sent the bill to Pemberley. I doubt my father knew, however, that it so closely resembled mine. I myself am uncertain why Wickham would want a walking stick identical to one I possessed."

"Envy. He wants what you have. Even now, after all your family has done for him, he still believes himself entitled to more. If he could not *be* a Darcy, he could own a walking stick adorned with the Darcy cinquefoil." She drew her brows together. "Of course, now we must explain how the cane found its way to Northanger Abbey. Mr. Wickham cannot have been Frederick's imposter—we know him too well. Even disguised by the bandages, we would have recognized his voice and manner."

"Wickham was stationed in Newcastle for a year before Captain Tilney's death, and he frequents the inn where I saw Mrs. Stanford. I have no doubt of their acquaintance, only the extent of Wickham's involvement in Mrs. Stanford's scheme."

"Lydia revealed that they have accumulated considerable debt again. He may have simply sold the cane to help satisfy his creditors."

"I believe another interview with Wickham is in order."

"You are not going to Newcastle again?"

"No. It will have to take place here." Though he loathed the very thought of Wickham coming to Pemberley, he would not leave Elizabeth with her time so near.

"What did Mr. Wickham say during your last meeting? Did he offer any information about your mother's strongbox?"

"He confessed to returning for it, but said Mr. Flynn

caught him and confiscated it. I shall speak to the gardener about it on the morrow."

"May I? You are indentured to your aunt after breakfast, and heaven only knows how long she will keep you. Too, if he does produce the casket, I should like to bring it in here while Lady Catherine is otherwise occupied."

"Very well."

"I hope he does indeed know where the ivory can be found. I must admit, Darcy—I should like to have it with me when our daughter is born. It lent your mother such confidence, and I could use a little more at present."

Something in her voice made him uneasy. "Have you and the child been well?"

"It is nothing over which to panic, but we did summon Dr. Severn in your absence. My right leg gave me a bit of trouble."

Dread crept over him. "What sort of trouble?"

"It fell numb for a short period." At his indication of alarm, she continued quickly. "Mrs. Godwin assured me that she has known other mothers to experience the same problem, with no ill effect on them or their babies."

"What did Dr. Severn say?"

"To walk less and sit more."

"And have you followed his instructions?"

"Yes. Though Darcy, I must say, he was most unpleasant throughout the visit. He is due to return this week and stay until I am brought to bed, and I do not know how I will tolerate him."

Darcy himself found the physician's arrogance disagreeable. He still had not quite recovered from his *shush*ing. "We have engaged him for his expertise, not his manner."

"Even so, he could at least make an effort to be congenial. He seems to regard me as an annoyance."

"Seat him next to my aunt at dinner. You will benefit from the comparison."

"Or they will recognize each other as kindred spirits and unite against me."

"If that is the case, you always have your mother as an ally."

"I wish I had yours as well." She paused. "Though in a sense, I feel as if I do. It almost seems at times that she is guiding me."

"Toward the statuette?"

"Yes. But also through this time of waiting. On several occasions when I have been in need of encouragement, I have found it in something of hers. After Dr. Severn's most recent call, for instance, I discovered a journal she kept while expecting Georgiana. You must read it, Darcy. Whatever unhappiness your parents endured, in your mother's final months, they were hopeful."

He was glad for it. From what he could recall of the period of Georgiana's anticipation, his mother *had* seemed to have found a measure of peace. Both of his parents had seemed more in accord. He had feared it was a memory more wishful than accurate.

"I look forward to reading it," he said.

"There have been times, too, when I—" A soft thump in Elizabeth's dressing room drew their attention.

"Wait here." Darcy took a candle and went to investigate. The chamber was empty, but he found the pounce pot on the floor beside the escritoire, its powder spilled onto the rug.

"Your pounce pot fell," he said.

"I moved it when I retrieved Mrs. Tilney's letters." She stood in the doorway, ignoring his direction to stay put. "I must have left it too close to the edge of the desk. I have been dropping things more and more often of late, but this is the first time I have managed to do so from such a distance."

He set the small vessel back to rights. The maid could attend to the powder in the morning.

They returned to the bedchamber. Elizabeth arched her back and put a hand to the base of her spine. He felt a twinge of guilt at having been away so long, forcing her to deal with Lady Catherine alone and work hard to cover his absence at a time when simply moving through each day presented enough challenges for her.

"Is my son a heavy burden?" he asked.

She smiled softly. "Our child is heavy, but no burden."

He helped her into bed and she lay on her side while he rubbed her back. "Is there anything more I can do to improve your comfort?"

"Inform your daughter that she can commence her dancing lessons *after* she is born."

"I shall, but I make no guarantee that the child will listen. What else?"

"Tell me I am not grown exceedingly fat. My mother says I am big as a house."

"You have far to go before you reach the size of Pemberley." He helped her roll onto her back so that he could meet her gaze. "And to me, you have never looked more handsome." He kissed her. "Anything more?"

"Solve this Northanger Abbey puzzle so that we can send your aunt back to Rosings—and never have to deal with the righteous Mr. Melbourne or that officious Mr. Chase again."

"All three of them would claim that they are only doing their duty."

"Perhaps they could do it with less zeal. Or redirect it. If Mr. Chase, for example, would only apply his sharp investigative talents to our cause instead of against it, the case would solve itself."

"It would have to."

She was pensive for a moment. "Darcy, what do you suppose happened to the nine ivories that disappeared from Northanger? General Tilney sounds by all accounts to have been an unpleasant man, but I have to agree with his logic. It seems terribly suspicious that the statuettes went missing at the same time Mrs. Tilney visited Pemberley, especially after she suggested giving one of them to your mother. And she was so certain after her return that the birth your mother anticipated would proceed smoothly—perhaps because she left behind nine ivories to replace the one Lady Catherine retained?"

"If my mother received the ivories from Mrs. Tilney, she would not have withheld them from their rightful owner when he demanded them back."

"Even to protect her friend from his wrath?"

He paused to contemplate. His mother had been a woman of strong loyalties, and the general, a harsh man. Darcy doubted she would knowingly abet theft, but if she had accepted the ivories from Mrs. Tilney with the false assurance of the general's sanction, then later learned he had not consented, might she have kept silent?

"If she did harbor the ivories, upon Mrs. Tilney's death she would have surrendered them to the general. But none of Mrs. Tilney's letters suggest any complicity on my mother's part. In fact, they indicate the opposite."

Elizabeth sat up. "Perhaps Lady Anne never knew she had them. Consider, Darcy—during her stay, Helen Tilney spent a great deal of time with her hands in the soil of your mother's new garden. She could have buried the statuettes without anyone's knowledge. Did you notice how often she referred to the garden after she returned to Northanger? And the quilt she created—it is in the nursery. Its pattern depicts the garden. I believe it possible that she was trying to tell Lady Anne the ivories were somewhere in the garden, without making an explicit statement that would compromise your mother. Perhaps the quilt holds a clue to their whereabouts."

He reviewed the letters. Indeed, Mrs. Tilney mentioned the garden in nearly every one. "She specifically refers to lilies of the valley and marigolds. The lilies of the valley appear in her condolence letter, but she brings up the marigolds repeatedly."

Elizabeth laughed softly. "The marigolds. Of course."

"Why 'of course'?"

"Marigolds—Mary's Gold. She buried her treasure with Mary's gold."

"If she did, we will unearth it tomorrow."

They then set aside thoughts of ivories and letters and people from the past. He asked what else had transpired during his absence, and enquired more closely about her health. He was glad Georgiana had seized the initiative and sent for Dr.

Severn. He was also glad the doctor was due to return soon and remain with them for the remainder of their wait. Elizabeth's time approached faster than he cared to contemplate.

The sound of a door opening in Elizabeth's dressing room drew their notice toward the open doorway. "Who enters?" Darcy asked.

One of the housemaids came to the doorway. "Begging your pardon, sir, ma'am." She offered a flustered curtsy. "I just banked Mrs. Wickham's fire one last time before retiring, and I thought I would check yours as well. I did not expect to find you awake. I am terribly sorry to have disturbed you."

"Thank you, Jenny," Elizabeth said. "Our fire is fine."

"Again, my apologies, ma'am. Good night." She left them, closing the door behind her.

"Lydia's fire is restored. One crisis addressed," Elizabeth said as she settled into bed. "Lavish some attention on Lady Catherine after breakfast and a second will be dispatched. I then need only find a husband for Mary sometime between dinner and tea, and all of our houseguests will be content."

Darcy snuffed out the candle and joined her. "How long do you expect that to last?"

"Approximately six minutes."

Thirty-three

Our garden is putting in order by a man who bears a remarkably good character.

—Jane Austen, letter to Cassandra

Elizabeth and Darcy found Lady Catherine waiting for them at the breakfast table, where Darcy's meal comprised three courses: an upbraiding for his neglect of his aunt, a litany of the evils Elizabeth had perpetrated against her, and a generous portion of indignation over her ladyship's being forced to coexist in the same house as Mrs. Wickham. Fortunately, only Elizabeth overheard her criticisms; Darcy moved their discussion to a more private venue when her parents entered the breakfast room, and Lydia slept so late that she missed breakfast altogether.

Utterly unable to occupy herself, Mrs. Bennet spent the morning following Elizabeth from room to room, prattling details of a scheme she had devised for introducing Mary to every eligible gentleman in Derbyshire. Elizabeth half-listened, until an absent nod of her own and subsequent squeal of delight on her mother's part awakened her to the danger of inattentive head movements. She was then forced to give her mother her full concentration lest she accidentally agree to something she would regret. She was still not altogether sure what had inspired the squeal, but felt certain she would find out at the worst possible moment in some horrifically mortifying manner.

Noon had passed before Elizabeth extricated herself to speak to Mr. Flynn in private. Mindful of her leg lest the unpredictable numbness occur again, she had intended to summon the gardener to the house. But four-and-twenty hours with her family had made her desperate to escape for at least a brief while, and she felt herself safe in walking the short distance to Lady Anne's garden.

She found Mr. Flynn near the marigold beds, which apparently had already undergone excavation. He was speaking to several of his undergardeners, his manner more agitated than she had ever witnessed in him, even when the Madonna lily had been stolen from the greenhouse. When he saw her, he dismissed his staff and came forward.

"You appear distressed, Mr. Flynn. What is the trouble?"

"Mrs. Darcy, some mischief-maker has dug up part of the garden. When I entered, I found an enormous pit and soil thrown everywhere. My staff can put it back together—by the time the marigolds bloom in summer no one will know the difference. But who would do such a thing?"

His news took her aback. At first sight, she had assumed Darcy had ordered the digging. But any such command would have gone through the head gardener, and would have been performed with greater care.

"None of your staff have any knowledge of it?"

"No, I have questioned them all. Whoever did this came during the night."

"Mr. Flynn, this might seem an odd query, but—was anything buried in that flower bed that the perpetrator might have wanted?"

"Nothing has ever been buried in this garden but plants, so far as I know."

Elizabeth regarded the gaping hole in the earth. Whoever had dug up the marigold beds had done a thorough job. If the ivories had indeed been buried there, they certainly had been found.

A sense of loss possessed her. Her belly constricted, as if her daughter, too, recognized it. Even worse than the ivories having slipped through her grasp was the fact that now she would never know whether Helen Tilney had hidden the treasure at Pemberley. She felt that she had let down Mrs. Tilney, missed by mere hours the revelation of a secret that had awaited discovery for more than twenty years.

She sighed heavily and turned back to Mr. Flynn. "I assure you, Mr. Darcy and I will endeavor to identify the culprit." She suspected Mrs. Stanford was somehow involved, but how Frederick Tilney's mistress had reached the same conclusion as Elizabeth about the marigolds and acted upon it was a matter about which she would have to speculate with Darcy. "In the meantime, Mr. Flynn, I need to speak with you on another subject."

"Of course, ma'am."

"Mr. Darcy and I have been seeking a strongbox that once belonged to Lady Anne. A carving of a Madonna lily graces its top, and a letter lock seals it shut. We have come to understand that on the day Lady Anne died, George Wickham had the box in his possession. Have you any knowledge of it?"

"That good-for-nothing bounder—I always knew he'd turn out a knave. Yes, I came upon him. Found him with a rock getting ready to smash the lock open. He tried to tell me it was his box and that he had simply forgotten the combination, but I took one look at the lily on the lid and suspected it belonged to Lady Anne. I snatched it up before he could damage it. He threatened to report me to his father and insist I be dismissed. I said, 'Go ahead, boy. Mr. Wickham is a good steward and a fair man. Let us see what he has to say about young scamps who repay the generosity of the Darcy family by stealing from them.' He blustered some more, but when I told him to get out of Lady Anne's garden and that I never wanted to catch sight of his worthless hide in it again, he took off fast enough."

That indeed sounded like Wickham. "What did you do with the strongbox?" she asked.

"Well, as I said, I thought it must belong to Lady Anne, but word had passed through the servants that the midwife was with her, so I could not ask her about it. And I did not want to leave it anywhere that scapegrace might find it again. I knew of a place in the garden where it would remain safe until her ladyship could retrieve it."

"Is it yet there?"

"Aye, it waits for her still. Or rather, I suppose it waits for you, Mrs. Darcy—as you are the lady of the house now."

He led her to one of the alcoves along the garden's perimeter. She remembered it well. This was where she had experienced the miraculous moment of quickening, where she had first felt her daughter stir within her. Without realizing it, she had been mere inches from the blessed statuette.

"Of the three alcoves, this was Lady Anne's favorite," he said. "When the Madonna lilies are in bloom, it offers the finest view. She spent a great deal of time here the summer before she died, resting or reading on this bench, sometimes simply contemplating."

With slow, deliberate actions, Mr. Flynn carefully mounted the stone bench and stood. Under ordinary circumstances, Elizabeth would have insisted on sparing him the climb, but given her shifting center of balance and the amount of grace with which she moved these days, the septuagenarian was probably the superior gymnast between them.

A large terra-cotta rosette adorned the wall behind the bench. With considerable effort, he lifted it away from the wall and set it down to reveal a niche behind.

Within the hollow rested a small rosewood box.

ELIZABETH AND DARCY stared at the small casket resting on the table between them. She had brought it straight to her dressing room, where Darcy had discovered her testing the letter lock.

"Would you care for a turn?" she offered.

"I have already attempted every word of four letters I could call to mind."

"That was nearly two decades ago. Surely your vocabulary has acquired a few more."

"None that my mother would have used."

So close and yet so far. She had first tried simply ANNE, which was apparently too simple. She had next tried Anne and George's initials without luck. So she'd tried LUCK, but the lock did not appreciate her sense of humor.

FITZ had failed, DEAR had disappointed, LADY had let her down. She had thought herself brilliant when LILY occurred to her, but evidently it had not occurred to Lady Anne. Nor had MARY or GOLD.

"We are opening this lock if I have to retrieve Dr. Johnson's dictionary from the library and attempt every word in it," she said.

"Actually, that idea has merit. At least we would be applying a method instead of random guesses. But perhaps my mother's correspondence would be a better place to start. Or her journal—particularly the entry where she mentions the lock."

She retrieved the journal, George and Anne's love notes, and the Tilney letters. She started with the journal. "The entry about the lock does not offer many inspiring four-letter choices. I doubt we shall meet success with *that, have, take,* or *whim.* Some of the other entries hold more promising possibilities. Try *baby.*"

He did, and shook his head.

"*Safe*? *Gift*? *Born*?"

No. No. No.

More failures followed. She abandoned the journal and turned to the love notes. She began with the last—the one George had written to Anne when Georgiana was conceived. For some reason, she was partial to it, perhaps because, unlike the breathless infatuation of the early letters, it bespoke a deeper, time-tested affection. She skimmed to the end of the now-familiar lines, to the final paragraph she had read countless times. It had never before made her gasp, as she did presently.

Of course! Why had she not thought of it?

"Darcy," she said, barely able to contain her excitement, "try *love*."

He rotated the four rings to L-O-V-E and tugged on the lock. It remained securely closed.

"Let me attempt it."

Darcy relinquished the box. Elizabeth spun the rings out and back into position—with the same result. The lock would not budge.

She deflated. "I was so certain." It had seemed such an obvious, natural word for Lady Anne to have chosen. So intuitive. *Love conquers all.* Apparently, today it did not.

They spent another half hour in futile attempts, interspersed with speculation about Helen Tilney's ivories and who had dug up the marigold beds. Darcy shared her opinion that somehow Mrs. Stanford and her accomplices were involved.

"I wish we knew Wickham's present whereabouts," Darcy said. "If he is in the neighborhood, he could easily have stolen onto the grounds last night."

"Lydia says he escorted her as far as Lambton, then returned to Newcastle."

"With Wickham, that means nothing. He could have lied to her, or prevailed upon her to lie to us."

"It would have to be the former. Lydia is incapable of keeping anything to herself." She rotated the rings to TALE, without reward. "Yet even if Wickham is the offender, how did he come to suspect the ivories lay beneath the marigolds only hours before we intended to seek them there ourselves?"

"Might your sister have eavesdropped on our conversation? She was up and about late last night—as were my aunt and your mother. She might have then slipped from the house to meet with Wickham. How did she appear at breakfast this morning?"

"She did not appear at all." Had a nocturnal rendezvous

with her husband led to Lydia's late rising? Her sister had never been one to welcome the day at an early hour. "I dislike contemplating Lydia practicing such deceit upon me. If we are casting a suspicious eye toward our relations, I would much rather blame your aunt."

"You believe my aunt conspires with Frederick Tilney's mistress?"

"No, with Mr. Wickham—he is such a favorite of hers." ROSE met with rejection. "I suggest that Mrs. Stanford and company might not be our culprits at all. I caught Lady Catherine prowling in my dressing room during your absence, and for a time I was unable to locate Helen Tilney's letters. Perhaps her ladyship borrowed the letters and drew her own conclusions from them. She may speculate that your mother hid her statuette with the others. Or she might want all the ivories for herself."

"Even if my aunt has taken up espionage, I doubt she has ever held a shovel in her life."

"No, but that would not prevent her from instructing someone else in its use. She has servants here at her command." She pushed the box away, having exhausted her four-letter vocabulary at present, and asked the question that weighed most heavily on her mind. "The culprit's identity aside, was he successful? Did he find the Northanger ivories?"

"If he did, he is long gone. If he did not"—an uneasy expression crossed Darcy's face—"he may yet lurk about Pemberley."

"Still trying to find the ivories before we do." She became more hopeful. Perhaps the Northanger ivories had not slipped through their grasp after all. But if Helen Tilney had not buried them beneath the marigolds, where had she hidden them? The crib quilt came to mind again. Mrs. Tilney could not have sewn the ivories themselves into it—they were too large to go unnoticed—but had she secreted within the stitches some key to their whereabouts?

"I should like to take a closer look at the quilt Helen Tilney made," she said.

They hid the strongbox in a secure location and went to the nursery. All was prepared for the imminently anticipated new Darcy, and Elizabeth realized that she had very little time remaining in which to contemplate such matters as ivories and letter locks. Tiny caps and tinier fingers, hungry cries and toothless smiles would soon consume her attention. She still contemplated the birth itself with apprehension, but the discovery of Lady Anne's strongbox lent her courage. Surely they would find a way to open it and access the Madonna and Child statuette before she was brought to bed. If they were also to solve the Northanger puzzle and clear the Darcy name before the birth, however, they would have to do so quickly.

She looked toward the windows for the quilt, but it no longer hung between them. It was on the floor.

Torn into countless pieces.

Thirty-four

Elizabeth suspected herself to be the first creature who had ever dared to trifle with so much dignified impertinence.

—Pride and Prejudice

The quilt was mutilated, the blocks torn apart, the top ripped from its backing. Whoever had visited destruction upon it had done a thorough job of profaning a gift whose stitches had bound together the fabric of two women's lives. And an equally effective job of robbing the quilt of any clue it might have held.

The sight sickened Elizabeth. Her stomach weakened; a low pain began in her back and radiated to her abdomen. She sank into a nearby rocking chair.

Darcy observed her with concern. "Has your leg fallen numb again?"

She shook her head. "I shall be fine in a moment." She looked at him in astonishment. "Who—"

"I do not know, but I intend to find out. Unlike the garden vandalism, this offense must have been committed by someone within the house, and no one will rest tonight until my questions have been answered."

When she recovered from the shock, Darcy escorted her

back to her dressing room. He ordered her some tea and sat with her awhile after Jenny brought it. Then he departed to begin his interrogation.

Elizabeth tried to distract herself by returning to the strongbox and its letter lock, but it could not hold her attention. She found herself repeating failed combinations as the image of Helen Tilney's destroyed handiwork continually intruded into her thoughts. The remains of the lovingly created baby quilt kept calling to mind another innocent victim of violence, the child she had read about yesterday in the Prioress's Tale. She shuddered again as she had upon reading it—what a dark story to be told by a character who wore a brooch inscribed with "Love conquers all." Or whatever the Latin words were that Georgiana had read aloud.

She paused. *I have taken the precaution of putting a lock on the casket. . . . I think Madame Eglentyne would approve.*

She scooped up the lockbox.

The large tome of Chaucer's complete works remained in her morning room. She found the chamber blessedly free of Lady Catherine, her mother, or anyone else who might have considered herself at liberty to make use of it. The book lay where she had left it, its massive weight apparently having rendered it immune from the susceptibility of other written material at Pemberley to disappear and reappear at unpredictable intervals. She set Lady Anne's box on the desk, went to the book, and rapidly flipped pages until she found what she sought.

And theron heng a brooch of gold ful sheene, on which ther was first write a crowned A, and after Amor vincit omnia.

She rotated the rings of the lock. A-M-O-R.

It opened.

Her heart pounding, she removed the lock from the hasp and lifted the lid. Velvet cushions surrounded a small cylindrical object covered in a soiled, tattered scrap of fabric. She held her breath as she reached inside and carefully lifted the treasure from its cradle. Slowly, she unwrapped the fragile mantle to reveal the Madonna and Child.

She released her breath. The statuette was exquisite, reflecting at once its medieval origins and an ageless veneration for its subject. The ivory captured the Christ child as a boy of perhaps two, offering Mary an apple as she held him. Her face reflected serenity Elizabeth wished she could borrow, and indeed, gazing upon the figurine, she felt a sense of calm envelop her.

Until a jarring voice shattered it.

"I see you have recovered my statue for me."

She turned so quickly that she almost dropped the ivory. Not trusting herself to keep a firm grasp on the statuette, she set it back in the cushioned box. She then walked toward Lady Catherine so that she blocked Darcy's aunt from the prize.

"It is not your ivory. Your mother gave it to Lady Anne, who in turn passed it to me."

"Insolent, grasping upstart! How dare you claim my mother's heirloom as your own? Your pretension exceeds all bounds of tolerance."

"And your selfishness surpasses even that of which I had thought you capable."

"Hand over my ivory or I shall take it for myself."

Elizabeth had done with her ladyship's riding roughshod over everyone in her path. Physical discomfort and the day's events had also rendered her cross in general. Women with swollen ankles should not be provoked.

"Attempt to seize it, and I shall have *you* arrested for theft."

Lady Catherine tried to circumvent her, but Elizabeth advanced, her enlarged abdomen leading the charge. Her ladyship retreated, backing through the room's main doorway and into the chamber beyond. Apparently, having achieved the size of a house held its advantages.

Darcy's aunt regarded her icily. "You shall regret this, Mrs. Darcy."

A noise behind Elizabeth momentarily drew her attention. In the pier glass beyond Lady Catherine, she saw Jenny enter the morning room to perform her daily duties. Elizabeth returned her gaze to Darcy's aunt and lowered her voice.

"I doubt it."

Her ladyship's own gaze swept over Elizabeth derisively. "I thank heaven my sister did not live to see what an unworthy creature has assumed her place at Pemberley. She would despise you."

"I doubt that, too."

Lady Catherine raised her chin, cast a final, dismissive glance at Elizabeth, and marched off. Elizabeth watched her go until she disappeared from view. Then she went back into the morning room to retrieve the statuette.

Jenny was gone.

So was the ivory.

Thirty-five

This seems to me the best plan, and the maid will be most conveniently near.

—Jane Austen, letter to Cassandra

Elizabeth peered into the box twice—thrice—as if repeatedly looking where the ivory ought to have been would make it reappear. She picked up the scrap of cloth that still lay in the bottom and stared at it. Then she turned in a slow circle, her gaze ricocheting around the room as her bewildered mind struggled to absorb the obvious. Jenny had stolen the ivory.

Jenny, cheerful Jenny.

Deceitful Jenny.

If Elizabeth had felt ill upon discovering the quilt, that sensation was nothing compared to the wave that passed through her now. Her insides turned to water. The pain in her lower back returned, spreading forward into her belly and upper legs. She shakily lowered herself into a chair, but sitting down did not help.

Her thoughts bounced from her discomfort to Jenny's betrayal and back. Had Jenny merely happened upon the statuette and taken advantage of the opportunity to steal it? Or had she been scheming against Elizabeth and Darcy since her arrival? Was Jenny responsible for the disappearance of other items? The destruction of the quilt? How closely was she working with the Northanger Abbey imposters?

Her pain eased but discomfort remained. She recalled with alarm Lucy and Graham's mysterious "illness" at Northanger, and that it had arisen after eating a meal the conspirators gave them. Jenny had served her tea earlier. Dear Lord—had she put something in it?

She felt steady enough to rise and pull the bell. Fear for the baby overwhelmed her. Dr. Severn was expected today but had not arrived. She needed help.

She asked the answering servant to summon Mrs. Godwin posthaste, and to locate both Darcy and Mrs. Reynolds for her. As she waited, she clutched the scrap of cloth that she still held in her hand and prayed for her child and herself.

By the time Darcy arrived, she was feeling better. The pain had subsided and she had gained control of her panic. He immediately read in her face, however, that all was not well.

"Tell me," he said.

The details came out in a rush. "I opened the lock—Lady Catherine found me—While we were arguing, Jenny stole the ivory. Now I feel ill—I fear she may have adulterated my tea."

Darcy turned white. "Dr. Severn—"

"Has not arrived yet. I have summoned Mrs. Godwin."

He nodded, still trying to digest all she had told him. "Describe what you mean by 'ill.' "

"Similar to what I experienced in the nursery. I am presently much improved over what I was a few minutes ago."

"How did the tea taste?"

"Strong. But not unusual."

"Let us hope Jenny's treachery ends with theft."

Mrs. Reynolds entered. "Mrs. Godwin has been sent for," she reported.

Darcy informed her that both Mrs. Godwin and Dr. Severn were to attend Elizabeth in her bedchamber directly they arrived. He also issued instructions, which he would repeat to the steward, for the apprehension of Jenny. The housekeeper departed to carry out his orders.

He had delivered the commands coolly, but when he turned to her and said, "Let us get you to bed," she could hear strain in his voice. And when he touched her, his hands betrayed a slight tremor.

Despite her assertions that she possessed sufficient strength to walk—not to mention sufficient girth to injure him—he insisted on carrying her to their bedchamber. Lucy helped her undress while he spoke to Mr. Clarke, and he returned just as she settled into bed. He kissed her forehead and held her hand and said all the things people say when assuring a loved one she will be fine while inwardly fearing she will not.

He studied her intently. "How do you feel now?"

She did not want to admit it, even to herself, but she was starting to feel worse again. Just then Mrs. Godwin arrived.

"Good afternoon, Mrs. Darcy. How are you today?"

"Unwell." And afraid.

Mrs. Godwin seemed to grasp her unvoiced reply along with the spoken. She sat on the edge of the bed and took one of Elizabeth's hands. The other, which yet held the scrap of cloth from Lady Anne's box, Darcy retained.

She explained her symptoms and the possibility that an unknown substance slipped into her tea might be its cause. Just as she finished, the pain began again. Mrs. Godwin asked her several questions about its location and intensity, listening closely to her replies and putting her hand on Elizabeth's abdomen. Though the ache was stronger this time than last, with Mrs. Godwin present she was not as frightened as before.

When the pain subsided again, Mrs. Godwin turned to Darcy.

"Sir, find this Jenny to settle any doubt. But I do not believe your wife has been poisoned." She looked at Elizabeth and smiled. "My dear, you are in labor."

Thirty-six

He cannot be the instigator of the three villains in horsemen's great coats, by whom she will hereafter be forced into a travelling-chaise and four, which will drive off with incredible speed.

—Northanger Abbey

With Elizabeth in Mrs. Godwin's care for the present, Darcy went in pursuit of more information about Jenny. His foremost concern was whether she had been found, but he also intended to learn everything Mrs. Reynolds could tell him about her, from her work habits to her parish of origin.

He berated himself for his blindness. He should have dismissed her the day he discovered her in the library with Wickham. Now God only knew the extremes to which her perfidy reached. They had not anticipated the child's arrival for another fortnight at least. He prayed Mrs. Godwin's diagnosis was accurate, that it was merely labor that incapacitated Elizabeth, with no complications caused by malice.

He rarely went belowstairs, but he wanted to speak to Mrs. Reynolds without delay, and also to search Jenny's room. He hoped to determine as much as he could as quickly as he could, so that he might return to Elizabeth. Mrs. Godwin had said that her pains were infrequent enough that the birth was still many hours off. He grew impatient for Dr. Severn's arrival. He would not be easy until the entire ordeal was over, but his anxiety would lessen with the physician in the house.

He found Mrs. Reynolds in the main servants' hall, and they moved to a spot just inside the exterior door where they could talk without danger of being overheard. Yes, Mr. Clarke had come and coordinated efforts with her. No, Jenny had not been found yet. Yes, the search was widespread but discreet. No, they did not believe she had escaped the house. Yes, several men swept the park even now.

As he talked to the housekeeper, an unfamiliar chaise and four stopped at the servants' entrance. He watched to see who emerged, but no one did. Instead, a thin figure darted toward the carriage from the hedges. Jenny.

He ran outside, reaching her just as she was about to climb into the carriage. He grabbed her shoulders and pulled her away from the vehicle, but not before she managed to thrust a small object to one of the passengers within. He looked into the gentleman's face.

"Wickham!"

Panic flashed across Wickham's countenance. The driver slapped the horses, and the carriage sped off. Gripping Jenny tightly by the shoulders, Darcy tried to get a glimpse of the other passenger, but he—or she—wore a hooded cloak that obscured the face.

A servant began closing Pemberley's gate. But the vehicle barreled through and continued at breakneck speed out of the park.

Impulse urged him to pursue—catching the conspirators meant clearing his name. But Elizabeth needed him within. And as far as his wife was concerned, he held the most important villain in his grasp.

Once the carriage disappeared from view, Jenny ceased struggling. He turned her around to look into her face. Her eyes were wide with fright.

He fought to maintain his calm, to remain composed

when he wanted to shout. "Answer my questions truthfully and it will go easier for you."

She nodded shakily.

"Did you adulterate Mrs. Darcy's tea this afternoon?"

She swallowed. "No—no, sir."

He studied her so intensely for signs of prevarication that she looked as if his gaze alone might knock her down. "Did you today, or at any time, administer anything to her without her knowledge? Any substance that could harm her or make her ill?"

"No, sir—nothing like that!"

"Has anyone else done so?"

"No! At least, not that anybody told me about. No one wants to hurt Mrs. Darcy."

"God help you if you are lying to me."

Her shoulders trembled. "I swear to you, I am not."

She appeared so rattled that he tended to believe her. Though she might practice duplicity when nobody watched, he doubted she could gather enough composure at present to deliver a falsehood convincingly. He relaxed his grip, but not his stance or expression.

"What did you give Mr. Wickham just now?"

"A statuette."

"That you stole from Pemberley."

"I'm sorry, sir. Truly—"

"*Sorry?* Do you know the value of that ivory? How long it has been in my family?"

"Please don't send me to gaol, sir!" She began to cry. "My sisters and I—we've got no one since our father died, and they said they would pay me well. All I had to do was keep my ears open and borrow a few things from time to time."

Gaol was the least of the evils she faced. Though the statuette's history rendered it priceless to him and Elizabeth, its monetary worth made its theft a transport or hanging offense for Jenny.

"What else have you taken?"

"N-Nothing, sir. Nothing I kept. I always returned the letters and such after they were finished looking at them."

So Jenny was responsible for all the misplaced correspondence. Elizabeth would be relieved to know their son had not deprived her of her wits after all.

"Who are 'they'?"

"Mr. Wickham and Mrs. Stanford."

That much he had surmised. But who was the third conspirator, the one who had posed as Frederick Tilney? "Does anyone else work for or with them?"

"I do not know all their business, sir. I only do what they tell me."

"How did you come to work for them?"

"My father owned an inn at Newcastle—the Boar's Head. I used to help with the serving—two of my sisters still do, working for the new owner, but he couldn't afford to keep all of us. Anyway, Mr. Wickham dines there frequently, and so did Mrs. Stanford's captain. One night Mr. Wickham and Captain Tilney got to talking, like gentlemen do after they've first got to drinking. Mr. Wickham mentions that he grew up at a place called Pemberley and brags about his connections to the Darcy family. The captain says he has heard of Pemberley and the Darcys from his father, and asks all sorts of questions about the late mistress and some statuettes she might have had. I kept my mouth shut and the tankards full, but Mr. Wickham, he can't be in a room without having his eyes on three girls at once and he noticed me listening.

"Well, then my father died and our money ran out, and after the captain's accident Mr. Wickham comes to me and asks do I remember that conversation, and I say yes. He says he can get me a position at Pemberley if I'm willing to help with some business the captain left unfinished. I ask what kind of business and he says the statuettes are hidden someplace at Pemberley and you and Mrs. Darcy are looking for them but if we find them first I shan't ever have to worry about money again. I say that sounds like stealing and he says the ivories really belonged to Captain Tilney, who wanted to give them to his lady except he got killed first. Nell was sick and the two littlest ones had no shoes and our landlord was at the door every day looking for his rent, so I agreed. Mr. Wickham brought me here and got me a position as a housemaid, just like he said."

Darcy would speak to Mrs. Reynolds later to learn how Jenny had come to be hired. The housekeeper knew Wickham was not to be trusted, so some intermediary sympathetic to the former steward's son must have brought Jenny to her attention.

"What instructions did you receive?"

"To use my access as a household servant to learn all I could about the ivories."

"In other words, you were to spy on Mrs. Darcy and me."

She dropped her gaze. "Yes, sir. Whenever I had news, I sent word to Mr. Wickham or Mrs. Stanford, and one of them would meet me. About a fortnight ago, Mrs. Stanford came to Lambton and has been there ever since. Mr. Wickham is there now, too."

Captain Tilney's mistress had probably come directly after Darcy had seen her in Newcastle, his visit having inadvertently alerted her to developments in his and Elizabeth's own investigations. Under different circumstances, Darcy might have appreciated the irony of Mrs. Stanford's being at Pemberley whilst he traveled the country searching for her.

"Where do they go now?"

"I do not know for certain, sir, but I think Northanger Abbey. When nothing turned up in the marigold beds last night after all of Mr. Wickham's digging, they said something about Mrs. Tilney's garden."

Wickham had violated the flower beds. He had suspected as much. "What can you tell me about the quilt in the nursery?"

She looked up quickly. Guilt flashed across her features. "I feel terrible about that, sir. Truly I do! It was such a pretty quilt. But after I told them what Mrs. Darcy said, about it maybe holding a clue, and then finding nothing in the garden with the marigolds, they insisted I see whether something was sewn inside. I didn't want to rip it apart, but they were terribly ugly about it. They said 'in for a penny, in for a pound,' and that I was already involved so deeply in their scheme that they had only to snitch to you and it would be Botany Bay for me." Her chin trembled again. "Please, sir—you won't send me to gaol, will you?"

Darcy, having experienced firsthand the horrors of gaol, could not lightly subject anybody to such an ordeal. Yet Jenny's offenses, particularly the theft of his mother's statuette, were grave.

"I shall have to give the matter further consideration. In the meantime, I will place you in the custody of Mr. Clarke." The steward would ensure Jenny was closely watched until Darcy could devote attention to her fate.

Just now, there was another woman at Pemberley whose welfare concerned him far more.

Thirty-seven

"I dare say we could do very well without you; but you men think yourselves of such consequence."

—*Isabella Thorpe,* Northanger Abbey

Mrs. Bennet waylaid Darcy en route to the bedchamber.

"Oh, Mr. Darcy, is it not exciting? Lizzy is brought to bed! I knew she was too fat to last another fortnight! But I do not believe my nerves can bear the waiting. Thank heaven the doctor is come—though he would not let me stay in the birthing room. Something about hearing himself think."

The news of Dr. Severn's arrival was most welcome. Darcy had not wanted to leave Elizabeth entirely in Mrs. Godwin's care while he dealt with Jenny, but he'd had no choice. Now the physician could take command.

He found the bedchamber scene much altered from what it had been when he departed. Tension greeted him at the door. Elizabeth was out of bed, leaning on Mrs. Godwin and Lucy for support. Dr. Severn stood beside them, pointing toward the bed and ordering her into it.

"Is aught amiss?" Darcy asked.

"I came in the room and found Mrs. Darcy walking

around, of all ridiculous notions," Dr. Severn said. "And this *midwife* encouraging her."

"I was uncomfortable in the bed," Elizabeth explained.

"Of course you are uncomfortable. You are giving birth, not hosting a ball. Now do as I tell you. Get back into bed and stay in your place."

"Indeed, Doctor," said Mrs. Godwin, "I do not see the harm in allowing Mrs. Darcy to—"

"Now that I am come, Mrs. Darcy has no further need of your learned advice. You may leave now."

"Perhaps Mrs. Godwin can assist you," Elizabeth said.

He glanced at both women disdainfully. "I do not require, nor desire, the assistance of an ignorant old woman. I have overseen hundreds of births."

"So have I," Mrs. Godwin said quietly. "And most benefit from additional sets of hands."

"Mrs. Darcy's maid and the other servants can perform any mundane tasks required."

Elizabeth looked at Dr. Severn with irritation. "But do you not think an experienced—"

"Get back in bed."

The physician clearly was not having the calming effect on Elizabeth—or himself, for that matter—that Darcy had intended when he'd engaged Dr. Severn last autumn. Indeed, the man's arrogance and conceit instead undermined Darcy's trust in his expertise. Increasing the distress of one's patient hardly seemed beneficial to anybody.

"Elizabeth, perhaps now that you have had your stretch, you might return to the bed," Darcy suggested, attempting to mollify both doctor and patient.

She cast him a look that said *Et tu, Darcy?* but acquiesced. While Dr. Severn glowered at the midwife, Darcy and Mrs. Godwin helped Elizabeth back into bed. Darcy noticed that she had secured the scrap of cloth from the statuette around her wrist.

"I found Jenny and questioned her thoroughly," he said. "She asserts that she added nothing to your tea, and I am inclined to believe her."

Relief crossed his wife's countenance, though plenty of distress remained. "Did she surrender the ivory?"

"Unfortunately, she had just passed it to Mr. Wickham and Mrs. Stanford when I discovered her, and I could not question her and pursue them at once. But we shall retrieve it, I promise you."

Another pain took hold of Elizabeth. A soft whimper escaped her. The pain was expected, but that fact did not make it any easier for Darcy to witness.

"Mrs. Darcy, will you cease that moaning?" Dr. Severn snapped. "It is most irritating, not to mention terribly unbecoming in a lady of your station."

"But I—" She gasped for breath between words. "*Hurt.*"

"You and every other woman in travail. What did you expect? Women are supposed to endure pain while giving birth. It is the natural way of things." He turned his back and began withdrawing his array of torture devices from his black bag. "Demonstrate some self-control, or we are in for a long night of it."

Elizabeth looked as if she were about to cry. She gripped Darcy's hand so tightly he thought his fingers would break. Did the doctor have no human compassion?

Mrs. Godwin took her other hand and rubbed the small of her back. "This one is almost over. Take a deep breath and release it slowly, as we did before. There now—it has passed. With the next pain, we shall count together again to distract you, all right?"

The midwife's words soothed Elizabeth, and she nodded. The afflicted expression left her face, replaced by one of trust and calm determination.

"You shall do nothing of the sort," Dr. Severn declared. "That ridiculous counting will drive *me* to distraction. Mrs. Godwin, I said you may leave. You as well, Mr. Darcy. The birthing chamber is no place for a man."

Darcy was beginning to think the same thing. At least, in regard to one man in particular.

"Dr. Severn, my wife's mother is downstairs in the yellow drawing room. I suspect you will find her in want of a tonic for her nerves. Kindly attend to her—and remain there unless Mrs. Godwin summons you."

"I do not understand you, sir."

"Then I shall speak more plainly. I am consigning my wife to Mrs. Godwin's care. You will assist her if she has need of you."

"*I* assist *her*? You cannot be serious!"

"Indeed, I am."

"I am a doctor—one of the most sought after in London. I received my training from the Royal College of Physicians. I will not be ordered about by some country midwife."

"I respect your training, Doctor. It is the reason I hired you. But your manner is adding to my wife's distress."

"So I am to take direction from a woman? I will not suffer such insult." He shoved his equipment back into his bag. "Mr. Darcy, I bid you good day. May your wife survive it."

Another pain seized Elizabeth, but the absence of Dr. Severn seemed to make this one easier for her to bear. When it had passed, she thanked him for banishing the physician. He was uneasy about the doctor's medical expertise walking out the door, but the departure of the man himself had also removed considerable anxiety from the room.

Mrs. Godwin helped Elizabeth find a more comfortable position in anticipation of her next pain. Then she turned to Darcy. "I have things well in hand here, sir, and your wife needs to focus on the work she has ahead. Bid her farewell for now."

He looked into Elizabeth's face. The last thing he wanted to do was leave her. He kissed her deeply, then continued to hold one hand to her cheek. He tried not to let the spectre of his mother's fate haunt him.

"You *will* see me again," she said.

"Is there anything else I can do for you? Would you like your mother with you after all?"

"I think perhaps I would."

"Lydia?"

She managed a laugh. "No. But if you would send for Jane?"

He should have thought of that himself. "Of course."

"And—" She hesitated.

"Name it, Elizabeth. If it is within my power, it is yours."

"It probably is not. But . . ." Beloved eyes, intense with the commencement of another pain, beseeched him. "I believe I would feel better if I had your mother's ivory."

The ivory that was even now speeding away. He could hardly bring himself to leave the room, let alone Pemberley. What if the unthinkable happened while he was gone?

Yet if he departed immediately and rode hell-for-leather, he might manage to overtake the fleeing carriage. He would be performing some useful function instead of impatiently pacing the gallery like a caged tiger. And if there were any truth in the family legends at all, he would be doing something to protect his wife and son through the danger of bringing him into the world.

Several servants entered, carrying in supplies. He turned to one of them. "Run to the stables as quickly as you can. Tell the groom to saddle Mercury."

Thirty-eight

"Do but look at my horse; did you ever see an animal so made for speed in your life?"

—*John Thorpe,* Northanger Abbey

Darcy urged his mount across the Derbyshire landscape, bleak and forlorn in the winter moonlight. Surely the villains' carriage could not be much farther ahead. He had stopped at Lambton to exchange Mercury for a fresh horse and enquire after the conspirators, and learned that they had just completed a stop of their own. They had paused to retrieve their luggage, and been further delayed by a quarrel amongst themselves as the trunks were loaded. Apparently, Wickham and Mrs. Stanford had been in favor of transferring to a post chaise, so as to benefit from the superior speed offered by a skilled postilion guiding rested animals, but their driver would not hear of it. He had insisted his horses could outstrip any post horses, that despite the short bait and additional encumbrance of luggage they should maintain a pace of fifteen miles per hour all the way to Gloucestershire, and that nothing ruins horses so much as rest.

Darcy was happy to let their driver attempt to prove his

point as he gained on them with every mile. He now watched for the carriage to come into view. What he would do when he at last overtook it, he had not quite worked out yet, but somehow he would come away from the encounter with Elizabeth's ivory in hand.

He reached the top of a rise and at last spotted a vehicle ahead. In the darkness, he could not at this distance identify it decisively as theirs, but the moon illuminated the road brightly enough that he could see it was no yellow bounder and carried no postboys. The carriage weaved across the road and back as it sped along, its driver apparently having trouble controlling the horses. He felt confident of its being the vehicle he pursued.

It approached a bend in the road. From his vantage point, Darcy could see a post chariot traveling from the opposite direction. This carriage seemed to be headed into the curve at a more sensible speed, under the control of a competent postilion. And thank goodness, for as the conspirators' chaise reached the bend, it overturned, and the oncoming chariot narrowly averted becoming part of the accident.

The undamaged vehicle stopped. The postboy sprang toward the wreckage; his passenger emerged just as Darcy himself reached the chariot. He was surprised to recognize the traveler.

"Mr. Tilney!"

"Mr. Darcy! I did not expect to see you until I reached Pemberley."

In all the distraction of the day's events, Darcy had utterly forgotten that this was the date upon which Henry Tilney was to have commenced his visit.

"I am in pursuit of our imposters. I believe them to be in that carriage."

"Oh, dear. Let us hope they have survived so as not to deprive the courts the pleasure of hanging them."

They soon determined that the villains indeed lived to lie another day. Somehow, the two passengers managed to escape serious injury, though Mr. Wickham complained of an injured ankle. Darcy could not say he felt the slightest bit of pity watching him grimace as he dragged himself out of the wreckage. As soon as he emerged, Darcy demanded the ivory from him. Having no choice, Wickham relinquished it.

"Mr. Tilney, it gives me no pleasure to introduce you to Mr. George Wickham, to whom I have the misfortune of being related by marriage."

"Fitz, you wound me."

"Address me in that manner again and I shall force you to walk home."

The other passenger had accepted the postilion's aid and leaned on his arm for support.

"This woman is, I believe, Mrs. Stanford," Darcy said, "also known as Dorothy the housekeeper. Mrs. Stanford, I understand you were acquainted with Mr. Tilney's late brother."

"Why—" Mr. Tilney peered at her intensely. And chuckled. "Isabella Thorpe!"

"Mr. Tilney!" She released the postboy and staggered to Henry with as much charm as one who has just been overturned in a carriage can muster. "How good it is to see you after all this time! I declare, it has been an age! How is your wife, my dear friend Catherine? I long to see her. Thank heavens you happened along when you did. I am sure you are wondering what Mr. Darcy can possibly be talking about. This is all the most frightful misunderstanding."

Darcy glanced enquiringly at Mr. Tilney. "I gather you have already met?"

"Let us say that Mrs. Stanford's interest in my family—and in Frederick in particular—considerably predates her marriage to the colonel. I see the years have altered you little, Mrs. Stanford. You are what you always were."

The accident had loosed several locks of her hair. She tucked one of these behind her ear and smiled coyly. "You flatter me, Mr. Tilney."

"Do I? That was not my intent." He turned to Darcy. "Is Mr. Wickham the man who posed as my brother, then?"

"No, merely a conspirator in the plot. I have not yet identified who impersonated the captain."

The driver of the overturned carriage had been thrown from the vehicle. He lay several yards distant, where the postilion found him.

"What the devil?" exclaimed a familiar voice. "Sneak up on a fellow in the dark, will you? Damn, but my wrist hurts!"

"I believe that is our imposter," said Darcy.

With the aid of Tilney's servant, the hapless driver stumbled toward their party. He was indeed the height and build of the false captain who had met them at Northanger. He appeared far less mysterious, however, with two eyes. "Devil take that curve! A hairpin turn if I ever saw one. A dozen coaches must roll on it each day. If I lived within a hundred miles of here, I would rebuild the road myself. I say—Tilney!"

"Mr. Thorpe." Henry turned to Darcy. "Mr. Darcy, meet Mr. John Thorpe, Mrs. Stanford's brother."

Mr. Thorpe was found to have suffered a sprained wrist, which he complained about to the point where one would think he had broken his arm. At least the injury relieved him of the danger of driving any vehicle through the treacherous curve again. That fact did not, however, prevent him from rattling on about its hazards. "The road positively bends in half. A death trap! Absolutely perilous!"

"Mr. Thorpe," Henry said, "if you must air your vocabulary, I would prefer you use it to explain the night you entertained the Darcys at Northanger Abbey. As my brother."

"Upon my soul, that was a jolly night, was it not, Mr. Darcy? Isabella always could design a wickedly clever scheme. The look on your faces when I first walked in the room—it was capital! Never had such an amusing evening in my life. So glad Captain Tilney issued the invitation before he died—I was happy to step in when he could not keep the engagement."

"To what end?" Darcy asked.

"To learn about those ivories the captain promised Belle, that's what."

"I somehow doubt my brother promised Mrs. Stanford anything of the sort."

"I am certain that he meant to give them to me," Isabella said. "Frederick had contemplated contacting the Darcys from the time he learned of Mr. Wickham's connection to the family. When Wickham heard from his wife that they were looking for some sort of treasure at Pemberley, I said, 'See? The Darcys know something about those ivories after all. If they find them, you should ask for them back.' He laughed and said, 'You would like that, would you not?' So I know he wanted me to have them." She sighed dramatically. "Since poor Frederick did not live long enough to give them to me himself, completing his unfinished business was the least I could do for him."

"You mean for yourself," Mr. Tilney said.

"Oh, Belle said she would share them," Mr. Thorpe said. "Once the captain died, she fretted that you would misunderstand Frederick's intentions, so we had to find them for ourselves. You are a cagey fellow, Mr. Darcy! Could not get much information from you directly, or find a thing in your trunks while you were at dinner, but Belle heard enough through the servants' doors. Shame you had to go and spoil everything by leaving our party before Wickham had the maid installed at Pemberley. He and Belle had a fix for that, though. What did you think of the cane? An exceedingly faithful copy, was it not?"

"It was." Darcy looked at Wickham. "I understand a Mr. George Darcy commissioned it."

Wickham grinned smugly. "Mr. George Darcy purchased a great many things that season. I never imagined at the time how useful that particular item would prove."

"But the diamonds were *my* inspiration," Isabella said boastfully. "They were the very thing to prevent your returning home too soon. The letter to the constable was mine, as well. Did it not work beautifully?"

"You always were a practiced letter writer," Mr. Tilney said.

"Just as well you did leave early, though," said Mr. Thorpe. "That plaguesome old butler returned before we were expecting him and we had to brush off."

Darcy could scarcely believe his ears. They had plunged him into a morass of dire legal difficulties simply to delay his return home for a few days? Moreover, they appeared utterly insensible to the consequences of their actions. "Do you comprehend that I faced hanging for the crime of which I stood accused?"

"Fiddlesticks!" said Mr. Thorpe. "You are a gentleman. What is the law to you? It will not give a gentleman trouble."

"We shall see whether you still believe that come the morrow."

"Mrs. Stanford," said Mr. Tilney, "if you wanted something by which to remember my brother, why did you not simply take the diamonds for yourself while you were at Northanger Abbey? You could have dispensed with the hunt for the statuettes altogether."

"The ivories held more value—*sentimental* value." Isabella adopted an innocent expression. "Besides, if I had kept those diamonds, that would be stealing. The statuettes, in addition to having been promised to me, were just lying around somewhere waiting to be found. We would have been rescuing them, really."

Darcy yet held his mother's statuette in his hand. "As you rescued this one?"

"I cannot imagine why that servant girl thrust that statue at us. Of course that one is yours. There must have been some misunderstanding."

Much as he wanted to interrogate the party further, Darcy was anxious to return home. He was also in serious doubt as to whether any of the accomplices had anything useful to say. He and Mr. Tilney determined that they would all proceed to the inn at Lambton, where they could send for the apothecary and the constable. The conspirators rode in Mr. Tilney's post chariot while Darcy followed on horseback.

By the time everybody emerged from Mr. Tilney's carriage at the inn, the party had apparently become engaged in a quarrel over who was to blame for their having been caught.

"We would not have overturned if you had not insisted upon driving."

"It was not my driving, it was the deuced road!"

"Had we traveled post, Mr. Darcy would not have overtaken us."

"You are the one who insisted we stop at Lambton to retrieve our belongings. . . ."

Darcy was rather glad for his own solitary journey to the inn. Henry Tilney appeared the way Darcy felt after an hour spent with his mother-in-law.

The conspirators entered the inn. After asking a servant to send for the constable, Mr. Tilney shook his head in bemusement and looked at Darcy. "One wonders how three such shallow, selfish people managed to devise a plot of such serious consequence."

"One wonders how the three of them managed to cooperate long enough to execute it."

"It must relieve you to apprehend them and settle the matter of the diamonds. Now they will stand trial in Gloucestershire instead of you."

"I am indeed glad for it, but I confess to distraction. When I left Pemberley to pursue them, Mrs. Darcy had just been brought to childbed."

Henry's face lit with genuine delight. "That is capital news. May I congratulate you on a son, or on a daughter?"

"I do not yet know."

"Good heavens, Mr. Darcy! You should be at home, not chasing ruffians about the countryside. Why did you not say something sooner?"

"I did not want to leave you alone with our merry trio."

"I have matters well in hand, and shall come to Pemberley in a few days with a report, if you like. But for now I bid you adieu. Get thee to your wife, my friend."

Thirty-nine

How well the expression of heart-felt delight, diffused over his face, became him.

—Pride and Prejudice

He arrived too late.

The moment he entered the house, Darcy sensed that something within it had changed. Elizabeth's trial had ended. Though he had won her prize back for her, returned with the ivory in hand, he had not reached her in time.

And she had come through her travail just fine.

His heart nearly stopped—and his breathing did—upon seeing her again. And upon beholding his child for the first time.

'Twas the darkest hour of night when he passed into the bedchamber. No sign remained of the struggle this room had witnessed just hours earlier. All in the household, save Mrs. Godwin and a nurse attending mother and child, had gone to bed. He was spared any noisy effusions of Mrs. Bennet or blunt declarations from Lydia and could behold his wife in quiet as she lightly dozed, a tiny bundle at her side.

"They are both well," Mrs. Godwin assured him. "It was an easy birth—if birth can ever be called easy."

"Have I a son or daughter?"

"I shall let her tell you."

"I do not wish to wake her."

"She wants to see you."

Mrs. Godwin and the nurse left them in privacy. He approached the bed, beside which a single candle burned. Elizabeth's arm encircled the baby, wrapped so snugly in a small blanket that he could see only the child's head—closed eyes, wrinkled cheeks, an impossibly tiny nose, tufts of dark downy hair. Carefully, afraid he would somehow break the delicate form, he lifted his child from the bed and into his arms.

So light. So fragile. So utterly dependent.

At the removal of the infant, Elizabeth's maternal instincts awakened, and so did she. Her lips formed a smile, and her eyes held a contented, if sleepy, expression.

"I see you have met your daughter."

A daughter. The most wondrous word in the English language.

"You smile—your ordeal was not so terrible that you resent me as its cause?"

"I can think of more pleasant ways to spend an evening, but none that yield so great a reward."

"I have something for you." Shifting his daughter to one arm, he produced the ivory. "I am sorry I did not return with it in time."

She accepted the statuette from him. "I am sorry I sent you on such a desperate errand when you no doubt would have preferred to remain here."

"As the alternative was waiting with Lydia, I was glad for the occupation. And glad to have rescued the Madonna from the three villains who kidnapped her, before they had an opportunity to sell or damage the ivory."

"Though it would have been a comfort to have your mother's treasure with me during the birth, I found strength in other sources. A skilled midwife. My own determination. Your devotion. Even this." She traced a finger over the scrap of fabric yet secured to her wrist. "If I could not have the statuette itself, at least I could keep its mantle close to me." She removed the cloth now and wrapped the ivory back within it. "I also had my mother, do not forget. For a short time, at least."

"That did not last?"

"*She* did not last. Just as I was about to suggest she return to my father and Lydia, she fretted herself into a fainting fit."

He could not suppress a laugh. "Forgive me. Is she all right?"

"Oh, yes. I believe her loss of consciousness to have been beneficial to all parties. By the time she awoke, all was over, and her effusions could communicate entirely felicitous content."

"I am glad she proved of some use to you. I imagine a woman would generally want her mother present during her travail, when possible."

"This may sound odd, but I also seemed to feel *your* mother's presence. Perhaps it is all the reading of her letters and journal, and knowing I labored in the same room as she, that fixed her so strongly in my thoughts. But I sensed that somehow she, too, supported me during my trial. At times, I even believed I detected the scent of lilies."

"Were my mother alive, she most certainly would have wanted to be here."

They both gazed at their daughter. He thought he saw his mother in the line of her chin, his wife in the shape of her brow. He wished the small eyes would open so he could ascertain whose resemblance they bore, but their child already demonstrated a will of her own by remaining quite determinedly asleep.

"You were so certain I carried a boy—and I, that I carried a girl—that we never settled upon a name for either," Elizabeth said. "What shall it be? Who shall *she* be?"

"I am still partial toward Elizabeth."

"Nay. She should not have to share her name with another member of the household, even her mother." His wife stroked their daughter's brow. "At least, not a living one." She looked up at him. "Perhaps Anne?"

Her desire to honor his mother pleased him. But having witnessed Elizabeth's struggle to establish her own identity at Pemberley, he hesitated to place this tiny being so directly in her grandmother's shadow, to invite a lifetime of comparison before the child even opened her eyes on the world. "Jane?"

Elizabeth contemplated a moment, then shook her head. "She does not look like a Jane." She sighed. "How do parents ever choose?"

Mrs. Godwin returned to check on Elizabeth one final time before retiring. A chamber had been prepared for the midwife, and she instructed Elizabeth to send for her if she required anything during what remained of the night. Darcy doubted he himself would sleep a moment.

"Mrs. Godwin," he said. "Were you present when Georgiana received her name?"

She smiled sadly and nodded. "Your parents were talking quietly, and I was trying to grant them privacy while making your mother as comfortable as I could. She knew she was dying; they both did. She was exhausted by her ordeal, he by anxiety and grief. He declared he would name their daughter Anne, that Pemberley *must* have an Anne or he could not bear to live here any longer.

"She said no, let us join our two names, as we joined Fitzwilliam and Darcy to name our son. Let us call our daughter Georgiana, and may our children embody our union. May they grow, and thrive, and show the world what is possible when love conquers all."

The glimpse of his parents' final moments together prompted him to take Elizabeth's hand and bring it to his lips. "Thank you for our daughter," he whispered fiercely.

As Mrs. Godwin left, she reminded him that their daughter still had no name.

"Much as I appreciate my parents' practice of combining their two, I am not quite enamored of Fitzabeth," he said.

Elizabeth caressed their daughter's cheek. "I have something else in mind."

Forty

It was doomed to be a day of trial.

—Northanger Abbey

Lady Catherine entered Elizabeth's bedchamber as if it were her own.

"You summoned me?"

Anticipating another volatile confrontation, Elizabeth had considered postponing this conversation until she had regained more strength. Her travail was but a day past, and she still experienced pain and fatigue from bringing her daughter into the world. But some pleasures should not be deferred, and the result of the communication she was about to make would be worth any unpleasantness arising from its delivery.

She glanced at the cradle, where her daughter was sleeping off the exhausting experience of having been born, and sat up as straight as possible in her bed. "I have the happiness of informing you that Mr. Darcy and Mr. Tilney apprehended the real thieves of the Northanger diamonds last night. While we appreciate your generous service these several months, we are no longer in need of a legal chaperone. You may return to Rosings."

Darcy's aunt appeared as satisfied by the news as Elizabeth. "I had myself decided that the custody arrangement had become insupportable, and was determined to devise a means by which Mr. Melbourne would release us from it. I only hope my own affairs have not suffered neglect while I sacrificed so much time and attention to yours."

Elizabeth reflected that she and Darcy would have been perfectly content with a smaller sacrifice on her ladyship's part, but graciously thanked Darcy's aunt for her kindness.

Lady Catherine scoffed. "It was not kindness. It was duty."

"Cannot duty be performed with kindness?"

Her ladyship did not immediately reply. Her gaze had fallen on the Madonna and Child statuette, which rested on the table beside Elizabeth's bed. "Sometimes in the performance of duty, one is forced to be unkind." She looked at Elizabeth. "My sister never realized that in withholding that ivory, I was saving her from herself. I could not allow those around her to know she believed in Popish nonsense."

Elizabeth struggled to comprehend her. "Lady Anne was a Catholic?"

"Never! Do not even utter such a thing. But our mother came from a family that secretly held on to the Catholic faith long after the Reformation, and a few of those beliefs passed through the generations. I would not have society thinking our family maintained any connection to its Catholic past."

"What difference would it have made? Catholics are no longer persecuted in England."

"It made a difference to me."

Elizabeth absorbed this revelation with disgust. Darcy's mother had suffered so that his aunt could prevent a scandal that would have existed only in her own head. Lady Catherine was so obsessed with the concept of family honor that she had lost all understanding of what honor meant.

The baby stirred. Elizabeth slowly swung her legs to one side of the bed and slid her feet to the floor. She crossed to her daughter and lifted her into her arms. Lady Catherine, meanwhile, took no apparent interest in the child.

"I think perhaps it would be best if you departed tomorrow morning," Elizabeth said.

"I shall depart this afternoon, as soon as my trunks are packed and my carriage readied." She moved toward the table with the statuette.

Elizabeth stepped in her way. "The ivory shall remain here."

"You dare to keep it for yourself?"

"I do not keep it for myself. I keep it for Lady Anne."

"*You?* The former Elizabeth Bennet—daughter of nobody and sister of scandal? Who are *you* that you believe yourself entitled to claim anything on Lady Anne's behalf?"

Elizabeth straightened her back, lifted her chin, and unflinchingly met Lady Catherine's imperious gaze.

"I am mistress of Pemberley."

DARCY SHIFTED IN his seat and did his best to ignore the stuffiness of the crowded courtroom. County assizes normally attracted large numbers of spectators, the trials offering merely one of many entertainments within the festival-like atmosphere that surrounded them. Twice a year, His Majesty's subjects indulged in days of public balls, private parties, and—oh, yes, the administration of law.

It seemed that all Gloucestershire had turned out this spring. After each day's elaborate procession—the judge in his great white wig and scarlet robe, accompanied by trumpeters and sheriff's men in full dress—down the city's main street, more men, women, and children than Darcy would have believed possible packed into the hall. The legal proceedings provided the best theatre most of the audience would see all year. Or, at least, until the next assizes. And like any theatrical, the grisly accounts of murder and dire pronouncements of death sentences would be followed by dinner and dancing.

Despite the crush, Darcy recognized a few individuals. He, of course, knew his companions; he sat wedged between Mr. Tilney and Mr. Wickham, the latter of whom attended at

Darcy's behest. Mr. Melbourne had been advising the judge all week of defendants' crimes and previous conduct, and Mr. Chase had swaggered forward to make exceedingly brilliant contributions to several trials.

Darcy also knew the faces of John Thorpe and Isabella Stanford, whose fate the judge would soon decree. The Thorpe siblings had stood trial earlier in the week for their misdeeds. After huddling for all of three minutes, the jury had pronounced them guilty.

They, along with all the other parties convicted in the course of the week, presently appeared for sentencing. Mr. Thorpe observed the current proceedings as if he were merely a spectator, exclaiming and murmuring along with the rest of the crowd as each punishment was declared. But Isabella, who had entered the room in a state of nervous agitation, stilled more with the calling of each name not her own.

"The Thorpes' trial was one of the first," whispered Mr. Tilney, who did not ordinarily attend assizes. "Why have they not had their turn?"

"Assize judges hand down sentences in order of severity, beginning with the lightest punishments and ending with executions," Darcy replied.

"Oh, my. That does not bode well for them, does it?" The judge was more than three-quarters finished, and had just pronounced another one-way excursion to Botany Bay.

More sentences were delivered. Darcy observed Wickham's response to each, wondering whether the scoundrel was absorbing the message Darcy had intended by commanding his attendance. Assize court truly was an awesome spectacle—the judge in his red, ermine-lined robe and traditional wig, meting out justice in rhetoric that rivaled parliamentary speeches. No one, surely not even Wickham, could come away without respect for the power of the law.

Wickham shifted restlessly. "I still do not understand why you insisted I accompany you here," he muttered. He had been annoyingly blithe throughout his accomplices' trial, but this afternoon he had turned ill-tempered.

"Because were it not for your wife's relationship to mine, you would be standing up there with the Thorpes."

"Oh, I see—I am to learn gratitude. There but for the grace of Darcy go I?"

Darcy glared at the insufferable snake. "I would not behave in such a cocksure manner were I you. The quarter sessions in Derbyshire are yet to come."

The Darcys and Mr. Tilney had decided not to pursue prosecution of Mr. Wickham to the full extent of the law. Mr. Tilney considered the Thorpe siblings' prosecution sufficient redress for the theft of the diamonds. In the matter of the ivory stolen from Pemberley, neither Darcy nor Elizabeth wanted to risk a death sentence for Lydia's husband, as his execution would only leave Mrs. Wickham more dependent than ever on the rest of the family.

Jenny, too, had escaped full punishment. As the misguided girl seemed to have learned her lesson, Darcy and Elizabeth had merely dismissed her and sent her back to Newcastle. But for Wickham, some deterrent to future misconduct was necessary. So he would stand trial at the quarter sessions, where Darcy hoped a few months' hard labor would be ordered. It was possible, though not probable, that the experience might build his character, but even should it not, Wickham had nothing better to do with his time—he had already been discharged from the army for interfering with the notification of Captain Tilney's death.

Only five sentences remained for the judge to hand down. At last, Mr. Thorpe and Mrs. Stanford were called forward.

"Have you anything to say?" the judge enquired.

"Upon my soul, I certainly do!"

Henry Tilney let slip a soft groan. "If John Thorpe speaks, he might as well hang himself."

"Your honor, I believe that during my trial, it was not made sufficiently clear that I am a gentleman. If it had been, the jury would not possibly have convicted me. Why, those old codgers probably could not even see who they were trying! If I were on the bench, I would conduct a new trial. By

Jove, I would! Juries cannot simply go round convicting gentlemen. What will England come to?"

"Fortunately, Mr. Thorpe, you need not concern yourself over the fate of England."

"Capital! I knew you were a fellow who would see things my way."

"Because you are being transported."

John Thorpe sputtered. "Transported?"

"Seven years in Sydney." The judge followed the pronouncement with a lecture on respect for the law as the cornerstone of social order, meant as much for the audience as Mr. Thorpe—which was just as well, as Thorpe himself did not seem to absorb it in the least and did his best to interrupt.

When his honor had finished, he turned to Isabella, who had paled at the pronouncement of her brother's sentence. "And you, Mrs. Stanford—"

"Your honor, please recall that I thought the whole scheme at Northanger was merely a charade. My brother arranged the whole thing. It was all—"

"A misunderstanding? So you said at the trial. The court hereby sentences you to seven years' transportation, same as Mr. Thorpe, and hopes that by the end of it, your understanding will be stronger."

"Seven years!" Mrs. Stanford appeared about to swoon. But as the judge orated further, she recovered herself, pulling back her shoulders and tilting her head coquettishly.

"Might I approach the bench?" she asked in a soft voice.

The judge, having ended his speech and, he had thought, his dealings with the Thorpes, released an impatient sigh. "What remains to be said, Mrs. Stanford?"

With all the grace she could muster, Isabella strolled to the judge and murmured something only he could hear. One finger stroked the sleeve of his robe.

His honor's brows rose. "Indeed? In that case, I *will* change your sentence."

She batted her eyes and smiled.

"Ten years."

The few remaining sentences required the longest amount

of time to deliver. The judge donned a black cap before handing them down, and spoke long and passionately about crimes too heinous to pardon on earth. The recipients of these fire-and-brimstone sermons would not be going to a penal colony, but to the gallows.

Wickham fidgeted throughout.

When court adjourned, Wickham was the first of their party to stand. He crossed his arms defiantly and looked down at Darcy.

"Am I dismissed?"

Darcy rose and met him eye to eye. Despite Wickham's bluff manner, Darcy detected disquiet within him. Perhaps in witnessing the fates of his friends, Wickham had finally glimpsed something unpleasant about himself.

"Go," he said. "I will see you at the quarter sessions."

Wickham acknowledged him with a nod. He then hobbled off, his injured ankle still troubling him.

"So," said Henry Tilney as they waited for the remainder of the crowd to file out of the hall, "Mr. Thorpe will be exchanging his famously swift horses for a slow boat to Australia."

"It would seem that his belief in the immunity of gentlemen from the law did not bear out," Darcy replied.

"No, but apparently the law—or, at least, the gentleman who administered it—did prove immune to Mrs. Stanford's charms."

"Poor Mrs. Stanford." Darcy met Tilney's eye and grinned. "There must have been a misunderstanding."

Forty-one

Have you remembered to collect pieces for the patchwork? We are now at a stand-still.

—Jane Austen, letter to Cassandra

"Thank you, Mr. Flynn, for coming all the way up here," Elizabeth said. A fortnight into her lying-in, she had yet to leave her apartment. But she had need of the gardener's knowledge and did not want to postpone consulting him.

"It is my pleasure, Mrs. Darcy."

Her daughter slept in a cradle nearby, and he gazed at the baby for a long time. "A pretty one, she is. Just like her namesake."

She smiled, never tired of hearing compliments about her daughter. "You would certainly know." Just as he would know how to put together the puzzle she could not quite assemble. She gingerly walked to the table where the pieces of Helen Tilney's quilt were laid out. Jane, her mother, even Lydia had offered to work together to help her restore it. With such a team working upon it, the result would be less than perfect. But the combined handiwork would make their creation more than a mere quilt. It would be an ideal legacy in which to place her daughter.

"Helen Tilney created a quilt whose pattern represented Lady Anne's garden," she explained to Mr. Flynn. "The quilt has been damaged, but I am piecing it back together. I have encountered difficulty, however, with several sections that do not seem to fit where they belong. Since you know Lady Anne's garden better than anybody else, I thought perhaps you could help me."

"I would be honored, Mrs. Darcy."

She showed him the sections she had arranged thus far, and the outstanding pieces that no longer fit. "The marigolds simply will not cooperate. Nor will the violets."

"That is because you have them in the wrong place," he said. "If Mrs. Tilney made this design, it reflects the original plan of the garden. I later moved the marigolds to a bed where they receive more sunlight. Here," he said, switching the pieces, "if you think of the garden's rosette shape as a compass, the marigolds as Mrs. Tilney knew them were at northwest by north."

The pieces now fell into place—in more ways than one. She not only knew where Lady Anne's friend had sewn the marigolds onto the quilt.

She knew where Helen Tilney had sown the ivories in the garden.

Epilogue

She looked forward with delight to the time when they should be removed from society so little pleasing to either, to all the comfort and elegance of their family party at Pemberley.

—Pride and Prejudice

A sweet perfume greeted Elizabeth and Darcy as they entered the south garden. It was a fine June day, and the Madonna lilies had just bloomed. Though Elizabeth often strolled with the baby in Lady Anne's garden, at last she and Darcy could introduce their daughter to the flower whose name she bore.

Lily-Anne Darcy took only casual interest in her surroundings as her father held her up to admire the lilies. She had, after all, recently discovered her own hands, and celebrated this extraordinary event by spending a good portion of her waking hours attempting to stuff all of her fingers into her mouth at once. The nursery maid had apologized repeatedly for not yet managing to break her of the habit. Elizabeth and Darcy found the practice adorable.

Elizabeth broke off a single flower and brought it to Lily-Anne for closer inspection. The baby smiled, grabbed its stem tightly in her small fist, and waved it round.

"I believe she approves," Darcy said. He looked to Elizabeth, but she yet observed their daughter.

"Rather too much. She is trying to eat it."

He pried the flower from Lily-Anne's fingers and returned it to Elizabeth. She tickled the baby's cheek with its petals, eliciting smiles from both daughter and husband.

When Lily tired of the game, Darcy placed her in Elizabeth's arms. "Unfortunately, I must leave now or I shall arrive late."

"This is such a perfect day that I refuse to allow your errand to spoil it. So long as you do not return from the quarter sessions with the news that Mr. Wickham has been released into *our* custody, I shall be satisfied."

Darcy shuddered at the very notion. "Responsibility for one child is enough." He met her eyes. "For now." He kissed his wife, bade Lily-Anne behave for her mother, and departed.

Left alone with her daughter, Elizabeth walked round the garden. The marigolds were preparing to bloom, and the first violets of spring had appeared none the worse for having been temporarily displaced to retrieve the nine statuettes Helen Tilney had hidden. Henry Tilney and his wife had come in person to collect the ivories, and all had taken such pleasure in the visit that the couple extended it twice before finally returning to Gloucestershire. It appeared that in burying her treasure at Pemberley, Helen Tilney had also planted seeds of a friendship between the next generations of Tilneys and Darcys that would be cherished as much as the one she had enjoyed with Lady Anne. The Darcys looked forward to calling upon the Tilneys later in the year, and had been assured that, this time, they would experience a perfectly ordinary reception at Northanger Abbey.

She carried the baby to the alcove that had sheltered Lady Anne's treasure for so many years. Despite the prominence of the summerhouse, Darcy's mother had been correct about this more understated corner offering a superior view of the lilies. She had also been right about the glare of the sun upon the desk in the morning room; Elizabeth had finally conceded the point and had it moved back to its original position. Apparently, the new Mrs. Darcy still had much to learn, but she no longer found herself overshadowed by the memory of Darcy's mother. Indeed, she had come to consider Lady Anne an ally.

The light breeze marshaled itself into a brief gust, carrying the scent of lilies even more strongly to her senses. A few dried leaves scudded into the alcove. A folded paper was among them.

"Lily, what have we found?" Elizabeth bent and retrieved the paper. It was a note in handwriting she now knew as well as her own.

My dear Mrs. Darcy,

My lifetime is ended; my days as Pemberley's mistress, past. I commit words to paper once more because it now falls to you to carry on my legacy.

For two and a half centuries, a treasure passed from mother to daughter. By the time my own mother placed in my hands a small chest containing the Madonna ivory, it had long been assumed that the statuette was this treasure. It is not.

When I made my pilgrimage to the cathedral library, I discovered that among the many riches held by Northanger Abbey before the Dissolution, the greatest had been the one most humble in appearance: a relic of Mary, a portion of her mantle brought from the Holy Land during the Crusades. It is this relic, which enfolds the Mother and Child I inherited, that constitutes the true treasure handed down through generations—for those who hold it, if they be of faithful heart and worthy spirit, receive the gift of grace.

A treasure such as this cannot be possessed, only held, and to you I entrust its stewardship. I could not commend it to a better caretaker. Guard it well. And in time pass it to your daughter.

Now tend to your garden, Mrs. Darcy—to your life with Fitzwilliam and the children you will raise, your own precious lilies. And know that one who has gone before you watches fondly from above.

—A. D.

Elizabeth studied the note. It bore no date. From its opening, she presumed it had been written while Lady Anne lay dying. Yet she could not imagine Darcy's mother exerting herself at such a time to pen a second letter to an unknown future daughter-in-law, let alone a note reflecting such serenity. Nor could she begin to account for its appearance in the garden, at this moment, blown in by the breath of summer.

Lily-Anne cooed, drawing her from reverie. The infant grasped her mother's finger and smiled.

"My own precious Lily," Elizabeth whispered. "Your grandmama practically called you by name. However did she know?"

Other phrases in the letter had suggested similar prescience. Either Lady Anne had seen what lay ahead, or her message had been composed more recently.

"Perhaps your grandmama's presence here is even stronger than I realized," she said. She made the sort of playful face that very young children somehow manage to elicit from otherwise dignified adults, to the glee of her daughter. Then she held up the baby so that they two were eye to eye. "What think you, Lily-Anne? Has your grandmama's spirit been about?"

Lily smiled again. Then her gaze moved past Elizabeth's shoulder and she giggled.

It was her daughter's first true laugh. Elizabeth turned round to see what had captured her delight. But nothing was behind her.

Nothing but the breeze and the fragrance of lilies.

Author's Note

I have now attained the true art of letter-writing, which we are always told is to express on paper exactly what one would say to the same person by word of mouth. I have been talking to you almost as fast as I could the whole of this letter.

—Jane Austen, letter to Cassandra

Dear Readers,

After writing so many letters between fictional characters in this story, it seems only fitting that I close the book with a letter to you.

Many of you have been kind enough to write and share your thoughts about the Darcy series, and I take great pleasure in your letters. One of the most common subjects of questions is the amount of research I do for each book. I strive to be as accurate as I can, performing research not only before I begin a new story, but also the whole time I'm writing it and even after completing the initial draft—still trying to find elusive answers, confirm details in multiple sources, or reconcile conflicting information. Research discoveries often create or shape plot ideas and sometimes even change the course of the book. Other times, the influence of historical facts is more subtle, such as in descriptions or word choices.

Which leads me to a confession. While researching for North by Northanger, *I was disappointed to learn that although* Lilium candidum *is a very old flower long associated with the Virgin Mary, it did not become known by the name "Madonna lily" until the second half of the nineteenth century—after my novel takes place. Therefore, to be historically accurate, Mr. Flynn, Lady Anne, Helen Tilney, and Elizabeth Darcy ought to call it by its older name, the Annunciation lily. I wrestled long and hard with this troublesome fact. Though William Shakespeare wrote that "a rose by any other name would smell as sweet," I felt that in the context of this story—one that resonates with the theme of maternal bonds—calling the Madonna lily by any other name would diminish its effect. So I took a little poetic license and, for the sake of storytelling, allowed my characters a vocabulary word slightly ahead of their time. I hope you will forgive me.*

I also hope you have enjoyed Elizabeth and Darcy's latest adventure, and the opportunity to become reacquainted with (or perhaps first meet) some of the characters from Northanger Abbey, *one of my favorite Austen novels. Alas, Austen wrote only six full-length books. But she also left behind numerous letters and minor works, and research for* North by Northanger *led me to study her letters more closely than I ever had before in order to capture the epistolary style of the era. I had forgotten how entertaining they were—as full of wit, irony, and incisive observations as her novels, with a whole new cast of characters to entertain us. If you are a fan of Austen but have never read her letters, you might want to give them a try.*

Meanwhile, you can find more information about the Mr. & Mrs. Darcy series and my forthcoming books at my Web site: www.carriebebris.com. And if, while you're there, you should happen to drop me a note, I'd be delighted to hear from you. No quill pen required!

Yours most sincerely,
Carrie Bebris

Turn the page for a preview of

Carrie Bebris's

Pride and Prescience

(0-765-31843-1)

Available May 2007 in trade paperback from
Tom Doherty Associates

Caroline Bingley's wedding indeed proved the talk of the *ton*, an event calculated in all respects to outdo the Bennet sisters' nuptials. Her gown featured more yards of lace, more beads, more ribbon, than Elizabeth's and Jane's combined. Her veil was longer, her bride's cake taller, her wedding breakfast a full twelve courses. The guest list included more "particular friends" than Mrs. Darcy thought it possible for one couple to have; in fact, Miss Bingley seemed to have invited any titled acquaintance whose card she'd ever received.

Elizabeth considered the whole event an exercise in ostentation, from the exotic foreign flowers in Miss Bingley's bouquet—she and Jane had chosen English roses—to the gaudy wedding ring the bride showed off to all. The solid gold band, engraved with a sunburst design, featured an enormous oval fire opal surrounded by six smaller diamonds. The main stone extended all the way to her first knuckle and perched in a setting so high that Elizabeth would have feared catching it on every piece of clothing she owned were the rock adorning her own hand. She much preferred the delicate engraved band Darcy had given her.

Unlike Darcy, Mr. Parrish had chosen also to wear a wedding band. Elizabeth didn't know whether the practice was common among American husbands, but Caroline made sure everyone in attendance was aware of this additional show of Parrish's devotion. For his part, Mr. Parrish appeared to take the matrimonial spectacle in stride. According to Jane, his contribution to planning the event had been limited to selecting the wedding rings and asking Professor Randolph to stand up with him. The latter choice had caused Elizabeth mild surprise—she had not realized, while conversing with the professor at dinner, that he and Parrish had so intimate an acquaintance. Randolph appeared in high spirits, genuinely delighted by his friend's marriage and choice of partner.

It was with relief that she watched the bridal couple quit the Pulteney Hotel, which had hosted the enormous gathering. As the guests dispersed, the Darcys indulged in a much longer and more heartfelt leave-taking of Jane and Bingley. Elizabeth and her closest sister had previously found themselves divided for months-long periods while paying individual visits to friends and relations, but this separation, with each departing for her own new, permanent situation, felt somehow more final. She knew, however, that the two couples would often visit each other's homes.

She and Darcy spent their last London evening in Drury Lane enjoying a performance of *The Rivals*. It was an older comedy, but neither had seen it performed before, and Sheridan's play provided a merrier conclusion to their London interlude than had Miss Bingley's dramatic production. Now Elizabeth looked forward to collecting Georgiana from the Gardiners early the next morning and setting off for Pemberley at last. Christmas was less than a fortnight away; already, cold air nipped fingers and toes, while Yuletide sights and smells filled every shop.

She gazed out the window as their carriage wended from

the theatre back to their townhouse through crowded lanes still wet from evening rain. Falling temperatures had turned the damp air into fog, which cloaked the many pedestrians and coaches in eerie greyness.

"Does London never sleep?" she asked. "This seems an extraordinary number of people filling the streets so late at night."

"Late? The hour is just past midnight."

"I think I prefer country hours."

"And here I thought I had married a woman of fashion."

She was grateful for her husband's presence as the driver turned onto a darker, seedier road. Though the members of London's social elite might believe they lived in their own little *beau monde,* in reality their world collided with the city's less desirable districts and denizens at nearly every corner. Fashionable streets lay within blocks of shabbier neighborhoods, and theatregoers could not travel from a Mayfair mansion to Covent Garden or Drury Lane without entering squalid surroundings thick with sights of desperation, sounds of debauchery, and the smells of unwashed bodies and horse excrement.

Fortunately, Elizabeth saw no children begging in the dim, flickering gaslight this evening. The little ones always tugged at her heart, and not a day of their London visit had passed without Darcy stopping the carriage at her behest to press coins into small, cold hands. No, tonight more sinister figures prowled the streets: unkempt wanderers, aggressive panhandlers, scarlet women, dark-clad rogues. Even as she watched, one dagger-wielding ruffian deprived another of his purse, while twenty paces away, a woman with painted lips called out offers that left little doubt of her moral character to a group of intoxicated dandies tumbling out of a gaming hall.

She shuddered and reached forward to draw the curtain, preferring to complete the journey in isolated darkness rather than observe more such sights from the window. No sooner had she grasped the fabric, however, than an inconceivable sight stayed her hand.

"That cannot be Caroline Bingley!" She gasped, staring at a woman walking unescorted along the dirty gutter. Unless the uneven light deceived her—surely it must!—the new Mrs. Parrish ambled toward them down the shadowed street. Despite the chilly mist, she wore no hat, no gloves, and no mantle or spencer over her short-sleeved muslin gown. Indeed, the sole accessory on her person was a bulging reticule that dangled from one arm. She strolled as if shopping on Bond Street in the broad light of day, oblivious to the peril around her.

The woman's face, bearing, and stride in all ways matched those of the former Miss Bingley. But whyever would Caroline Parrish be walking half-dressed down a menacing London street alone on her wedding night?

"Good heavens, it *is* her." Darcy rapped a signal to their driver. "Stay here," he told Elizabeth as the coach slowed.

The thief Elizabeth had seen earlier, a ragged youth of perhaps fifteen, spotted Caroline's unguarded handbag. He darted toward her, snatching the reticule as he passed. But the strings of the overstuffed bag became wrapped around her wrist. The force of the swiping attempt spun her round, at last making her sensible of her surroundings. She cried out as she struggled with the criminal, but she did not let go of the reticule.

Darcy leapt out of the still-moving carriage. "He has a knife!" Elizabeth warned, but her words proved unnecessary. The criminal, malice radiating from every line of his dirty, pockmarked face, already brandished the weapon in his bony hand. It glinted in the sputtering light.

"Leave this lady alone." Darcy, his back to Elizabeth, faced the ruffian. Her heart hammered so loudly in her ears that she scarcely heard his words. Nearby chatter died as people turned their attention to the evening's latest entertainment.

The young rogue ceased his struggle with Miss Bingley to take Darcy's measure. Darcy made no move forward, but drew himself up to his full height, over a foot taller than his adversary. She could imagine the forbidding expression on her husband's face—the piercing gaze, the impassive jaw. She had seen it before. But would it carry the same power on a dark, dangerous street that it did in a drawing room?

It did, thank heaven. The would-be purse snatcher spat on the ground in an impotent display of resistance, then darted into the mist.

Elizabeth released breath she hadn't realized she held. Praise God the thief had been so young—she doubted even Darcy could have subdued an older criminal with the force of his presence alone. As her husband whisked their friend into the carriage, the surrounding cacophony of begging and bawdiness resumed as if nothing had happened. Indeed, by the standards of these witnesses, nothing had.

Their coachman quickly set the horses in motion. To Elizabeth it seemed they couldn't move fast enough. Once the scene behind them melted into the fog, Darcy directed the driver to Mr. Parrish's townhouse.

The incident had shaken Caroline, but otherwise, as far as could be discerned inside the dark coach, had left her physically unharmed. She sat stiffly beside Elizabeth, clutching the reticule in her lap, and nodded in mute acceptance at Darcy's offer of his cloak.

"Are you all right, Mrs. Parrish?" Darcy asked.

She did not answer, but rather gazed straight ahead as if she hadn't heard the question.

"Mrs. Parrish?" Darcy echoed. She merely pulled the cloak farther round her shoulders.

"Caroline?" Elizabeth tried. Though the two women had never been intimate enough to use their Christian names, she thought perhaps the new bride had not yet grown accustomed to being addressed by her married name.

Mrs. Parrish at last responded. She turned toward Elizabeth and stared at her as if trying to remember something. "Miss Elizabeth Bennet," she said finally. Then she looked at the coach's third passenger. "Mr. Darcy."

Elizabeth regarded her in shocked silence. Had it really taken her that long to realize who they were? The robbery attempt must have unsettled her more than was visible.

Darcy leaned forward. "Mrs. Parrish, did that thief harm you?"

She shook her head slowly. "No, I just . . . No." She straightened in her seat, as if remembering her posture. Her chin recovered its usual tilt. "Thank you, though, for interceding."

Elizabeth waited, hoping Caroline would now offer some explanation of what she had been doing on the street in the first place. Where was her husband? Had the couple gone out together and become separated? Had she fled their house—the marriage? This was all so exceedingly strange.

When no account appeared forthcoming, she ventured the subject herself. "We were surprised to see you as we passed. Does Mr. Parrish wait for you at home?"

Caroline raised a hand to her temple. "Forgive me, Mrs. Darcy," she said, her voice as haughty as ever. "I feel a headache coming on."

The remark silenced Elizabeth as effectively as it no doubt had been intended. She withdrew into the corner of the carriage, the rebuff having smothered all sympathy toward her seatmate. In the year or so she'd known Caroline Bingley Parrish, she'd never aspired to enter the woman's confidence, never wished to number her among intimate friends. But really! When concerned acquaintances rescued one from robbery and who-knows-what-other harm, some word of explanation seemed a not-unreasonable expectation.

She was tempted to leave Mrs. Parrish and her "headache" to face alone whatever predicament had led to her midnight stroll. Obviously, Elizabeth's concern was neither solicited nor welcome. Yet she sensed something different about tonight's rudeness—that it stemmed not, as usual, from disdain toward herself, but from a desire to keep some private anxiety private. For that she could not fault her.

The fact did, however, set one's mind to wondering what could so trouble a woman who, twelve hours earlier, had declared herself the happiest, most fortunate bride in all England. A glance at Darcy's face revealed that he, too, knew not what to make of their companion's behavior. He started to speak, stopped, then began once more. "Mrs. Parrish, is *everything* quite all right?"

Caroline met his gaze. For a moment, confusion clouded her countenance, and she looked as if she might confide in Darcy. But then her features smoothed and she tilted her chin once more.

"Yes, Mr. Darcy. Quite."